Wish of the Wicked

Also by Danielle Paige

Stealing Snow

Before the Snow

Queen Rising

WISH OF THE WICKED

DANIELLE PAIGE

BLOOMSBURY
NEW YORK LONDON OXFORD NEW DELHI SYDNEY

BLOOMSBURY YA
Bloomsbury Publishing Inc., part of Bloomsbury Publishing Plc
1385 Broadway, New York, NY 10018

First published in the United States of America in November 2023
by Bloomsbury YA

Library of Congress Cataloging-in-Publication Data
Names: Paige, Danielle (Novelist), author.
Title: Wish of the wicked / by Danielle Paige.
Description: New York : Bloomsbury Children's Books, 2023
Summary: Eighteen-year-old Farrow hatches a dangerous plan to seek revenge on Queen Magrit and regain her magic, but when Farrow finds herself falling for the one person who could ruin everything, she must decide whether it is more important to live in the past or forge a new future.
Identifiers: LCCN 2022009820 (print) | LCCN 2022009821 (e-book)
ISBN 978-1-68119-686-2 (hardcover) • ISBN 978-1-68119-687-9 (e-book)
Subjects: CYAC: Magic—Fiction. | Revenge—Fiction. | Fantasy. | LCGFT: Fantasy fiction. | Romance fiction.
Classification: LCC PZ7.P154 Wi 2022 (print) | LCC PZ7.P154 (e-book) | DDC [Fic]—dc23
LC record available at https://lccn.loc.gov/2022009820
LC e-book record available at https://lccn.loc.gov/2022009821

Book design by John Candell
Typeset by Westchester Publishing Services
Printed and bound in the U.S.A.
2 4 6 8 10 9 7 5 3 1

For my beautiful mother, Shirley Paige,
you are my fairy godmother, I know you watch over all our family still . . . Chris, Andrea, Daddy, Josh, Sienna & Fi.

Wish of the Wicked

WANTED—DEAD OR ALIVE!

REWARD FOR THE CAPTURE OF FUGITIVES

By edict of Her Royal Highness Queen Magrit, members of the Entente and all users of magic are now and hereafter considered outlaws of Hinter and the Thirteen Queendoms. All enemies of the Crown will be burned at the stake. Protecting any such outlaws is considered high treason, punishable by death.

PART I
THE PAST

The Entente will rise again. We have a plan, and you are just in time.
—Galatea, La Soeur of the Past

PROLOGUE

The End. And Also the Beginning.

The Queen created the word "witch" and cursed my people in one breath. And in the next she condemned Hecate, my Hecate, to die.

We had been walking through the square when the Queen's guards grabbed her. Hecate went with them, even though she was stronger. Even though she could have stopped them with a breath, a whisper, or a turn of her wrist. She let them lead her to the square and tie her up. She let them start a fire beneath the pyre. She kept her lips sealed. She did not move a muscle in protest. She let them take her from me. From all of us.

From me especially.

Hecate was the most powerful of us. She was the Future of Les Soeurs, my mentor, and sister to us all. But I didn't know she was my mother until the moment before her last breath.

When I could move again, I touched my face. It was wet. I realized that I was crying. I had never seen another member of the Entente cry—not Hecate on the pyre, not Galatea as she was watching her. But I was crying now.

I should have known she was my mother, but Hecate had always been so powerful that her wishes were opaque to me—like she never wanted or felt anything other than what she was doing at the time. But as she burned, her eyes met mine. The flames curled around her. She should have been screaming—instead, she spoke to me in a voice I could only hear in my head.

I wish I'd told you, Farrow. But it is not our way.

I tried to scream, to get to her, but I was paralyzed where I stood. As a man dressed in the livery of the Queen's guard read off a list of offenses, saying things like "malevolent sorcery against the Queen" and "treasonous inciter," my mouth would not open; my legs would not move. I didn't know if Hecate was using what power she had left to stop me from fighting when she should have been fighting to stay alive.

Don't fight.

Suddenly Galatea, my older sister and the Past of Les Soeurs, appeared in the center of the square. If Hecate expired, there would be only two of them left. The three Les Soeurs led the rest of the Entente, each with a different gift. Iolanta, the Present, was in isolation. But she would feel Hecate die the moment it happened. Galatea, as the Sister of the Past, would remember every second of Hecate's death without the kindness of time to help it fade. Even though it was thought that my gift would be the Present someday, it felt like I would be remembering every detail of it forever too. I prayed for them to be able to stop it, but that was all for naught.

The other sisters began to appear. The army raised their swords against them. I still could not move.

Iolanta was there suddenly—Iolanta, who never left the confines of her isolation. Iolanta, who knew the Present and clearly could feel Hecate on the pyre.

South and Amantha and Bari were there too, making their own desperate attempts at saving her while I stood frozen.

I had no choice. I did not blink once as I watched the flames engulf her body, her face, and her hair. As her skin charred black and her eye sockets filled with fire, and as my eyes stung and teared from the smoke, I could not unsee. But I didn't know why Hecate would have wanted me to have this be the last image that I would have of her, my mother.

Iolanta raised her wand, and Black Fire coursed out of it. Unfortunately for all of us, that fire met with the store of cannon fire nearby. Everything was chaos; everything was burning and ash in an instant.

When it was over, when the Entente were all ash and the Queen's guard had left on horseback, I tried to turn and leave, to get away. But something stalled me. I wanted, I needed, to take her home. I waited until dark; I waited until every last onlooker had dispersed.

I gathered the ashes from the pyre and put them in the pouch I wore around my neck, making sure I left no part of her behind. When I was done, I held her in my hands. I could not feel her—not her power, not her essence, not her electricity.

My mother.

In the Entente, we were all sisters. There were no mothers. But now I knew mine, and I didn't know how to feel about it. I slipped my wand out of my pocket and tried to use it to make a path to the Hiding Place. But it was no use. The wand did not work.

I had to go on foot. I ran the whole way to the Hiding Place. It was where we had been born, where we were raised until we were ready for placement, and where we were to go if anything catastrophic ever was to happen. Losing Hecate was worse.

The interior of the Place mirrored that of the palaces we were sent to—marble floors, high ceilings, opulent silks—but everything here was made of magic.

It wasn't until after the ashes were in the glass coffin in the center of the room that I realized something I could not reconcile. How had any of this happened without Les Soeurs stopping it? How was it that we could correct the fates of others and not do the same for ourselves? My mother saw this coming.

"You could have stopped this," I said as I closed the lid with a spell. "We could have avoided the square today altogether."

She was gone, and the Queendom wants us all dead, not just her. How is that Fate's plan?

We were Entente. For centuries we had been at the side of every queen and king in every Queendom, as advisors, confidants, leaders. We were the whispers. We were the details, tiny arrows that you couldn't ignore. We were strings of moments, coincidences, and happenstances that led you to yesterday and today and tomorrow. We were the Fates.

Nothing was the way it was supposed to be. There had always been the three of them directing us: Past, Present, and Future. Though no one ever saw Iolanta except for Hecate and Galatea, we always felt her influence in the directives we were given. It had always been the three Les Soeurs, but now . . .

"Hecate," I whispered to the glass casket. "I know there isn't a happily ever after for us, but I never expected this." As I looked through the glass before me, something seemed to . . . stir.

I closed my eyes tight, doubting them.

But when I opened them again, the ashes were indeed moving, forming the shape that I knew so well to be Hecate's.

"Hecate?" I said, feeling slightly foolish. Despite a lifetime of magic up close, I had never seen anything like this. Dead was dead. There was no "after," we all knew that. But as I watched Hecate's ashes swirling around in the glass coffin, what I knew slipped away.

The ashes began to swirl around the case in a frenzy. They formed a kind of funnel that increased in velocity.

I leaned in just as the glass shattered and the funnel tornadoed out of the case and smashed about the room. I landed on the floor, pushed by the force of air that the ashes had created.

"Hecate!" I screamed, wondering if the ashes were conscious, wondering if the ashes were dangerous, wondering if the ashes were still Hecate.

I got back to my feet, my eyes still on the swirling gray. Glass clattered around me, and yet somehow I had not felt a single cut. I half expected the ashes to try and escape. Perhaps the coffin disagreed with her. Perhaps, they/she was seeking peace. But as they spun down from the ceiling they began to form the Hecate shape all over again. And when the ashes had settled completely into her form, they finally stood still, and I took a step toward them.

I had not known that she was my mother, but I had always felt closer to her than the other Older Sisters. It was her favor I sought, her approval I wanted. For a moment, the ashes began to make up her face, and then her neck, her shoulders, and so on, until my Hecate was before me, completely formed.

"Why didn't you tell me?" I blurted.

My mother made of ash did not answer. Or maybe she could not. Then the ashes broke apart and came back together in the shape of a heart.

Was this her way of telling me that she loved me? Or was this her way of saying goodbye?

The ashes broke apart again and came back together as her silhouette.

"I don't want to say goodbye to you," I said finally.

I didn't know magic could do this. That it could continue beyond the grave. There were rules and limits. Things that we did and did not do. But here was Hecate, my mother, standing in front of me made of ash.

Suddenly, behind me I heard footsteps against the marble. I turned back. Someone was coming. Lots of someones.

Hecate beckoned me closer with a wave of her arm. I stepped forward, and she lowered down beside me. Her ashes brushed my ear.

Leave everything behind, the ashes whispered in Hecate's voice . . .

Run!

This time the voice was louder, and the ashes burst apart.

RUN!

I ran.

CHAPTER 1

The night before

Whose power would you rather have?" Bari asked, cross-legged on the bed in the room we shared.

"Hecate's, no question," I said automatically.

"Knowing the Future is better than the Past. Everyone knows that," Bari responded.

"But I would take either Hecate's or Galatea's over Iolanta's power," I said.

"Iolanta's is the worst," Bari agreed.

I felt something lift inside me.

At seven and a half, Bari was only six months older than I was but somehow miles ahead of me in magic. It was a small victory to have even an ounce of her approval. I imagined everyone in the Entente would agree with me, including Iolanta herself; the gift of the Present wasn't a gift at all. It seemed much closer to a curse.

I pictured Iolanta in her isolation room, sitting in the dark quiet and letting the world go by, her homemade things around her. Because outside the Reverie, Iolanta felt every single human from the Hinter to the Thirteenth Queendom and beyond all at once. For even the strongest Entente, the weight of all those Presents was too hard to bear.

"But the Future is more interesting than the Past. You can't do anything about the Past," Bari argued.

I thought about Hecate, who was stoic and watchful and stern. You wouldn't know that, when she looked at you, she could see your entire life stretched before you in a single touch—all the possible futures, all the possible twists and turns.

And I thought about Galatea, who was different from her sisters. She bore her gift like a shield. She could look at a human and know every bad and good thing they had ever done. The Past was set. And she had little reverence for humans because of it.

And I thought of the mantle that Galatea, Iolanta, and Hecate were charged with—the heavy responsibility of advising the queens of every Queendom.

Before I could respond to Bari, a large beetle with glowing blue wings landed on the tip of my nose. We were taught not to kill insects, but I instinctually raised my hand to swat it.

"Don't move, Farrow," Bari said. "If you crush them, you crush me."

"What did you do?" I asked as my concern rose for Bari. I tapped my wand against my leg nervously.

Bari lifted her skirt, revealing that her legs were now completely composed of the same kind of beetles as the one perched on me. The beetles' wings were the same blue. If the insects hadn't been moving, I would have thought that Bari was wearing a glamorous pair of pantaloons.

She had been experimenting with transformation for months, but she had started turning her wand on herself. In contrast, I had only managed to give a beetle a single butterfly wing. Every Entente practiced with insects before they moved on to animals. But we were not supposed to turn our wands on ourselves until we had mastered smaller magic. Bari was always trying bigger and bigger spells.

I had turned my wand on myself countless times, but I never strayed past the small spells, like cosmetics, and I dabbled in minor weather changes. I could make my light-brown skin and dark hair any color or texture—from my impossible curls to an updo. I could touch the hem of my dress and make it any style I wanted, from its default gray to a gown worthy of a princess. My biggest feat to date was filling the courtyard with fog.

Bari could do more with her wand than I could with mine. All the young Entente could—except South, who was human and could do nothing. He was adopted by the Entente and he had no magic. But he still had a wand. He carved new ones constantly, holding out hope that one day a wand would work.

What Bari had done I had never seen another Entente attempt to do. I was pretty sure we weren't meant to do it at all.

"Have you told Les Soeurs yet?" I asked in a whisper as I looked for the beetle, which had flown away. It circled over our heads just out of reach. Amazingly, Bari seemed unbothered that a part of her was buzzing above us in beetle form.

"Not yet. I can only do the extremities," she said. "I want to try with something larger . . . maybe birds or butterflies."

Bari had a penchant for winged things, be it a butterfly or a sparrow. If it flew, it garnered her attention. But what would make her concoct a spell like this? There had to be a rule against beetles for legs . . . What would Hecate say when she saw what Bari had done?

Bari waved her wand again. The errant beetle returned dutifully to its place among the others on the bed. Another wave. This time the blue beetles transformed into her flesh again.

"Bari, it's dangerous. You've made yourself too vulnerable. What if you complete the spell? How would the insect version of you be able to hold a wand? What if you got stuck like that?" An image of her with a beetle head and an Entente body flashed in my imagination.

"Then you would change me back. You worry too much, Farrow," she said confidently. "You could do it too if you tried. How do you think the Fates became the Fates? We don't just wake up one day ready for big magic. We have to prepare."

"I don't want to turn into beetles. Besides, I could have crushed part of you."

If my words affected Bari in the slightest, her face didn't betray it. Before she could mount another defense, she suddenly put a finger in front of her lips and threw the dress back down over her legs. She raised her wand and the door swung open, and South tumbled in after it. He had been listening.

"You're both wrong," he cried. "Iolanta's is the best. If you know the Present, you'd know if someone is lying or telling the truth." South, seemingly immune from embarrassment, plopped down on the floor near the foot of my bed.

He was always doing this. He didn't understand that we wanted him to stay as far away from us as possible.

"No one asked you, South. Besides, you'd be lucky to have any magic at all," I snapped.

South's hair was a mess of brown curls that always seemed too long and were rarely combed. His eyes were big and brown and too often looking at me. He was the only boy—the only human—ever allowed past the Veil, the magic that hid the Reverie from the rest of the world. I didn't remember when Les Soeurs brought him home. But with a single touch, Galatea had known his Past, Iolanta his Present, and Hecate his Future, and together they had known there was no one else in all the Queendoms with whom he belonged.

"Farrow! That's not fair," Bari said suddenly. "We may never be lucky enough to be chosen as Fates, but South will never be touched by magic at all."

"I'm glad I'm nothing like you." South looked right at me as he said it. "I would rather be anything than an Entente."

South had never said anything like that before. He was lucky to be here.

I felt my cheeks go red and my heart pick up its pace. South had always liked me the best. What if South liked me so much because he thought I was the closest one to him, the closest to being human? What if Bari thought the same thing? My magic was late, not absent altogether. There was a difference. If only I could show them that I was like my sisters and not like him . . .

Bari's eyes flashed with anger, and they caught mine with what felt like a challenge. I knew what she was thinking too: *We can't let him talk about the Entente that way.*

"What's going on?" a voice asked from the far corner of the room.

We glanced over to see nothing but an empty chair. A second ticked by and the air blurred in front of it, and then Amantha stepped out of the center of the blur.

Traveling was a prized gift that sometimes took years to master. I could make it from one room to another in the Entente but never any farther than a few feet. Amantha had been as far as the next Queendom.

"South doesn't want to be part of the Entente. He wants to be anything else," Bari explained.

"Anything else, huh?" Amantha asked.

South glanced at me wistfully, as if he was expecting me to come to his aid.

Bari caught his glance and seized upon it.

"I think South thinks maybe our Farrow would want the same," Bari said with an edge of mischief in her voice.

Amantha chimed in. "What do you say, Farrow?"

South looked at me again, expectant.

"Just take it back, South," I said, breaking his eye contact and finding the wall. But out of the corner of my eye, I could see him slump with disappointment.

"I would rather be anything else than Entente," he said firmly.

"Be careful what you wish for, South," I said with a flourish. I spotted a moth poised on the edge of the windowsill and got an idea.

South laughed and then got still, his eyes widening.

"What are you doing?" he asked, his voice pitching a hair higher with concern.

"*Quiet your smile, stop your laugh, and don't be so daft . . .*"

I raised my wand and began to chant some words under my breath. It wasn't a real spell, but South didn't know that. South was always there, a constant reminder of what it would be like to be completely ordinary. He wasn't one of us. He was a boy. He had no magic. He was a stray who Iolanta had taken in even though she couldn't take care of herself.

I thought that the second I raised my wand he would run, but South's eyes were defiant. He stood firm. The only indication that he was at all upset was the more-pronounced-than-usual rise and fall of his chest through his shirt.

I began again.

Quiet your smile, stop your laugh, and don't be so daft.
If not the Entente, what do you want?
If not here, then where?
I know—why not the sky?
When I open my eyes, you can fly.
Like the pesky moth that you are,
You will have wings so you can fly far . . .

He began to back away, then suddenly screamed in pain.

I heard a crunch of bone. He fell to the floor and began writhing around.

What was happening?

"It wasn't a real spell, South," I said as panic seized me. "I just wanted to teach you a lesson.

"South?" I called his name. But if he could hear me, I couldn't tell. He tried to stand up, but his legs buckled under him.

I reached down to try to help him, but he recoiled from my touch.

"Leave me alone," he said, his voice hoarse and full of reproach. He got to his feet again and turned toward the door.

Beneath his gray shirt something rippled. The rustling stopped and the cracking began. It sounded like bones breaking and re-forming.

A second later a pair of black-and-flesh-colored wings tore open the shirt, unfurling toward the ceiling. South stared at the shadow the wings made on the floor of the room. He stretched an arm around to touch the wings, but they were just out of reach.

South glanced back at me, his eyes meeting mine again. I felt the crush of guilt.

Hecate appeared in the doorway, watching me with disappointment so deep, it hurt almost as much as my guilt.

What had I done?

"Wings . . . You gave him wings," Bari said, her eyes wide in wonder. Amantha pointed and did not say a word. Her pale skin had gone paler.

"It was an accident," I blurted out. "I'm sorry, South."

But South was already running past Hecate as fast as his little red shoes could carry him.

"How did she do this?" Amantha asked Hecate.

"With enough will and enough magic, anything is possible," she replied.

"I didn't mean to, Hecate," I tried to explain.

Hecate looked directly at me. "Like I said, be careful what you wish for, Farrow."

CHAPTER 2

Imagine yourself without a hint of magic," Hecate said sternly.

"Impossible. I'm made of magic," I said, with more bravado than I felt.

I was in serious trouble. I had broken a major rule.

I looked back at Bari, who did not dare look up at me. Instead she patted down her skirt, as if it hadn't just had hundreds of beetles beneath it.

"Come with me, Farrow," Hecate commanded.

"Just me?" I asked.

"Next time I see the two of you, I expect both of you to be on your feet. Understood?"

She knew about the spell Bari had used to make her legs into beetles. Bari and Amantha shared a guilty look, then answered in chorus.

"Yes, Hecate."

"What about South?" I asked, not moving.

"Galatea will find him."

"I mean . . . the spell . . . his wings . . . ?" I explained.

"The magic will run out, like it always does," Hecate reminded me.

The Entente's magic had limits. Spells expired based on the power of the one wielding it. And I barely had any power.

I breathed a quiet sigh of relief. I hadn't caused any permanent damage. But the look on South's face stuck with me. He was more than hurt. And I had done that to him.

"Come, she's waiting," Hecate said.

"She?"

Hecate didn't answer as she led me down the hall. I had to take two steps for every one of hers. I was in that much trouble. We passed by the courtyard, which stood in the center of the Reverie's many buildings, as we wound our way through the labyrinth of rooms that made up our home.

Tere, one of my sisters, was experimenting with the weather in the courtyard as Galatea looked on. Tere's eyes were closed, her wand raised to the sky, and she pulled the clouds above closer with concentration alone. I wished that I had chosen to play with clouds instead of South's flesh.

Galatea advised, "Think of your wand as a lightning rod. The power is within you. The wand merely channels and conducts it."

The clouds darkened from white to gray in an instant, and drops of rain began falling from the sky. Tere opened her eyes and held up her hands, marveling at her own handiwork. Galatea looked on approvingly. It looked like play, but it was practice. We believed that the atmosphere was just one of a million things that determined a moment and that every moment could change the course of Fate.

What I had done to South just now . . . What had it done to his fate? What had it done to mine?

A few minutes later we were outside the one room we were forbidden to enter without permission—Iolanta's.

"We never get to go in there," I whispered, feeling trepidatious as Hecate beckoned me to the door.

"I know the Future, Farrow. Galatea knows the Past. But Iolanta is the only one who knows your heart right now."

"That's not true. I know it too," I countered, straightening my spine.

I took a deep breath and stepped toward the door.

Hecate leaned down and I felt her lips brush past my ear as she whispered, "Remember to keep your distance."

She opened the door to the room and pushed me inside. I felt the *whoosh* of the door behind me, shutting. I was alone with Iolanta.

The room was completely pitch-black. I pulled my wand out of my pocket and illuminated it with a whisper.

"Make your mark on the dark . . ."

I could barely make out Iolanta on the floor in the dark. But her pale-gray dress stood out against the shadows. It was made by her own hands, and shabbily so. I could see the seams and I felt my wand twitch, wanting to fix it with magic. Iolanta made her clothes and her furniture and absolutely anything she touched herself so nothing around her would be tainted by human or magical hands, and they wouldn't elicit visions of the Presents of so many lives. She had transformed the wood of the darkest part of the forest into a wooden goblet and a wooden bed. None of it would elicit the Present. But Iolanta was not a carpenter or a tailor, and the results were crude compared to the relative beauty of the rest of the Reverie, with a design limited only by Hecate's and Galatea's imaginations.

I remembered Hecate's directive and Iolanta's delicate condition. She could not be touched—not by humans, not by us or our magic.

"What has Hecate brought me?" she asked, her voice a harsh whisper. "Ah, I see . . . Farrow."

Iolanta clapped her hands and illuminated herself with a handful of flame. I knew she was powerful. I just hadn't seen it up close.

I gasped when I looked around. There were words and drawings scratched into the walls. The sketches were of all kinds of people captured in the moment that called to Iolanta. There was no rhyme or reason to the images. There was no discriminating: rich or poor, happy or sad, bakers, soldiers, husbands, wives, and children. There were a few of Les Soeurs, my sisters, and South. Some of the scenes were pleasant: couples kissing, families sitting down to dinner, a wedding. Others violent: a fight between men, the drowning of a woman, a man on his deathbed. It didn't matter how high up or low down the person was—Iolanta could see them. How she chose what to record I did not know. Perhaps she did not either.

On the wall behind her there was one freshly drawn, the paint still wet—South running away from the Reverie with his wings. Just like the others, Iolanta must have drawn it as she saw it.

"My, how you have grown," she said, focusing on me as her pupils constricted in response to the light.

"I didn't mean to do it—" I stopped myself. I knew I was supposed to be quiet and let Iolanta read me.

"You gave South wings, and Hecate did not appreciate your gift."

"Neither did South," I said sadly.

"But part of you is pleased to know exactly what you are capable of."

Was that what she saw in me?

I shook my head. "I hate that I did that to South. It was not what I meant to do."

"Wasn't it, though? You wanted to show him that you were not like him. I believe that you succeeded."

Iolanta had seen not just the moment. She had felt the ugly truth inside me as well.

I shook my head again.

"That is what I felt. But I did not know I had the power. I did not know . . . Before today I could not *hurt* a moth, let alone turn South into one."

Iolanta did not respond. She stared straight forward almost as if she could see right through me to the door behind me. Her eyes glassed over. Was I so wretched that she wouldn't even respond? Or had she drifted off to one of the other Presents?

"Please, you have to believe me. If you could feel what I felt, you had to feel that too . . . Iolanta?" I pleaded.

"Have you ever thought about what it's like for South, not just here with us but out there? A boy unlike any other in a world run by women."

I was struck. South didn't really belong anywhere. And I had just made him feel that even more acutely.

"But there's a prince now," I said. "A boy is going to do something that only women have done. A boy is going to be king. That has to change things for South."

"Does it . . . ? The boy prince and South are the rarest of things. And sometimes rare things spark fear where there need not be . . ."

I didn't understand. Boys had always been treated fairly. There was only one place in the Queendoms that they couldn't sit: the throne. And now even that was going to change.

"People are afraid the world is going to change—and when they get afraid, they do desperate things that might just change it after all."

Suddenly Iolanta held her head in her hands as if she were in some kind of pain.

"Iolanta? Can I help you? What can I do?" I asked, rushing to her side. I touched her skin. She was burning up.

Iolanta swatted me away, sending me flying against the wall.

"Too close, my dear," she said in a singsong voice, the lightness of which contrasted with the obvious agony she had been experiencing seconds before.

"I'm sorry," I said as a shock of pain coursed through me, radiating from the base of my tailbone.

"That is your gift, Farrow. You knew you were not supposed to touch me, but your instinct was to help no matter the consequences. Now, come closer."

I shook my head and remained plastered against the wall. I'd learned my lesson and it still hurt. Being with Iolanta meant having someone see you, possibly even better than you saw yourself, and I was still feeling guilty about today. I wasn't sure if I wanted to be seen.

"Run away, little mouse. But know this: you think magic is the most important gift now, but it's the heart that is your strength—your true gift. One day you will see."

Then just like that she became confused.

"Bari needs you. Hurry, child," she ordered before closing her eyes.

I backed out of the room and found Hecate wasn't waiting for me. I turned and raced for the room I shared with Bari.

When I got there, Bari's face was filled with frustration and in her hands she was holding her wand. It took me a second to realize what she was doing. She was trying to break it in half.

"No, Bari!" I said. Whatever she had seen, it couldn't be awful enough to make her stop using magic.

She looked up, surprised to see me. Then she turned her attention back to the wand, redoubling her efforts. The wand gave way and broke into two pieces.

"Why?" I asked.

"Hecate came back when you were with Iolanta," Bari said. "She showed me something from my Future. I looked scary."

I didn't understand. I couldn't imagine voluntarily choosing to be scary, whatever that meant. "I'm sure that you can still fix it. That's why she showed you."

"I don't want to change a thing," she asserted.

"Why not?"

"I am going to be so very powerful." Bari seemed to have missed the point of Hecate's lesson.

"Then why did you break your wand?" I asked.

"I need a new one, one that can rule Fate itself."

CHAPTER 3

The next day, the sound of chimes rang throughout the Reverie. It was time for our lessons. Bari and I raced to meet our sisters in the courtyard. When we got there, everyone was chattering as we took our places. Usually I'd be nervous about how they all would inevitably outshine me with their magic. But not today. Today I knew I wasn't behind my sisters in magic. And the reason why I knew wasn't there.

South usually sat in on every magic class even though he didn't have magic. Today he wasn't here because he'd been touched by mine. I longed to see him restored to his old self. The moth wings I'd given him must have left him overnight. But he must have been too mad or too embarrassed to share our company. And who was I to blame him?

"Why does he even bother?" Amantha had asked once.

"There is a value in knowing about magic even if you can't wield it," Galatea had said then.

Now Galatea looked around for him.

"Where's South?" she demanded.

My other sisters tittered again.

"Very well, let's begin without him." Galatea's voice was bright, but her eyes, as always, were haunted by the Pasts that she was constantly flooded with.

Hecate was stoic and stern, Iolanta was mad, and Galatea was simply beautiful and sad.

I asked her once, "Don't you see the happy Pasts as much as the sad ones?"

"I've found that sad things form longer shadows than happy ones, I'm afraid."

Galatea faced her Pasts as bravely as she could manage—dutifully trying to stay in the Present.

As usual, Galatea wore a dress that was made of seeds about to bud. Sometimes in the course of a day her whole dress would bloom. Today the dress was a pale green with seeds arranged in a tiny polka-dot pattern. Along the bodice, there were a few specks of white where the tiny flowers had begun to open to the morning sun. She surrounded herself with growing things—they helped her stay as grounded as possible in the *now*, while her mind was filled with the *then*.

Galatea also loved teaching us—because there was nothing more present than us in her mind. Children were more likely than adults not to be harping on things left behind.

Now she stood in front of us in the courtyard where we usually met for lessons with the rise of the sun.

"Fate turns in an instant . . . Fate turns on the tip of your wand . . . Fate is determined in seconds. In gusts of wind, in broken carriage spokes, in lost and returned gloves, in stolen moments and found ones. We create the moments. Sometimes we steal them. We shift destinies. It can be an arrow missing its mark or landing squarely in the center of a heart. We deal in small bits of magic. And the smallest infinitesimal magic can change the Queendoms. Never underestimate your power. Do not underestimate even an iota of magic. Don't forget that the weight of the world rests on your wand."

We stood a few feet apart in our dresses of gray, giving each of us room for our magic. Galatea stood before us, either showing us new spells or waiting for us to show her what we'd learned on our own. Today, she was focused on the latter. Each sister got up one by one and showed what her wand could do—what she could do.

Selina made a tree rise in the center of the garden with a large branch that lifted up Galatea like she was in the palm of its hand. Galatea laughed.

Tere made snow, which rained down as Selina lowered Galatea back to the ground.

Effie made her face that of a bear—and then roared, scaring us all except Galatea, who was not fazed by anything at all.

Amantha disappeared and reappeared with something concealed in her hand. "How far did you get this time?" Galatea asked, opening her hand to receive whatever Amantha had brought.

Amantha poured white sand from her hand into Galatea's. Galatea reacted with a hum of pleasure as she surmised that the sand was from Tourlais, the Ninth Queendom.

"All the way to Tourlais. You'll make it across all the Queendoms by the end of the year at this rate."

Amantha beamed.

Sistine hummed a tune that made us laugh. Her magic was music that could turn a moment, change our mood, make us happy or angry.

Still reeling from my encounter with South, I tried to hide behind the others. If I was lucky, it would be time for lunch soon and I could get through this lesson unnoticed.

Meanwhile, Odette disappeared then reappeared with some freshly baked bread.

"What do you have for me today?" Galatea asked. "Is it a basketful of kisses or something else?"

"Something else," Odette said with a broad smile.

"Ouch," Galatea said as she chewed. She grabbed her knee. "How clever," she added, lifting her skirt and revealing that the bread hadn't just given her the feeling of a skinned knee; one had actually appeared on her body.

Odette clapped her hands together, her pride evident.

"However, I am not sure how practical . . . ," Galatea began, deflating Odette's moment.

Inflicting pain was not something that the sisters embraced no matter what the outcome. But Galatea seemed to weigh her choice, maybe because the pain itself was so minimal.

"Do you not teach us that a wound as small as a paper cut can change the course of a life?" Odette protested.

Galatea laughed.

"That is true. But work on a painless distraction next time. I've found that while the human response to fear is quite profound, we prefer to deal in more positive methods unless there is no other choice."

Odette bowed her head. We all wanted to please Les Soeurs, and disappointing them stung.

The lesson was nearly over. I was already shuffling away, hoping to sneak out before I had to go.

"Not so fast . . . Now it's your turn, Farrow."

"Show us your new trick," Amantha demanded. "I want to fly too."

I felt my cheeks go warm. Of course they all knew.

"I would like to skip today," I said, gulping some air after declaring this to Galatea.

"Magic does not skip a day."

"Please, Galatea," I said, my bottom lip trembling. I had disappointed all Les Soeurs and myself. And raising my wand again felt like I was opening myself up to doing it all over again. Or worse.

"Very well, but tomorrow I expect to see your wand back in the air."

"Yes, Galatea," I said.

Before she dismissed us, she said, "Remember what it is to be Entente. From what I have seen today, I feel that we have forgotten."

She was talking about me and South—of course she knew. Either Hecate had told her or she had looked at my Past.

"There is no need for laughter. South not only belongs to us. He represents an opportunity to show empathy—a skill essential for our duty to the Queendoms."

"Now—who are we?" she asked us as she had a million times before. And after each line she stopped and we followed her, our voices rising louder with every line. This was our creed.

We are the Entente.
We have no fathers or mothers—only sisters and
 The Three—
We are defenders of destiny.
Our hearts have no function other than to serve.
Our hearts do not beat for ourselves—our hearts
 beat for the Hinter.
We are the Entente . . . now and Ever After.

Saying the words gave me a sense of calm. But then a butterfly flew into the courtyard, and I was back in my misery again. The sight of wings made me think of South.

"Everyone, that's it for the day. Farrow, stay," Galatea said as she allowed the rest of my sisters to leave the courtyard.

I stepped forward and put her wand to my temple.

"What you said up there, that was about me, right? It's my fault. See for yourself."

Galatea took the other end of the wand and watched my Past.

"It matters that you did not intend to hurt him, Farrow."

"It doesn't matter to South."

"It matters to you. It matters to who you are. Farrow, I know it doesn't seem like it, but what I said up there, I was talking about me. I used to be the one with the small magic while Hecate and Iolanta far outpaced me. And then one day, just like you, I realized what I could do. You have to figure out what to do with it. Now that you have all that power, you have to figure out how to use it. And sometimes just a little bit goes a long way . . . Now, go."

"Go where?"

"I don't think it's me that you need to be telling all this to."

CHAPTER 4

After leaving Galatea, I looked for South. I found him at the edge of the cliff that overlooked the stream running through the Reverie. Inexplicably, his shirt was off; his wings were outstretched.

I gasped. How did South still have his wings?

It was my first spell on a human. Before yesterday I hadn't even managed to change any living thing except myself. How had my spell seen the light of a second day? There were rumors of spells lasting longer, but that was the stuff of Fates and the Fates did not dare overuse their powers. If there were exceptions, they did not tell us about them. And yet I, the youngest of the Entente, had somehow cast a spell that had lasted another day.

I stared at South's wings, which looked different in the sunlight. They were a deeper purple than I'd thought. They were beautiful and luminescent, like a moth's. Part of me marveled at my handiwork, but I winced as I saw where the wings connected in the center of South's spine. His flesh strained against the new weight of his wings.

My eyes fell to the ground beside him, where his wand lay. He must have tried to fix it himself.

"South," I said quietly as I sat down, far enough to give him room to spread his wings. I looked past him to the trees we used to make our wands. He saw my face next to his in the water and frowned.

"How are they still here?" I asked.

The wings flapped once, causing a draft of air that blew my hair back. For a second I thought he was going to take flight.

But instead he twisted around and tried to reach his wings with his left hand. In it was a knife. I gasped again.

He gave me a withering look and tried to explain. "They won't come off."

"South, stop!" I got up and ran to him but stopped short, looking at the knife.

"Why do you hate me so much?" he demanded.

"I don't . . ."

"When Amantha and Bari and the other sisters are around, you are one Farrow. When they're not . . . you're another."

He wasn't wrong. When my sisters weren't around, I had played with South—human games like hopscotch and catch, and I'd shown him spells. But when my sisters were around, I shunned him. I felt the same shame I'd felt with Iolanta and with Galatea creep in all over again.

"South . . . I . . . ," I began but "sorry" did not seem enough.

"I wish you were the same Farrow all the time."

His words cut into me with the same pain I imagined he felt when he'd cut into his flesh.

"You have to do it," he demanded, holding the knife out to me.

I took the knife and threw it into the water.

"Why did you do that?" he asked.

"Because I don't want to hurt you," I said.

"Then use your wand. Help me, Farrow."

I shook my head. The best thing to do was to wait for the spell to wear off.

"I'm getting these off, with or without your help. If you don't do it, then I'll just get another knife," he countered. The look on his face said that he was serious.

"Okay." I pulled my wand out of my pocket and pointed it at him. "Hold still."

He opened his arms to me, as if to welcome my magic.

"Why don't you hate me?" I asked. Wasn't he afraid I would maim him further?

"Who says I don't? But you did this. You can undo it. Stop being a chicken and just do it."

I tried to think of a new spell, but the words did not come.

"What if I turn you into something worse? We need help, South. We need to talk to Hecate."

"You have to do it. I can't spend another day like this." He looked at his reflection in the water. "I look like a monster."

"I can't. I'm sorry, South."

He stormed toward the main house, but his wings slowed him down as a strong gust of wind pulled him back with every step. I looked away, feeling responsible for further humiliating him.

I looked at the water again, my face distorted.

He wasn't the monster.

I was.

"Hecate, please," I pleaded when I found her in her room.

It was the opposite of Iolanta's room. Things from other people surrounded her. Dead people. There was a collection of brushes that lined her dressing table. Each one belonged to a dead Fate. She said that they kept her anchored to the Past. As the Fate of the Future, she was always in danger of getting lost in the visions of what was to come, just as Iolanta had gotten lost in all the Presents. Similarly, Galatea's room was designed to keep her in the Present, just like her dresses. Her room was alive. Her furniture was made of live trees. Every fabric and surface was embedded with seeds, from the carpets underfoot to the curtain that wove itself together to open and close at the whim of Galatea's wand.

I walked by Hecate's dressing table like I would a graveyard, carefully and with deference. But I was also curious.

What would it be like to be Galatea, to touch one single hair and see the whole of someone's life so far? What would it be like to be Hecate and see the whole of their future? What would it be like to be Iolanta and see their every truth right now?

"Farrow? Surely you did not come here to stare at my brushes?" Hecate asked brusquely.

I turned my back on the brushes and faced her. "It's South. Somehow the magic hasn't worn off. He still has his wings."

"I know," she said without blinking.

Of course she knew. She had to have seen it before it happened. She had to have known that his wings had stuck. But she'd also have to know when and how they would be remedied.

"Can you tell me how I did this?"

"Marry your words to your will and you can do almost anything, but that doesn't mean that you should," she said.

"Why are you punishing him when I am the one who messed up?" The words came out in a rush. I had never contradicted Hecate before. But the image of South struggling with his wings was there every time I shut my eyes.

"What *we* do has consequences. If you are to become a Fate, you have to know that. You all do," Hecate countered.

"But why should he pay the price for what I've done?" I dug in, unable to let this go.

"We are all tied together. For better or worse. And you know that."

"But South is human. He isn't really Entente." Even as I said it, I knew the words were unkind.

Hecate frowned. "South is just as much Entente as you or me. He was raised under our roof. But even if he weren't . . . being a Fate means caring about everyone, not just the Entente. It means caring about everything in the Hinter and the Queendoms and beyond. It means that what you do matters. And what you undo matters."

"Hecate," I said, fighting a sigh. Hearing her logic, I thought of what Iolanta had said: imagine what it's like to be South. And just then I imagined I had made everything that much worse for him. I was quite simply the worst Entente ever.

I pushed my wand in Hecate's direction.

"Maybe you should just take it away from me for a while."

"Why would I do that, when you're going to need it where we're going?"

How could she possibly want to take me anyplace now? I wondered.

"You're coming with me to the palace today," she said.

"What?" I asked.

"It's time to pay our respects to the new Queen," Hecate said as she gently took my wand and deposited it in my dress pocket.

"I thought we did that last week," I protested, confused and a little relieved to feel the weight of my wand at my side again. If

Hecate wanted to take me with her, then I wasn't a complete waste of magic after all.

Queen Meena had died just a week ago, and the Entente, along with the rest of the Queendom, had been in attendance at the funeral. There were Entente at the side of every Queen, but Meena had been the most powerful. Hinter was the most powerful Queendom, which was why the Reverie was seated here. It was Les Soeurs' duty to keep that power in check for the good of all the Queendoms. Hecate and Galatea had helped us with our glamours and we had mixed into the crowd in the square, along with what seemed like all of Hinter. Only Iolanta had stayed behind, because that many bodies filled with so much sadness in her proximity would have been too much for her senses. But she could see their interactions from the Reverie.

"Magrit was a princess then. Now she is the Queen," Hecate explained.

"What's the difference?" I asked. Wasn't she the same person this week as she was the last?

"I don't think she's changed, but I fear she might change all of us."

CHAPTER 5

A few minutes later I watched as Hecate added wrinkles to her face with her wand. Then she began to gray her jet-black hair with another stroke of her wand. Whenever we left the Reverie, we always took on new faces. It was imperative that our identities be kept secret from the royals.

"Why do you pick a skin that is so ancient?" I asked.

"We don't value vanity in the Entente. It's dangerous," Hecate said as she touched another section of her hair. It became gray with a tinge of pale green. "And no one looks at an old woman.

"There," she said, seemingly done. She got up and made room for me at the dressing table. Our reflections stared back at us in the mirror that sat atop it.

I started to reach for my wand but hesitated. This was what I did best. But after what had happened with South, I wasn't sure if I could do it anymore.

"It's okay to make mistakes, Farrow. But you can't let the mistakes make you. In time, South will be fine. But you have to forgive yourself and use your gift."

I picked up the wand and hesitated again. It was too much. The image of South and his wings and scrunched-up face stopped me.

She sighed. "Okay, just this once. But next time . . ."

I nodded and smiled at her, grateful for this small reprieve. "Can I have green eyes this time?"

She touched her wand to my temple and I closed my eyes. When I opened them, my gray eyes were now a piercing shade of green, matching the shade in my imagination perfectly.

"The idea is not to stand out, Farrow," she said, tapping her wand against the side of my head again.

I pouted as my eyes dulled back to their usual shade of gray.

"But the Entente and the Queendom are friends," I said. I had been told about the Entente's connection to the palace and the royals my whole life.

"No. The Entente and the Queendom have a covenant," Hecate corrected. "It means 'agreement.' And agreements are not always honored."

When Hecate's wand passed over my features, they changed too. She slimmed out my face, broadened my nose, and darkened my eyebrows and eyelashes to match the long dark hair she'd replaced my brown hair with. To finish, she raised my cheekbones and increased my pout. It never hurt when Hecate transformed my face.

"I know this feels like a game, Farrow. But it's not. Picking up a wand should never be for your own satisfaction. It should be for good." She bent to touch the hem of my dress.

I watched it change from the gray that we all wore every day to a pale shade of blue. I opened my mouth to ask for a pale shade of yellow, knowing I would be met with the same denial.

She took me in for a beat before touching the dress again. The yellow appeared.

"Why?" I asked as joy filled me. Was this pity because of my near tears? "I thought we couldn't take the risk."

"I know you think me hard, Farrow. But everything I have done is to give you the armor and tools you will need for what is to come."

"What is to come?" I asked, knowing she would never tell me.

"Let's take the long way," she said, putting her hand over mine.

I was still surprised that Hecate had suggested I go with her. But I shouldn't have been. She was a creature of the Future. She let go of the Past and even the Present easier than her sisters did.

"Hurry up—time won't wait for us," she said with a wry smile.

Hecate could be stern, but she was not without humor. She smiled at her own joke as I followed her out to the Veil.

The air flickered before Hecate could tap the magical Veil that shielded the Reverie from the world. Iolanta appeared, blocking Hecate's wand and our way.

The Veil was created by Les Soeurs to protect us. No human could find it or us unless we wanted them to. Les Soeurs cast the Veil with the rise of the moon, and it lasted until the next moonrise. All three Les Soeurs had to be present to complete the spell. All of us could enter and exit at will with our wands. South had to be accompanied by one of us to enter or to exit. Looking at the shimmering air, I wondered for the first time how it must have felt for him not to be able to come and go from his home as he liked. Even if South truly had wanted to fly away from here, the Veil would have stopped him.

"Iolanta, what are you doing out of your room?" Hecate asked, her voice filled with concern. "Let me help get you back to bed."

Iolanta never left her quarters. What would make her leave them now? Seeing her twice in as many days was more than unusual. It was unsettling.

"Don't go. Please," Iolanta said, her lids heavy, as if they were trying to shut out the light.

Galatea showed up beside Iolanta.

"Iolanta and I discussed it. I agree with her. You should not go," Galatea said firmly.

Hecate looked from one Fate to the other. She and Galatea were usually on the same side.

"You know what we saw at the funeral," Iolanta continued.

"Let's give her some time," offered Galatea gently.

"Time for what?" Hecate asked. "We know better than anyone that time is not the salve for what we saw in Magrit. She isn't right. She lacks more than she is. Empathy and morality are necessities of the Crown and she is without them."

"And you think that talk will be the answer?" Galatea countered.

"We have known many a heart to change," Hecate said.

"Not one as stubborn as this," Iolanta added. "I can see the new Queen's heart and it is dark."

"That's the beauty of the heart," Hecate said. "It can change from moment to moment and from one day to the next. Besides, tomorrow is my concern, sister. Today is yours."

"Hecate." Iolanta grabbed her arm again. "Her heart will not change. Usually, in a moment, I see the flickers . . . flickers of doubt . . . the seeds of change. There is no change in her." Iolanta sounded clearer and more certain than ever.

"We did not see any tears, but we also didn't feel them," Galatea agreed. "Not in her Past, Present, or Future."

"She is not the first daughter to fail to honor her mother," Hecate countered. "Perhaps this lack of sentimentality will make her a better ruler."

"That would be easier to believe if she'd shown compassion for a single person in her entire life," Galatea argued. "She did not cry when her own husband expired after returning from the war with the Thirteenth Queendom. She did not cry at the birth of little Prince Mather. Even when he was the first male heir born to any Queen in any Queendom in all recorded time. And she did not cry when her mother fell ill or when she died."

"I would think that her defense of her son would be a point in her favor. Or at the very least a glimmer of hope," Hecate countered.

"Unless she sees her son as a possession, not a flesh-and-blood love. When she was small, she loved her dolls to death and would let no one else play with them. That did not stop her from beheading them all."

Galatea knew everything about every royal, every indiscretion, and that knowledge of every bad thing had left her skeptical of what good lay in their Futures.

"She was a child. They were dolls. You cannot make that the standard."

"Why not? We judge our own by the highest of codes. Why should humans be different? I have measured every moment of Magrit's life, and she has yet to show us something other than selfishness."

"Then what do you suggest?" Hecate asked.

"If the Crown has changed, then perhaps we must change to meet the Crown," Galatea offered. "If she scares us all this much, then let's find another way to deal with her."

"And what way would that be?" Hecate pressed, sounding genuinely curious.

"You think that they can change. But you don't allow for us to, Hecate," Galatea corrected. "I hope that isn't the death of us."

"You worry too much, sisters. We all have a part to play, and I know better than anyone that this is mine . . ."

"Hecate . . . Please . . ." Iolanta's face contorted as if she was fighting tears.

"Know this, we are always together, sisters. Even if we are far apart," Hecate said, resolute.

"Then take this with you." Galatea surprised all of us by giving her a kiss on the forehead.

Hecate looked at her sharply. The mark where Galatea had kissed her lit up like the glow of the moon and then washed over the rest of her skin with white light. Was it a protection spell?

"What did you do, sister?" Hecate demanded.

Galatea smiled. "Just making sure that you come back to me."

~

Hecate and I walked the short distance to town in silence. In the week since Queen Meena's death, the Queendom had been under a constant state of reconstruction. Workers were tearing down the white stone face of the palace.

I pulled at Hecate's hand. "What are they doing?"

"The new Queen is replacing the stone with Black Glass," Hecate said.

Black Glass was the black metal found only in the Hinter, the First Queendom. It was stronger than any metal known to man or to the Entente. It was the reason the Hinter was considered the most powerful of the Queendoms. The guards' weapons were forged with Black Glass, and so were the walls that fortified the Queendom.

"It is so very ugly," I commented.

Before we could move on, Hecate whispered a warning. "Avoid the glass; do not look upon it in the company of humans."

"Why? Will it hurt us?"

"The Queen thinks it can hurt our bodies, but she is wrong. But there is more than one way to hurt."

I cocked my head. I didn't understand. We had magic. Hecate and Galatea seemed invincible. Iolanta was another story. But the cause was not humankind; it was her gift itself.

"How can we be hurt by it?"

"It can reveal our faces."

The impulse to do the opposite of Hecate's directive seized me. I wanted to see how the glass worked up close. I wanted to see my face transform back to itself. But Hecate's stern look stilled me as it always did. The elaborate act of disguise had seemed like a game to me that the Entente played with the Queens, not something more sinister—until now.

"This is not pretend for the sake of pretending—as delightful as it can be to wear a dress of yellow or the face of someone else. It is a protection just as much as the Veil—know that and remember it." She looked at me intently, deflating our adventure just a bit.

"Yes, Hecate," I said dutifully.

But Hecate, seemingly responding to my shift in mood, added, "The Queen is not erecting the glass with us in mind. She has another objective."

"What objective?"

"The glass is strong. She is making a fortress," Hecate assessed.

"What do we need a fortress for?"

Hecate looked solemn. "War."

CHAPTER 6

This wasn't my first time in the palace, but it was the first time I had been there since Magrit had taken power. And even though she had been in mourning, she had somehow found time to completely redecorate. The last time I was there, it had been decorated in pastels and ornate brocade. Now the Black Glass I had seen in the square was everywhere. Giant friezes of it carved with flowers and figures were replacing former Queen Meena's pretty wallpaper. Workmen were fortifying the palace from the inside out.

The Queen's lady-in-waiting appeared. She wore a full black mourning dress in honor of the dead Queen. She was plump with a round face, which lit up after she studied Hecate for a quick beat. Over the years, Hecate had presented herself to the palace wearing dozens of different faces, but all she had to do was whisper the word "Entente" and she was brought to the Crown.

In the past, some royals had disagreed with the Entente, while others had followed their advice to the letter. But they always accepted the Entente into their drawing rooms, and they always listened. Today should not have been any different, but I could not help but think about Galatea's and Iolanta's warnings.

Hecate smiled and curtsied. We were required to act like nobility when we were at the palace, so that our visits to the Queen and our influence on her could remain our secret, save for a few trusted insiders. Still, Hecate was the most powerful being I had ever known, and despite being told it was custom, it was odd seeing her bow down to anyone.

To the people, the Entente were a rumor, a bedtime story. But for those close to the royals, they were real and revered.

"I am glad you are here. Princess . . . Queen Magrit is not well. Perhaps she never has been." The lady's words came in a rushed whisper, and she looked behind her as if she were worried that someone might be listening.

This was not what Hecate wanted to hear, but she smiled nonetheless. "Lady Sadie, it is indeed a difficult time. But even in the most difficult times, there is still opportunity for good."

"I see you brought another. I can take her to the kitchen and get her some sweets," Sadie offered.

"Thank you, but she stays with me," Hecate said.

I felt a wave of pride. I wasn't a human child. I was Entente.

Suddenly Hecate whirled around and pulled out her wand. I felt her tense beside me, and then the flash of movement as she stabbed her wand into the air in front of her just as a line of soldiers came charging around the corner. The men froze in place in response to Hecate's wand.

Hecate could stop time, but it wasn't something she did lightly. Were they a threat? Were the soldiers attacking us? I could hear my heart beating in my ears.

Next to her, the lady-in-waiting gasped and fanned herself as she marveled at Hecate's magic. "Oh my. That's incredible! You really are Entente . . . But it isn't necessary," she exclaimed.

I studied Hecate's handiwork. The soldiers were completely still. But upon closer examination, I noticed something strange . . . They were carrying wooden swords.

"They're playing with the prince," Lady Sadie said.

Hecate closed her eyes like she did when she caught a glimpse of the Future to confirm.

"Hide-and-seek," Lady Sadie explained. "Prince Mather makes the staff play with him. The Queen doesn't allow him to have friends."

Hecate's power, like the powers of all the sisters, had to be focused on a few people at a time. If Hecate looked at too many Futures at once, she would end up in a dark room like Iolanta. It was possible for her to miss something—like the intent of the advancing soldiers. Hecate, Galatea, and Iolanta called them glimpses for a reason. Images and feelings flooded all their senses, and sometimes they didn't have enough or they had too much information about what had, could, or would happen. Just now, I had witnessed Hecate get a glimpse wrong. She smiled down at me as if she knew what it meant for me to see that even a Fate could make a mistake.

A little boy who looked to be my age ran behind me. He had dark-brown hair, wild brown eyes, and a smile that spread from ear to ear. I recognized him from the funeral—Prince Mather.

To my surprise, he stopped in his tracks.

"Whoa!" He was mesmerized by the frozen soldiers. "Magic."

He reached out and touched the arm of one of the soldiers. The soldier did not move. "Are you Entente?" the prince asked, looking squarely at me.

I glanced up at Hecate for permission.

She nodded.

"Can you play?" he asked, forgetting about the soldiers and focusing on me.

"I'm sorry. The Entente don't play," I said reflexively, and at the same time ardently wishing it weren't true.

The prince looked up at Hecate in disbelief. He had probably never met another child who didn't play before.

"We have to see the Queen. Perhaps some other time," she said.

The prince's face fell, but then he brightened.

"If I say you have to play, then you have to play. Everything and everyone here is mine," he said matter-of-factly.

"No one owns anyone," I snapped as the goodwill I felt for him a second before began to fade away. "You certainly don't own the Entente."

Lady Sadie gasped. There were protocols for dealing with royals and I had clearly broken one of them.

"That is not the way we speak to His Highness," Lady Sadie said sternly.

"That's not the way he should speak to the Entente," I retorted, putting my hands on my hips.

Hecate cleared her throat beside me. I looked up at her, expecting admonishment. Instead, she bent down and addressed the prince.

"I know that you are mourning your grandmother, but this is no way to behave. The people are not your playthings, and neither are the Entente. You should consider it your honor to one day be king . . . not the other way around."

Prince Mather's bottom lip quivered. The arrogance and the smile were gone. All that remained was a sad little boy. I felt a pang of sympathy for him. It had not occurred to me that the prince's behavior could be tied to missing his grandmother.

"The Queendom must move on," he said. "We should all be happy for our new Queen." The words sounded rehearsed, as if they were not his own.

"It's okay to miss her," I told him, just as Hecate had told me at Queen Meena's funeral. "The Past is never gone. We carry it with us now and into the Future."

"Farrow is right," Hecate said. "When someone truly loves you, some part of them never leaves you."

Prince Mather absorbed my words and Hecate's with a sniffle. "Are you sure you can't play? I'm asking, not ordering," he added quickly.

"We have to go, Prince Mather," Hecate said, her voice gentle now.

The prince's face fell again, but this time without the petulance.

Hecate bent down and whispered something to him, and he smiled.

"She says we'll meet again," he told me.

I wondered if she meant that I would be his Entente. Until I made South wings, I'd thought that I would be lucky to be sent to one of the other Queendoms to use my magic to aid and advise another queen. But if I was capable of that, perhaps I was capable of being a Fate after all. The thought was chased immediately by guilt. Nothing good should come out of the bad thing I had done to South. I wish I had found out how powerful I could be some other way.

"I'll take you to the Queen. But first we must make you presentable," Lady Sadie said.

"But what about them?" Prince Mather asked, pointing at the still-frozen soldiers.

Hecate lifted her wand. "I'll count to five and give you a bit of a head start."

The little prince ran ahead of the soldiers with a squeal. He took a peek back at them and his eyes connected with mine just as Hecate reanimated the soldiers, who picked up exactly where they had left off.

~

"Now, to what do we owe the honor?" Queen Magrit was seated on a chaise in the center of the room. Her angular face did not hide her displeasure.

"Your Majesty, we just wanted to pay our respects. I fear we did not get off to the best start after the funeral. The Entente and the royals have a great history. And my sisters and I want only for the Present and Future to have the same fruitfulness.

"Last week I showed you that if you don't change course, you will lose your life. And the lives of many of your subjects. And yet you do not believe me."

"You told me to give up my crown. You might as well have asked me to give up my life," the Queen said.

Hecate approached her with her wand. "May I?"

The Queen recoiled and then she reconsidered, leaning forward. Magrit couldn't resist. She wanted to see. Hecate put her wand to her temple as Magrit closed her eyes. Queen Magrit shuddered at what she saw and her eyes flew open.

"Enough!" the Queen screamed, her eyes wild. "How can I believe what you say and what you show me when you won't show your true face to me?" she said angrily.

"This is the way it has always been done. For your sake and for ours," Hecate explained calmly.

"If you hadn't noticed, things are different now. I am different from my predecessors. And the Future will be different from the one you magicked for me."

Hecate raised her wand again. "I don't make up the Future. I am merely a conduit."

"You are more than that. You and your kind have meddled too much and for too long in human affairs. I believe it's time for you to leave."

I expected Hecate to keep fighting. To make her case. The way she had with me about South. But, instead, she crossed to me and took my hand.

"I pray you heed my advice, dear Queen. Or Hinter will pay for your folly."

We slipped out into the square among the crowd. I glanced back at the palace.

"Don't look back, Farrow. Don't ever look back," Hecate said with an urgency that frightened me. "Promise me that you will look to the Future no matter what happens."

She touched her wand to my forehead; I closed my eyes, and I got a glimpse.

I could see the interior of the palace and my hand extended, holding a wand. Somehow I knew it was mine. It was different from the one that was in my pocket now. It was completely covered in carvings. The chime of a clock tower rang in my ears.

When Hecate removed the wand from my temple, I looked at her.

"I don't understand," I said, searching her face for meaning.

"One day you will. I wish we had more time, Farrow."

She kissed me on the cheek then. I felt warmth wash over me, and I could see the faint glow of the kiss's light emanating from my skin. I remembered the kiss that Galatea had given Hecate. A kiss of protection.

Then she did something that no one in the Entente had ever done before. She hugged me.

"We don't do that," I said as her arms came around me. *We cannot do what we must for others if there is no light between us. If we love each other too much there will be no room for us to love all humanity.* Hecate and the other sisters had told us that countless times. We were supposed to be sisters, but we were not supposed to be attached to one another. But right then she pulled me close. I put my arms around her awkwardly and inhaled the smell of her hair. She smelled like the lavender soapstone we all used.

"It's time to go," she said, straightening. She touched my face and dress again and then her own. I could feel us both transforming into the appearance of commoners. To my shock, she had chosen her own face.

I touched my face. I was wearing my own too. "We never show our real faces."

Hecate abruptly let go of my hand.

The Queen was sweeping into the square with her guard twenty-deep behind her. At her side there was a boy about my age dressed in a guard's uniform.

"That's not the prince," I said.

"Be quiet. Be still. You have to hide, until . . . ," Hecate whispered, drifting off.

I protested, reaching for her hand, but she pushed me backward with a wave of her wand and suddenly I was beneath one of the carts in the square. I tried to move forward, but it was as if an invisible wall blocked me from moving. She had spelled me.

"Witch!" the Queen said, her eyes locked on Hecate.

Hecate stood her ground, but she did not raise her wand. She did not stop time. Hecate was not running.

"Witch," Magrit repeated as she stepped still closer.

From my position under the cart, I could see the soldiers surround my mentor.

"Take her."

CHAPTER 7

A few minutes later Hecate was standing on a pyre, her hands tied to a post behind her.

A guard began reading out charges from a scroll. It seemed impossible that the list was made after our visit to the Queen today; it was so long and dreadfully detailed. I couldn't make sense of any of it. The only crime the Entente were guilty of was sacrificing generation after generation to help the Queendoms.

But Hecate ignored the guard and focused on the Queen.

"Do you have anything else to say, witch?" Magrit asked.

"You have already seen what I have to show you," Hecate said simply.

"Just because my mother and her mother before her believed in fairy tales doesn't mean that I will follow in their folly . . . Do you really expect an entire Queendom to turn on your word?"

"This is how it has been done for generations. The Entente exist to serve and guide you, our Crown. Do you argue with that legacy, that history?" Hecate asked.

The Queen shook her head. "History is in the eye of the beholder. And from where I am standing, you have done nothing for the

Queens before me that they couldn't have accomplished on their own."

"If you don't trust my words, then trust my wand—you have seen what the Future holds for you if you do not listen."

"Our memories are our own—and so are our destinies. You don't get to take them from us."

No. I could hear my own voice in my head, but I couldn't get the word across my lips. I tried to move toward Hecate, but my limbs were no longer my own. They were still. Just as Hecate wanted them to be.

She looked the Queen straight in the eye.

"You don't have to do this, Magrit."

"But it is my Fate. According to you."

The Queen waved at the guard reading the charges, and then snatched the scroll from her hands, taking over.

"You are charged with performing sorcery with the intention of usurping the Crown. What say you?" the Queen pressed.

Hecate did not answer. The Queen continued to pace around her.

"Did you or did you not come to me and ask me to take off my crown in the name of your dark magic?"

As she spoke, people began to gather. It was a rare thing to see the Queen in the square. It was an even rarer thing to see a real, live Entente.

Most people in Hinter were aware of magic. And of the Entente. But no one, except the royals, was sure that we really existed. Until now.

They did know the Queen, and they believed in her. And if she said that we were bad . . . then perhaps they would believe that the world was better off without us.

I waited for someone to stop her. There were gasps. But then there was quiet—the worst kind of quiet, where fear holds everyone hostage and no one breaks free of it.

Not a soul stopped what was happening. Not even Hecate. I'd seen Hecate perform magic without touching her wand before. Why not now? Was it the fault of the Black Glass or was it Hecate herself? Was Hecate wrong before? Did the Black Glass have the power not just to reveal our faces but also to stop our magic in its tracks? And if it could, how could Hecate not have foreseen this? How could she not know that the war that Magrit sought was not just on the other Queendoms but on us as well?

Please, Hecate, help yourself. Save yourself. Please.

"You claim to love the people. But you told me you would choose a piece of metal over them," Hecate said.

Suddenly Hecate's face began to transform itself into the Queen's.

She spoke in the Queen's voice: *"The people belong to me. They would gladly give their lives for me. I am the Crown. I am everything to them. I could run the streets with their blood and they would line up and offer up their veins for me."*

The real Magrit did not flinch, but the people reacted. There was a murmur of dissent. Was their beloved Queen admitting that she could put them on the pyre too? The guards shifted closer to them, quelling their din before it could grow. Their faces were awash with confusion.

"Who do you believe—a witch who can change her face and voice at will or your Queen?" the Queen countered.

The people shifted uncomfortably, looking from Hecate to the Queen and back again. The Entente had not been real to them until today. And their Queen was everything to them, as her mother was before her. But they had known only peace during Meena's reign. And Queen Magrit was bringing them chaos in their public square.

Hecate's face returned to her own.

And the crowd inhaled collectively, inscrutable. They had not seen magic before. Hecate was magic in the flesh.

"*We* always tell the truth, no matter what face we wear."

"The people know me. And my heart. Who are you? How can they believe you when you want nothing, love nothing, hate nothing? Who are you?"

In the interminable pause, the crowd made a decision between the Queen they thought they knew and the Entente they had believed were a thing from childhood tales. In the stories, they had been magical saviors, but in the flesh, when the Queen rewrote the story, she made the Entente the villains. A murmur rose that became a chant of "witch." Hecate had miscalculated. By showing her magic to the people, she had given them cause to fear her.

The Queen concluded her list of offenses. "I don't trust you or the Entente. And what I do not trust must be extinguished for the good of the Crown. For the good of us all."

The Queen's man raised a torch and prepared to light the pyre.

In my mind, I thrashed against that which bound me, tried with all my might to scream and wail, but Hecate had trapped my anguish inside me. Hecate remained calm. A single tear ran down her cheek.

I cannot lose you like this. Please, stop this for me.

Everything I have done, I have done for you and your sisters. You will see, she said in my mind.

Hecate finally said out loud, "We are forever. No one can take us from one another. We *are* Entente."

But I knew that Hecate wasn't talking to the Queen. She was talking to me.

The crowd resumed their chant with more force. *"Witch! Witch! Witch! Witch!"*

My heart was the only thing that could move, and it began beating so hard it echoed through my paralyzed form. But it wasn't enough to drown out the words.

I focused again on the boy in full guard's uniform next to the Queen. His skin and hair were brown. His face was round. His eyes were piercing green, but they reflected back the darkness of the new buildings made of Black Glass around the square. His mouth remained in a fully pursed line. He had not joined in the chant.

Thunder crackled, followed by a flash of lightning that lit up the already bright sky, meeting Hecate's hand in one of the pockets of her skirts. Hecate didn't need her wand to wield her power. It only aided her in being more precise.

I willed her to strike again and use the lightning to break the bonds that held her. But the sky remained dark for a beat.

The Queen nodded at the soldiers to light the torches. The flames went up, and I watched in horror as the pyre began to burn beneath Hecate.

Lightning struck again. This time near the Queen, but if Hecate was responsible for it, she did not show it.

From my hiding spot, I didn't understand.

We had been walking through the square when the Queen's guards grabbed her. Hecate went with them, even though she was stronger. Even though she could have stopped them with a breath, a whisper, or a turn of her wrist. She let them lead her to the square and tie her up. She let them start a fire beneath the pyre. She kept her lips sealed. She did not move a muscle in protest. She let them take her from me. From all of us.

From me especially.

Hecate was the most powerful of us. She was the Future of Les Soeurs, my mentor, and sister to us all. But I didn't know she was my mother until the moment before her last breath.

When I could move again, I touched my face. It was wet. I realized that I was crying. I had never seen another member of the Entente cry—not Hecate on the pyre, not Galatea as she was watching her. But I was crying now.

I should have known she was my mother, but Hecate had always been so powerful that her wishes were opaque to me—like she never wanted or felt anything other than what she was doing at the time. But as she burned, her eyes met mine. The flames curled around her. She should have been screaming—instead, she spoke to me in a voice I could only hear in my head.

I wish I'd told you, Farrow. But it is not our way.

I tried to scream, to get to her, but I was paralyzed where I stood. As a man dressed in the livery of the Queen's guard read off a list of offenses, saying things like "malevolent sorcery against the Queen" and "treasonous inciter," my mouth would not open; my legs would not move. I didn't know if Hecate was using what power she had left to stop me from fighting when she should have been fighting to stay alive.

Don't fight.

Suddenly Galatea, my older sister and the Past of Les Soeurs, appeared in the center of the square. If Hecate expired, there would be only two of them. The three Les Soeurs led the rest of the Entente. Iolanta, the Present, was in isolation. But she would feel Hecate die the moment it happened. Galatea, as the Sister of the Past, would remember every second of Hecate's death without the kindness of time to help it fade. Even though it was thought that my gift would be the Present someday, it felt like I would be remembering every detail of it forever too. I prayed for them to be able to stop it, but that was all for naught.

The other sisters began to appear. The army raised their swords against them. I still could not move.

Iolanta appeared suddenly—Iolanta, who never left the confines of her isolation. Iolanta, who knew the Present and clearly could feel Hecate on the pyre.

South and Amantha and Bari were there too, making their own desperate attempts at saving her while I stood frozen.

I had no choice. I did not blink once as I watched the flames engulf her body, her face, and her hair. As her skin charred black and her eye sockets filled with fire, and as my eyes stung and teared from the smoke, I could not unsee. But I didn't know why Hecate would have wanted me to have this be the last image that I would have of her, my mother.

Now there were only two Fates left.

The Queen took in Galatea. The twisted look of satisfaction she wore dissipated at the sight of Galatea standing there. Another Entente holding a wand.

"Hecate, what have you done?" Galatea whispered, looking up at the pyre, which had now completely consumed our sister. My mother. She was ash.

"What have you done?" Galatea demanded again, this time to the Queen.

The square filled with Entente. Galatea stood defiantly in front of them all, her blond hair standing up in the wind.

"The Entente will rain the hells down on you," Galatea vowed as she raised her wand to the sky.

The Entente replicated the gesture, raising theirs to the sky too. Even South raised his wand—tiny, ill equipped, and utterly without magic. He was the only boy among them. His face was changed too. He'd traded his brown hair for red. And his skin was a ghostly pale. But even with the new face, I would have still known him. And as he stood strong, his wings concealed beneath a coat, he lowered his wand. Now he was holding it like a knife, perhaps readying himself to fight the only way he could—the way a human would.

The Queen seemed almost more curious than afraid as she looked at my sisters and South. "Which one are you? The Present or the Past? Unfortunately, the Future is no longer with us."

"I am the one who is going to end you," Galatea said, her voice hollow and cold.

"Perhaps. But your sister already told me that my death is not today."

Galatea's face clouded, and the sky darkened with it. "We also told you that Fate can change."

"Kill them all!" the Queen commanded.

The soldiers fanned out, heading for my sisters and South.

I had never seen Entente fight. Our wands were meant for creating good things in the world, not for combat. As the troops advanced, Galatea pushed the younger Entente behind her.

Bari stumbled backward, landing on the ground near the cart behind which Hecate had pushed me. She saw me and reached for me, her face a mask of confusion.

"Come on, Farrow. Don't be afraid." Her hand stretched out toward me, but I still couldn't move. I didn't understand why the spell hadn't expired with Hecate. "What's wrong with you? Why are you just standing there like that?"

I couldn't even move my eyes enough to convey that I was frozen—frozen as my sisters fought, which was what we were never supposed to do.

Bari's hand hit Hecate's invisible wall. "It's a spell." She raised her wand and tried to undo it.

Listen to my wand.
Break her spell.
I won't tell.

But nothing happened.

A dagger whizzed by Bari's head, and she ducked. It bounced off the invisible shield in front of me and landed on the ground.

"I'll come back for you," she whispered before she raced off, wand raised.

"Advance!" Magrit commanded.

"She is your Queen, but this is your choice!" Galatea yelled at the line of soldiers, daring them to choose peace. She summoned another lightning strike. This one ripped a line in the stone in front of the soldiers. They stopped in their tracks and stared down at the cracked stone, steam rising from it. Galatea had given them a line to cross and an opportunity to turn back.

The Queen gave a condescending laugh. "My people are the Crown."

One of the soldiers cast a worshipful look at the Queen and stepped across the line.

"We are the Crown!" he shouted, the Queen's words on his lips. The others followed him across the line.

The commoners began running and screaming, trying to get out of the way as the guards advanced.

The soldiers' swords should have been no match for our wands. We were stronger than any human. We had magic. But we were taught never to hurt another soul, human or Entente. There was hesitation in our actions, enough to leave us at a disadvantage.

Except for Galatea. She did not hesitate.

Her wand seemed to crack open the sky, and white lightning flashed wherever she wielded it, crackling and sparking toward the line of soldiers. There were screams from their ranks, but they held their formation. They raised their shields defensively.

The lightning hit one shield and went straight through the metal. The shield dropped, revealing that the soldier had been hit squarely in the chest. I could see another soldier's uniform moving behind him through the gaping, burning hole. The soldier stood for a moment, somehow still conscious. He looked down at the hollow in his chest. He crumpled to the ground and was finally still, his face frozen forever in a look of horrified surprise.

I felt the pressure of more tears welling up behind my eyes. This was a new horror. Within seconds of losing Hecate, I had seen one of Les Soeurs become a killer. I felt another tear roll down my cheek, even though I couldn't move a muscle to wipe it away.

The other Entente stood still, none of them ready to do what Galatea had demonstrated. They improvised, using their gifts to fend off their attackers instead of killing them.

Amantha appeared and disappeared next to the soldiers in formation, brandishing her wand and freezing individual soldiers one at a time.

Despite Galatea's deadly might, the Entente were still struggling against the sheer number of soldiers around them. Galatea's wand moved swiftly, and she struck down more soldiers with her lightning strikes. But for every felled soldier, there was another to take his place.

Behind her soldiers, Queen Magrit was watching, pleased at their progress. The small, strange boy was still at her side.

Who was he?

Suddenly Iolanta appeared at the edge of the square. Her skin was so pale it almost glowed in the daylight. She blinked heavily. But she raised her wand and Black Fire splayed from it, dancing across the cobblestones of the square before it reached its first victim.

South spotted Iolanta and ran toward her, but a line of soldiers stood in his way. For a moment he looked panicked. Then he pulled off his coat and his wings unfurled. The soldiers stopped in their tracks. They raised their swords and charged at him.

He flapped his wings and began to rise, higher and higher, above the fray.

I searched for Bari, and my breath hitched when I saw that a soldier was holding his knife to her throat. Not Bari too! I couldn't lose her.

"Please, I'm just a child," she wailed so loudly that I could hear her from my involuntary hiding spot. She made a face that seemed so vulnerable, so unlike her, I was shocked.

The soldier's face softened, and he pulled the knife from her throat. Bari took the opportunity to raise her wand enough to touch the soldier's skin. The soldier gasped as he realized too late that she had tricked him, and then began choking.

A scorpion emerged from his mouth. He tossed it away from him in horror. He coughed again and another emerged. His arms flailed helplessly as the creature climbed out onto his face. He could not scream, only gurgle, as it was followed by another and another. His head was engulfed in scorpions in mere seconds. But they were not *on* him, I realized. A few more seconds and he didn't appear human at all. He was a pile of scorpions. The pile wobbled under its own weight, then cascaded onto the ground and surrounded Bari.

Bari looked at her wandwork, her chest heaving with effort and adrenaline.

I realized before she did that the scorpions were about to attack her, their tails raised in unison, ready to strike.

Bari turned toward me as if she could hear me, then turned back and looked down at the army of scorpions. She stomped on one of them defensively. A human scream seemed to come from the carpet of bugs, which began to scatter. Other humans screamed too as they saw what had become of the man.

The crunch of the scorpion's exoskeleton reminded me of what Bari had said about her beetles: *If you crush them, you crush me.*

Queen Magrit yelled for her men to regroup.

Galatea motioned toward Iolanta to stop.

"She's happy she did this. I can feel it," Iolanta said to the others. Then she looked at the remaining townspeople, who had been trapped in the square by the battle. "Some of them are joyous. Some of them are relieved. Some of them are scared. But not a single one of them is going to help us."

Above, South changed course and headed back into the fray. He was too far away for me to see his expression. But I imagined it to be what I felt: a mix of fury and impossible hurt. He had something in his hand.

As he got closer, I saw it was a rock. He began taking more rocks from his pockets and pelting them at the soldiers, providing some nonmagical cover for his sisters fighting below.

One of the soldiers spotted him and raised an arrow lit with fire. I tried to scream again, but still I had no voice.

An arrow arced through the sky and whizzed by one of his wings. He spotted it and turned over in the sky, evading it. But just as he righted himself, another lighted arrow arced toward him. This one hit its mark.

A hole burned clean through his wing. He screamed in agony, and then he began to fall.

There were too many people in my way to see where and, more important, *how* he landed. I imagined him crushed and tangled up in his newfound wings.

Iolanta's expression darkened, and she raised her wand. I thought she was turning her rage toward the townspeople who were in her direct line of vision. But then I spotted them. There were two soldiers pushing cannons toward the Entente.

Iolanta's Black Fire collided with the cannon fire. An explosion tore through the square as the black plumes reached out like smoky tentacles, destroying everything in their reach. The force of the explosion pushed me backward, and the spell Hecate had bound me with shattered.

When the smoke began to clear, I saw a gulf of earth and debris between the pyre and where the Queen and her men stood. The Entente and most of the soldiers were gone. The explosion had wiped them out.

All that was left was one of South's bloody shoes lying in a pile of ash. Were they all gone? Had any of them managed to travel away in time? I prayed that they had. But looking at the ashes, my heart sank.

I pointed my wand at the Queen, my hand shaking with effort. She would pay for what she had done.

But nothing happened.

The magic wasn't there.

The Queen approached me. "Leave this one alone. She's not Entente. She's human." She snatched the wand from my hand and dropped it on the ground like trash. "You should know better than to play at being a witch, little girl."

~

After the dust settled, after the soldiers were gone, after every person I loved had been struck down, I picked up my wand from the ground and clambered down to the pyre, where I could still make out some semblance of Hecate's form. But when I reached to touch her, the ashes crumbled into the pyre and my insides felt as if they crumbled with them. I put the ashes into the pouch I wore around my neck.

How could I still be here when they were gone? How could I have been frozen while they fought? It was all too much.

We were the Entente. We were the architects of Fate. How could this be our end? For centuries we had been at the side of every queen in every Queendom, as advisors, confidants, leaders. And now we were all gone.

Except me. And the ashes.

CHAPTER 8

I took Hecate to the Reverie, our hiding place. I put her in the glass coffin. I said some words over her. Impossibly . . . Thankfully . . . she came back to me in ash form. The soldiers came, and I ran like she told me to. I ran as far and as fast as I could, and I took refuge in the Enchanted Forest. There, I felt myself begin to crumble as the Reverie had when I was leaving it.

Everything was lost.

The tears began to flow. Again.

What would become of me?

Had my sisters somehow survived? Would they come back for me?

As the sun set, the dark crept in. The dark had never held any fear for me when I had a wand in my hand that could illuminate it in an instant. But now was a different story. It was scarier than I imagined. For the first time in my life, I was truly alone.

And there were sounds. The rustling of leaves. Or was it something else? I knew I couldn't stay there forever. At most, I would be lucky to survive a few nights, especially with no magic. My useless wand could not make a fire or light the dark or make a bed of feathers. And it could not bring my sisters back to me.

As I curled up in the hollow of a large tree, my now-gray dress my only warmth, I told myself that I wouldn't sleep. That maybe I would never sleep again. But somehow I finally gave in to the dark.

When the sun rose with a searing glare, the grief crashed in on me again. My sisters, gone. Hecate, ash. The Reverie, no longer home. But suddenly a shadow blocked the sun. I looked up and she was there. The ashes. Hecate as ashes had returned to me. She'd somehow found me in the middle of the forest.

"How can this be? How can you be?" I asked her.

This time there was no fear as I looked upon her.

"Are you really you?" I asked.

Hecate stood in front of me motionless for a beat. Did this mean she had no answers in death as she had in life, or was she keeping them close even now? I put my hand out, and she mirrored my gesture with her own. I moved my other, and she matched my hand. I stooped in one direction, and she followed. Somehow the small pantomime felt like comfort. But I still needed more.

"Hecate, please. Please speak again—please tell me something. Anything."

The figure shook her head.

"Is it that you can't or you won't? Which is it? Can't—" She nodded.

"Do you know why this happened? Do you know why you're here?"

Her shoulders shrugged.

I reached out to touch her and the ashes made room for my finger, closing around it. I put my hand right through her. What madness was this? How?

She broke apart and made a question mark.

"You had to know—why didn't you stop it? Why didn't you save us all?" I demanded.

"Will I ever see the others again? Are they dead or just gone? Will they come back for me?"

Hecate did not answer. She just stood still.

She was as enigmatic in death as she had been in life. But she was still here. She was all I had.

That was the moment that something broke in me. I let myself fall to my knees. Hecate had come back to me from the Burning. She had somehow fought death itself to be here with me. If my sisters were alive, they would have done the same. Which meant they weren't alive. They were gone.

The next morning, my grief was still there but it had a companion: vengeance. I didn't just miss my sisters. I didn't just want them back. I wanted the person responsible to pay for taking them from me. That want sharpened the dull ache in me into something new. Not a wand. A weapon.

Hungry and grieving, I had an errant thought. And I asked Hecate, "What if we could get to the Rookery?"

The ashes cocked their head as if they did not know what I was talking about. But when Hecate was alive, she knew.

The Rookery was an underground band of rebels who supposedly didn't support the Queendoms or the Entente. It was said that they were tricksters who lived in the Thirteenth Queendom, on the outermost edge. It may as well have been the end of the world. But I didn't know if the Rookery was even real or just a groom's tale. When Hecate or Galatea spoke of them it always seemed it was in jest. I recalled a moment a few months ago, after Tere had not been paying attention in training. Hecate had warned, *Perhaps you'd prefer to live with the Rooks... See how you like their rogue magic... You'll end up with noses where your ears should be.* My sisters and I laughed at the time, but now I considered the Rookery. Could the Rooks offer protection? Could they help me get my magic back? Could they help us get payback on the Queen?

But without an answer from Hecate and without magic, traveling between Queendoms seemed an impossible distance to venture for a rumor. So I pushed the thought of the Rooks aside and focused on my immediate survival.

I was alone in the world with only Hecate's ashes to keep me company. But I knew what I needed to do.

The covenant between humans and Entente had been extinguished with my Hecate. There were no more rules. I would somehow get my magic back, and I would have my revenge.

Magrit had tried to put magic in the shadows. I was prepared to hide there until the moment I could strike.

When the men came with their dogs and their swords, the ashes seemed to know before I could say anything. They hid in the trees.

I feigned interest in the dirt as the soldiers came upon me, mistaking me for a normal girl.

"Leave her—she's just a vagrant."

"We can't just leave her."

"The Entente are all dust—no one could have survived that explosion. The Queen is just obsessed."

"Well, she'll have our heads if we don't keep looking."

The second guard sighed and repeated, "We can't leave her like this."

"Very well, but we'll lose half a day."

The guard grabbed my hand roughly and dragged me along.

Panic seized me—at first I did not want to leave Hecate. Then I remembered that she had walked through death itself to come back to me. I didn't look back as I walked away with the men. I knew somehow that she would follow me anywhere.

PART II
THE PRESENT

Love is what saves you. Love is what saves you and the Hinter.

—Iolanta, La Soeur of the Present

CHAPTER 9

I spent the next five years in an orphanage among human children. I looked like any other orphan, and I let them believe that I was. What was I without my sisters, without my mother, without magic?

That girl I once was might as well have been dead. I was the day without sun. I did not feel. I was empty instead of full. Lost instead of found. I didn't cry after the day of the Burning. But I didn't laugh or smile either. I was a witch without everything that made her so. I needed a place to hide. And what better place than in plain sight?

The orphanage was run by a woman named Madame Viola, who was kind but mostly indifferent to me and to all the other children. I kept to myself. But Hecate was always with me in the pouch I hid around my neck.

As I grew, the anger that was born the day of the Burning grew too. I had no magic. But I would have my revenge. I would wait. Until I was bigger and stronger. Until I could find a way back into that palace and take the life of the one who took everything from me.

But as I grew so did Queen Magrit's reign. Stronger, bolder, and more powerful. And so did her new word for us. She had killed us twice that day. Once with physical death and once by killing our good name. Entente was the name that we had given ourselves long before I was born. Witch was the name that she had handed us. Entente was a whisper, a prayer, a wish for a better Fate. Witch was a scream, a slur, a denigration.

In naming us, she had accomplished two things—labeled us as villains and made us a target for all that the people didn't understand. Every bad thing that happened. Every bump in the night. Every crop that went unharvested, every storm that touched a town, every famine that brought hunger. It gave the people a place to put all their hurt and blame and sadness. It was not true for the heart of every woman and man in the Hinter, but it was true for some. And the Queen exploited that, and the word spread from person to person, from Queendom to Queendom, until it was a part of the vocabulary of the world. So much so that you could not say the word "Entente" without someone coupling it with the word "witch."

It was in essence another Burning, another death for all of us . . . And even though humans were not capable of curse, it was a curse that would haunt us that day and for years to come.

And then, after five years of waiting, Fate stepped in.

I was twelve and in the middle of an unappetizing breakfast of porridge when a woman swept in with a boy my age in tow.

"Ladies and gentlemen, this is Madame Linea. She's here to adopt one of you," explained Madame Viola.

Madame Linea was dressed like a noblewoman, her hair an architectural masterpiece of braids and curls. Her skin and hair were almost the same shade of white. And the boy was dressed in finery that could have matched the prince's. He was pale too, with brownish-blond hair, a narrow face, and big eyes that held the promise of a very handsome man.

"And I'm Tork . . . ," the boy volunteered, a twinkle in his blue eyes.

Linea cast him a sidelong glance that quieted him but not his smile, which got wider.

Madame Viola lined us up, and Linea took a look at all of us.

She shook her head when Linea stopped in front of me and looked down. She made me turn around and inspected me like she was inspecting a prized horse.

You don't want Farrow, Madame Viola's headshake said. She went over to Linea and whispered something.

I knew what she said without hearing it. I was not fit for taking. I had not made friends with the other kids at the orphanage. I had kept to myself from the day soldiers had discovered me in the forest and brought me there.

"But with a little polish and paint, she's the closest match," Madame Linea said.

"But, Madame . . ."

"I can make any girl into something else."

"I don't doubt your skills. I just think you should know she's not like the other girls."

Linea frowned. "When men say that about women, it's meant to be a compliment, and when women say it about other women, it's meant to be an insult. But from my experience, there are no two girls who are exactly the same . . . But I can make her look that way," she said with certainty.

I glanced from Linea to Madame Viola, confused. But I was sure that somehow Linea had put Madame Viola in her place.

"Do you know what a Couterie is?" Madame Linea asked me.

I shook my head.

"Every princess and every prince, every duchess and every duke, every person whose blood is deemed noble has a Couterie."

Some part of me bristled at her choice of words. It sounded like the Couterie were possessions.

"What does a Couterie do?"

"She or he trains to become the perfect companion to the royals—from the moment they reach adulthood and until their Ever After."

"Companion?"

"Advisor, friend, lover... Whatever they need... A perfectly matched soul who knows their every like and every whim. Who knows their history and the history of the Queendoms. Who advises and protects them and helps them *become* who they are supposed to be."

"Isn't that a wife? Or a husband? Isn't that what love is supposed to be?" I had read the same tales filled with romance and promising Ever Afters that every child read in the orphanage, though I never imagined love for myself—only revenge.

"Madame Viola keeps you all so very naive," Linea assessed. "You've clearly never met a royal." The corners of her mouth tugged upward with amusement.

She could not be more wrong.

"There are very few marriages of true love in the Queendoms. Rather, they are contracts of land and troops. The Couterie offer an opportunity for a queen or nobleperson to feel loved without condition," she continued.

"And what about the Couterie? Do they get love in return?"

Linea paused and then said, finally, "We do not expect love. But we get comfort for the rest of our lives."

I nodded, but I truly was surprised. The Entente had spent their lifetimes giving to humankind. I had never imagined that the

Entente had a human counterpart that was equally dedicated to the whims of the Crown.

"How are they chosen? Why me?"

"The Couterie have been around as long as there were crowns. It is an ancient art that has been passed down for generations. Couterie are chosen to be perfect matches to the royals. They spend their days studying and training to be companions. And when they are both of age and if they both so choose, the Couterie help them cross the line into adulthood . . . and seal the bond between them forever. It's called Becoming."

"Surely, you don't mean . . . ," I said, my mind filling in the blank.

"It is a great honor to be a royal's first. Of course, it is purely a matter of choice. The royal's and the Couterie's. But the best Couterie do anticipate and fulfill every need of the royals—hearts and minds and bodies alike."

Behind her, the boy, Tork, pulled a face, breaking the seriousness of the moment. He seemed to want to make me smile. Despite myself, I felt a bit brighter.

Sensing something of what he was up to reflected in my face, Linea turned to the boy, but by then he was all seriousness again.

"She looks just like her, doesn't she, Tork?" she continued.

The boy nodded. "It's uncanny."

"You will be the perfect Shadow for Lavendra."

"I don't understand," I said. "What is a Shadow then?"

"If a Couterie falls ill, or dies, or for any reason chooses not to fulfill his or her duties, there is a contingency plan. A Shadow is there to take the place of the Couterie if he or she cannot be there. He or she *shadows* the Couterie and serves him or her every day."

"Kind of like an understudy in a play."

"Yes, what an apt analogy."

Madame Viola cleared her throat, nudging me.

"You'd think the girl had better offers... Hurry up, girl—say 'yes' already. You're wasting Madame's time."

Linea smiled and focused on me.

"This is a lifelong commitment. The choice has to be yours, and yours alone. I can promise you a home. You can stay with your Couterie for the rest of your life. Or you can take your purse and make a life of your own one day. Or you can challenge her and become Couterie yourself. Whatever you do, you will be rewarded. It is a life of waiting and servitude, but it is also one that will take you to places you wouldn't be able to otherwise go. The insides of palaces."

I perked up at the word "palaces."

"This Lavendra, who is she the Couterie to?"

"The prince."

There was only one prince in all the Queendoms. And he was the son of the woman I intended to kill.

Ever since I had seen Hecate on the pyre, I knew I had to find a way to get to the Queen. I had been waiting to get my magic back. I had been waiting to be old enough or strong enough. And just like that, Linea and the Couterie had offered me a way into the palace.

"I would be honored to be a Shadow," I said.

"Welcome to the Couterie." Linea opened her arms to me and gave me the briefest of hugs. My nose filled with the scent of some flower I'd never smelled before. It was sweet and rich and rare. She smelled like freedom.

An hour later, I was walked into the Couterie. There was a line of girls and boys waiting to greet me. They stood in pairs of what looked like identical twins. Only, they weren't twins. They were matched together, Couterie and Shadow, by Madame Linea. Each duo seemed identical at first glance. But upon closer inspection, I could see the slight differences between them.

There were a few more boys than girls at the Couterie because there had always been a Couterie for every Queen, and until now there had never been a prince in need of one. But there were plenty of other noble persons of every sex in need of Couterie so there were still a healthy number of girls. And of course there were Queens who chose female companions. And dukes and other noblemen who chose males.

A girl stepped forward from the end of the line. Her face matched mine.

"Meet Lavendra, Shadow," Linea said.

Madame Linea had left out this part of the equation. When she'd said there was a resemblance between me and the prince's Couterie, I didn't think she meant someone who was almost a mirror image.

Tork, the boy with Madame Linea, winked at me, then leaned into my ear and whispered, "It's going to be okay. You'll get used to it."

I assumed Linea had chosen him to accompany her to the orphanage by design, to ease my fear of going off to a new life with a stranger. There was indeed something about him that was comforting. Unlike the others, who stood perfectly poised in line, Tork was somehow more relaxed and more animated.

Lavendra stepped closer to me.

"She's almost perfect. But her nose and her ears!" Lavendra said, wrinkling up her own nose.

She was right. Lavendra's was a perky button of a nose

compared to my wider, flatter one. I clamped my hands over my ears reflexively. She was right about them too; her ears were considerably smaller than my own. Was that cause to send me back to the orphanage? Would I lose my chance?

"Don't worry, Farrow. I've already called the doctor," Linea said without missing a beat.

Tork whispered to me again. "Don't worry—the doctor is very gentle."

It took me a moment to understand what they meant. Becoming Couterie was my way to avenge Hecate and kill the Queen. But first, I would have to give my flesh.

CHAPTER 10

The next day and for months and five long years after that, I dove headfirst into learning my duties as a Shadow. Life here wasn't so different from the Reverie—but instead of learning magic, I was learning the life of a Couterie.

Couterie were a royal's best friend. Someone who knew them through and through. No Couterie ever married their royal. Marriages were arranged for political gain and monetary power or to strengthen the lineage for the next Queendom. But there could be friendship or love between royals and Couterie.

A Shadow was part maid, part mimic. Each Shadow was trained to take a Couterie's place for good if he or she could not fulfill his or her duties, but it had never happened in the history of the Couterie.

Lavendra was Prince Mather's Couterie. She spent her time studying the Ana, a book that included everything there was to know about the royal palace and Prince Mather: his favorite foods, his battle strategy, what his every expression meant. One day soon she would move into the palace and be just steps away from Queen Magrit.

And as Lavendra's Shadow, I would go with her. I couldn't have planned this better if I had tried. *Praise the Fates.* Wherever they were.

Being Lavendra's Shadow meant being with her for almost all her waking moments. Aside from her daily walk, which she insisted on taking by herself, I was with Lavendra from dusk till dawn.

"What are you doing, Farrow?" Lavendra said, suddenly appearing in the mirror behind me in my room, her arched brows furrowed.

My fingers tapped against my leg. It was a nervous habit I couldn't shake. I touched my nose, flinching as I remembered what the doctor had done to it. I touched my ears too. The doctor had been as gentle as she could be when constructing my nose to match Lavendra's. But human surgery was painful compared to the magical transformation that once upon a time Hecate could perform with a wave of her wand.

"I just wanted to try your dress on," I blurted, running my hand down the pale-yellow gown. Its delicate boning was accentuated by hundreds of petals made out of the same delicate fabric.

Lavendra put her hand on my shoulder and gave it a playful squeeze.

I felt my muscles tense.

"Keep it. It looks better on you . . . ," she began.

"No . . . that's not . . ." When I heard the compliment, I reached for the buttons at the back of the dress. Lavendra's hand stopped me. Compliments might as well be curses coming from Lavendra's lips. I knew that there would be an insult coming. I just didn't know how soon, which made it all the more torturous.

"I insist. You have the frame for it," she said matter-of-factly and took a step back.

We both had light-brown skin and curly hair, but I was slighter and taller than she was, while Lavendra was more voluptuous. Shadows were supposed to look as much like their Couterie as cosmetically possible, and Lavendra's recent blossoming had caused us to look less alike, which left Madame Linea less than pleased. Most of my wardrobe was hand-me-downs from Lavendra. But never anything as fine as this.

I had reminded her of what Linea saw as a flaw, and now she would have to remind me of my place.

"Stop slouching and pretend a ruler is tied to your back, like we practiced in class," she said, modulating her voice into a perfect imitation of Madame Linea's.

I obeyed and looked at myself in the mirror again.

"There, now you look more like a real Couterie instead of a Shadow . . . Wait—there's just one more thing."

In a couple of swift motions, she untied the corset and pulled the strings so tight that I could hear my ribs crack.

I smiled through the pain.

In the glass, we looked like twins, but we were worlds apart on the inside. Lavendra was only a year older than I was, but she seemed miles ahead of me in beauty and education, grace and selfishness, impatience and temper. And Lavendra never let me forget how far apart we were.

I reminded myself again that she was a means to an end, but there were still moments when she tested me and threatened my will. But I would not throw away all the years I'd worked for my chance at vengeance on her selfish self. I had already sacrificed too much to lose it all on her.

"Too bad you and that dress will never see the inside of the palace," Lavendra said. "Now, bring me some honeybread. I'm famished."

"You know that Madame Linea will kill me if I let you have another bite of it," I began.

"Then you're in a bind, because I'll kill you if you don't," Lavendra said and plopped down on the chaise in the corner.

"How come I'll never see the inside of the palace? I'll never be a Couterie, but as your Shadow, it's my duty to be at your side on your day of Becoming and beyond."

"Tell that to the Queen of Paranoia. Only true Couterie are allowed inside the gates of the palace from now on. I think Magrit's still afraid of the Entente. But imagine her thinking that anyone in the Couterie could be a *w-i-t-c-h*."

"Imagine . . . ," I repeated. My mind raced as I saw my window of opportunity for revenge closing after years of preparation and sacrifice. Years of honeybread and servitude. Years of pretending to be something I was not. Lavendra had not delivered an insult. Instead, she'd delivered a near death blow to my plot.

I took a breath, and when I did, Lavendra pulled the strings tighter as I tried and failed to turn the new information over in my mind and find a way around it or through it.

Magrit's reclusiveness was not new. It had begun the second she took the throne and started erecting the Black Glass fortress around her. She had wiped out the Entente. She had begun to take down the other Queendoms. She was rarely seen, and Prince Mather was not seen at all. But she had not made any noises against the practices of the Couterie until this very day.

My mind hit a wall. I did not see another way into the palace. And without it, I did not see another way to get to the Queen.

The dress suddenly felt even tighter, even though Lavendra had stopped pulling on the strings. She didn't have to continue, since Queen Magrit had already unknowingly cut off my oxygen. Vengeance was the only air I breathed.

Studying me, Lavendra began to loosen the corset.

"Farrow, you look like a ghost. I'm sorry, little Shadow, that you aren't coming with me to the palace. Only Madame Linea can come with me. No strangers are allowed in the palace anymore, including servants. No exceptions."

"The Queen is outlawing Shadows?"

"No, just banning them from living in the palace. Other queens and noblemen have no such qualms for their palaces and estates. But you, lucky you, will remain here unless some tragedy befalls me and only then can you swoop in and take my place."

"No . . ."

"Yes . . . The Queen gets more paranoid by the day. Anyone not essential is no longer welcome in the palace. The real tragedy is my hair, Shadow. There is no way that Madame Linea can work the magic that you do," Lavendra continued, oblivious.

She gave me a sharp look when I didn't react to her compliment or thank her for releasing me from the corset.

"Why are you so sad, Shadow? I swear you look as if you lost your best friend. Not that you have any . . ." She laughed. Her gray eyes blazed with sudden interest.

We weren't friends, but she knew me well enough to notice my disappointment. It was a Couterie's job to know what people were thinking.

I didn't answer her. I slammed out of the room and out of the Couterie without saying a word.

Lavendra leaned out the open window and called down, "What

about my honeybread, Farrow? You can't honestly expect me to get it myself."

I ran away from Lavendra as fast as my feet could carry me. *What now?* I thought. *There must be another way to get to the Queen.*

CHAPTER 11

I wasn't looking where I was running and as I was leaving the grounds, I ran headlong into Tork, almost toppling him over.

"Perfect timing, Farrow. I need your womanly advice this instant!" Tork exclaimed, holding on to me. He looked deeply into my eyes before tearing his gaze away and offering up a smile.

Was it my imagination or was he becoming handsomer every day? But right now he was standing in my way. Just as with the orphanage, I had tried not to get too close to the humans I found myself living with. But Tork had made it his mission to be the center of attention no matter what the room or who was in it. And there were times like these that his persistence out willed my resistance.

"I have written a letter and I need to know if it will make a lady swoon," he said as he released me.

"I'm not the lady, am I?" I said lightly.

"Certainly not; your heart is harder than those pearls around Linea's neck. And please don't take offense. Being heartless is what every Couterie strives for," he returned, and I laughed.

Tork was the first Couterie I met the day that he and Madame Linea had come to the orphanage, and yet he and I were not friends, but I was always friendly with him. It wasn't his fault. Shadows and Couterie kept to their stations. As far as humans went, I found him more harmless and more amusing than most, and even Madame Linea was not immune to Tork's charms. He was her favorite no matter what he did. But right now he was behaving oddly, even for a human. Still, I didn't have time for his crisis; I had one of my own.

"I don't have time to help you make the Queen of Blenheim swoon. I have to go. Romancing the Third Queendom will have to wait," I said curtly, pushing past him and breaking into another run.

A half hour later I found myself in front of Queen Magrit's palace.

Queen Magrit's city had indeed become a fortress. Black Glass now covered every wall of the palace. Trying to break in without magic would be pointless. The only people in and out of the palace were those who belonged there by birth. Even the servants' line was based on inheritance. And the Queen and her son rarely left the royal grounds. All of which made my mission nearly impossible.

Unable to face Lavendra and the Couterie just yet, I took the long walk back to the Enchanted Forest. One of the many advantages of the Couterie over the orphanage was my autonomy. I was free to go anywhere in the Queendom so long as I disguised it as an errand for Lavendra. I usually only returned to my childhood home in the dead of night, but today I made an exception.

Today, I found my favorite spot in the woods behind the structures where my sisters and I had learned our magic and lived our lives. But it hurt too much to go inside. Instead, I headed straight to the place I had played with South all those years ago when Bari and Amantha didn't want to play with me.

I felt a rustling around my neck and retrieved the silk pouch I had kept secreted beneath my clothes since the day of the Burning. I gently pulled the strings open to free Hecate's ashes.

"Hello, Hecate."

I hated keeping Hecate cooped up. But whenever I was alone, I let her out.

Hecate's ashes materialized from the pouch and danced around me. They dispersed again before settling into a sitting pose on a nearby rock. My breath still caught every time I saw her silhouette.

I tried not to make more of what she was. Was she leftover magic? Just remnants of who Hecate used to be? Or was she still truly conscious with every thought and emotion intact? Even in death, Hecate still held her cards close to the vest.

But she was always with me. I didn't know how I could have made it through the intervening years without her in whatever form she was in. So I chose to believe in the ashes because they and my vengeance were all I had.

I had a piece of Hecate. Or I suppose really it was a million pieces. I hung the memory of her on the ashes and held on as tightly as I could. But it was not enough. The ashes could not truly answer the anger that still lived in me for the secrets Hecate had kept from me when she was alive. And she could not be the mother I longed for when I ached for her and my sisters or when the reality of being the last Entente in the world hit me all over again.

Hecate cast a look back toward the buildings. She wanted to go back inside the Reverie. Sometimes, I would comply. But not today. While the tomb room had crumbled the day of the Burning, some of the other buildings remained intact but were in disrepair. And without Les Soeurs' magic, all the magical details of the Reverie were gone. Without all three present to recast the spell, the Reverie had become ruins.

Still, I would curl up in my old bed. And I would sit in front of Hecate's mirror. I would raise my useless wand in the courtyard. I would stand by the water where South stretched his wings. My sisters never joined me. But Hecate did. She'd be by my side in front of the mirror as if ready to give me a brand-new yellow dress. She would fill the doorway of the bedroom I shared with Amantha, ready to admonish me for giving South wings. And she would stand next to me by the river as if she was catching me with South all over again. I never reentered Iolanta's room, because it made me too sad. But when I opened the door before closing it again, I could see that the pictures Iolanta had drawn were still there. I could almost hear my sisters' laughter. I could see their magic. I could taste the food—but they were not there. I would raise my wand to play Entente since I could no longer truly be one.

"Not today, Hecate," I whispered. "We have a problem."

The ashes shifted and turned away from me as if she could not be bothered to listen.

"Please don't start," I said, looking at them. At her.

Hecate had never seemed to like my plan for vengeance. But getting into the palace to kill the Queen was the only thing that had kept me alive since the day I'd watched Hecate burn in the square.

The ashes dispersed and flew back into the pouch. Even if we disagreed, Hecate would never leave my side, not after she had defied death to stay with me.

Sighing, I pulled a branch down from the tree above, hoping this time would be different. I snapped off a piece of wood and began to whittle a wand.

I doubted the wand would work. I had tried countless times

before, to no avail. I couldn't stop myself from trying to rekindle my magic any more than I could stop myself from coming back here—no matter how dangerous it was. Soldiers still swept through periodically, hoping to find a "witch" dumb enough to come home again. They did not and could not know the Reverie's precise location. But judging from the boot prints I'd found nearby over the years, they had come close—and there was always the danger of being found near it. Not that even if I were discovered would I likely be recognized as a witch.

Iolanta had once said that magic never really died. If I found the right branch . . . If I said the right words . . . Maybe then magic would come back to me. I hadn't given up on magic. Even though it had clearly given up on me.

I thought of Bari, Amantha, and South. Sweet South, with his brown eyes, long brown curls, and plump little face, always naively waiting for magic to come to him. Then I remembered his bloody shoe lying in the rubble.

I focused on the task at hand. If nothing else, it was comforting to feel the wood move beneath my knife. We were supposed to carve the story of our lives on each wand. Instead, I carved a wand for each sister I had lost. I tried to re-create their wands as I remembered them. Just as I had tried to re-create the memory of each of my sisters, even though sometimes it felt as if they were fading no matter how tightly I held on to them.

Hecate's, Iolanta's, and Galatea's wands were filled with tales of queens and armies and romances and wars. Bari's wand was made of the oldest oak in all of Hinter and had a small beetle and a bird on the hilt. Her first successful spell had been turning a beetle into a bird and back again.

Amantha's appeared blank, but if you looked closely, you could see a gust of wind. Odette's had food, representing her magical cuisine, which I missed no matter how many bites of honeybread I snuck. Tere's was sun and clouds and rain. Sistine's was a music note. And on and on the wands went . . .

Finally, I carved my own out of baby redwood, which was barely part of the century. It had a series of faces on the hilt, because the only magic I'd done well as a child had been transforming my own features and making some minor apparitions.

I held out the wand in front of me. I closed my eyes and wished for magic, like I had hundreds of times before. Magic was supposed to be a gift, one we used to serve humanity. It wasn't meant to wield power.

But humans, or at least the ones we'd trusted most, had betrayed us. Now I needed just a little magic. Just enough to finish this.

I cast a spell, and then opened my eyes.

Nothing had changed. Nothing had happened. Nothing ever happened. I threw the wand down onto the ground in frustration.

I had been so absorbed, I hadn't noticed the man standing on the other side of the clearing. He was striking-looking, with dark hair and eyes, and an easy smile of someone comfortable in his skin.

"I'll trade you, miss?"

The man was tall, and his eyes were kind. He took a step toward me.

I picked up the useless wand defensively.

"Hello there," he called, and I immediately relaxed.

What was he doing here? My lessons from the Entente had taught me to pay attention to details. The finery of his coat. The perfect crop of his hair. The manicured arch of his nails told the story of a man well taken care of. He wasn't a soldier. He was a noble.

"My horse got tuckered out and I was looking for some water," he offered, holding up a leather canteen gingerly. "But instead it looks like I found an artist."

I looked around and saw a white-and-brown spotted stallion trailing behind him.

"I apologize. I didn't mean to startle you, miss."

He made a small bow and withdrew a step, which I assumed was meant to make me feel more comfortable.

"The spring is through there," I said, pointing in the opposite direction, toward the stream where I'd once played. I made eye contact with the horse, who bent his head toward me almost in greeting. I smiled and the horse seemed encouraged, pulling his owner toward me. The man steadied himself and gently pulled the horse back.

"So sorry, he usually doesn't take to anyone . . ."

"Well, that makes two of us . . . ," I said lightly.

"Thank you again. I'll be on my way then," he said, turning to go, but something seemed to stop him and he turned back.

He looked down, spotting one of the wands that I had apparently dropped before I settled on the rock. He leaned down to pick it up and hand it back to me.

Inside, I cursed my mistake. If the wrong person found these and knew what they were, I might be found out.

"Is this yours?"

"It . . ." I stopped myself. I had been caught carving the wand. What lie could I tell to extricate myself from this?

"May I say that your work is exquisite? I've never seen carvings like these. Do you think I could buy one for my daughter?" the man asked.

"Buy?" I asked, trying to grasp the question. "Don't you know these things are forbidden?" I countered. "What could you possibly want with a wand? If the guards caught you, there would be hell to pay."

He shrugged as if he could not be bothered, or perhaps he was of such a high rank that he believed he was untouchable to the Queen and her guard.

"Not everyone in the Hinter is happy about what happened to the Entente. Some of us think that they were the only thing keeping us from the darkness."

"Well, they're gone. Long live the Queen," I said, feigning indifference.

The man ignored my sarcasm and studied me a beat.

"I don't think everyone in the Hinter or the other Queendoms agrees with that sentiment. I want my daughter to know that once upon a time there was magic in Hinter. And that perhaps there is magic still. The Entente were a brave, generous people. They served the Queendoms well. And they were rewarded with nothing but pain. I want Ella to know that they existed and were brave enough to challenge the Queen. They were more than a fairy tale."

"Very well," I said.

Putting my own wand safely in my dress pocket, I considered the other wands. I picked up the one that represented South. I ran my fingers over the wings I'd carved into the wood. He'd grown up with us. But aside from Les Soeurs, the other Entente never made him, a human, feel truly welcome. And I had played my own cruel part in that. Giving his wand a home suddenly seemed fitting.

"For your daughter. But I cannot take a single coin."

I turned and left the woods. I didn't know why I'd given the man the wand. He was human. But something about him pushed me forward. Something he said gave me a glimmer of hope.

I had not figured out the puzzle of my magic. But I would not lose my chance at getting into the palace.

There was another way to kill the Queen.

CHAPTER 12

When I got back to the Couterie, I was met with another surprise. There were members of the Queen's guard posted outside the front door. I surmised that it was another search. While I was all but certain that my sisters were gone, the Queen had continued to search all the Queendoms for the Entente.

Instinctually I retreated and plastered myself against one of the trees on the side of the ornate pale-pink stone face of the Couterie. Once again, my vengeance was postponed. I knew that there was no real way to detect my magic. You can't detect what isn't there. But I had Hecate with me. I needed to release her so that she would not be found.

Suddenly, a voice came up beside me.

"Don't mind me . . ."

I gasped.

It was Tork. He was sharing my tree—leaning casually against it as if there was nothing at all going on.

"What are you hiding from? Oh, I see . . . The Witch Finder's found us," he said, his voice filled with amusement.

"The what?" I asked in a whisper. "There's no such thing."

"There is if the Queen says there is. She's created a new unit of the guard. They're going to finish what the Queen started with the Burning that day."

I should not have been surprised, but still this news felt like a slap in the face. While I had been busy growing up without my magic, Magrit had been amassing her power. According to rumor—which was all we had—after the Burning, she had demanded that the Queens of the other Queendoms pledge their allegiance to her and give up their Entente for burning. But there were no Entente at their sides anymore. They had come to Hecate's side the day of the Burning, only to meet an explosive, undeserving end. The Queen claimed they were in hiding, and she used the specter of the Entente as a means to subdue the people and wrest control of the Queendoms. This was just the next step in her tyrannical rule. A magic finder.

"Relax, they're not looking for us—they're looking for magical people. The Queen really is getting madder by the day."

"Don't—Madame Linea says never disparage the Queen," I said dutifully.

Tork's face suddenly shifted. "It's okay . . . I understand, Farrow," he whispered.

How could he possibly know that I would have reason to fear the Witch Finder? Even if that fear was irrational. I had no magic, after all.

I decided to feign ignorance.

"What do you mean?" I asked finally.

"Unlike the rest of us, you came here late. I can't imagine which tragedies brought you here. The rest of us were brought here from the orphanage before we could even speak. Before we had anything awful to remember. You must have faced things in the world, in the orphanage, that we can't even fathom. That's why the guard looks scary to you—that's why you hold yourself apart from the other Shadows."

He was unintentionally right about what came before. My past before the orphanage had been horrific. But he was wrong about the orphanage. There had been a kind of peace in waiting there after the shock wore off. Little was expected of me except to eat and attend classes. Orphans were not expected to have much of a future in the Hinter, and no one really talked about the past because they had their own demons.

"I don't like talking about that part of my life. I want to put it behind me. I want to keep my eyes on the future."

"I respect that. I didn't mean to pry."

We stayed like that until the Witch Finder left. I was surprised that Tork could be good at being quiet and still when I needed him to be. The sight of the new guard in their new uniforms filing out of the Couterie empty-handed allowed me a sigh of relief. They looked like normal soldiers. There was nothing discernable about them that looked at all special. There was a cloaked figure, whose face I could not see, and the guard quickly closed ranks around him or her. I assumed that this was the Witch Finder. The Witch Finder was ushered into a carriage and the guard whisked him or her away. And since I was the last of the Entente, I had nothing to fear from them, I told myself, willing myself to believe it. It was the Queen who was going to be afraid.

Tork and I peeled ourselves off the tree and walked back into the Couterie as if nothing had happened. Because nothing had.

Like I said, Tork wasn't my friend. But I could tolerate him a little more now. Perhaps it wasn't a bad thing to have allies. Especially given what I was about to do next.

CHAPTER 13

There she is! So nice of you to finally join us," Lavendra drawled as she looked up from the Ana when I walked into the sitting room that night. She pulled it close to her chest protectively. The Ana was indeed a Couterie's most prized possession. And studying it the most important part of their duties. Madame Linea herself gathered all the information for the Ana and even sewed and bound the pages so that no other hands than the Couterie's and her own were ever in possession of it. But the Couterie helped too in filling them—pasting in portraits and letters and even handwritten bits of information Linea delivered. As much as the Ana could be seen as a labor of love, it was also a tool of memory. What better way to remember the facts if you literally had your hands or pen on every single scrap of your royal's life?

She was on a chaise in the center of the other Couterie and Shadows, who were playing games, knitting, and singing songs at the piano.

"Lucky for you, my craving for honeybread has passed. Get me some hibiscus water, would you?" she asked, and returned to the book.

Usually my feet would reflexively take me to the kitchen to

respond to her latest whim. But my feet did not move. Ire filled me again. I had given five years of service to this plan. I had nothing to show for it, except a penchant to serve a spoiled girl.

Instead I steeled myself and said through gritted teeth, "Lavendra, I challenge you."

The room fell silent. Knitting needles stopped clicking, a chess piece was dropped back on the board, and whoever was at the piano stopped mid-concerto.

Lavendra laughed, breaking the silence.

"You can't possibly be this ridiculous," she assessed after a long pause.

All the other Couterie, except Tork, joined in her laughter.

"What's all the commotion?" Madame Linea demanded, entering the room.

"Farrow just told the most amazing joke. Do share it with Madame Linea."

"It's not a joke," I said. I straightened my spine, checking my own posture as Lavendra had instructed mere hours ago. "I challenge Lavendra. I want to take her place as Couterie to Prince Mather."

Madame Linea took a shallow breath. From everything she'd told us, even though the ability to challenge existed, not one Shadow had ever exercised it in all the years she'd been Madame.

"Very well, I will contact the Queen."

"The Queen?" I asked.

"Who do you think administers the Challenge?"

The truth was, I didn't actually know what the Challenge entailed. I'd tried to pick up hints about it from my fellow Shadows, other

Couterie, and Linea herself. The best explanation came from Jacoby, Tork's twin and Shadow.

Twins were rare in the Queendom but common in the Couterie, because neither twin would ever be required to go under the knife. I wondered sometimes if that was why Tork was different, lighter somehow. He had family. Even if I never saw them behave as anything other than Couterie and Shadow.

"It's a test of who knows the royal best," Jacoby said while folding Tork's laundry perfectly. "But it's an unpassable test. Because the Couterie have the advantage of possessing the Ana, and the Shadows were left only whatever scraps of knowledge they have learned from their Couterie. It's an impossible test that the Couterie is destined to win— What possessed you anyway?" He asked suddenly.

"I wanted to wear something before Lavendra does. It's my raison d'être," I said lightly. But Jacoby was serious.

"You should challenge Tork. No Shadow has studied his Couterie as closely as you. And no one could match their Couterie as closely as you."

"It would be like the moon pretending to be the sun. Everyone would know the light I cast was just a reflection. Not the real thing," he said matter-of-factly.

"That's not true," I countered.

"I am awkward and exacting. He's a star."

"Only because he was always in the way of your light," I said, using his metaphor.

He took this in and softened as if considering it.

Then he shut down.

"It doesn't matter. He is not going anywhere except to Queen

Papillion's palace. At least I get to go with him, even if I am in the shadows where I belong."

"But you can't forget your light, Jacoby, wherever you are. I won't."

He took me in for a beat before folding the last piece of laundry. "It would have been nice to wear something first though. Come on. It's time for dinner."

I let my encounter with Jacoby sink in and arrived at dinner five minutes late. Even after years of pretending to be one of them, sometimes seeing all the matching faces reminded me of the pain from the doctor's knife, as well as the breadth and depth of human cruelty. And seeing Jacoby think so little of himself made me see another pain I hadn't really imagined. What it must be like to be in a literal sibling's shadow like Jacoby was.

I touched my nose, missing my old one—one that I realized too late had been identical to Hecate's. The doctor did more than change our physical appearances. With every cut of the knife, she told us that our Couterie was above us and we Shadows were not as good. Not as worthy. I had my own sense of worth. I was Entente. The other Shadows did not have that.

The dining room was the size of a ballroom and was the heart of the Couterie's manse. The table itself was a marvel, unlike anything I'd seen. All the Couterie ate every meal together at the hand-carved table of three concentric rings, which must have taken carpenters months to construct and claimed at least three giant ElmWoods from the Dark Wood at the edge of the Enchanted Forest. The middle circle had fifty seats, one for each Queendom's Couterie. The outer ring had one for each of their Shadows. We Shadows sat and ate behind the Couterie, both to learn from them and to attend to their every need. Madame Linea sat at her own circle in the center of the other two rings. The outer circles and their seats moved in tandem around Madame Linea's like the rings of a planet, with the aid of an intricate set of gears installed beneath the circular floorboards by a watchmaker. The purpose: for Linea to observe all.

Lavendra wasn't there. She was still sulking in her bedroom. Looking around one last time, I took a deep breath, mustering up every ounce of courage I had, and sat in Lavendra's seat next to Tork just before the table's gears began to shift.

There was an audible gasp from Couterie and Shadows alike. I was challenging more than Lavendra. I was challenging the Couterie way of life.

"Enough of this drama, ladies and gentlemen," Madame Linea ordered. "Dinner is served."

As the room filled with chatter and the sound of forks against plates, Tork leaned close and whispered lightly, "So you're really going through with this?"

I swallowed hard, feeling a hint of nausea that had nothing to do with the movement of the table, and took a swig of the lavender nectar.

Tork took me in before saying, "Maybe *you* really are Entente. First a challenge. And now you're really taking her place."

He looked at me as if he were seeing me for the first time. His eyes were wide, and he blinked hard.

I shrugged it off. "Maybe we're all overdue for a change."

"How does it feel to be in the seat of a Couterie?"

"No different," I demurred, sinking farther back into the tufted chair.

"Well, I think it's time we Couterie had some new blood."

I studied him a beat. Was he messing with me? Couterie never sided with Shadows over other Couterie. I found myself strangely nervous under everyone's gazes and wondered where this conversation was going.

"Since when did Lavendra fall out of your favor?" I asked.

As soon as the words left my lips, Tork's cheeks reddened, suggesting that it was quite the opposite. I stared at him a beat, surprised. It had never occurred to me that anyone could love Lavendra, let alone Tork. And love was just as foreign to Couterie as it was to the Entente.

"You don't want her to be Couterie, because you like her," I tested.

"Let me know if you need any help preparing for the Challenge. Relax, Farrow. I am not pining away for you. I have another reason to be invested in the outcome of this contest," Tork said, ending the conversation just in time for dessert. I took this in.

Apparently I wasn't the only one with secrets.

CHAPTER 14

I went back to my room and released Hecate's ashes.

"What do you think, Mother? Can I beat Lavendra?"

Competition wasn't something that was encouraged among my sisters. Nor was revenge, for that matter. Hecate took a form of repose at the foot of my bed as if she were too tired for all my scheming.

I plopped down on the bed beside her.

I sighed, wanting praise from the ashes that never seemed to come. Hecate was judging me in death as she had in life.

"I did this. I brought her here. The Queen doesn't come to the Couterie. The Couterie come to the Queen . . ."

But the ashes were unmoved. Hecate's silhouette was defiantly still.

I flashed back to the day I had performed my biggest feat of magic—giving South wings. It was the worst thing I had ever done, and then I remembered the words Hecate had said: *Be careful what you wish for, Farrow.*

"'With enough will and enough magic, anything is possible,'" I whispered, thinking of Hecate's words that day. But I hadn't any magic. My will would have to be enough.

There was a knock on the door. It was Holocene, one of the maids. Hecate dutifully flew up to the ceiling, hovering overhead while Holocene peeked into my room. If the Shadows were beneath the Couterie, then the maids were even further down the hierarchy. If we were shadows, they were practically ghosts.

"Madame Linea wants you to know that the Challenge is set for two days from today. The Queen and the prince will be in attendance."

CHAPTER 15

What in the hells are you doing down here? Do you want the Queen to think that I am a monster?" Linea said when she found me alongside the other Shadows and maids preparing the drawing room for the royal visit. Apparently, today was an exception. Linea was perfectly okay with being perceived as a monster on days the Queen wasn't visiting.

She ushered me into Lavendra's bedroom and made me put on one of her dresses.

Linea had decided she wanted the Queen to think that her Shadows wore ballgowns while they served their Couterie.

"There. That's the best we can do," she said, frowning as she examined me in the dress. Not the one I had coveted, sadly, but a simple gray silk that she deemed appropriate for the occasion. "Why are you putting us all through this, Farrow? What possibly possessed you? You'll only embarrass us all."

"You said once that this life could take me inside palaces. I really want to see the inside of the palace," I deadpanned.

Linea swallowed a laugh at the irony of me using her own spiel against her.

"Go on then, it's only our funeral," she said, patting down my hair and leading me back to the drawing room like we were going to the gallows.

The prince wasn't supposed to meet his Couterie for another year. It was tradition for the royal heirs to meet their Couterie on their eighteenth birthdays. Technically, I still was not allowed to meet him.

And, apparently, the prince would not see me or Lavendra—or anyone, for that matter. He was led into the room wearing a blindfold of black silk that was as fine as any Couterie gown.

My furious heart threatened to beat through my corset when I saw the Queen entering behind him. Her face still had the same sharp edges. Her eyes were still the same hollow pools of gray that I remembered. She looked older, though, no longer the girl queen with the young son. Now she had fully grown into her long neck and limbs—and they were encased in Black Glass. I had never seen anything like it. Her gown, from its bodice to its belled skirt, was armored by Black Glass that was spun into thread and woven into the fabric. The result—a shimmering gown that was as cold and black as her heart.

The rumors of the Queen's increased paranoia were not just rumors. Her very person was cloaked in proof.

"I do not want to ruin the first time he sees his Couterie with this circus," Queen Magrit said to Linea as Prince Mather was helped inside by two of his valets.

They settled him into a chair, and he laughed.

Lavendra and I took our places in front of him. She wouldn't look at me. She wouldn't speak to me. She hadn't from the moment I'd challenged her. From what I knew of her ego, she thought that depriving me of her attention was the ultimate punishment. But for me, it was the most peace I'd had since I'd become her Shadow. And I knew something else: a quiet Lavendra was a scared Lavendra.

The prince put his hands on the blindfold.

"Don't you dare!" the Queen said.

He put his hands down at his sides, but a mischievous smile remained on his lips.

It was the first time I had seen either of them in so many years. I was so close. I could take my sharpened wand and stab the Queen here and now and have my revenge—but there was no way I could pierce the Black Glass of her dress in a roomful of guards, Couterie, and Shadows.

The Queen was obviously annoyed, but she seemed to enjoy being in charge of the proceedings.

"As a Couterie, you are tasked with protecting the future king's honor, heart, and body. The Challenge is comprised of three parts. The first is a question of love. The second: influence, and the third: devotion.

"Let us begin."

We flipped a coin to determine who would go first. I lost the toss and waited for the Queen to propose the first question to Lavendra.

"I will set the scene and you will tell me what you would advise the prince to do in this situation. Do you understand?"

"I do, Your Highness," Lavendra said.

"The first question is one that deals with the heart of the prince."

The Couterie and Shadows leaned in a bit, clearly interested in the subject matter.

"Prince Mather must choose his bride one day. When that day comes, if he is presented with a choice between love and a match that furthers the interests of the Queendom, which should he choose?"

Lavendra smiled as if she knew the answer.

"The prince has no choice. His heart never comes before the Queendom. He will make the match that ensures our sovereignty."

The Queen clapped her hands together, obviously pleased with her answer.

I held in a sigh. I took a long look at the prince's body language. Even with the blindfold, I could see he was not in agreement with Lavendra's words.

"Why can't the prince have both?" I asked. "A marriage of love that benefits the Queendom. I think that he deserves both. I think we all do. After all, that is what Queen Magrit had and what Queen Meena had before her."

There was an interminable pause. Had I overstepped?

"Well, son, what say you?"

"The Queendom comes first. Always first. But I do hope that my heart doesn't go unused. The second answer is the victorious one," the prince said.

His body turned toward the Queen. He wanted her approval.

"The first point goes to Farrow," the Queen said, "and as such, she will answer the next question first: A landowner accuses the new king of overcollecting taxes. What say you?"

I remembered the prince when he was young, running around the palace. He'd said to me that "everything and everyone here is mine."

I used his childish sentiment and said, "The Crown owns everyone and everything in the land. It is impossible for the Crown to take from the people when it has given everything to us."

The Queen turned to Linea.

"Very astute."

Lavendra cleared her throat and smiled.

"I think my lady is mistaken; there should be a crime for theft."

"Pardon? The prince has done nothing wrong."

"But the landowner has. He has stolen the prince's good name and should be punished accordingly, at His Highness's discretion, of course."

The Queen laughed at this and turned to her son, whose expression was harder to read.

"What say you, son?" she asked pointedly.

"Who am I to argue with such logic? The second answer wins."

I almost cursed Lavendra underneath my breath. How could the prince like her answer better?

A murmur went through the room. The Queen rapped her chair's arm for attention before speaking again.

"I see we have come to an impasse. The final question will decide your fates, quite literally. Lavendra will answer first."

A beautiful young servant brought out a tray with two apples covered in what appeared to be gold leaf.

"The prince's life is in danger. Someone has poisoned one of these apples. You must save the prince. Choose wisely. The prince's life depends on it, as does your own. And please be warned—there is real poison in one of the apples," the Queen added.

The other Couterie gasped. I felt my heart begin to race.

I was the only one in this room who truly knew her cruelty, and still I was surprised by the depth of it.

I knew that my plan for revenge would one day put my life in danger. I never imagined that day would be today.

The prince himself reflexively protested. "No, Mother!"

Queen Magrit looked at him sharply. She was unaccustomed to dissent, even from her own son.

Madame Linea's left eyebrow twitched. But she remained silent.

"Fret not, ladies, the poison is fast-acting. You will know your fate within minutes." The Queen laughed, clearly pleased with her deathly scheme.

"Mother, you can't," the prince objected again, rising from his chair.

"Relax, my son. There is an antidote."

She nodded, and another servant stepped forward, holding a tray with a vial on it. He lifted it high for all to see. The sparkling blue liquid inside caught the light.

"The vial will be administered only if the prince sees fit. These lives were cultivated for you, and so shall their fates be."

"Thank you, Mother," the prince said, bowing his head to her.

Linea cleared her throat as if she wanted to say something. But her lips remained firmly sealed.

Lavendra's face was ashen. Silently, she picked up the apple on the right side of the tray and took a bite. With a shaking hand, she replaced the apple to its original position.

"Lavendra has chosen the apple on the right," the Queen announced.

Then it was my turn.

From this distance, the apples appeared identical. And they remained so as the servant brought them closer. It was a life-and-death decision for more than just me. If I didn't win this challenge, then I would not get to end the Queen's life.

"Which one do you choose?"

I looked from one apple to the other. How was I to pick?

I tapped my fingers against the pocket of Lavendra's dress,

wishing for my wand, which wouldn't work even if it were here. I stopped myself.

"There is only one way to be sure that the prince is safe."

I took one apple in each hand. I looked between them. I took a bite from the one on the left. Then I lifted the apple on the right and bit that one too.

Tork and the rest of the room gasped. Linea fanned herself with her hand.

"Farrow has eaten both apples," the Queen announced.

"Then the prince has made his decision," Mather said. "Lavendra bit only one apple. She wanted to be applauded for risking her life. But she left herself a chance to live. A real Couterie would not leave the chance. She would put the prince's life before her own. Lavendra, you are a Shadow now."

The Queen turned to me. "That means you, Farrow, are Couterie."

Lavendra shook her head.

"This is a mistake. This cannot be . . . ," Lavendra began, and then she fell silent, seemingly realizing what she had done. She'd questioned the Queen.

She bowed low.

"Both apples are poisonous—but when eaten together, they cancel each other out. A rather elegant riddle," the Queen said, congratulating herself.

"You poisoned me . . ." Lavendra drifted off. But it wasn't that she'd lost her words. It was the poison taking them from her, stealing away her breath.

Lavendra's hand went to her neck, and she made a gasping sound. Her dewy face turned ashen, and she fell to the ground.

I rushed to her side. I spotted Tork in the gallery, ready to help, but his Shadow and brother, Jacoby, pulled him down.

"Help her!" I screamed.

I looked up at the Queen, who cocked her head at me, as if the scene before her were a curiosity at a fair. My stomach turned.

"What are you waiting for?" I demanded.

"As I said, it is the prince's decision. Mather, should she live or should she die?"

A razor-sharp edge laced through her voice. I wondered if maybe this was a test for the prince too.

I remembered what the Queen had said about the apples. Apart, they were poisonous. Together, they canceled each other out. I reached for the second apple to put it to Lavendra's lips, but one of the guards stopped me.

I looked past him. It was up to the prince to determine Lavendra's fate. And it was up to me to convince him.

"Please, Your Highness. Mercy is the ultimate power. You get to show that it is your will that determines her fate," I pleaded, trying to appeal to his ego.

Would the prince let Lavendra die? Was that the cost of answering wrong? Was this the cost of my vengeance?

My eyes fell on the prince, who was still, so very still. What was he thinking? Was he his mother's son? Would he let Lavendra die to prove his mother's point? Or to prove something to her?

He answered without emotion and without urgency.

"Give her the antidote," he said.

The Queen sighed as if she were disappointed. The guard handed me the antidote, and I poured it into Lavendra's open mouth.

I held my breath as I waited for hers to return.

One, two, three, four... I counted in my head as the moment ached on.

"Lavendra...," I demanded.

Come back to me, come back and challenge me, I thought. It was part prayer, part wish, part spell, even though I knew I couldn't make one anymore.

A few interminable seconds passed, and her eyes fluttered open.

When she spotted me, I could see the truth of what had just happened hit her all at once. She glared at me.

I helped Lavendra to her feet. She was weak, but she wrested away from me and began to stumble again. Linea rushed to Lavendra's side and shifted her weight over to her.

The Queen got up quickly, and her guards trailed behind her.

She walked past me, and then looked back.

"You are a strange one. She is your competition, and yet you moved to aid her after her defeat. You should savor your victory. A true victor leaves no one behind to rise again."

She was right. But there was no way she could know she had made that mistake already by leaving me behind. There was no way for her to know that her mistake was going to be fatal. I was someone she'd left behind, and I was going to kill her.

"Linea, you have the year to get your house in order. Couterie, I look forward to seeing you in the spring."

"Your Highness, may I escort Lavendra to her room?" Linea asked the prince.

"You may, but the victor stays," he said.

The royals and their pomp and circumstance. He couldn't even see me, but he still needed an audience for his exit.

Linea shuffled Lavendra out of the room.

It was supposed to be the prince's turn to exit. Two guards

moved to either side of him to help him out of the room, since he was still wearing his blindfold. But a couple of seconds ticked by, and he did not rise from his seat.

"Your Highness?" one of the guards prompted.

"Clear the room. I'd like a moment alone with my Couterie," he said. "I believe she's earned it."

The guards froze in place, but then one whispered to him, "Her Majesty will have both our heads if we don't get you back to the palace. She does not wait."

"Then you are in a quandary, because I will have your heads if you don't," the prince said with a mischievous smile below the blindfold.

"Of course, Your Highness," the guard said with a bow. He and the other guard retreated to the back of the room. They threw open the doors and the Couterie filed out. I caught a grateful glance from Tork as he crossed the room beside Jacoby.

"Farrow?" the prince called.

I realized that I hadn't moved a muscle since the Queen had left the room.

"Yes, Prince Mather," I said finally.

"Come a little closer," he demanded.

He couldn't possibly see me through the blindfold. But I obeyed, inching closer.

He put his hands up to the blindfold but then put them back down again without removing it.

"Cook always says that I would enjoy my food better if I waited and savored it," he quipped lightly.

But I felt the weight of the joke. Part of me rose up in protest. He was still the little boy I'd met in the hall of the palace. He still thought of people as possessions for his entertainment or his consumption. Just like his mother.

"I must know what possessed you to take both apples. How did you know my mother's riddle called for such sacrifice? How did you know that the sacrifice was the remedy itself?" he asked. His voice was filled with curiosity, like he genuinely wanted an answer.

"I didn't know. I hoped."

"Hope? Not a word heard often in our Queendom."

And I trusted in the Fates, I thought. But I didn't dare say the words out loud.

"I am closer to everything that I want than when I woke this morning," I said, choosing my words carefully.

"I'm afraid that you have the advantage here," he said.

"You are the prince. How could I possibly have any advantage over you?" I asked.

"I cannot see your every expression, and yet you can see mine." He gestured toward his blindfold. "But I prefer it this way. If I could see you, my opinion of you might be clouded by your beauty."

"How would you know that I am in possession of beauty?" I asked.

"Beauty isn't just in the face. It's in the content of your character. It's in the way you carry yourself through the world. You are clever. You are brave. Hence, you are beautiful."

It was strange. Prince Mather wasn't what I had expected. In fact, he was . . . charming. Where did he get it from? It certainly wasn't something he'd learned from his mother.

"That is an easy statement to make when I am also in possession of the face chosen to match the features deemed most pleasing to you."

Before he could answer, Madame Linea returned to the room. In the last hour I had seen her morph from the authoritative instructress to the Couterie into something else. Something obsequious. Something afraid. Instead of gathering satisfaction, I felt something else stir in me. I had never been on Linea's side, exactly. She was a means to the Queen's end. But seeing her bow before the blindfolded prince made me remember myself and bristle toward him.

"Pardon the interruption, Your Highness, but the Queen is waiting," Linea whispered.

The prince sighed as if he were annoyed by either Linea's presence or his mother's impatience. Or some combination of both. I found myself annoyed by his annoyance.

I marveled at the luxury he had of being the one person in the world who could dare upset the Queen and be greeted only with sighs.

I could hear the sound of the door closing behind me after Linea's exit.

"Till we meet again, fair Farrow," he said.

He reached out his hand and I put mine in it. He took my hand to his lips. I felt myself tremble. I told myself it was because I was still coming down from the poison. It had to be that and not the sensation of his lips grazing over my skin. But even when he dropped my hand, I felt the absence of his and I found myself tapping my fingers together nervously.

"You never answered my question," he added, running his hands through his hair. "Why would you risk your life with a challenge?"

"I am closer to everything I want than when I woke this morning," I repeated.

The prince paused and pursed his lips. I could not see his eyes, but I felt like if I could, they would be staring into mine.

"I feel like I am closer too," he breathed.

And despite myself, I felt the tremble again.

"Gerard . . . Thornton . . . it is time." The two guards raced to his sides to guide him out. He let himself be led.

"Not the most dashing of exits, I'm afraid," he said.

I laughed for his benefit.

When the door finally shut behind them, I looked at the tray with the apples. I knocked them to the floor. My instincts as a Shadow and an Entente made me kneel to begin cleaning up the mess. But when my knees met the ground, the cold wood floor shocked me awake, like a slap of water to the face in the morning. I righted myself and got to my feet. I stepped over the golden fruit. I would not kneel.

I was Couterie now.

CHAPTER 16

I woke with a start.

Lavendra's face stared down at me in the dark. Behind her, through my room's window, I could see the moon still sitting in the middle of the sky.

"Lavendra, what are you . . . ? Do you need something?" I said as I tried to orient myself. I wasn't dreaming. Lavendra was really here. But why? What was she doing here in the middle of the night?

"You're going to take my place, Shadow," she said without preamble. "I don't know whether you saved me or cursed me when you took my place. But I have decided it's the former. You gave me my freedom. You gave me a reason to leave this place. Can I let you in on a little secret?"

I sat up in the bed. I saw her valise stuffed messily to the brim. She was leaving. This was her version of goodbye.

I nodded.

"There was part of me that always envied Shadows," she said in a hush.

"How? Why?" I asked, thinking of the time we'd spent together. There had never been a moment when it felt like she wanted to trade places with me.

"Before, you got to live here without any expectations. You never had to Become. You could just be," she explained.

I had never just been. I had been born into the expectations of the Entente, and since they were gone I had lived under my own self-imposed expectation for vengeance. There was no rest for me.

"But have you thought of what it really means to Become? What it really means to devote your whole life to another who you don't really know? Take away the pomp and circumstance and the big black palace. And he's just another boy. One that you never got to choose for yourself."

Lavendra's words struck a chord. I had never thought about what it was like for her. But I was still on the defensive, thinking of how it had been for me.

"You have no idea who I am. You never bothered to ask," I returned. I couldn't help it—the words tumbled out of me after five long years of staying quiet for Lavendra, copying her every gesture, serving her every whim.

"You're right," she said.

I was stunned. Lavendra had never backed down to a contrary idea once in all our time together.

"And maybe I have no idea who I am either. I've spent my whole life preparing to be loved by one person, and you've spent so much of yours trying to please me . . . It is such a mess. But neither one of us created it," she added.

I felt my chest constrict with guilt. I had not created the Couterie, but I had created the circumstances that were sending Lavendra out into the night and away from everything she had ever known.

"I never really thought about you and me having anything in common except our faces. But I couldn't have been more wrong.

I've been serving the idea of the prince. And you've been serving me . . . What could I have done with all those years—all that energy? What could I have made, or built, or learned? What could you have? I know more about the prince than I know about myself. I am the product of his likes and dislikes, not my own. What else do you know, Farrow?"

I inhaled sharply. I'd actually been serving my own revenge. But she was right, we had both devoted ourselves wholly and entirely to a cause. In her case, she'd decided that cause was no longer worth pursuing.

Had she really changed? Was this a trick? If Lavendra could change her mind and heart, what else was I wrong about . . . about humans . . . about my plan . . . ?

"You don't have to go," I blurted, refocusing on her. I stilled my hand, which I realized was tapping at my leg.

I wanted to tell her that this was temporary. That I only needed to be Couterie for one night. Just long enough to get to the Queen. But I couldn't tell her. I couldn't risk the plan. But as much as I didn't like her, as much as I remembered her selfishness and her moments of unkindness, I didn't necessarily want to send her out into the harsh realities of the Queendom.

"I know we have never been friends, Farrow. But if you want to come with me, I think that my purse would be enough to cover your passage as well . . ."

I forced myself to breathe. I had never imagined this. She was extending her hand to me. I could feel the call of what she was suggesting . . . Run away from the plan, run away from the Hinter. Run away from the pain and loss and hurt. And just start over . . .

"I know this sounds crazy. I know I have been less than kind."

"That is an understatement."

"Yes, it is," she said, with meaning. "But there is a whole world out there. One where we make our own expectations."

"I can't. My place is here."

"But if I deserve more . . . then so do you, Farrow."

I shook my head. "I can't explain it. But this is where I need to be," I said.

She took a long beat to consider me.

"Then maybe you'll be a better me than I was," she added. And with that, she gave me a kiss on the cheek.

"Goodbye, Farrow."

"Goodbye, Lavendra," I returned as she closed the door behind her.

I rushed to the window. A few minutes later I saw her emerge from the back door of the Couterie, suitcase in hand, and disappear into the night.

CHAPTER 17

In the morning, after a near sleepless night, I woke up to Madame Linea's screams. They echoed through the halls, loud enough to wake everyone under the Couterie's roof. I could hear the patter of slippers and doors opening up and down the hallways.

I raced upstairs to Linea's room, where the other Couterie were gathering. Couterie and Shadows alike exchanged confused, sleepy looks. I played along. Linea had to have discovered that Lavendra had run. I could not let her know that I already knew. Linea never emerged from her quarters before brunch, but here she was screaming at the crack of dawn. Everyone was there—everyone except Lavendra.

One of the Shadows, Sypress, knocked on the open door after patting down the wisps of blond hair that had escaped her braid.

"Madame?" she said as loudly as she dared.

Madame Linea paced away from us. She was still in her night silks, and she was holding a letter. Even from a distance, I knew it must be from Lavendra.

"She's gone," Madame Linea said, pacing the room and dropping the letter to the floor.

I managed to contain a smile and ask, "Who? What are you talking about, Madame?"

"Lavendra . . . Rather than live the life of a Shadow, she snuck away in the night. No one has ever left the Couterie."

Madame Linea pulled her robe closer around her, seeming to come to her senses and realize she had an audience. "Everyone, what are you standing there for? Lavendra is gone, but we must go on," she ordered. "Go, except for Farrow."

There was a murmur of disbelief as the crowd shuffled off to breakfast.

I had changed Lavendra's, Madame Linea's, and possibly even Tork's life course when I changed my own. Hecate had once said that one change made so many ripples. She was right.

When everyone was gone, Madame Linea turned her focus to me. I couldn't remember ever being alone with her in her room before now.

"Farrow, what would make her act so foolishly? What will become of her?"

"I don't know, Madame . . . You have taught her well. She is resourceful."

But if Madame Linea was hearing me, it did not register on her face. She wrung her hands in frustration. I had never seen her to be anything other than calm.

"We don't need her anymore," I said. "I won the Challenge. I will be Couterie."

She suddenly leaned toward me. "Have you ever been to the circus?" she asked, picking up a brush from her dressing table as she spoke. "My favorites were always the trapeze artists. I was obsessed. I spent whatever allowance I had to go see them . . .

"There was one artist, Ophelia the Grace, who wore the most beautiful costumes, and she walked the high wire like she was crossing the room. She was so effortless. I thought she was magical. I thought she might even have been Entente."

I took a shallow breath at the mention of the Entente. There was no way for her to know about me, but that did not stop my skin from prickling in alarm.

"But it turned out she was not. I was sitting in the back row of the theater when she fell from the wire and clear through the net . . ."

"Did she . . . ?" I asked.

"Deader than Lavendra will be if I ever set eyes on her again," she said. She dropped the brush to the floor, and it landed with a thud. I instinctually wanted to reach for it and pick it up, but Linea's face told me not to.

"That's awful, Madame Linea. The net failed?" I asked, horrified.

"No, the net did its job," she countered.

"I don't understand. You said the trapeze artist got hurt. The net obviously failed."

"There is no net strong enough to catch someone from that height. The net was a placebo. It gave the artist the illusion of safety. It allowed her to step out onto the wire. But it was never meant to actually catch anything. Or save anyone."

It took me a second, but I realized what she was trying to say. "So, we . . . the Shadows are a net?"

She nodded. "Having a Shadow a step behind you keeps you on your toes. If you know that someone is waiting to take your place, you are that much more careful to keep it. More than that. You give the Couterie the illusion of choice."

"And you get free labor and free competition. We were never meant to take anyone's place," I said.

It was clever and cruel. But it was effective. Madame Linea didn't nod this time. She was done being coy with me. There was no point now.

"I know Lavendra better than anyone. I have studied her almost every minute I've been here. I can be her. Challenge or no challenge, I can be Couterie," I said.

Madame Linea outstretched a hand, a slow smile crossing her face. "You surprise me, Farrow. You *are* Couterie, after all."

I took her hand and shook it.

CHAPTER 18

From that moment on, I was Couterie. And from that moment on, I planned my attack on Queen Magrit.

My first order of business was moving into Lavendra's room, where I would finally be able to read the Ana. The book held the key to my mission. In its pages were maps of the royal palace, daily routines of both Prince Mather and the Queen, and other essential information I needed to kill the Queen.

But when I closed and locked the door behind me, I saw the room with new eyes. It was the first time that I wasn't worried about Lavendra coming in to chastise me. The first time I wasn't anticipating her every single need. Instead, someone else would wait upon me.

I opened the doors to the closet and ran my fingers along the dresses. I touched the bed that I had made a million times. Finally, I threw myself upon the chaise where I had waited on Lavendra for so many years.

I opened the pouch, wanting to show Hecate our change of fate. "Hecate?"

She didn't stir. She'd been cooped up so long during all my machinations the last few days.

"Hecate?" I said again, and she finally rushed out.

"We have all this space now," I boasted as the ashes zigzagged around the room, making a slight breeze that rustled my dresses.

She continued to speed up, creating a funnel of ashes in the center of the room, which blew a few pieces of stationery across the desk and knocked over a tray.

"Hecate," I whispered again, and the whizzing cloud of her ashes finally slowed down in front of me.

I put my hand out, and she mirrored me like she had when I was small. When I moved my other hand, she did the same.

"Why can't you just talk to me? Why can't you just tell me that I am doing the right thing?"

I finally moved again, and she moved with me.

"You're infuriating," I said, but some part of me wondered if what she'd done then was to let me know I wasn't alone.

A few seconds later she returned to her pouch, and I picked up the Ana from the bedside table. Holding the leather-bound book in my hands, I thought about Lavendra.

Only Couterie were given permission to read the Ana—never Shadows. I had stolen glimpses before, but I had never gotten to read it in its entirety. Now I could pore over every detail. Now I could plan. Whether the ashes liked it or not.

Settling in on the bed, I cracked open the Ana. There were lists of things that Prince Mather liked and disliked. His abilities and failings. His opinions on politics. And stories from maids and ladies, valets and footmen, and interviews with the prince and Queen Magrit.

> ... Speaks in perfect paragraphs ... Curses but only himself when he finds himself at fault. Unnervingly polite ... Remarkable physical specimen from a rigid diet and exercise routine insisted

upon by the Queen. He steals sweets from the kitchen, but the patisserie chef knows and leaves his favorites for him. Until he protested, he was assisted up and down staircases to ensure that he did not have a fall . . . Examined daily by the royal doctor . . . Without a spare heir the prince's physical safety is the Queen's most vital concern, second only to her own.

As the only heir, everything is designed to make sure that he survives to succeed.

The prince was forbidden to leave the palace. But there were a handful of incidents in recent months of him sneaking out with no report of where he had been. He was admonished by the Queen for his unsanctioned absences and put under twenty-four-hour guard.

"Where do you go?" I wondered aloud as I looked at this puzzle of stories and facts.

The result was a picture of a young man who seemed in some ways the same as the sad, petulant little boy I had seen in the palace the day of the Burning, and, in others, seemed all grown up. Had he ended up like his grandmother, the kindly Queen Meena, or his mother, the evil Queen?

"Who are you now?" I asked as I turned the pages.

I stopped on a passage that startled me.

Many people are afraid of what the prince's future holds. Will he take the throne? Is he a harbinger of the end of Queendoms? And the beginning of kingdoms?

I guffawed at the idea. There had been no such possibility of a "kingdom" until Prince Mather. From the beginning of Hinter, and maybe even from the beginning of time, our lands had always been ruled by queens.

> There have been several attempts on the prince's life by other Queendoms to ensure that he will never be king.

Part of me felt a surge of pity for the prince. No child deserved to have his or her life threatened. I knew that better than anyone as a child of the Entente.

I flipped through the pages, searching for one thing: his feelings on the Entente.

> Agrees with Queen Magrit on what should be done: eradication. Sworn to help the Queen take over the Thirteenth Queendom, her greatest threat, since it's an unknown land that will not denounce magic.

He had grown up to be just as his mother had trained him to be. The proof was on the page.

Each entry was initialed and annotated. Overheard. Seen. Experienced. And by whom. Staff. Ladies-in-waiting. Or signed by Madame Linea herself.

He hadn't learned from his brief encounter with us. Those tears he had cried for his grandmother were probably his last. His heart had hardened.

I flipped to another page.

> His Court of Gentlemen is charged with constant companionship and vigilance of the prince, but friendship has eluded the prince except for Hark, the Queen's Right Hand.

"So you never made friends—except for someone paid to serve your mother," I murmured.

> The prince spends his time reading. He is happiest in the palace kitchen curled up in the window nook. He is often seen walking or riding his horse around the grounds. There is a window in his bedroom that overlooks the gardens, and he is said to haunt it, looking out at the world that he will one day rule but is forbidden to play in...

"No wonder he sneaks out," I murmured, feeling an involuntary pull toward the necessary chess piece in my plan. But I stopped myself. I reminded myself that the prince was not an object of sympathy. He was a means to an end.

I was deep into my research on Prince Mather when Tork pushed open the door. He jumped back in surprise upon seeing me. "Farrow! Oh, I was just... I mean... I didn't realize you had already...," he muttered, wiping his eyes quickly.

"Do you miss Lavendra? I am sorry, Tork," I said.

And I was sincere. I had no bone to pick with Tork. I could see that he was hurting because of what I had done. I patted the chaise, encouraging him to sit next to me.

"My heart. My stupid heart," he exclaimed.

My brow furrowed. Lavendra, despite her uncharacteristically graceful exit, had always been selfish and insufferable. And Tork was probably the kindest of all the Couterie. But it was more than the unlikelihood of their connection that puzzled me. It was the unlikelihood of any connection. After thinking of only revenge for years, and as an Entente who did not believe in romantic love for herself, love was as foreign to me as the Thirteenth Queendom.

And falling in love was something that Entente did not do. Even if I was the last of us. But whatever I knew or didn't know of love, the idea of Lavendra and Tork together just did not make sense.

There were all those secret walks and that distant look that Lavendra had had of late, which I had attributed to her musing about the prince. But I couldn't have been more wrong. When Tork and Lavendra were together, they did nothing but trade barbs... I felt the realization hit me in the face and my cheeks burned from missing what was now obvious. Under all that animosity, there was love.

Tork must have seen my confused look because he began to try and explain.

"It started as practice."

"Practice?"

"We kissed a few times. It was supposed to be practice. But after a while, when I kissed her and she kissed me, I was never thinking of the Queen of Blenheim and she was never thinking of the prince. We were thinking of each other. Or at least that's what I believed... But how could she leave if she felt anything at all for me?"

Maybe she didn't have feelings, I thought first, snarkily.

"I am sorry, Tork," I repeated.

"Don't be—you didn't make her run. And yes, I was in love with her. But I was too scared to tell her. I was such a fool, Farrow."

"You are many things, but never a fool," I countered.

"After you won the Challenge, I decided to give up being Couterie. So we could be Shadows together and live out our lives here. But now she's gone, and I never told her how I felt. I never had the courage to give this to her," Tork said, pulling a folded paper from his pocket.

I looked down at the letter. "A love letter? May I?"

He nodded.

I was surprised by the beauty of the prose, and I read a particularly gorgeous line out loud.

"'I would forgo today if we could have forever . . . between barbs . . . between lessons . . . between dares . . . between airs . . . between kisses . . . I know not when I went from loathing you to knowing there was no in between with you. There's only you . . .' You're a poet, Tork."

Tork blushed. "Maybe if she had read this, she wouldn't have run. But who really knows?" He took the letter back.

"Maybe she didn't know what she felt. Maybe it had nothing to do with you or maybe it had everything to do with you, but maybe she had something she needed to do for herself," I said out loud as I felt around for an answer.

Tork cocked his head and looked at me. Maybe I'd said too much about a subject I clearly knew nothing about.

"Thank you, Farrow . . . ," he said, sounding like he meant it. Like, maybe, just maybe, I'd helped him feel a little better.

"She would have made a terrible Shadow," he added, brightening.

"And I am going to make a terrible Couterie," I returned, hoping the sentiment made him feel better.

"You will be perfection. But you must learn to be a better liar," Tork said as he got up and made his way to the door.

If only he knew.

"Can you do me a favor?" Tork said.

"Anything."

"Don't look at me like there's a cloud over my head, Farrow. I can't stand it. I can't take your pity for the rest of my time here."

"I promise. You're not the center of everything, Tork . . . ," I said, trying to lighten the mood. But instead my mind went to Lavendra, out there on her own. I hadn't thought about what would become of Lavendra or the Couterie before I enacted my plan.

"You're the center of everything now, Farrow. You're the prince's Couterie," Tork said with a smile, before he made his way into the hall.

I got up and closed the door.

I felt the ashes rustle around my neck again.

"Mother! Please," I said, pulling open the string on the pouch.

The ashes continued to rustle, but Hecate did not—would not—emerge.

"I'm sorry, Hecate. I know you do not like what I am doing. But I have spent my life waiting for the chance to make things right. To balance the scales. I will make her pay for what she did to you."

The ashes went still.

Again, I was grateful that Hecate could no longer see my future the way she used to when she was fully alive. Or at least she had never hinted that she could. If she didn't like this part, I didn't know how she would handle what was to come.

CHAPTER 19

The right dress or the right suit can change the course of a Queendom. You think I jest. But there are queens and dukes who fell in love at first sight. Without the right tailor, they would have faded right into the wallpaper."

Madame Linea was dressing me for the part of Couterie as if her life and mine depended upon it. She'd spent the better part of the week after the Challenge filling up my closet with gowns in a rainbow of colors and styles. There were tailors and fittings and it all seemed so ridiculous. I wasn't used to being fussed over, especially by humans. There was a very big difference between being a Shadow to the Couterie and being one of them.

If Couterie and Shadow were miles apart, then being Entente was another planet. I remembered dresses that floated from closets and shimmied down over my dark, curly hair with a flick of my wand. And bracelets of flowers.

As I stood in front of a pile of colorful clothes Madame Linea had left for me to try on, memories of my Entente life flooded my consciousness. I remembered Bari using her own wand and instead of decorating herself with blooms, she'd replaced her limbs with glowing beetles.

"Don't move, Farrow. If you crush them, you crush me," she'd said. *"We don't just wake up one day ready for big magic. We have to prepare."*

Bari believed that no one ever became a Fate without some risk. The same seemed to apply to avenging them.

In my head I could see Bari beside Galatea after one of our lessons in the courtyard.

"What if I am never as good as you?" I asked Bari as she created and spun a spiderweb around her finger the way human girls twisted curls around theirs.

Across the courtyard, Selina was making herself a crown of flowers with her wand. Em had turned her wand on herself and was making a face with wolf teeth. Freya was blowing fire rings. Everyone was better than I was.

"That's human talk. You are made of magic. You might even surpass me one day," Bari said with a wry smile.

"Liar," I said.

"Hardly. I have faith in you. Every day my magic gets stronger. It's just a matter of time for you. If the sisters haven't taught us that, then they have taught us nothing. The Past informs the Present and the Future."

"But doesn't the Past inform the Present and the Present informs the Future?"

"Iolanta can't inform anyone," Bari blurted with a laugh.

I remembered how her face had fallen. As if she had regretted her words.

"But you're right. Look at what I can do today that I couldn't do yesterday. And who knows what I can do tomorrow? There is no such thing as bad or good magic. There's what you can do and what you cannot," she said.

"Just promise me that you'll be more careful," I said gently.

"Only if you promise that you will be the opposite." She smiled.

I tried to shut out the memories. Bari hadn't been careful the day of the Burning and she was gone. And I wasn't being careful now.

I reopened my eyes, and then moved to put the dresses away as Linea walked by my open door.

"Leave them for your Shadow," she commanded. Linea had not gone to the orphanage to look for another match for me as she had before. She had chosen one of the maids instead. After a few surgeries, the resemblance was close enough. But seeing her altered face wounded me every time.

"Where is Holocene?" I wondered aloud. In all the excitement, I realized she hadn't returned since breakfast.

"You aren't supposed to be concerned about where your Shadow is. It is her job to be concerned about where you are," Linea instructed.

Everything felt like a lesson or a test from Linea. It was another tightrope that I was expected to walk. And like Linea had said, I knew that there was no net beneath me.

After all the clothes and shoes were bought, after my hair was braided and my skin polished, Madame Linea turned her attention to my education. Being Couterie meant more than knowing the Ana. I also had to entertain, advise, and be able to defend the prince. All this was the price of entry.

Singing was quickly dismissed. Lavendra sang like a bell, and I sang like some sort of wounded animal, according to Madame Linea. It was one of the few things that the doctor could not fix. So my lessons were focused on dancing, as well as the defensive arts, which were the hardest skills to master.

I still felt like I was part servant, part Shadow. No Shadow had ever had to step in for her Couterie. And absolutely no one let me forget that. I felt my frustration rise at being defined by the prince's whims, even when I had a plan of my own.

"It's just the first day. You will improve, my dear. There is a difference between having all eyes on you and you having your eyes on another. You will learn," Madame Linea counseled.

At least fencing gave me an excuse to wield a sword. Perhaps it would come in handy when I faced off with the Queen.

I was a scrappy fighter, not an elegant one. It felt good to let my foil fly and concentrate on movement and power.

When the session was finally done, I presented myself in front of Madame Linea, triumphant.

"Effective. But the royals expect more flare."

"Wouldn't they prefer to be alive?" I asked.

"If you are royal, you don't expect to have to choose between any two things. You can have them all."

I tapped my fingers against the handle of the blade and stopped myself.

"You still fight like an orphan, not like a Couterie."

I didn't care about artistry. I cared only about killing the Queen. But I had to please Madame Linea or I would never actually make it to the palace.

I raised my blade again.

CHAPTER 20

Hecate used to say that the Future was the one thing you spent forever waiting for but most were not ready when it arrived. Madame Linea had filled my days with so many lessons and so much training that all the seasons had run their course again, and the spring was again upon us. The days and nights ran together, with me waking with the sun to train and falling asleep with my head in the Ana and Hecate watching over me. I wasn't sure how ready I was yet, but I would not let even a second be wasted.

On the first night of spring, my Shadow, Holocene, was late again for getting me ready for dinner. After waiting, I laced up my own corset, but I left my hair for her to tackle. She came in a rush and shut the door behind her hard. She was carrying a tray of fruit.

"I'm sorry I'm late, Farrow."

"No apologies. Only reason," I instructed gently.

"There was another burning. I didn't get your honeybread. I couldn't walk past the square," she said, sounding ashamed.

I took an automatic deep breath after she said it, and I immediately regretted it. The acrid smell clinging to her clothes filled my lungs and triggered my memories. The smell of flesh on the pyre. The Queen was at it again.

She had begun burning girls a couple of years after the Burning in the square. I snuck away from the orphanage each time, certain that somehow she had found one of my sisters. But each time it had been a human girl tied to the stake and not my sister. I never stayed to watch the girls burn. But their screams had followed me and stayed with me. I felt as if I could hear them now as Holocene apologized.

"No apologies. Only results," I said again.

She nodded. I could see her stall another apology as she opened her lips and closed them again. She then laid out my brushes, combs, and hair adornments like I had hundreds of times for Lavendra. Holocene then smoothed out her skirt with her hands, which trembled as she did so. She was obviously still shaken by what she had seen in the square.

"One of the girls was only fifteen. Imagine. That's younger than us," she said as she approached and stood next to me in the mirror. She began braiding my hair. Her fingers were clumsy and the braids imperfect.

I frowned at our reflections. The Queen was keeping the story of the Entente alive, even though I was the only one left. She was using it now, as she had then, as a way to control the Queendoms. I had no love lost for humans. And there was a certain irony in the Queen burning her own in search of the Entente. I had held firm in my belief that my sisters were gone. Otherwise they would have come back for me. But the burning smell still reached inside me and unsettled me. It brought back the day of Hecate's Burning over and over again. I assured myself that the feeling came more from the idea of the Past than the Present.

"Here," I said, and retwisted my bun into one that was identical to hers. When I leaned over to fix an errant stray hair at the nape of

Holocene's neck, I flinched when I noticed the scarring behind her ears from her last alteration.

Holocene was trying. I could feel the effort in the strain of her voice and in the carefulness of her step. She was trying so hard to live up to the standards of the Couterie, but the real her was bucking against the imitation and making herself visible and heard with every gesture and sound she made.

"Thank you. But Madame Linea said I had to braid it myself. I'm not Couterie."

"What Madame Linea doesn't know won't hurt her," I said. But as I looked again at the girl's scars and as I took in the smell of her hair, I got a flash of that very bad day again. I shook it off, but not before Holocene noticed that my hands were shaking.

"At least no one would dare burn one of the Couterie. We're too important," Holocene said.

"The Entente used to think that too," I said quietly.

"What?" she asked, unsure.

"Never mind," I said. I knew better than to speak of the Entente here. But the knowledge of Magrit's actions against her own people loosened my tongue.

"You can take the girl out of the Shadows, but she will always be one . . . ," a voice said as the door opened behind us.

I turned around, ready to admonish someone, but instead found myself face-to-face with Tork.

"When you stand still, I wouldn't know that you weren't Couterie all your life," he teased. Tork walked into the room as I admired myself in the mirror.

"Don't be kind," I countered as Holocene bowed and exited.

"I'm never kind, remember?" he said sternly, but his eyes were smiling.

"I think you protest too much, Tork."

"I think once you open your mouth, you most definitely are still a Shadow," he said.

I laughed.

Tork and I had fallen into a routine of preparing each other for our Becomings. Tork was promised to Queen Papillion of the Third Queendom, Blenheim. Somehow what I had done to Tork and Lavendra had bonded us to each other. I was grateful for his friendship. It made me feel just a bit less guilty for breaking his heart.

We spent hours talking about Queen Papillion and the prince. Tork also had the inside track on what was happening outside Madame Linea's walls. He knew about the wave of people who had been burned at the stake in search of the Entente. He even told me about a group of underground Resistance fighters.

I wished I could tell Tork that I was planning to put an end to it all. But I kept my secret sealed. Instead, I always turned the conversation back to love and Lavendra.

"It was just a crush," Tork said.

"You're always thinking about her. She's in the room. She's in every room. I can see it on your face," I said.

"Love isn't for our kind," Tork replied. "We can't afford to fall in love. Not with each other, and certainly not with our queen or prince."

I nodded in agreement. There was zero chance of that happening. You can't fall in love with a dead boy.

CHAPTER 21

The day before my Becoming, I got up early and walked out of the house. Madame Linea had assumed I would spend my last day and the few coins she'd given me to pamper myself and say goodbye to my youth. But I wasn't doing that at all. Instead, I was preparing. It wasn't an easy thing to kill a queen.

I took the long way back to the Enchanted Forest. I had not been there since the day I had decided to stop being a Shadow and become a Couterie.

I had so much to do to get ready, but I allowed myself one indulgence before my life changed completely—again.

I let Hecate's ashes roam free in the Reverie. They flew away from me in a rush and took a tour through every room of the ruins before soaring back and taking form in front of me.

"We're home, Hecate. At least for today," I said.

I didn't know if Hecate was happy anywhere. But I believed that if she could be, it was here.

"Tomorrow we finally get our revenge. But I could use a little help. Do you think you could put in a word for me with Fate?"

The ashes separated and then reconfigured themselves in her

favorite spot—the rock near the tree where I kept the wands I'd whittled.

"I'll take that as a yes," I said firmly. I needed her to be with me on this.

I took the wands out of their hiding place, deep in the hollow of one of the oldest wand trees. The wands for every Entente, with images that reminded me of them—the powers we had and the things we loved. I had carved them hoping that perhaps the spirit of the Entente would somehow help me regain my magic.

Magic never really dies. You can wield it, but it is never really yours, Iolanta had said. But after a time, I think I was really just memorializing my lost family.

Even though he wasn't a true Entente, my first wand had been for South. My last had been mine. I had one more wand to make. My own, for the new me. For the me I had become.

I began with the faces of my glamours . . . then the wings that I had created for South . . . his shoe . . . Hecate's ashes . . . a letter to represent Tork and Lavendra . . . and I ended with a carving of a crown.

I stretched out the wand again. This was what I'd come here for. To try again.

Maybe Fate wanted me to wait till I needed it most.

"One last time," I whispered.

I called on my lost magic, I called on my lost sisters, and I called on my lost self. I squeezed my eyes shut so tightly, my face hurt, and I whispered to them all.

Come back to me
One last time.

Let this be the instrument of the Future
And the Queen's Fate.
It's not too late.

"'Marry your words to your will and you can do almost anything.' You said it then. I need it to be true now . . . ," I added.

I tried to change the leaves from green to any other color. I was attempting a beginner spell—the kind we'd learned when we were small. But there was no change in the leaves at all.

I looked down at the wand in my hand and the others on the ground. I thought I had come here to try again. But maybe I had really come to say goodbye.

"Hecate, it looks like we have to make our own fate this time."

Hecate cocked her head, seemingly looking at me.

I pulled the knife out of my pocket and added something to my new wand.

We were supposed to carve only what had happened—not what we wanted to have happen. But I made an exception in case this was my very last carving. "There," I said out loud as I etched a dagger through it. The dagger through the crown was my Future. Or at least I hoped it would be.

Then when I was done, I carved the wand itself to a very sharp point. It was a crude weapon, but hopefully an effective one. I would use it to kill her. Fates willing.

I slipped the wand into my pocket and looked up at Hecate.

Hecate's ashes were sitting on a rock, hunched over, as if she were crying.

"Hecate, I'm sorry. But I am doing this for you. For all of us."

I remembered Hecate, my Hecate, as she once was, after I had given South wings. She was in her room, pulling a dress out of her closet. She had sent Bari and Amantha to dinner but had kept me behind. I had pleaded with her to fix him.

Hecate had not moved a muscle. She was my mother, even if I hadn't known it. And she was my teacher, even if I never fully understood what she wanted me to learn. She had refused to fix South, which I could not understand. Why did Hecate make everything so hard when she could fix anything with the wave of her wand?

I wondered what the consequences of killing the Queen would be. Would the world be saved? Or would it be the start of something else entirely? We were taught to only make small gestures to keep Fate on course. But what I was going to do was bigger than what I had done with the Challenge. I wasn't just changing lives; I was taking one. What would that do to the Queendoms? What would it do to me?

I noticed the sun was meeting the horizon line and the forest was becoming dark. It was time to go back. I got to my feet and shouted to Hecate.

"If you don't come back now, I'm heading to the Couterie without you," I threatened. "You have to be a little proud of me, Hecate. After all these years, we're going back to the palace. I'm going to make her pay, Hecate. For you. For my sisters. For the life I should have had. *We* should have had . . . Everything is happening now."

The darkening sky broke and her ashes came at me all at once. Hecate didn't agree with me, but she wasn't leaving me either.

❧

The day of my Becoming would bring me one step closer to completing my mission, which was in odd contrast to the grand celebration Madame Linea and the Couterie had prepared.

The sitting room was filled with champagne and a spread of the prince's favorite foods. Couterie and Shadow alike congratulated me on my Becoming.

The day of the Becoming was also Prince Mather's eighteenth birthday. My own had come and gone without an ounce of fanfare, which was the Entente's way, as well as the Couterie's. But I could not help but note the disparity. Noble people's lives were celebrated in ways our own never would be. The prince was literally being given another person for his birthday, one raised for his every whim, and on our own birthdays we received not so much as a piece of cake. But on the day before I was to be given to him, I was given the first and only party in my honor in all my years.

"You are transformed. You are Couterie," Madame Linea said, raising a glass in my direction. "Cheers to Farrow's Becoming. May she make the prince's every dream come true."

"Cheers to Farrow!" Tork said, sidling up next to me. He took my hand and gave it a squeeze before slipping a small packet into my palm.

"What's this?" I asked.

"I have treasured our time together. Call it a thank-you from a friend," he said in a low voice. "They're sleeping pills. You know, in case things get out of hand with the prince tonight. One if you want not to care. Two if you want to forget. Three if you want to sleep through till sunrise."

"You are a friend, indeed," I said, suddenly sad that I might never see Tork again.

"Here's to you," Tork said, touching his glass to mine.

I raised my glass back and toasted to my future success.

"Now I want you to give me a present in return," Tork said.

"You do know that is not how presents work," I countered.

"Not a present then, a promise."

"What do you want me to promise?"

"That you won't fall in love. I think we Couterie are highly susceptible to getting our hearts broken. I made up a connection with Lavendra in my head because I was lonely. A connection she never encouraged and never returned in her heart. Because we have been told our whole lives not to love. I just want you to avoid making the same mistake I made," Tork said gently.

"And what mistake was that? Falling in love? I assure you that I am in no danger."

"I saw him in the drawing room. Even I'm a little in love with the prince," he said.

The prince was undoubtedly handsome, brilliant, and kind to other humans. But he was also his mother's son.

"No, you're not," I said pointedly, changing the subject back to Lavendra.

"No, I'm not. You're relentless. But you're not being realistic about how the Hinter works—about how the world works, about how people work."

"Then explain it to me."

"I stood outside Lavendra's door with my stupid letter night after night because I was afraid of love. Of how we would survive outside the Couterie. And I have to live with that cowardice for the rest of my life."

"Tork . . ." I wasn't pretending now. I felt genuinely sorry for this human and the pain I'd inflicted on him.

"Please, Farrow. I want better for you."

"I promise you, the only heart that is in danger is the prince's."

He raised his glass and clinked it against mine.

While the rest of the Couterie celebrated, Madame Linea took me aside.

"Come, Farrow," she said, sweeping me out to the hall and into her private chambers. "There's one last thing to do, and there are things you should know. Things I must tell you before you leave for the royal palace."

Linea's suite was decorated like her: tasteful but a bit stuffy.

She led me into her bathroom and told me to disrobe. She wanted to paint something special on my back. She told me it would be a surprise for the prince.

"Your time with us has come to an end," Madame Linea said as she carefully brushed henna ink across my body. "The rest is up to you."

When she was finished, I took a seat on the chaise in her room.

"Now I will share something very important with you before you Become."

She went to her dresser drawer. When she returned, she was holding a large golden box. She opened the box and handed me the mirror inside.

I turned the mirror over and over in my hand. It weirdly did not show my reflection. "This mirror doesn't work."

"It's Gray Glass. It's from the Entente."

I had never heard of Gray Glass. I didn't understand. I knew all about Black Glass, but this was something else.

"With it, *she* could show me the Future. She could show me who belonged to each other," Madame Linea continued.

Only one Entente could show the Future. Hecate. My Hecate.

I reached for the pouch where I kept Hecate, but I came up empty. I'd left her pouch in my dress pocket.

"You're saying that the Entente picked your Couterie? They picked me?" I asked, incredulous.

Madame Linea nodded. "The prince, every queen, every nobleperson held the mirror, and the name or face of the matching Couterie would appear in it. And then I would go to the orphanage and find him or her. How do you think I have always chosen so well? Never a Couterie rejected. Never a Shadow used. Until Lavendra."

"But once the Entente disappeared . . . It's been years. What did you do? How did you match up the Couterie with their royal counterparts?"

"Once Hecate was burned in the square, the Gray Glass stopped working. So I improvised. And no one has been the wiser. You were the last Couterie who was chosen. You were chosen long ago. That was your fate. Hecate told me that your case would be different, that I wouldn't find you for several summers. And she was right."

My mind was blown. Hecate knew I would come to be Couterie. And more than that, she had sent Madame Linea to find me.

"And now that you're about to head off to Prince Mather and Queen Magrit to meet your fate, you should know what happened to Queen Magrit's Couterie."

It had never occurred to me that Magrit had gone through the same process of Becoming as every other royal and that she would also have a Couterie.

"What happened?" I asked, dread rising.

"Elon was a kind soul, filled with empathy to counter her lack of it. And she was rather fond of him. But she realized how very much her Couterie knew about her, and she didn't like that. Then one day he disappeared . . . Nobody knows what really happened to him."

I digested this and realized Madame Linea was giving me a warning.

"You think Prince Mather will do the same to me?" I guessed.

"Prince Mather is harmless, but Queen Magrit could wake up

tomorrow and decide that what you know far outweighs the service you provide."

"I can handle myself. You taught me how," I reassured her.

"Against the prince, but not the Queen and her army. I taught Elon too."

"It won't be the same. I'm not Elon."

Madame Linea sighed. "I wish you all the luck in the Queendoms, Farrow," she said, taking the mirror and dismissing me.

As I walked back to my room, I thought about Prince Mather and the Queen.

I couldn't tell Madame Linea that it wouldn't be an issue. I did not plan on having a lifetime of being his Couterie. Only a single night.

There was still one thing left to do. I locked my door and released Hecate's ashes from her pouch.

"What the hells, Hecate? This is what my Fate is? You knew this whole time and didn't tell me?" I asked.

She remained infuriatingly still. Was this my Fate? Or did she still think I could change it?

"Hecate, please, why did you send me here if you did not want me to kill the Queen?"

The ashes finally moved, and she put her arms around me. There was no warmth in the embrace, but the gesture itself caused a tingly rush of feeling over me. In all these years, Hecate's ashes had never tried to hug me.

We stayed like that for the longest time, and when we broke apart again, I felt nothing but forgiveness for her. Hecate had done whatever she had done for me. I only wished she could tell me what would happen next.

CHAPTER 22

The day of the Becoming, I felt every pore of my skin tingle. We arrived at the palace doors in the morning, as scheduled. My entourage, per Queen Magrit's instructions, did not contain a single Shadow.

Linea had brought seven Couterie chosen specifically to accompany me. Despite the Queen's penchant for caution, it would be offensive to the other Queens not to have their Couterie present. But they were blindfolded for the journey into and out of the palace as an extra precaution. And Linea had warned them all that though they had loyalty to their own respective royals and nobles, it would be a mistake to cross their royal host. The fatal kind.

I had said goodbye to Holocene in the morning, and I'd left half of my remaining purse with a note: *For the Future, in case you find yourself in want of one*. Dutiful Holocene would probably return the money to Madame Linea, but I hoped for once she would choose her own interests over the Couterie's.

The grand palace door swung open, and a woman I knew was Sadie greeted us with glasses of champagne and insistent offers for her staff to show us to our rooms. She was older, but I recognized her from my visit to the palace all those years ago. I stopped myself from calling her by name.

"I'm Sadie. Welcome to the palace. If you need anything at all, please ring me," she said as we followed her into the vast foyer.

There was no way for her to recognize me. I'd had a different face then and a different life. She smiled and bowed and led us through the palace's many halls.

The Couterie was opulent, but Queen Magrit's palace made it look like a stable in comparison. The building was enormous, and every inch of it was gilded, tufted, embroidered, mirrored, or painted. Queen Magrit's idea of design was apparently "more." Behind every beautiful piece of furniture and sculpture was the specter of Black Glass. Every wall had been lined with the shiny black surface. It was the backdrop for everything. I was almost surprised that Sadie herself had not been dipped in it. The palace had certainly changed in the years since Hecate and I had been here.

I looked into the glass with trepidation. But there was nothing alarming in my reflection. I looked every bit the Couterie I was pretending to be.

The maids led the others to their quarters, and I was left with Sadie.

"Aren't you a beauty," she said.

"Thank you," I replied.

"Funny how girls always assume it's a compliment," she said sternly.

I sensed suddenly that she did not approve of me, or perhaps she didn't approve of Couterie altogether. Or was her cynicism because the intervening years had been unkind to her? I was certain that Queen Magrit had been. But had the prince been as well?

"Pardon me?"

"Beauty isn't what the prince needs. He has been starved of so many other things that are far more important."

"Like what?"

"Kindness. Friendship. Love . . ." Then she added quickly, "Pardon me, I speak out of turn."

I remembered the way she had looked at the prince when he was young. She wore the same expression now. She wanted to protect him.

"I will take care of him. I promise."

With a nod, Sadie pushed open a bedroom door at the end of a hall past a grand ballroom. "You can get ready in here," she said.

A guard was posted outside the room that had been prepared for me. His eyes were trained on the ground. I was immediately annoyed. Did he think he was too good to treat the Couterie with respect?

"Eyes up here, soldier," I said loudly in his direction.

"I wasn't looking at anything," he protested.

When his eyes met mine, I dropped the champagne flute that I had been holding.

It was South.

South, alive and all grown up. I searched his eyes, but there wasn't even the briefest flicker of acknowledgment.

"It's you," I whispered.

"Is there a problem?" one of the other guards, presumably his superior, boomed from down the hall.

"The beautiful lady mistakenly believes that she has met me before," South said.

The guard came closer, towering over us both.

"He's right. I must have been mistaken," I said quickly.

"No, please indulge me, miss. Step into the light, soldier, and turn around. There is no way you would ever forget this one."

"That's perfectly all right . . ."

"Your commander has given you an order, soldier," the guard said, no longer listening to me. "Do not make me repeat myself."

South stepped out of the shadows and into the light. The outline of his wings was encased in leather. The top points stuck up slightly above his shoulders. It was definitely him. South was alive.

"South is one of the Fallen from the day of the Burning. Our benevolent Queen welcomed him into our ranks," Sadie explained.

I pasted on a smile. South lowered his head and when he finally looked up, his eyes did not meet mine. My head clouded. I did not understand. Why was South here, in Queen Magrit's army?

"All hail the Queen's generosity," I managed, despite the pounding of my heart in my chest.

The guard, having enjoyed humiliating South, ordered him to step back into place.

"Forgive his insolence, my lady."

South gave a deep bow of apology. "Forgive me, miss," he said quietly.

"I can have him removed from your service, miss," Sadie offered, looking back and forth between us with interest.

I raised my neck haughtily, as I had been taught by Madame Linea.

"The Couterie believe that forgiveness is just another transaction. I know how he can make it up to me . . . ," I said, pausing dramatically for her benefit, and buying myself time.

"How's that, miss?" Sadie said expectantly.

"Make him bring me another glass of champagne."

"Certainly, miss," she said, her curiosity replaced by boredom. She of all humans would be accustomed to people humiliating the help.

I strode into the room, slamming the door behind me for effect.

I leaned against the door for a moment as I caught my breath. South was alive! I was not alone in the world after all. But how? And if he was alive, were any others? My heart was torn in two by Fate's delivery of South now after all this time. Was it a sign or cruelty? I tried to make sense of the irony of finding out I wasn't alone on possibly the very last night of my life.

A moment later, South knocked on the door.

"Come in," I ordered, making my voice as nonchalant as possible. South entered, carrying a glass of champagne on a tray. I closed the door firmly behind him.

South moved with grace and balance. Gone was the clumsy boy from all those years ago.

"South, I know it's you. Admit it," I demanded.

He was quiet for a second, and then he put his finger to his lips.

"Farrow, is it really you? The eyes are the same but there's something . . ."

I remembered my surgery. I shuddered reflexively, closing my eyes. The doctor's knife hovered over me in my memory. I forced open my lids and South came into focus again.

"It's me . . . How are you here? I thought you didn't make it," I said.

"I thought *you* didn't make it," he echoed.

I wrapped my arms around him. He smelled grown-up and clean, a mixture of soapy sandalwood. I could feel the wings on his back, which made no sense. The Entente's magic had limits. Spells expired based on the power of the one wielding them. And I had barely had any power.

"What are you doing here?" he asked.

"I'm here to kill the Queen."

"So am I," he said, without missing a beat.

CHAPTER 23

I don't understand any of this. You're one of her guards. How could you have joined them?" I demanded, backing away from South.

He flinched as if my words had hurt him, and then his face hardened.

"The day that Hecate burned, the Entente used whatever magic they could. Bari turned some of the Queen's soldiers into half-man beetles, and then there was the one she made into scorpions . . ." South hesitated as if he was remembering that moment. That day and all its horrors. When he spoke again, his voice caught. "The Queen rounded me up with the men touched by the Entente's magic. And since the Entente's magic held past that day to this very one . . . keeping them half insect/half man . . . she thinks I'm like them. She thinks that what happened to me happened during the Burning. We're called the Fallen."

Bari's magic had lasted just like mine had with South's wings. *Why? How?* I thought, trying to wrap my head around what this new information meant about our magic.

"She thinks that I, that we, are all abominations. But we are also an example of what the Entente can do . . . of what the whole Queendom should be afraid of," he said resolutely.

"She's using you."

"I'm allowing myself to be used."

"Against us? Against the Entente?" I asked, not understanding.

"*For* us. So that I could avenge *us*. I thought everyone was gone. Getting back at the Queen is all I've lived for since that day. And if I've had to pretend to be someone I'm not, that is the price. I've been waiting for the right moment to kill the Queen, but that's not an easy task. Not even from inside the palace walls."

"I saw your shoe. It was covered in blood."

"I lost it in flight, I guess."

The shoe was his. But he was alive. All these years, I had been wrong.

"The last time I saw you, you were hiding underneath that cart. I always assumed the guards found you there," he said.

I felt shame wash over me again. For not being able to act in that moment. For not being able to fight.

South studied me a beat and softened as if he could see my guilt.

"Hecate and the others wanted you to survive. Wanted the Entente to survive," he said finally. "I am so glad to see you, Farrow . . ."

"Me too," I said, meaning it.

"If I'd known you'd been forced into a place like the Couterie, I would have spent my time saving you—not trying to kill the Queen."

"You think I need rescuing? I chose the Couterie. It was my way into the palace."

"I didn't mean to insult you, Farrow."

I shushed him. "No more apologies. You're here. I'm here, South."

"We are," he said with a sheepish smile that was filled with emotion. "But you have to go. You have to leave."

"What are you talking about? I have spent the last six years planning for tonight," I said, caught up short.

"And I have spent the last ten. Let me handle it. Let me kill the Queen. It's too dangerous for you to be here," he said protectively.

"I could say the same for you," I countered.

"Just because you have magic, you think you are the only one who can take down the Queen," South said.

His voice was colder, the hug we'd shared seemingly forgotten. We had been apart for so long, and I realized that this was how he remembered me. I was his childhood tormentor. I had hurt him.

"No, that's not it, South. You don't understand."

"I understand plenty," he said defiantly, his voice rising. "You won't get near the Queen without her knowing you are Entente. There is more Black Glass now than there was when you were young. It is everywhere. You shouldn't be here at all, Farrow. I don't know how she does it, but she can sniff out a witch like a swine can sniff out truffles."

"I'm like you now, South," I confessed.

"What do you mean?" he asked. The familiar crease between his brown eyes that had annoyed me as a child suddenly seemed charming now.

"I think Hecate bound me with a kiss of protection when she was dying. That's why the Queen couldn't detect me," I explained.

"You don't have magic?" he asked.

"I don't have magic," I repeated. "Not since the Burning."

"Being Entente means more than just having magic," he said gently. "I always felt like I was Entente. I still do."

South paused and looked at me a long beat. "I don't think you'd be doing this if you didn't feel the same way," he added.

And for the first time in a long time, I felt like I had more to hold on to than my pouch of ashes.

I nodded.

"So how are you going to kill her? With a dance? Or with one of those heels of yours?" he asked boldly, breaking the moment.

I pulled the sharpened wand out of my garter. In one quick motion, South reached for it. Suddenly, the wand was at my throat.

"Two things: In order to get to the Queen, you might have to go through the prince. And the prince is one hell of a swordsman," he whispered.

I could feel South's warm breath on my neck, and my face flushed.

"I'll make sure his sword isn't within his reach. What's number two?"

"There's a difference between defending yourself and killing someone," South said.

I stomped on his foot. South loosened his grip on the wand, and I chopped at his arm with my own. The wand dropped through the air, and I caught it before he could recover. I raised it, victorious.

"I can handle myself."

South pulled something out of his pocket. He pressed a blade into my hands. "In case you need something other than a wand," he said, teasing. "I'd heard that the Couterie could fight, but I've never seen it until now."

"And yet you still doubt me?"

"I know you . . . or at least once upon a time I did, and the girl I knew would have had trouble killing someone innocent. Someone like Prince Mather."

"I will do what I have to do for Hecate. For all of us."

"How?"

"The prince's quarters are right next to the Queen's. In fact, she has a private door that accesses his bedchambers through hers. I will slit the prince's throat, slip into the Queen's chambers, and then I will slit her throat."

"Actually, the Queen moved his quarters," South corrected.

"No, that's not possible," I said. "It's in the Ana. She keeps the prince close for his protection."

I felt panic rise in me. I had studied the prince. I knew he was straining against the Queen's reins on his life. But I had not anticipated this.

South shook his head. "I've seen it with my own eyes. The prince no longer wants to share a wall with his mother. The Queen had a brand-new room prepared for him yesterday. But even if he hadn't moved, I don't think you would go through with it," South said with a rueful smile.

"How dare you presume to know what I will or won't do!" I whispered loudly, but the sight of his scrunched-up face made me smile too. "You still have the same expression when you think you're right," I said.

"So do you . . . ," he said, pausing and looking at me.

When our eyes met, it felt like we were back in the Entente again, our seven-year-old selves facing off.

"What happens after you kill the Queen and the prince? There are a hundred guards between you and the palace's front door. The Queen has almost hourly checks."

Killing the Queen was all that mattered. I hadn't thought about the after. Well, I had thought about it. But I had made a decision not to think about it anymore.

"South, all that matters is that Hecate is gone. And the Queen killed her."

"I know. But you matter too . . . ," he said resolutely. "I have a plan, Farrow, and in mine I get out. *We* get out," he said firmly. "You aren't alone anymore."

I looked at South for what seemed like minutes, but it could only have been seconds. We were strangers now. It had been so many years. But still, he was South. He was the only person in the whole world who wanted the Queen dead as much as I did. And he was the only person alive who knew me at all.

"Yes," I said finally. "We do this together."

He smiled broadly. But we didn't have time to celebrate our new partnership. Before South could share his plan, there was a rap on the door. Perhaps South had stayed too long. It could not have been customary for a Couterie to be alone this long with a guard.

As it swung open, I planted a kiss on South's lips.

When we parted, he looked back at me in surprise. It took just a second for him to realize the kiss was for the guard's benefit, not his or mine. The guard wouldn't say anything to jeopardize the Becoming and risk getting thrown into the dungeon.

South's eyes flashed with understanding. Was I flattering myself to think that there was something else along the edges? Something that approached disappointment that the kiss wasn't real?

South slipped out of the room, and I leaned against the door again. For the first time since the day of the Burning in the square, I had something other than revenge on my mind. I had hope. I tried to stuff it down, concerned that it would cause me to lose focus.

Despite myself, despite my plans, I had a new image in my mind beyond the dead Queen. For the first time, I thought about the day *after* revenge.

Me standing in the light with South.

CHAPTER 24

A few minutes later there was another knock on the door. I opened it, exasperated at South for taking the risk of visiting again.

But it wasn't South. Instead, Queen Magrit herself and a squadron of guards stood in the doorway. I froze, startled.

"Leave us," she commanded, and the guards reluctantly backed away.

The day of the Challenge, there had been distance between us. All of the Couterie, the guards, and the prince had been there. Now I was all alone with the Queen. The woman who had taken everything from me. The woman I was about to take everything from.

I didn't want her here. Not like this. It was too soon. What if I did or said something to give myself away? What if my anger overcame my reason and she called for her guards before I could wrest the life out of her?

"I see that the new position has not improved you," the Queen said. "Where are your manners? Aren't you going to invite me in?"

I stood back and opened the door wider. I held on to it as I curtsied to steady myself, and then shut it behind her.

"Your Majesty does not have to be asked. Every inch of this palace belongs to you. I am just lucky to be your guest," I said, offering a small smile while my insides raged more than the Cusata River.

"I promise you, I have devoted every bit of my being to readying myself for the honor that has been bestowed upon me," I vowed.

The Queen nodded and glided past me, the train of her ridiculously ornate gown flowing behind her. She took a seat just steps away from where South had stood.

"Do you have everything you need?" she asked.

"The staff has been even more accommodating than I imagined," I said.

"The prince means everything to me," she said, studying me. "I have seen him through all his milestones. Are you prepared for tonight to go off without a hitch?"

"Of course," I said, but I wasn't paying attention. I was trying to do the math. Could I kill her here and now? How would I escape with all those guards just steps away? How would I find South?

"Couterie are prepared for any circumstance," I added.

I bowed my head again. Being servile to her pained me, but I had to forgo the immediate satisfaction of killing her now for a better chance of success later tonight.

"Forgive me, Your Excellency. It is just an honor to be in your presence."

"I hope you spare the obsequiousness with my son. He is completely without airs. He abhors flattery of any kind," she said firmly.

"I assure you, Madame Linea has taught me all I could learn from the Ana. But only a mother can truly know her child's heart. If there is anything you care to share about Prince Mather, I would be ever so grateful."

It was the Queen's turn to be surprised. She looked at me hard, as if trying to determine if I was sincere. I held her gaze and she softened.

"That is true," she confirmed.

"I know what he reads and eats and what he listens to, but who is he really? What does he want?"

"He wants for nothing. He is the Crown Prince. But you will see that. Now I have a question for you."

"Anything, Your Majesty."

"What is the most important thing to remember about my son?"

I hesitated. "From what I can ascertain from the Ana, His Highness has friends, but no one close. He's been hidden from the world for his protection. He is lonely, starved for attention."

"Very few realize how lonely the Crown is. Mather has led a rather solitary existence until now. It was an unprecedented thing, you challenging your Couterie. I think I am rather glad you did," Queen Magrit said approvingly.

"Me too," I said, meaning it for myself and for my plan. But a tiny part of me prickled at the idea of hurting the lonely boy she had just described.

"I think you will be a good match for my son before he is married. You have haunted eyes, like you've lived. My son has been so very sheltered because of the dangers out there. One day he will rule us all."

He will never rule, I thought. My mind went to the prince, but I stuffed away the thought of him. He was still alive while Hecate and all my sisters were dead.

I wanted to say: *You took my mother. I am going to take your son, and then I am going to slit your throat.*

But I held back my words.

CHAPTER 25

Night fell.

"You may be my greatest creation, Farrow," Linea said.

She was perhaps the only person I'd ever met who could give a compliment that still complimented herself at the same time.

After hours of painstaking attention to my makeup and gown, Madame Linea deemed me ready. I was carried into the banquet hall on a sedan chair held by four Couterie.

They set my chair down in the center of the long dining table as if I were the main course. Before the Couterie could help me out of the carriage, my eyes met those of the man on the ornate golden throne.

The prince was much changed from the boy I had seen the day of the Burning. He was taller and lankier. His face was more angular, his jaw square—all of which I knew from seeing him at the Challenge. But now I could see that his eyes were a brilliant green. His smile was toothy and without care. His tanned skin made it seem as if he had just been out in the sun.

He seemed so different from the day of the Challenge. His skin was darker. His jaw was sharper. Perhaps I had misremembered him? The blindfold and the stress of being nearly dead must have clouded my memory.

We weren't alone. There were five other noble boys of varying degrees of handsomeness lounging around the room.

"He's quite the fool, isn't he?" one of the boys said, suddenly next to me. I did not risk a glance. He was so close, I could feel the heat radiating off him.

"Everyone looks a bit silly in a crown," I said, wanting the boy to go away.

"I couldn't agree more," he said, and I realized he wouldn't stop staring at me.

"Have we met before? There's something about you that seems so familiar."

I laughed at his audacity. He was persistent. Although I couldn't shake the feeling that I had also seen him before.

"I don't think the prince would appreciate you trying to pilfer his present."

"Oh, I think the prince would be just fine with it. We share everything," the boy said.

"Hark, the prince has indulged you long enough. Give him his seat," one of the other boys said. "Just because you're the Queen's Right Hand doesn't mean you can take the throne."

I watched Hark get up from the throne and then realized my mistake.

I knew from the Ana that Hark was the Queen's Right Hand and the prince's best friend. It was an unusual choice to have a Hand so young and for the Hand to be male. In lieu of the Entente, the Queen had created the position of Hand to advise her in all matters of politics and war. The Queen had gone through her court and found most of them wanting, and the rest she left for dead. It was rumored that she'd taken a servant boy and made him her Right Hand as a show of her strength and as a punishment for her court. I was struck by his familiarity with the prince. And with his audacity to take the prince's seat. Even in jest, I could not imagine that that kind of comfort could last for long in the orbit of the Queen. She could not take kindly to this, could she?

Turning to the boy at my side, the real prince, I bowed my head to him. "I beg your pardon, Your Highness," I said. I had gotten everything wrong. The Couterie prided themselves on knowing the details, and I had missed the most important one.

Hark handed the crown to the prince . . . who proceeded to place it on my head.

The boy next to me was the real prince. I took in his sharp features; brown eyes; deep, throaty laugh; and glowing skin. Even through my mortification, I was not immune to his questioning gaze.

"It looks decidedly better on you," he said.

Out of the side of my eye, I could see Linea entering. She took her seat in the back of the room.

No apologies. Only results. I swallowed an "I'm sorry." I needed to salvage the moment.

I stood up and jumped down from the table, landing beside the prince.

Before he could react, I kissed him. Kissing someone when you had exchanged only a handful of words was both incredibly intimate and the exact opposite—even when you were the one who initiated the kissing.

Or so I told myself.

The prince's lips were more responsive than South's. The prince was the enemy. But my lips did not seem to know or care about that distinction. We were not Couterie and prince, or Entente and enemy. We were lips and breaths.

When his hands moved around my waist and he pulled me

closer, I couldn't help myself from leaning in. He looked into my eyes for a long beat, and I suddenly wanted to know what he was thinking and feeling.

Then he blinked and looked away, toward his waiting audience.

For a second I had forgotten where we were. There were only his lips.

"She tastes like the heavens," the prince announced. "Madame Linea, you have outdone yourself," he added, with a wave to her.

Madame Linea smiled with satisfaction. "Farrow is responsible for herself. Her gifts are her own."

But even as she defended me, a tiny smile of pride played on her lips. Then, with a wave and a bow to us, she exited.

After the door closed, and the other Couterie fanned out to mingle with the prince's court, the prince finally looked at me again. My pulse quickened, but this time with annoyance at myself for caring about how long it took for his gaze to return to me after our kiss.

"I thought she'd never leave," I said. "What does the prince want to do next?"

"Perhaps we start with a dance," he said finally.

The others responded with hoots and hollers. One of the Couterie began playing a bombastic tune on a piano.

I pushed the prince down in his chair and began to sway my hips to the music, backing away so the whole room could see me. I could feel the rest of the room looking at me, but I kept my eyes on Prince Mather.

As I danced to the beat in front of the prince, arching my back, sweeping my arms near my curves, and drawing attention to the sinuous way I moved, his eyes roved down to follow my body.

The prince leaned forward to take me all in.

The other Couterie joined me in a dance that was a variation on a peasant dance, only we'd sped up the tempo.

As the music ended, the prince got to his feet. He walked over to me, and the others parted to make room for him.

"I did enjoy that immensely, but when I asked for you to dance, I meant that I wanted to dance with you. I didn't want you to dance *for* me."

"Oh . . . ," I said. I felt my cheeks warm, but I knew that my body's betrayal could actually act to help me. He would think I couldn't fake the response. He would know that he was indeed having an effect on me.

He took my hand in his and began to lead me in a few steps of a slow dance. The Couterie at the piano took up the tune. Every step took us closer to the door.

I was suddenly aware of every breath, every move he made.

"You don't have to be nervous," he said.

"I'm not," I countered.

"Then tell that to your fingers," he said with a laugh.

I looked down to see I was tapping my fingers against his.

"It's not nerves. It's just a habit," I demurred, and began to pull my hand away, but he held on to it gently.

"I like it. The idea of a Couterie being nervous with me is charming."

"You are the prince. Every girl in the Queendoms wants to be where I am," I said, flattering him.

The script almost wrote itself. That was the beauty of my training. That was the beauty of being Couterie—knowing what to say and how to say it and how your subject would respond.

His laugh was filled with surprise. It seemed genuine and just for me, even though there were so many people around.

"I am not a prince tonight. I am putty beneath your fingers." He brought my hand to his chest and pressed my palm into him. "Can you feel that? I'm terrified."

His heart raced beneath my fingertips.

"Of what?" I asked.

"Of you," he said simply. "It's not every day that the one you've dreamed of walks through the door."

My breath caught. I had thought about him as a means to an end. I had never really thought of him at all.

The prince glanced at the door. Then he looked at me. "Shall we?"

I nodded.

CHAPTER 26

We were an entourage headed to the prince's bedroom. I was flanked by the prince, South, and his guards. The moment of truth had come.

"Surely you cannot leave without letting us see your present unwrapped, Your Highness?" Hark said, stepping in front of us before we could actually leave. He directed his question at the prince, but he was looking at me.

"Fair Farrow, would you mind making every man in the room jealous?" Prince Mather said finally.

"As you wish, fair prince," I said.

I had been prepared for this by Madame Linea. By the years in the Couterie.

He put his hand on the sash of my gown and untied it before I could do it myself. I stopped his hands.

"No, let me," I purred. But I felt a flare of anger in me. Not just for myself but for every Couterie who had walked into rooms like this before me.

I was like all of them, but there was one difference. At the end of the night the prince and the Queen would be dead.

I hesitated for a moment. I had been naked in front of the

Couterie and had not felt an ounce of shame. I didn't feel shame now. Not for myself—but for the boys surrounding me, with their hungry eyes waiting for me to disrobe for their entertainment. The anger rose in me when I looked at them. The Couterie had not prepared me for that.

I sauntered away from the prince as if the pause were on purpose. I turned my back to him, then slowly slipped my dress to my shoulders, revealing the paint that Madame Linea had painstakingly brushed over me this morning. The boys seemed to hold their breath. I let the silk fall to my waist, unveiling the map across my body: Hinter. And then I dropped my gown to the floor, exhibiting the fluttering silk drawers barely covering my buttocks, painted like the churning sea and mountains, and my legs. The boys reacted again. Hark was the most vocal with a long whistle.

But when I turned around, I was looking at only the prince. There was longing in his eyes and appreciation. The paint served as another layer of mystery between me and his court and was the ultimate salute to the prince.

"I pledge my allegiance to the future king," I said.

A cheer went up from the boys in attendance. All eyes were on me.

The prince broke into a wide smile. "I pledge allegiance to the kingdom laid bare before me," he said, and he bowed down to me.

"Take your prize, Prince Mather," one of the other boys chimed in.

Without asking, he kissed me again. This time I felt his hands exploring my back and beyond. As his hands inched lower, I wondered for the briefest of moments just how far he intended to take it with all of the court watching.

But he stopped suddenly and draped his own jacket around me. He picked me up and carried me down the hallway.

We didn't speak. I could feel his heart beating through the thin cotton shirt he wore, and I could feel his musculature too.

The hallway turned. We reached the prince's bedroom.

Prince Mather pushed the door inward. The door shut and the lock clicked closed behind us.

And then we were alone.

CHAPTER 27

But when the door closed behind him, the prince did the one thing I did not expect. He took his hands off me. His smile, which had been so close to mine a moment ago, fell as he deposited me gently on my feet and pulled farther away.

"What is it, Your Highness?" I asked.

I thought I'd sensed longing as he'd pulled away from me, but I wasn't certain. The frown on his face confused me.

"I'm sorry, Farrow. I can't."

I blinked hard, confused by this turn of events. "The Couterie is supposed to anticipate— I fear I have failed you," I said.

"It is I who have failed myself. I did not mean to take it that far out there," he said.

"I don't understand—"

"Sadie brought your things. I hope everything is to your liking," he said quickly, and pointed to my cases, including the makeup case, which sat on his dresser. "If there's anything else that you need . . ."

"I have everything I need," I said, stepping closer to him again. "I'll just be a minute." I picked up the case and quickly strode across the room and into the bathroom.

Opening the case's false bottom, I was relieved to see that Hecate's ashes and South's knife were still there, as well as the little box Tork had given me. I slipped the knife into the hem of my stocking and left the rest inside.

He will be king one day, I reminded myself. He was the Queen's son.

When I returned and placed the case back on the dresser, the prince was sitting in a large, pillowed chair by the window. "Tell me about yourself. How did you come to be Couterie?"

"It is an honor to be chosen," I said.

"Based on what? You don't know me, Farrow. I could be a monster."

"I do know you." I ticked off the list of facts I had gathered from the Ana and what Lavendra had heard from the staff.

"You have three eggs prepared every morning. One fried, one boiled, and an omelet. And you eat only one of them. You don't know what you want until it's right in front of you. You play three instruments. Speak every language in the Queendoms except Urdish, because you used to skip your lessons and go visit your horses. You love to ride. You hate to fence, but you're good at it. You're allergic to crustaceans, but you eat them anyway because you love the taste. You like to stay up late, but you sleep even later . . . You hate the new novels the Queen has commissioned in an attempt to make you seem like a hero and not a curse . . . but you love to read history novels. I think stories are how you make sense of people, since you aren't able to get close to them . . ."

"The valets talk to the ladies' maids and the ladies' maids talk to Madame Linea." He chuckled. "And I do hate those novels about me . . . *The Prince and the Stable Woman* . . . it's just so embarrassing . . ."

And I found myself laughing with him. This was not the way I had planned this. He was not what I'd expected. He was wittier than I'd imagined. He talked more, smelled better, felt better... and kissed better.

"That is a collection of facts. A recitation of the Ana. Not who I am."

Why did the prince want me to think he was different from how he appeared? Different from the Crown? He was a royal and I was a Couterie. He did not need to impress me. This was not part of anything that Madame Linea had taught me. I was supposed to be seducing him. Not the other way around.

"I think a collection of facts is all that we are. Facts and actions," I countered.

"Then tell me your facts."

"I'm eighteen. I'm Couterie. I am here to be your companion until the day you are married and until Ever After if you so choose. Isn't that all you need to know?"

"You don't like talking about yourself, do you?" he said.

"I'm parched. There. That's something about me. Why don't I get us something more to drink?" I offered, moving away from him and his questions. I needed time, and at the exact same moment I didn't need any more time. South was right: Killing wasn't a wave of the wand. Without magic, it would be a slice of the knife. And Madame Linea never offered any lessons about how to kill someone after you had kissed them.

I could smell his breath, and I could still taste his mouth and feel his arms around me. This would be so much more intimate than I'd thought.

I poured two glasses. When I returned, I took the seat across from him.

We were sitting too far apart. I couldn't stab him without giving him too much warning.

I thought of the small packet that Tork had given me. *One if you want not to care. Two if you want to forget. Three if you want to sleep through till sunrise.*

Maybe if the prince was asleep it would make the stabbing part easier.

"I want to hear about you," the prince said.

"Me? Ah, you want all the salacious secrets of the Couterie," I said suggestively.

"No, I want to know about you, Farrow. What is your story? Where did you grow up? Where were your parents? How did you get here? In this palace?"

The prince leaned in. His expression was earnest, as if knowing the answers to these questions about me really mattered to him. As if he truly cared who I was.

I frowned after a beat.

"You think something bad happened to me and that's why I joined the Couterie?" I assessed, feigning defense. But as my cheeks reddened, I wondered where my training ended and where I began. Tork was perhaps the only person who had asked me about myself in all the years since the Burning. Being the subject of attention instead of the one attending brought warmth to my cheeks and caused my heart to knock against my rib cage.

"No, you misunderstand me. I want to know about your experience because I want to change the Couterie when I take the crown. The Couterie are the brightest and most accomplished people in our Queendom. No one has your education in history or in the arts. I believe that the Couterie definitely deserve a place by the king or Queen's side. But not their beds."

I took in his words. I had never expected anyone royal to say them. The Couterie system had been in place for generations, and no one in power ever publicly questioned or considered changing it.

"So what do you think? I want a Couterie's opinion."

He leaned back, away from me. He was different from what the Ana had led me to believe. He seemed kind and true and good. I blinked hard at him, studying him.

Except for South, humans weren't kind. Humans weren't good. But without my magic, wasn't I closer to human than Entente?

"I don't know if it is up to you to change the Couterie," I said, finally offering up an opinion on what he confessed to me.

"They have a way of life that depends on the Crown, just like the Entente. And I would never do what my mother did."

My cheeks flushed. What was wrong with me? I needed to remember my Couterie training. I reminded myself that underneath all this paint, I was still Entente. And yet somehow the prince had managed to fluster me. I stuffed my emotions down and reminded myself of the knife that was hidden in my stocking.

"I saw magic once," the prince said. "Down that very hall. I saw a girl with one of the Fates and they looked just as human as you or me . . ."

The prince got to his feet and walked toward the door. I half expected him to take me to the very spot where Hecate and I had seen him playing hide-and-seek with his guard. The memory of me and Hecate had stuck with him.

What he was saying was practically treason. Why would he share it with me now? Did some part of him know that I had been there that day? I wondered. But that was impossible.

"Are you sure you should be telling me this? Your mother's

feelings on magic are very . . . She wouldn't like it," I asked from my seat.

"From my understanding of your code, I am supposed to be able to tell you anything and trust you won't tell a soul. Not even my mother," he said, turning back to me.

"That is true. And I would never tell her. But I wonder, how can you trust me so easily?"

"I don't know if I trust you yet. But I would like to. And there is one thing I do trust."

"And what's that?"

"If you tell my mother, then she will kill both of us. Me, for treason, and you, for knowing. So I think I'm safe sharing anything with you."

It wasn't some connection between us that unlocked his tongue. It was the knowledge he had of how twisted his mother was. And yet when he looked at me, I could swear he meant every word.

"And it's more than that—I guess I'm telling you because of what the Entente told me that day."

"And what was that?" I asked, even though I remembered.

"I was being a bit of a brat. I was so distraught over my grandmother. They reminded me that her death was no excuse to be unkind. They were maybe the first to ever suggest that having the crown didn't mean that I owned anyone or anything. In essence, they were the first and only to ever tell me to try and be better than my mother. They didn't deserve what happened to them. They were just trying to protect the Queendom from her. I saw for myself how innocent they were, and I knew what my mother did to them. I will never forget them. I only wish I'd been old enough to stop what she started that day."

I felt shaken, but I tried to cover it.

"She claims she's done all this for me. But I don't want that burden."

"Do you believe that?"

"I don't want to. But some think that I am the cause of how my mother is."

"How?"

"I am the first male heir in the history of the Thirteen Queendoms. They say that my mother's inability to produce a female heir drove her mad."

He broke eye contact when he said this and looked down at his hands, which he wrung together. It seemed clear that he was blaming himself for this.

"That's ridiculous. You don't believe that, do you?"

Mather was silent for a moment; then he looked up. His eyes were full of sadness.

"My mother feels vulnerable to the other Queendoms because of me. What if that is behind her every decision and not the prophecy of the Entente?"

I rocked back in my seat. As much as I had been surprised by the whole encounter, I was doubly surprised by his guilt.

"You are not to blame. Your mother's choices are her own," I said firmly. I patted the seat next to me. And he returned to sit by me.

"But if I . . . Perhaps if I had never drawn breath, then there would be a lot of other people still breathing in Hinter."

But then there would be no you, I thought selfishly. I kept the thought in.

"Can I tell you something?" he said.

"Anything," I whispered, and nodded. But I wasn't sure if I could take any more truth right now.

"I actually thought about running away tonight. This is the first night of my adult life that I am not under her thumb."

"And what stopped you?"

"The second I saw you, I couldn't go anywhere."

"Because my face was made to match your ideal."

"It's more than your face, Farrow. It's you . . ." He drifted off, but his eyes never left mine.

I looked away. I had to remind myself why I was here.

"You don't know me . . . not really."

"What I know, I like. And I want to know more."

I took a few seconds then pushed past the compliment.

"Mather, what happens if you stay? Would you really make things better if she isn't on the throne forever . . . ?"

I hadn't intended to say any of that, but the words came in response to his sincerity.

"I would—but she'll probably live forever," he said, studying me in the pause that followed.

I had said too much.

"No Queen lives forever. Long live the king," I covered.

He smiled, but there was sadness in it. I reached out and took his hand. I let it rest there a moment too long before taking it away.

"Farrow . . . ," he whispered, his voice laced with longing, as if my hand leaving his pained him.

I felt it too. But I knew I had to push it away. I got to my feet.

"We need another drink."

It was time. No more stalling. I went over to the dresser and picked up the pills that Tork had given me. I slipped them into the prince's glass as I poured him a drink.

"Here's to change," I said, raising my glass to his.

He took a sip, and I finally felt myself exhale. I just had to wait for the drug to take effect. He got up again and walked over to where I'd rested the crown.

"I wish that we had met in the square, like normal people," he said. He reached for his crown. "That we could be Mather and Farrow. Not prince and Couterie. That's what I want. And I would trade this piece of metal for that."

Mather wanted a clean slate. He didn't long for power or magic. He didn't long for the crown or a wand. He wanted to meet a girl in the square and fall in love. He was that simple. He was that good.

For the briefest second I imagined myself in the square, bumping into Mather as Mather and me as just Farrow. Not Entente; not Couterie. Me without the burden of vengeance. But that would mean I would not ever have had Hecate or South or even Tork and Lavendra. I don't know who I would be without them, for better or for worse. And as tempting as it was, a life that simple was not possible. I would lose myself in the bargain. For the briefest of seconds that had seemed tempting to me . . . but I pushed the temptation aside.

"Mather, you aren't normal. You're a prince. Some things can't be," I said sadly.

"When I saw you in that room tonight, I felt like I knew you already. I felt like you were—like you are—the closest thing to Fate I have ever felt."

I inhaled sharply. I wasn't supposed to believe him. I wasn't supposed to get swept up in this. In him. But the more he spoke, the harder it was going to be to use the knife. I thought of Tork's warnings and of Linea's about not falling for the prince. I had thought myself immune. What was wrong with me? I knew him on paper in the pages of the Ana . . .

Behind him I noticed the moon peeking through the heavy silk curtains. It was almost morning. Where had the night gone? What was I doing? He was supposed to be dead, and I was supposed to have moved on to my real target, his mother.

But instead I was watching the sun come up with the prince. I was betraying my own plan and the Entente all at once.

"Kiss me again because you want to," I said.

I dropped the knife behind the bed. And I kissed him. At first he responded, and the kiss was urgent and sweet and filled with longing. We knew something of each other now and we both wanted so much more.

Suddenly he stopped responding. I pulled back. Mather was fast asleep.

I had learned in the worst way possible that Fate could be both cruel and kind. I wondered for the briefest of seconds if perhaps he had been sent to grant my wishes instead of the other way around.

He had said the exact thing that had stopped me from killing him. But I still had a job to do. I slipped the knife back inside my stocking and retrieved Hecate's ashes.

It was time to kill the Queen.

CHAPTER 28

I left the prince sleeping. Deep down, I knew that it would be a mistake to kill him. He had proven tonight that he was better than his mother. That he would not do what his mother had done. But once he knew that I had killed her, would I inspire the same feelings of vengeance in him that his mother had inspired in me? He had somehow dodged being as evil as her all these years. Would I ironically change all that tonight? Would I be giving him a whole new burden that would blight the rest of his life and all his dreams? No matter what, the idea of just Farrow and Mather running into each other in the square would be gone forever.

"Good night, sweet prince," I said before I tiptoed out the door and into the hall.

South was not at his post. In fact, no guards stood at the door. I craned my neck in either direction, but I did not see a soul.

Where was he? Had something happened to him? Was I wrong to trust him?

I turned down two corridors, not knowing which room was the Queen's. I kept going around turns and a maze of hallways. I could almost feel the hairs on my arms standing straight up. I'd memorized the layout from the Ana. But all the Black Glass made one hallway look almost identical to the next, and I cursed myself for taking too long. As I contemplated each turn, I wished I could let Hecate out of the pouch so she could walk the halls of the palace with me again, hand in hand. *Hecate, here we are,* I thought. *We're almost there.*

I turned another corner and saw a uniformed figure approaching from down the hall. I prepared to admonish him, but I realized too late that the boy coming toward me wasn't South. It was Hark, the prince's friend and the Queen's Right Hand.

"I did not expect to see either of you until well into the afternoon," Hark said as he stepped into the torchlight.

"I don't think that when I emerge is anyone's business other than His Highness's," I said back evenly.

"My apologies, fair Farrow. I cannot seem to stop insulting you," Hark said.

I was caught far from the prince's room, with no obvious reason for being there. And Hark was apologizing to me. If I could keep him focused on his guilt over his impropriety, then perhaps he wouldn't focus on the fact that I was not where I belonged.

"Is that apology for impersonating the prince or for whistling while I disrobed?" I managed as haughtily as I could manage.

"For both," he said, surprising me. "We all have a role to play."

"Oh? And what is yours?"

"To be whatever they need me to be. I think you understand that. But I think you are far more than a Couterie."

"And you are more than the prince's best friend?"

"I am the Queen's Hand."

"An odd position to begin at the tender age of six?" I countered.

"And how would you know at what age I was enlisted, fair Farrow?" he asked, raising his eyebrows.

"The prince must have mentioned it," I said, too quickly. I had not realized it at first, but now I was almost certain that Hark had been the boy next to the Queen the day that Hecate burned. Had the Queen raised him to be her Hand because that was the only way to ensure he was someone she could trust? Magrit certainly was not above stealing someone's childhood. She had done much, much worse.

He took me in for a moment. "I suppose I should be flattered that you and the prince were talking about me on the night of his Becoming."

I felt that same flash of outrage as when he had asked me to disrobe before everyone. But I didn't let him see it.

"You may forget that the Couterie are masters at more than just Becomings. We are also known for our conversational gifts. A gift that you do not necessarily possess . . . You still have not answered my question, Right Hand."

"Forgive me. I don't mean to offend you, and yet there I go again," he began. "It is far easier to raise an army from childhood than to make one submit after years of serving another. She merely did the same with me. It seems to me that the Couterie and my station are in similar predicaments, beholden to others."

I studied him. He seemed sincere. And if he didn't annoy me, I might even feel sorry for him. But if my time in the Couterie had taught me anything, it was when to know that there was more to someone than met the eye.

"There are no chains on either of us. I am free to leave this place. Just as you are. I am here by choice," I said firmly.

"Are you? There are all kinds of chains. Some are invisible ones . . . the promises made to our child selves that bind us tighter than our own will."

For a second I wondered if he could see inside my heart. That he somehow knew what I was really doing here.

He changed the subject. "Has tonight not been all that you imagined? Is that why you wander now?"

"What an odd choice of words. The Couterie are in the business of pleasing others, not ourselves. I assure you that the prince went to sleep satisfied. I just wanted to see the palace."

Hark looked up at the ceiling, on which artists had etched a painstakingly accurate depiction of the constellations. Flecks of diamonds stood in for stars and planets.

"It is beautiful," he said, softening.

"Stunning," I echoed, careful to keep the sarcasm out of my voice. There were people starving while Queen Magrit decorated with precious jewels.

"Do you want me to show you around? The gardens are lovely at this hour."

"I don't really think that's a good idea. If the prince wakes and finds me gone, I wouldn't want to offend him," I said as I tried to size Hark up.

What did he want from me? And did he really believe that I was just taking a stroll through the palace at dawn without the prince?

"The prince isn't like that. He is as gentle as they come. Nothing like his mother. He wouldn't begrudge you a tour of the palace. Especially by his most trusted companion."

"I thought you were the Queen's most trusted companion."

"I work for the Queen. But I am the prince's friend." Hark paused. "It's late, Farrow, and I fear I should let you go. You are much closer to the Queen's room than to the prince's. You see, hers is right down there. You want to turn around and head north down this corridor, and then make the first right. His will be the only door."

"Thank you for putting me back on course," I added for good measure as he turned to walk away.

He bowed deeply. "Only you can do that, Farrow."

We parted. I walked a few steps back toward the prince's bedroom when someone snuck up behind me.

"Hey, it's me," South's voice whispered in my ear. He turned me to him. "Did you kill him?" he asked.

"No, but I could kill you for scaring the hells out of me. I could have hurt you," I said.

I thought of his wings, which were standing up in his specially tailored uniform, and in my mind added, *again.*

He laughed at the idea of me hurting him, but then seemed to remember something, his face growing serious.

"That's a good thing, Farrow. I knew you couldn't."

"But I could have, South. I chose not to," I said firmly.

None of this was going the way I had imagined. All those years of plotting and planning had never involved South at my side. I was grateful for his presence, but the rush of emotion that came from having him here made everything complicated. I wanted to stop the world and sit with South to hear every second of our time apart. He had given me the facts, but I wanted all the details of how he felt, how he'd dealt with being in the belly of the Queen's palace. I wanted to take him back to the Reverie with me and properly mourn the rest of the Entente together. But, instead, we were here. And despite what he said, there was no guarantee that there would ever be another time for us to do any of that.

And at the same time, I could still feel the residual effects of the prince—the boy I'd decided not to kill. I still felt his kiss on my lips and his arms around my waist. I had left him alive. But I had not left him. He was somehow still with me, and now so was South.

"Why didn't you?"

"He isn't her."

"Exactly. I know it's been a long time, Farrow. But you haven't changed that much."

"You better hope that I have for this next part..."

"Don't worry, I'll finish her if you don't. This way; I've got access to her royal quarters," South said defiantly as he pulled a key from his pocket and shifted the rucksack on his shoulder. "There's a secret door to her suite."

"I'm sorry for being short with you. I haven't relied on anyone for anything in a really long time."

"Neither have I," he said gently. "Well, we won't have the Queen to worry about anymore... She won't be waking up tonight. Or ever," he added.

"The South I remember wouldn't joke at a time like this."

"I don't think there has ever been 'a time like this,'" he said.

South smiled as we continued down a different hall, as if he were filled with confidence even though we were facing near impossible odds. This was not the meek boy Bari and I had shoved aside when we were young. This was a very different South than I remembered.

"Come on! Her room's through here," he said, his voice an excited whisper.

I took South's hand and allowed him to pull me down one corridor and then another. He paused abruptly in front of one of the smaller rooms.

"You have to change clothes," he said, producing a guard's uniform, freshly pressed, from his rucksack. "Our chances of escape will be better if you try to blend in."

He pushed open the door to what looked like a small storage closet and handed me a torch.

Neither of us was prepared for what was inside.

CHAPTER 29

The room was just as opulent as all the others. Something glistened in the dark as South cracked open the door wider. The light from his torch found a shimmering cage that took up half of the space. Inside, it was empty, but there were all the accoutrements of a royal bedroom. There was a four-poster bed made of gold. Tapestry-laden silk bedding. Hand-painted furniture. Why would the Queen have a cage decorated with such care?

Someone was living here.

"I don't understand," South said. "The dungeon is downstairs . . . What does the Queen keep in here?"

"Or who?"

"Maybe it's someone else like me, someone affected by the Entente," South said.

"But why would they be locked up?"

"She keeps all the Fallen in the dungeon. This doesn't make sense. The bars are made of a metal I haven't seen before. It's not Black Glass."

"Magrit kept you away from the rest of the guards?" I asked.

"Initially. Once I proved myself, she moved me to regular

quarters. I haven't been back since," South said, his voice even. "Most of the Fallen weren't capable of service."

I digested this, horrified. How long had South spent in the dungeon? What had that done to him?

"Oh, South," I said, but South wasn't interested in my sympathy. He was focused on the cage, still trying to figure it out.

"Could it be someone with magic?" he asked.

"The Entente are gone, remember? This doesn't make any sense."

"Not us . . . ," South said. "The Rookery."

I laughed. "The Rookery hasn't been seen in a hundred years. And the Rooks wouldn't dare come to the Hinter, where magical beings are massacred."

"Then give me another explanation."

"A pet bear? A mountain lion? I don't know. You've seen how crazy Magrit is."

"I don't know either," he said, frustration wrinkling his brow.

"We don't have time to figure it out now," I said.

"No, we don't. You need to change," he replied, not moving from the cage.

I waved him away.

"Right, sorry!" South apologized and backed out the door.

Alone in the bedroom, I slipped into the guard's uniform. It felt strange to be so covered. The Couterie and Shadows usually bared their shoulders no matter the temperature. The fabric was stiff and a size too large. I had to fold the waist of the pants to make them stay up. Despite the looseness, wearing the uniform felt more constricting than any corset.

I was wearing the same uniform as those who had killed my mother. I took a look in the glass and exhaled, reminding myself why I was doing this. Hecate. The Entente. All that we'd lost.

"Farrow! Hurry up," South whispered from outside the door.

When I emerged, his eyes met mine. There was a sadness in them. He understood better than anyone how it felt to wear the clothes of the enemy.

Suddenly a noise sounded close by. It was mournful and strained.

"Did you hear that?" I asked.

"I think it's coming from in there," South said, nodding toward the door to the next room.

"Maybe we should ignore it. It's not what we came for," I said.

There was another moan and a knocking sound.

"Someone is in pain," he said, his hand on the knob.

"You and I are the only two people alive who I care about, and I'm not completely sure about you," I said, putting my hand over his.

"The Entente believed in helping all of Hinter, not just themselves," he countered firmly.

"And look where it got us . . . ," I warned.

South pushed a shoulder into the door, and it opened with more force than he'd intended. Together, we toppled to the ground inside.

CHAPTER 30

Inside, there was a second cage and a second bedroom. Only, this one wasn't empty. Just like the first room, the cage had a bed, a settee, and a wardrobe. But unlike the first, every inch of the floor was covered in objects. There were gowns, music boxes, diamond necklaces, heels . . . And in the center of it all was . . . Iolanta.

She was sitting on a tufted mattress, her legs curled up to her chest. Her hair was gone. Only a fuzz of red remained. She was wearing a gray gown like the ones we wore in the Entente before we'd enhanced them with magic. Her round face was gaunt. But it was unmistakably Iolanta. I fought a wave of guilt. I had almost made us miss her. If South hadn't insisted, we wouldn't have seen her at all.

She was alive.

"Iolanta," I whispered as I looked at my sister, who I had not seen for eleven years, and knelt down in front of the cage.

Iolanta didn't stir. Her eyes were glassed over, and she hummed under her breath. She didn't seem to see us.

"We have to get her out," South said to me, his voice cracking. He pulled at the cage door with both hands, but it held firm.

"South . . . ," Iolanta murmured, her eyes fluttering open and finding his.

It was as if the sound of his voice had wakened her. With great difficulty,

Iolanta raised her hand and the door to the cage swung open. Whatever dark powers had held back her magic, she was fighting against them.

South rushed to her side, and she recoiled as if she'd touched fire.

"Step back, South! We're hurting her . . ."

South responded, and I remembered how much it pained Iolanta when anyone got too close.

"What's all this?" I asked, taking in the collection of strange items that surrounded her. There were teacups, perfume atomizers, silk handkerchief, and furs, things that seemed to belong to noble people. But there were other things too—lamps, clocks. There was even a saddle. It made no sense.

Iolanta tried to whisper something. I leaned in closer. I could feel her breath on my ear. "Each thing has a different owner," she said in a hush. "She wanted me to tell her where you all were."

She? Iolanta must have meant the Queen. Queen Magrit was torturing her in hopes of finding more Entente.

Iolanta laughed a guttural laugh that was somehow not at all filled with bitterness.

South looked around, a quizzical expression on his face. I followed his gaze as he seemed to study the crush of things around her.

"We have to break them," South said, suddenly lifting a vase and crashing it on the floor.

He began to make a path, crushing the bottles and baubles. He was too loud. He was going to call attention, I thought.

"You're making too much noise. What the hells, South?"

"Think of Iolanta's Reverie. All the objects from the past . . . from the Dead . . . to distract her from all those Presents. These are not that . . ."

It hit me as he said it. Every single thing in this room tied Iolanta to a different person, a different Present.

He turned to me and mouthed, "What do we do? We have to get her out of here.

"The Queen wants to find you. She somehow knows that there is still magic in the world," South guessed, looking at me.

I shook my head. If he was right, all those girls in the square had been burned because she knew we still lived.

"No, Magrit wants to torture Iolanta. There is no way she could know we were still here. We didn't even know . . . ," I countered.

Iolanta nodded and added, "Why can't it be both? Two birds, one stone . . . one evil Queen."

But it wasn't one stone, it was hundreds. And I didn't even know how many "witches" had burned. South and I shared a look. He was stricken by the Queen's cruelty. But I think he, like me, was comforted by the fact that the Iolanta we remembered was still in there and she was surfacing. I joined in smashing another vase. I was struck at once with the Queen's ingenuity, as well as her cruelty. She had devised a jail that also delivered constant pain, from the day of Iolanta's capture until now.

I glanced back at Iolanta. Her limbs were moving freely now and before I could return to her, she had gotten to her feet. She stood. Free.

Iolanta sighed with relief. "There's no point trying to hide anything from Les Soeurs. We see it before or when or after. There is no escaping all of us."

Us? Was it possible that Iolanta, whose gift was knowing the Present, did not know that Hecate and Galatea were both gone?

"Iolanta, Galatea and Hecate . . . They're . . . ," I tried to explain.

She held up her hand. The ashes in my pouch rustled, telling me now was not the time. We needed to get Iolanta out of here. And I needed to get to the Queen's room before she woke.

"I know," she said, and closed her eyes. There was a wild look on her face.

"Iolanta, I am so sorry. If I had known you were here, I would have found a way to get you out," I said as I approached slowly.

"You could not have known," she said with the authority of the Present.

"I could have tried," I countered.

"Could have, should have, would have . . . There is only what you do and don't do in this life. You cannot live in the Past. The Present is already too much as it is. Or at least, that's my biased opinion," she said, sounding more assured with every word.

"Instead, you spent every day planning for today . . . plotting to kill the Queen," she added. "If you knew, would you have planned my escape or her death?"

I gulped. For a second it was like being back in the Entente, in Iolanta's room in the Reverie. I never knew how to answer her. I always felt like I was on the verge of choosing wrong.

"Don't worry, child. You have another chance to choose."

"We have to go," South warned. "Now!"

My mind raced. I hated Queen Magrit for what she had done to Iolanta all these years almost as much as for what she had done to my Hecate. Now I wanted to avenge Iolanta too.

"Hush your vengeance if you can. Long enough to let love in.

Love is what saves you. Love is what saves you and the Hinter," Iolanta said solemnly, reading my mind.

"Okay, we all agree. Love is good. But we have to save ourselves, and right now that means we're leaving," South said.

In one smooth movement, he picked up Iolanta and carried her into the palace hall, with me trailing right behind. The pain of him touching her was less than that of being Magrit's prisoner.

As South led us toward the maid's entrance, I couldn't help but wonder if anyone else was alive. Iolanta must know. Bari's face popped into my head, and then Amantha's. I felt another swell of emotion rise up in me. Longing, mixed with guilt because I never looked for them. I let myself believe that they were gone, and I was wrong.

"Don't abandon the Present for the Future, child. You need your wits about you right now. What you've just gained is far from certain," Iolanta commented, and looked at South meaningfully. "*We* are all in danger. There is no safe place anywhere in the Hinter. Not while Magrit sits on the throne."

CHAPTER 31

There was no time for talking as we raced through the shadows of the halls, but Iolanta didn't seem to care. Or maybe she knew better.

"There are things you must know," she continued. "Meena and the Entente coexisted peacefully because she wasn't interested in seeing the Future. She trusted us to keep the balance of Ever After. But her daughter . . . Magrit is a different story. Hecate foretold her Future, which ends in death, as it does for all of us. And that is why the Entente are banished. As for me, I never saw good in any version of Magrit's Presents. She never chooses good."

Then she leaned into South's ear and whispered something that made him stop in his tracks.

I shuddered and came to a halt too. I already knew that Queen Magrit was pure evil. Killing her was the right thing—not just for the Entente but for the other Queendoms as well. And the farther South led us to the exit, the further I was from fulfilling my mission.

South looked at me, clearly shaken by whatever Iolanta had told him. But all he said was, "Farrow, we have to keep moving."

Iolanta grabbed my hand. "Anger can take you where you need

to go until it holds you back. I hope when it's time, you can let it go." She looked at me, reading me like she had all those years ago.

"I can't leave until I kill the Queen," I said haltingly.

"I told you once: Do not lift the knife or the wand unless you are prepared to do what you must with it. Otherwise, it can be used against you," Iolanta mused, still staring at me.

I thought back to when she first gave me that advice. I had let my emotions control me—and my magic. But that was then.

"It is time to choose between your family and your revenge. The Entente live. If you want to find them, you have to go right this second. If you stay, you can have your revenge, but you will lose your chance to find them."

"But can't I do both?" I pleaded, knowing her answer.

"You have to choose," she repeated.

I took a deep breath and looked at the family I never thought I would see again.

"We just got you back, Iolanta. We're not going to lose you now. I choose you. I choose the Entente. I choose us," I said forcefully.

Out of nowhere I remembered the words that Tork had written for Lavendra: *I would forgo today if we could have forever.* He had written those words about love, not revenge, but they still applied.

"Better to fight for what we have, not what we've lost," Iolanta said quietly.

South cleared his throat. "*Now* can we get out of here?"

"Yes," she commanded. "I know the Present. I know every step of every soldier in the palace at this moment. I can feel their breath. I know their thoughts. They know that there are Entente in the palace." She pointed a crooked finger and said, "That way."

With Iolanta's guidance, we found the kitchen and wound

through the countertops, stoves, and prep stations until we reached a locked door covered in Black Glass.

"It's an entrance to the Fallen's wing. She kept us apart from the rest."

South dropped Iolanta to her feet. She waved her hand over the lock, and the door swung open.

It took me a minute to understand as we rushed through and the door closed behind us. The Queen had made a mini prison between the kitchen and the entrance to the larger dungeon. The corridor opened to ten cells, each with Black Glass doors.

"The guards are here. You and Farrow need to run. I will hold them off," Iolanta said.

"I won't leave you. I just found you," South said desperately.

She put up both hands. "Go," she said.

"I won't leave you," South repeated.

But before Iolanta could respond, the door we were headed toward swung open and there were guards behind it. We turned back, but it was too late—the other door we had come from creaked behind us. More guards.

We were trapped on all sides.

"What an incredibly sweet picture," Queen Magrit said, standing in the doorway with a victorious smile.

She was wearing a nightdress and slippers, not her usual armor of a corset and heels. Her hair was down, and her face was bare. She looked older than she had this afternoon. I could see every line that the years had marked upon her.

"A Couterie, a witch, and a Fallen . . . This is quite the alliance. I must say, I am surprised. But you've made a grave mistake breaking Iolanta out. She's hardly a witch at all anymore. Are you, pet?"

Iolanta's eyes bore into her captor's. She'd been kept in a cage, surrounded with Presents, and yet she had survived.

"Iolanta couldn't perform magic to save her life. Or yours," Magrit taunted.

"You never knew the difference between a broken thing and a patient one," Iolanta said. "My sister saw it before the rest of us. She was right about you. Your hubris will be your undoing. You've completely underestimated us."

As she spoke, I felt a wave of pride for Iolanta and for the Entente.

The Queen laughed as Iolanta raised her hand.

"Kill them," ordered the Queen to the soldiers.

The guards in the back let loose a wave of arrows, and we ducked. I checked Iolanta and South for arrows, but we were all clear. Iolanta closed her eyes and recited a spell under her breath. With a wave of her arm she let loose an arc of Pale Fire. But the Queen's soldiers were ready with their shields.

Iolanta raised her arm again and whispered.

Open the Black Doors,
And the Fallen will be free forever more . . .

As she spoke, loud noises echoed through the halls: all the Black Glass doors in the palace must have opened. Iolanta had unlocked the cages in the dungeon. The Fallen had been freed.

"What have you done?" the Queen cried as a man with a face comprised half of beetles and half flesh lumbered into the corridor joined by a half-scorpion creature.

A soldier raised his sword. But the beetles left the man's face and began to devour the soldier.

The Queen ordered another soldier to advance, only to watch him meet the same gory fate.

More and more of the Fallen attacked the Queen's army, who sent arrows into the crowd. Scorpions and beetles began climbing and attacking the soldiers' flesh.

"Now we run," South said, looking at the clear path that the monsters had created for us.

South led us back through the palace, taking every shortcut he knew from his years there. Iolanta helped guide him, stopping him with a wave of her hand when she sensed soldiers around the corner. There were soldiers everywhere. And arrows. We kept moving. More whizzed by us with every step we took.

Suddenly Iolanta sank to the floor.

South leaned over her, but she waved him off.

Then I saw the blood. The right side of her dress had a blooming dark-red stain, and when I peered closer, I saw that there was an arrow sticking out of it.

"I can pull it out. You can heal it with your magic," I said.

"The Entente do not step between life and death," Iolanta said.

"That's not true," I argued, thinking of Hecate. She'd defied death for me.

"Ashes, ashes, we all fall down," she whispered to me. She reached for the pouch beneath my dress, where Hecate's ashes rustled in response.

"Hecate couldn't leave you, not even in death," she whispered. "I'm afraid it's too late for me, children." She looked at South. "But not for you. It's yours now, child. Guard it well."

I followed her gaze to South.

"No, Iolanta. Stay with me," he pleaded.

The ashes exploded from the pouch on their own. Hecate's silhouette leaned over Iolanta, her hand reaching for Iolanta's.

Her eyes fluttered. She looked up at Hecate and smiled.

"Hello, Sister," Iolanta said.

I reached for them at the same time as South did, trying to help Iolanta back up. But the second our hands met, we were all somewhere else.

PART III
THE FUTURE

We can all be saved or lost by a kiss or a kill.
Either takes seconds and changes everything.
—Hecate, La Soeur of the Future

CHAPTER 32

We were in the woods. Iolanta must have transported us here.

"You need help. You're hurt . . . ," I whispered, looking down at her.

The Fate of the Present gently extricated herself from South and stood on her own. With a wave of her wand, the arrow in her side fell to the ground. She waved the wand again, and her wound disappeared.

"You healed yourself," I said, elated. She had listened to me after all.

She looked down at her wand. "Ah, I have missed doing that . . ."

She waved her wand a third time, and her ragged dress changed into a pretty poplin gown.

I felt myself relax seeing Iolanta healed and looking like she had in our childhood. In fact, Iolanta looked better than she did all those years ago. She'd never used magic on her clothes back then. Instead, she'd tried to make clothes and furniture with her own hands so that no other Presents could touch her. I felt myself tense up again, remembering that we were all still very much in danger.

"Where are we?" I asked.

"You know in your heart where we are, Farrow," Iolanta said softly.

And I did. We were where the Veil in the Enchanted Forest used to be, the entrance to the Reverie.

"We can't be here, Iolanta," I protested, looking to South to back me up, but he was still and silent. "The guards still patrol here. We'll be discovered. They'll come looking for us."

"The spell will hold. I will make it so they cannot find us. We have until tonight," Iolanta vowed.

I realized what she meant to do. It used to take the Three to cast the spell of the Veil. Iolanta was going to do it all by herself, with an arrow wound.

"We could use that time to put distance between us and the Queen's army. A whole night of distance," I said gently.

"We have other work to do."

She waved her wand and the Veil went down, cloaking the entrance to the Reverie. After all these years, I felt a rush just seeing the translucent skim that looked like the forest cover.

With another wave of her wand, the Reverie was returned to its former glory. The buildings that the guards had destroyed reappeared. The trees from which we had gotten the wood to make our wands filled the courtyard.

"It's just an illusion," she explained. "But I guess in some ways it always was . . ."

"It was real to me," I countered.

"It was real to all of us," she admitted, and moved on to where the garden used to be.

Iolanta looked at me a long beat.

"Don't fret. Hecate is on her way back to you. And your face! Would you like your nose and ears returned to you?"

I paused, thinking. I wasn't sure. I hated what I had sacrificed for the Couterie. But erasing the evidence felt like I would be erasing scars.

She pulled her wand back.

"Why don't you try it out for a while, and then you can decide?"

I nodded and felt my face transform.

I leaned over the river and took in my reflection. I could see Hecate in my features again. My nose was hers.

I felt my eyes well up with emotion, and I wiped away a tear.

Iolanta returned her attention to South, who remained eerily quiet. Was he just in shock from the events of the last few hours or was it something else entirely?

Iolanta turned to him. "And you, South, would you like to finally get rid of those wings of yours?"

"Do you think I care about my wings?"

"Wings are a pretty serious decision for anyone . . . ," she mused, raising her wand again.

South shook his head. "You don't get to pretend like nothing happened. What you said before, Iolanta—is it true?"

She stopped smiling, and as she relaxed, I could see the effort behind her expression.

"I am your mother, South. I should have told you . . ."

I gasped and looked from South to Iolanta.

"Why didn't you? Because of some arbitrary rule barring favoritism?"

Iolanta shook her head. "South, you wouldn't have existed if I cared about the rules. In hundreds of years of Entente, there had never been a boy born to any of us. When I had you and we could detect no magic in you, the others wanted me to leave you among the humans on a doorstep of a church. I refused."

"Then why? Why keep me in the dark when you knew better than anyone that the only thing I wanted was to feel like I belonged? You knew that I wanted to belong to you. Instead, I spent my whole life thinking I was human."

"Hecate foretold that the Entente would be endangered someday. To be a boy Entente with Rook blood . . . born of love . . . love between me and my Rook . . . and our love for you . . . you would have been the rarest of things. The biggest prize someone targeting magical beings—someone like Magrit—would have set her evil heart to capture. We thought it best that you thought you were human. So at least you could have a Future hidden among them if we could not keep you safe. Believing you were human didn't hurt you; it made you who you are."

South shook his head. Her answer clearly did not satisfy him.

I ached for both of them. Iolanta had robbed them both of a lifetime of love. Like Hecate before her, she had thought she had no other choice. In making the Entente strong, they had both forgone a family.

Iolanta sighed as if what she was going to say next took everything in her to reveal. "I wasn't fit to be your mother. I wasn't fit to be around anyone. No matter how much I wanted to be. I know you must have so many questions, but humor one of mine."

South didn't look at her, but he nodded.

"I felt every moment of your life. Every heartache, every victory . . . but you deserved a mother who was there to kiss your knee—not one who could barely leave her room. Do you think you can ever forgive me?"

South wordlessly turned to Iolanta and wrapped his arms around her. She pulled him to her chest. When he released her, they were both crying.

But as they parted, I noticed something that made my heart sink. There was a red stain in the center of South's shirt. Blood.

South read my face. "What's wrong, Farrow?"

Iolanta sighed beside him, and the illusion dissipated. A bloodstain bloomed on her new dress. The arrow reappeared. She had never removed it.

Some part of me must have known it was too good to be true. It had felt too good to be beside South and Iolanta, walking through the Reverie. It was as close to whole as I had been since the day of the Burning. But it wasn't real.

"No . . . ," South whispered as Iolanta sank to the ground.

"I need my sisters. We need to make a circle," she whispered.

"But South and I . . . We don't have any powers."

"I know. That's why we have to make haste and call the others."

The others? Had she really meant what she'd said back there in the palace? Were more of the Entente alive?

"Just get me to the circle," she commanded.

South picked her up and carried her to the center of the courtyard under the never-ending sky. The courtyard was where we had trained when we were small. This was where the sisters drew power from one another when Fate was far off course.

South laid Iolanta gently on the ground. She opened her arms and began to chant.

I drew the circle in the dirt with my wand while South lit the candles. He was still incredibly quiet. Iolanta asked us to join hands, and we sat with her on the floor of the courtyard.

Was she right? Were our sisters still out there somewhere?

Her eyes closed, she chanted.

We have waited so long. East, West, North, South, Sisters,
Come back . . .
Heed my song, come back to me, where we belong.

We followed suit. We repeated her words over and over again until Iolanta finally squeezed our hands. Then she dropped hers into her lap and looked to the sky.

We waited for a seemingly interminable pause.

"They're here."

I looked around. I didn't see anything. South's eyes met mine. I could see the doubt in them. But there was something else too—something I couldn't quite put my finger on.

"Take a closer look," Iolanta ordered hoarsely.

I followed her intense gaze and still saw nothing.

There was a strike of lightning behind us that seemed to last seconds too long. It was as if it were somehow frozen in time. And then, out of that sliver of jagged light, a person slipped into the sunlight. It was Galatea.

She took us in for a split second as the light dissipated, and then she rushed to Iolanta's side.

"Sister . . ."

"You are just in time . . . ," Iolanta whispered, collapsing.

South caught her and helped her sit back up.

Galatea's eyes fell on South and then me. "South . . . Farrow . . . You're alive."

Iolanta moaned again.

I found my voice. "She was shot with one of the Queen's arrows.

She used her wand. But it's not working. Maybe she used too much power transporting us here."

Galatea knelt beside Iolanta. She touched her face as if she were trying to determine if she was really there. If she was really real.

"Hecate is here too . . . ," Iolanta whispered.

Hecate's ash form stepped forward into the center of the circle and grasped Galatea's hands.

They stayed like that, palm against palm, for what felt like an age—as if they were looking into each other's souls.

"You're really here," Galatea said. "How I have missed you, sister. We are so close to having everything we want . . ."

"She doesn't talk," I explained.

"Why couldn't I feel your presence all those years?" she asked Iolanta, taking her hand.

"Long story. Let me tell it to you." Iolanta pulled Galatea's hand and put it over her heart.

I knew what she was doing. She was letting her in. She was letting her read her Past.

Next, Galatea put her palms over the arrow in Iolanta's side. She began to chant under her breath.

Make right what was done.
We have just begun.

Despite the horror for Iolanta that blanketed me, I found myself struck by the image before me. The three sisters reunited was something I had dreamed of since the day we had been separated. But I had never imagined it could happen. Future, Past, and Present. Ashes, alive, and half dead.

Iolanta just had to live, to hang on and have more of this, a Future with us all. After all these years, the Fates could not have brought us together only to lose one of them again.

But a few moments of chanting later, Galatea began to cry.

"I don't understand."

She tried again.

Make right what was done.
We have just begun.

I could hear Iolanta gasp for air and whisper something.

"This is the way of the Fates. Take care of one another— Take . . . take care of our sisters," Iolanta said softly, gasping for air.

"Shh—you need your strength—we will save you," Galatea whispered.

"Can't you do something?" I could hear my voice breaking.

"The Entente do not step between life and death. You know that," Iolanta said.

"I will not lose you again," Galatea argued, putting her wand to the sky. Lightning came off it.

A second later, two more figures slipped out of the lightning bolt and joined us in the courtyard. They were older, but I recognized them immediately: Amantha and Bari.

A smile broke across Bari's face when her eyes met mine.

"Farrow . . ."

Then she saw Iolanta.

"No!"

"Go, get your sisters. Hurry," Galatea ordered.

I watched a blur form in the center of the circle, and Amantha went into it.

Within seconds Bari's flesh began to dissolve, and in its place were thousands of bees with shimmering blue wings. Her dress dropped to the ground as the bees made a furious fluttering line back up to the sky. Just as quickly as Bari and Amantha had appeared, they were gone.

I felt relief well in me. Bari and Amantha were alive.

Iolanta reached out to me and South. She held his hand.

Around the courtyard we watched as my sisters came back to the Reverie. Each slipped out of the lightning and into the circle.

When the lightning stopped, there were fourteen figures wearing hooded robes standing around us in the circle. My sisters had returned.

As Galatea invoked their names, each girl stepped forward. Sistine, Effie, Perpetua, Selina, Odette, Xtina, Horatia, Tere, Freya, Walla, Em . . .

Their faces were the same as I remembered them—only older. Their eyes looked different, and I imagined mine did too. The contented, peaceful look of the Entente had been replaced by something more tortured. More haunted.

"The rest of the fifteen," I whispered out loud.

"In the flesh," quipped Tere.

"You're all here . . . ," I said as I felt my heart flood with emotion. Iolanta had been right about everything. The Entente were alive.

"Join hands, sisters. There isn't a moment to waste . . . ," Galatea commanded.

Iolanta laughed softly beside me.

"Stop, sister. Just be with me. All I ever wanted was to be back here with my family. I am home." Iolanta looked out at all the Entente, and then she squeezed South's hand.

A tear rolled down his cheek.

"My beautiful boy . . . my son . . ."

She turned her head to me.

"I feel your anger, young Farrow," Iolanta said to me. "It is so strong. But it is your love that is stronger than the Queen.

"Love is all," she whispered, then turned back to South and all of us. "I know the truth of this moment better than anyone. It's time. Right now."

And just like that, we watched the light go out in Iolanta.

CHAPTER 33

The Fates of the Present and the Future were gone.

South broke from us and ran from the courtyard toward Iolanta's room, where she had spent most of her days. I got to my feet and followed him. The grief was too much. When I got inside, I found South as he fell onto the bed, moaning in obvious pain.

"South?"

Beneath South's uniform, his wings sounded a crack. They made jerky movements as if they were trying to unfurl, as if he were trying to fly.

I grabbed his hand and tried to get him to his feet but couldn't. He pulled his arm away reflexively.

Something was wrong.

South sat up and tore off his jacket to free his wings. There was a chaotic pattern of scars where the wings met his back, a map or timeline of every time he'd tried to get rid of them. I had witnessed the aftermath of South's first attempt to remove them by the river when he begged me to take them off. He'd apparently never stopped trying. I shuddered at the thought.

With another cracking sound, the wings extended and stretched out. His scars smoothed and his crooked and gnarled wing bones righted themselves. Tears streamed down his face.

As his wings mended themselves, I realized what was happening.

It was more than grief that had struck him.

It was magic.

It was Fate.

"It's okay, South . . . I think Iolanta healed you," I said at his side.

His wings were still there. But every scar was gone. The wings had grown as South had grown, and they unfurled and extended to their full span. I was struck by their beauty as I stood in the shadows they cast.

Perhaps that was what Iolanta had done with her last breath, the way Hecate had protected me with a kiss, I thought.

"Not like Hecate," he said softly.

I hadn't said it out loud, but somehow South knew what I was thinking.

I have to go get Galatea, I thought. I didn't know how long we had until the guards would find us. But could South walk?

"Don't go. Stay with me," he said, trying to get to his feet.

I gasped. "You're reading my thoughts, South."

"Not just yours . . . ," he replied, holding his head suddenly and falling backward. "I can feel everything. I can hear everything. I can . . . ," he said painfully.

I tried touching him and he flinched again.

"South," I said. "Hecate stripped me of my magic in her last gasp at life, but Iolanta did the opposite. You have Iolanta's gift. When she passed into the Ever After, she gave her power to you."

South held his head in his hands. "That can't be possible. From the beginning of Time, the Fates have always been female."

He was right. There had never been a male Entente. But there was no other explanation.

"I don't think magic cares what you are. It just cares if you are worthy. Iolanta has made you a Fate."

"Iolanta is my mother," South said. "I'm not a human after all. Or an orphan. I always felt closest to her. Now I know why."

"Oh, South," I said, knowing exactly how he felt. I might be the only person in all the Queendoms who did. "You were never an orphan to me."

"I found her and I lost her, all in a matter of hours," South grieved.

"It was fated," Galatea offered suddenly from the doorway. She lit her wand to illuminate the room.

I gasped again, looking at the walls. I looked closer at the scribbles and drawings. There were the Presents that I half remembered from when Hecate had sent me to see Iolanta after I had given South wings. I realized now what I should have seen then, that among all those other images there were those that told a story—one that neither South nor I knew at the time. There were drawings of Queen Magrit at the funeral of her mother and the years before. But there were also drawings of South from when he was a baby to when he got his wings. And a drawing of a golden palace . . . one that I had never seen before. Not in our lessons with the Entente or my studies at the Couterie. This was Iolanta's story, a story of a mother who loved her son.

"She loved you very much," I whispered.

South took in the walls and sobbed. I almost reached for him again, but I stopped myself. He sobbed louder and recoiled as if I had actually made contact.

His grief combined with the Presents pressing in were too much.

"You're feeling all your sisters' pain on top of your own, aren't you, South?" Galatea said as she moved to the side of the bed.

South grabbed his head and whimpered again.

"Can you help him?" I begged.

Galatea placed her wand over South's long, brown curls and whispered into his ear: "South, listen to me and only me. Think of the moment that you were happiest."

He closed his eyes. A smile crept across his face.

Find your place in time and space, where your cares are strangers,
and you know no danger . . .
The spell is cast.
You decide how long it lasts.

She tapped his forehead with the wand.

His breathing slowed, and for the first time since all of this happened, he seemed at peace. She let her wand rest at her side, and she whispered to South.

Stay in that moment.
Rest in that moment.
You never have to leave that moment.
Not until you want to.
Or until I do this again.

"It's a sleeping spell," Galatea said. "Or rather, a dreaming spell. He can stay in that moment until I wake him from it. I promise you he is perfectly content. He is living in the Past, which is less painful than all the Presents. See for yourself."

She tapped her wand against his temple, and then against my own. I could feel my cheeks warm as an image formed in my mind's eye.

It was the moment in the palace when the guard had come in. It was my kiss with South. I gasped despite myself. I didn't know that I had made so much of an impression on him. Not in that way.

"Can you fix him? Is he going to be okay?"

"We will tend to him, but first we must tend to Iolanta," she said resolutely. "Magic isn't always easy, child. And South is going to have to handle all those Presents without being in a nap forever."

"And what if he can't?"

"Then his mother's fate will be his."

CHAPTER 34

The hours stretched long into the night.

We placed Iolanta in the glass casket at the back of the Reverie, the final resting place for all Fates. We said our tearful goodbyes, all except South, who would do the same when he was ready.

"May her blood be the last the Entente ever spill," Galatea said as Hecate's ashes floated next to the casket. Her hand caressed the glass.

"Here, here!" the other girls agreed, and raised their wands to the sky.

I closed my eyes in the moment of silence and thought of Iolanta, knowing the dull ache I felt for her could not compare to South's. I wished Iolanta to come back to us by magic or ash, as Hecate did. But that was not to be.

"*When the sun rises, so does the seal. No one but Entente can enter here*," Galatea announced.

We stood in silence and waited for the moon to set on Iolanta and for the sun to seal the spell. I could have sworn the sun shone brighter than I had ever seen it when it broke the horizon. It shone for Iolanta.

In the morning light, I looked at my lost—and now found—family. I noticed something I hadn't before. Freya's cherubic, dark-brown face was exactly the same as the day of the Burning. She hadn't aged a day.

"How can it be that you look exactly the same?" I asked.

"Time stopped for me on the day of the Burning. The explosion of magic when Iolanta's fire met the Black Glass and all the energy flowing from all of us . . . We don't know the exact cause . . . And we have yet to find a remedy," she said.

"Oh, Freya."

"My malady is nothing compared to what was taken from us that day. There are much worse things than being forever seventeen."

I took this in. Hecate, Iolanta, now Freya—how many of us had been hurt and changed forever?

Galatea jumped in. "Our scars can either hurt us or make us stronger. They are our history. They remind us what we have survived and that we are alive to tell the tale."

"Since the day of the Burning I can stop time," Freya boasted.

I frowned. I was not like Freya. I had lost my magic then.

Galatea looked squarely at me. "Tell me of your scars, child. I know they must be plentiful for you to have made it this far on your own."

"Hecate gave me a kiss of protection the day of the Burning. I lost her and all my magic in one fell swoop. But she came back to me, sort of."

"I searched for you, but I could find no trace of you. It must have been because of Hecate's spell. We assumed you were dead. Everyone survived except the Entente on the pyre. And you, Iolanta, and South, or so we thought. If I had known you were alive, I would have stopped at nothing to find you," Galatea explained. "The indignities you must have suffered . . . living among humans . . ."

I inhaled deeply, and my mind flew to the prince. I did not regret meeting Prince Mather. I flashed back to the moment he kissed me—

"We've been in hiding. Not all together, of course. That would have been too dangerous. It was safer if we spread out. Not just in Hinter but over all the Queendoms," Bari said, putting her arms around me.

It felt strange, but in a good way. The embrace told me the Entente were changed. There was a time when the idea of an Entente hugging another Entente was unheard of. But that had changed with the Burning and all the years in between. Apparently, Galatea had given them permission to throw out the old ways in exchange for the new.

"We've been biding our time, gathering our strength," Amantha said. "I'm so glad you both survived and found each other."

"I didn't find South until yesterday . . . I'm so glad you're all . . . I never thought I would . . . ," I began, but the words didn't come. A gasping sound escaped me as I looked at their faces. Faces I thought I would never see again. Amantha put her hand on my back, a gesture she never would have made when we were small.

"All these years you were all alone . . . Oh, Farrow," she whispered, her voice full of emotion.

And then, looking at my sisters, my entire story came tumbling out. Everything that had happened since the day of the Burning: the discovery that I was Hecate's daughter, my time as an orphan and then as Couterie, Queen Magrit and her Black Glass, and South being a Fate.

My story told out loud sounded fantastical. But my heart lifted seeing my sisters respond with looks of empathy, wonder, and perhaps even pride at how I had handled myself without them and without magic.

Amantha touched my nose.

"All that you went through . . . I can't believe they did that to you."

I shrugged. The nose felt like the least of all the years' wounds.

"I just wish I had my magic back," I said. "I kept whittling wands, but none of them worked."

"Hecate saved you, and she protected your Future the only way she knew how," Galatea said firmly.

I heaved a heavy sigh. I knew that what she was saying was true, but if I had had my powers, maybe I wouldn't have been alone all these years. My sisters had one another, and all I had was my vengeance.

"The Entente will rise again. We have a plan, and you are just in time," Galatea said. A smile crept across her face.

"But I don't have any power. I won't be of much help."

"I can't promise your Future. I deal in the Past. But it is my hope that you will be wielding your wand again. And South will be doing it for the first time. This is how we honor Iolanta."

I embraced Galatea quickly and released her. Then we all took our places in the circle.

"Farrow, there is no guarantee that the spell will work . . . but it will hurt," Galatea warned.

"That's not at all comforting. But any amount of pain is worth having magic again."

"Then let's begin," Galatea said.

I stepped into the circle, tapping my fingers against my wand. I felt adrenaline course through me. I was impatient and anxious at the same time. This was what I had waited and hoped for all these years. This was my chance to get my magic back.

Return the magic that was lost,
Put it where it longs to be,

Give this girl back
What makes her Entente—

With that, we raised our wands to meet one another's.

The dawn sky opened up again, not with rain but with a streak of lightning that met our wands.

We all fell backward from the strength of the force. I closed my eyes as the lightning coursed through my entire body.

It hurt—like my insides were on fire. At the same time, I felt more alive than I'd ever been. It was a pain that bordered on pleasure and returned to pain again.

My heart stopped beating. I heard a crack of thunder and saw another flash through my eyelids. My wand had been struck again. Suddenly, I felt my heart restart. The wand fell from my hand.

When I opened my eyes, my vision was filled with the faces of my sisters.

"You okay, Farrow?" Bari asked.

"You could have warned me that you were going to kill me," I said.

Amantha shrugged. "What's the fun in that?"

Galatea corrected, "I did tell you that this would hurt."

"You could have mentioned the bolt of lightning . . . ," I countered, my ego somehow smarting just as much as my entire body.

"Anticipation can make pain that much more acute. I wanted to spare you that," she said matter-of-factly.

Now that we had all made sure I was not dead, it was time to see if the spell had worked.

"Can I have my wand?" I asked.

CHAPTER 35

Think of your wand as a lightning rod. The power is within you. The wand merely channels and conducts it.

The Entente's teachings flooded back to me. Galatea's words came to me now. I closed my eyes and held my wand up, trying to illuminate it. I wished for light just as I had a million times when I was a kid. It was beginner magic, like tying your shoes.

"Remember, there is magic everywhere. You just have to master it. Use your words and your wand and bring it into submission," Galatea offered, trying to be helpful.

I waved the wand, but nothing happened.

I waved the wand again and again. Concentrating harder, closing my eyes again. Trying to summon every bit of will.

Finally I stabbed the air in frustration, using the wand like a foil. What if my magic had not returned?

"Stop trying, child," Galatea said softly.

The other sisters slipped back into the Reverie. I wondered if they'd left because they were embarrassed for me. Or if they just felt there was no reason to stay since I clearly didn't have magic. I wasn't sure which was worse.

"It's possible. Anything's possible. You may just have more

healing to do. I thought I felt the lightning unbind the spell, but there was so much resistance. It's not my spell to break. It's Hecate's."

"So only she can break it?"

"I thought her death would have loosened its hold. But it's possible that her spell is stronger than death. There is a theory that love is another kind of magic. I have never believed it or seen it. But perhaps Hecate's love for you is how the spell has held on."

And perhaps that's how Hecate herself has held on, I thought.

As if in answer, Hecate's ashes dispersed and rushed toward me, back into her pouch.

"Let's go home," Galatea said finally, taking my hand and raising her wand.

CHAPTER 36

Galatea broke South's dreaming spell. As soon as she did, he shot up from the bed, screaming.

"They're coming!" His jaw stiffened and his shoulders tensed. "Queen Magrit and her soldiers. She's so angry. And she's coming for us, Farrow," he said with urgency, as if he expected them to breach the Veil at any moment.

Galatea spoke up beside him. "Like I said. It's time to go home."

The word sounded strange to me. This place, the Reverie, was the only place that truly felt like home.

Everyone rushed out to the circle in the courtyard, and one by one, my sisters disappeared from where they'd come into the morning haze until only Bari, Amantha, Galatea, South, and I remained.

We—even South, though it pained him—joined hands, and Galatea and Amantha chanted under their breaths. Suddenly we were elsewhere.

"This is where you live?" I asked as I took in the outline of the large manor house before us.

It was rustically beautiful. It wasn't as formal as the Reverie.

The main house itself was the size of the Couterie, but its face was comprised of gray stones puzzled together with peach grout. The house was large with a long, sloping roof covered in red-clay tiles. Tall, rectangular windows were spaced a few feet apart along the house's face, except for around an unfinished oaken door that was a couple of stories high with a large, iron family-crest knocker.

I had told my story, but I had not even begun to hear those of my sisters. They had dispersed throughout the Queendoms. Most of them stayed as far apart as possible to avoid discovery, but Bari and Amantha had stayed with Galatea. I asked why.

"Yes, the three of us came here right after the Burning. Amantha and I were wounded from the explosion, and Galatea needed someplace that no one would look to use her powers to heal us," Bari said.

"Wounded how?" I asked, thinking of Freya.

Our wounds used to be wiped away with a single wave of a wand.

Bari shrugged off the question. "Galatea fixed us, but without the power of the three sisters it took longer than normal. Still, I think our wounds served us . . . When we arrived, Mr. Gray, a nobleman, and his wife could not deny us. They took one look at us and they welcomed us into their home. Even with all the rumors about what really happened in the square. Then the wife fell ill, and we had to take care of their daughter, Cinder, um, Ella—"

"Cin-der-ella . . . ," Amantha chimed in a singsong. For a split second I was transported back to our childhood room, and I remembered how Amantha, Bari, and I teased South. Perhaps they were not so grown-up after all.

"Ella. The girls gave her a nickname that I refuse to use," Galatea corrected.

"Because she is forever getting dirty," Amantha explained. But I was left with more questions than answers. Judging by the finery of the house, Ella should be very much refined. But Amantha and now Bari seemed to be on the verge of a fit of giggles at the mere mention of the nickname they had given her.

"Anyway, it was all terribly tragic. After the wife died, Galatea married Mr. Gray—" Bari straightened her face and resumed her story.

"You're *married*?" I asked, spinning around to look at Galatea.

"Was married. Heathcliff... Mr. Gray died of the same illness," she said somberly.

"Did you love him?"

Galatea laughed. "Mr. Gray was very good for a human. He and his wife took us in not knowing what we were."

The Entente were not supposed to indulge in romantic love. But they weren't supposed to get married either.

"But did you love him?" I asked plainly. Entente did not marry. Entente did not love. That was the way we were brought up. But Iolanta's story about loving a Rook and having South had changed my perception of what an Entente was capable of. Of course, Iolanta, bless her to the Fates, was different from any other Entente... But the intervening years had left us all so changed—what if this had changed too?

As a surprised Galatea considered my question, I wondered what I wanted her answer to be. Did I want Galatea to have loved? And I wondered why the answer mattered to me.

"I loved him for what he gave us. Safety and opportunity," she said noncommittally.

Love and gratitude aren't the same things, I thought. But I did not say the words out loud. What did I know of love anyway, being not quite Couterie and not quite Entente?

"There were also servants living with us, but they've . . . they've all gone. Ella's still here, though, so we need to keep South from prying eyes," Galatea explained, leading us inside the adjacent barn.

We climbed a rickety set of wooden stairs to the uppermost portion of the barn. I could still smell the horse below.

"You want to keep him here?" I asked, incredulous.

The Fate waved her wand and turned a blanket and a bale of hay into a proper bedroom with a wrought-iron bed and a nightstand.

"There are no traces of humans here except for Ella. This is the best place for South right now," Galatea said matter-of-factly.

"Can't you fix him? I thought you were going to do a spell to help him deal with all the Presents?"

South looked up at her, expectant.

"There is no spell to help South. I would have explained it earlier, but you were in so much pain."

"Just like there was no spell for Iolanta," South said. He dropped his head, resolute.

"I can't cure him, but I can shield him. We will make a spell to make sure that no one outside this household will even dare look up when they enter the barn. And if they do, they will see only bales of hay."

Galatea led us in the chant, which we repeated over and over.

Protect our brother from the light;
Make it so those outside the grounds can never see his might,
Until the time is right.

After a couple of seconds, it began to rain in the center of the barn. The rain seemed to fall in slow motion. Every drop clung to South. And after he was completely covered, the rain seemed to meld into his skin.

Protect our brother from the light;
Make it so those outside the grounds can never see his might,
Until the time is right.

And then the rain stopped falling.

"South, you are not healed, but you are shielded," Galatea announced. "No one can see you or your magic unless you want them to."

South looked at me, his eyes still filled with excitement about the magic he had just experienced.

"Do you feel any different?" I asked.

He shrugged. "Everything's different. We got our family back," he said simply.

I smiled and a warm rush of feeling washed over me. South was right—we had our family back.

Our next chapter was beginning.

CHAPTER 37

Come in, Farrow. And Hecate," Galatea beckoned. "We have much to discuss."

She opened the door to her room with a wave of her wand and took a seat in a big, tufted armchair, inviting me to sit opposite her.

The room was pretty and rustic like the others in the mansion. Everything was covered in different floral patterns. The bedspread was a deep, calming blue with rosebushes. There were tiny poppies on the light-blue chairs and forget-me-nots on the walls.

Her eyes fell on the pouch around my neck.

"May I?" she asked, gesturing to it.

"Of course," I said, loosening the strings. In all the excitement, I had forgotten what this meant for her and Hecate.

Hecate's ashes re-formed in front of her sister. Galatea's calm expression melted away and her bottom lip quivered.

"Hecate . . ."

Hecate's hands met Galatea's again.

"I still can't reconcile that you're really here," Galatea said, her voice filled with wonder.

Hecate leaned in and touched my cheek. It felt like a shock. Even after years of being around humans who were constantly touching one another, it was odd to see and feel the Entente expressing physical affection.

Galatea never took her eyes off Hecate.

"I am glad, sister. I thought I had lost you, but bless Fate, there is more for us after all . . . Then I guess you knew that."

The ashes suddenly funneled together and whooshed away from Galatea toward the ceiling and then out the window.

Galatea's face fell.

"She does that. Hecate hasn't been around anyone but me in so long," I said as an excuse when Galatea tried to mask her disappointment with a smile. "Sometimes I get mad at her too," I added.

"I've been mad at her for all these years," Galatea admitted.

Then Galatea did something quite unexpected. She burst into tears.

"Galatea?"

But when she looked up, she was smiling at me.

"I don't understand. Are you happy or are you sad?" I asked.

"Both. I never thought that I would get to have a squabble with my sister again."

I reached over and squeezed her hand.

I tried to remember Galatea as she was before the day of the Burning. When we were small, it always felt like she was judging everyone. She knew every secret of your Past. Just like Iolanta knew every lie. And unlike the Future or the Present—there was no way to change the Past.

The result had always been that Galatea was completely and totally disappointed in humans. But when she disappeared into the facade of Madame Gray years ago, maybe she emerged as something less Entente. Something more human, capable of showing emotion and getting rid of years of secrets.

"*We are always together, sisters. Even if we are far apart,*" Galatea whispered.

Through my fog of memory, I recalled that Hecate had said those words on the day of the Burning when Galatea and Iolanta had tried to stop us from visiting the Queen. It was clear from Galatea's face that she remembered it as if it were yesterday.

"I know every word she ever said to me. I remember all Iolanta said too."

"That must have been a comfort," I offered.

"And a curse," she said. "I relived every word, knowing I would never hear from them again, searching for some meaning, some clue as to what Hecate had given us of the Future, some clue of whether or not Iolanta was still out there somewhere . . . And you and South. But I could not find anything in any Past that could help me or restore us, and I could not put the memories behind me either. They are still here. As vivid and real as you standing before me."

"I'm sorry, Galatea."

My eyes stung with emotion and, as I looked away from Galatea, I noticed the walls weren't covered in flowered wallpaper. Upon closer inspection, there were tiny flowers growing out of the walls. I looked around the room and saw live flowers on every surface. Even the chair I was sitting on. The patterns were intricate and deliberate.

"These flowers. Are they Selina's handiwork?" I asked, referring to my sister who had a penchant for growing things.

Galatea nodded as she recomposed herself.

"It had to take so much control to make that design. And it's very pretty," I said.

But I knew it was more than that. It was my sister Selina's

attempt to give Galatea some peace. To keep her from the Past. Hecate had her brushes from the dead, which helped keep her from the Future. Iolanta had her bones, which she believed drew her to the Past. And Galatea had flowers and seeds—the closest thing to a Future that any Entente could come up with.

"Do they help?" I asked.

"Sometimes it helps that someone wants to help," she said bravely, but I wondered if it was enough.

"I don't think Hecate was capable of telling me where you were or that Iolanta was alive. I think mainly she shelters me," I offered, wanting to give Galatea some peace, even though I knew from my own experience how slippery and elusive it was. Peace had been a stranger to us since the day of the Burning and perhaps it would remain that way even when our mission was complete. Still, standing beside her, I longed for her to be a friend.

"I can see that now. I don't blame Hecate. How could I? I blame the humans. I blame our ancestors for making so many concessions that it was our code for her not to share a Future this important with all of us. I only pieced this together after the Burning. In that second she died, I saw all this."

Galatea was different. I just hadn't realized how much. When I was young, Galatea had carried around the sadness and horrors of all the Pasts that she experienced. Now, it seemed like the weight of the Pasts was eclipsed by her anger, which burned as sharp and bright as my own. If the sadness was still there it was buried.

Then she put her wand to my temple. I closed my eyes and gasped as an image of Galatea, Iolanta, and Hecate filled my field of vision. It was a Past.

"Why are you showing me this, Galatea?" I said, opening my eyes and raising my hand to remove the wand.

"Because I wish she had shown me," she said softly.

I released her wand, and when my eyes were shut I could see them. It hurt to see Hecate in the flesh, but it filled me with joy in the same instant.

They were all so young. Probably my age. I gasped again when I saw Hecate laugh and smile, the others joining in. I had never seen any of them so carefree. They were standing on the path to the palace. As they got closer, I could see it in the distance. It looked as it used to before Magrit covered it in Black Glass.

"Time to be serious. We have a Queendom to save," Hecate, ever the leader, whispered to her sisters. "Iolanta, you have to get rid of that before we get to the palace."

Iolanta, looking happier than I ever saw her in life, save when she looked at South, suddenly frowned and clutched her pocket. She produced a skull.

"It helps," she said with a pout.

"It won't help for the Queens to see us carting around body parts," Galatea added, siding with Hecate.

Iolanta sighed, conceding her point. She closed her eyes and disappeared.

Hecate and Galatea shared a look filled with concern.

Galatea spoke first: "She's getting worse."

Hecate, ever the optimist, said, "She's stronger than she knows."

Iolanta reappeared a second later, her hands empty. "Let's go," she said with a nervous smile.

"Dare I ask where you put it?" Hecate said, raising her eyebrows.

Iolanta smiled a rueful smile and Galatea and Iolanta returned it.

The Fates put their wands to their faces and within seconds had new ones. Iolanta and Galatea both picked the faces of pretty, young women. Galatea had made herself taller and darker. Iolanta made herself shorter and stouter and gave herself a face that reminded me of the local blacksmith. Hecate chose the face of an old lady.

I almost laughed as Galatea admonished her. Even when she was young, Hecate still preferred old faces.

"Can you once pick someone born this century?" Galatea asked.

"The humans respect this face," Hecate said, slightly on the defensive.

Galatea tapped her wand again and the vision flashed to the throne room, where a young Queen Meena was meeting with the young Queen of Malle, the Second Queendom. I recognized her from the Couterie history books.

There was a large audience. The two Queens sat at opposite ends of a long table.

Hecate, with her new face, sat in the center of the table. Iolanta stood next to Queen Meena, and Galatea stood next to Queen Raina.

I recognized all the markers of the Entente. Each whispered something in the ear of her Queen.

Hecate was apparently posing as Regent, and the others as respective Right Hands.

"What say you to the treaty?" Hecate asked.

"We agree to the terms," they said in unison.

The Queens signed with flourishes. Their courts cheered.

A young Princess Magrit slipped into the room with her younger sister in tow. They curtsied to their mother, who looked up.

Hecate suddenly brought her hands to her head. Iolanta opened her mouth to say something, but then wobbled on her feet. Her eyes closed and she fell backward, landing on the marble floor with a dull thud. She had fainted.

Galatea rushed to Iolanta's side while Hecate steadied herself.

"It must be all the excitement," Galatea lied.

"But it wasn't," Galatea said beside me. "We set the scene. We armed the Queens with every bit of knowledge to make the best deal with each other. We brokered peace—we stopped a war. We had won the day. But we had lost our Future. And only Hecate knew."

"What do you mean?" I asked, dread rising in me.

Galatea tapped the wand again, and I saw Hecate alone with Queen Meena.

"What is it? What did you see? I saw you bristle when my daughters entered."

"You cannot let Magrit have the crown. Not ever."

"Why not?"

She put her wand to Meena's temple. A single tear rolled down the Queen's cheek as Hecate showed her her daughter's fate.

Galatea tapped her wand against my temple again. The next image was years later; both the Queen and Princess Magrit were much older.

Outside the window, Prince Mather was playing with his only friends, the guards. It was before I'd met him the first time. Before he'd lost his beloved grandmother. Before he'd been left all alone with Magrit.

"I had hoped your Future would change. We waited and watched. But it has not. You have not. I know this is hard . . . but it's for the best."

"You think the Entente know me better than you do? You know my heart, Mother."

"A mother knows her daughter's heart better than anyone, and that is precisely why I am saying this, as much as it hurts my own."

"Mother, no . . . This is the Entente talking. They tricked you . . ."

"I'm sorry, my dear. My decision is final. I will take care of you and Mather, but you will never take the throne."

I saw a flash of Magrit's signature anger in her eyes. I waited for the explosion, but Magrit stayed calm, which surprised me.

She got to her feet.

"We will make the transition as seamless as possible. Your sister will take the crown. For the Queendom. Please don't leave angry. I can see you're upset."

"I'm not going anywhere, Mother."

Then Magrit crossed over to the tea set, piping hot on the bureau.

"Good, we'll talk this out. I am going to take care of you and Mather, I promise."

"I know you will. But first let's have some tea. Everything's better after a good cup of tea."

Before the pour, Magrit opened a secret compartment in her ring. She tipped some blue liquid into the steaming cup.

I recognized the color from the day of the Challenge. The antidote was the same blue. Was the poison that color too? It had to be.

My stomach turned.

I knew about her penchant for poison. I'd seen it up close in my Challenge with Lavendra. But to poison her own mother?

"What happened to her sister? She's not in exile, is she?"

I had had to memorize the prince's family tree when I was Couterie, but I had never paid much mind to Magrit's sister. No one had seen her in years.

"After they buried their mother, Magrit encouraged her to take a trip to reassure peace with the other Queendoms . . ."

She tapped my temple again with her wand. I saw a tearful

goodbye between Magrit and her sister as she boarded a ship in the harbor.

Magrit waved as the boat pulled away. Then she whispered to one of the guards, "Sink it."

Then she smiled and waved a second time.

I gasped again. In the middle of digesting this horror, I thought of the prince. I wondered if she would hurt him one day too.

Galatea removed her wand. "She is more dangerous than we ever imagined. She is human. That is their way. And she is the worst of them. But we are not without fault."

"What do you mean?"

"I see it now—all these histories—all these compromises we made for peace with the humans. We sacrificed our power for their comfort. We agreed to serve them because they were afraid. It was our first folly."

I corrected my earlier assessment in my mind. Maybe Galatea wasn't less Entente. Maybe she was more so.

"We need to get you to bed. I'm just glad to see you and Hecate again, in whatever form she's in," Galatea said, busying herself, covering her momentary hurt.

She led me to a guest room down the hall from her, Bari's, and Amantha's rooms. This was not as opulent as the palace or the Couterie or even the Entente. But it felt much more like a home. Instead of the silks and brocades that I had grown up with, there were quilts of cotton woven together in intricate patterns. My room had rustic charm, with whitewashed furniture and a pretty, quilted bedspread that looked handmade, though it was missing live flowers like Galatea's.

Galatea opened the closet, which was filled with dresses that I knew would be magicked to fit me perfectly. Galatea touched the sleeve of a nightdress and in a blink I was wearing it. She waved her wand over it and the waist cinched in tighter and the collar adjusted itself.

"Tomorrow night we will start to ready our attack. Tonight you should rest from your journey. I'll tend to South," Galatea vowed.

I hesitated, wanting to watch South myself.

"I should stay with him," I said.

"You'll need your strength for tomorrow. And even with the sleeping spell I cast, the fewer Presents around him . . ."

She was telling me to stay away from South. Something sank in me. We had only been reunited a couple of days ago. But the thought of being separated now made me uneasy.

"Galatea, you've done so much for me and South, but can I ask for one other thing . . . ?"

"Of course. What is it?"

"Can I have my nose back? The one the doctor gave me. I know it sounds strange, but hearing your story made me think of mine. What the doctor did to my face is part of me now. I don't want to pretend it didn't happen."

"You don't want to pretend it isn't part of you. I understand. Say no more."

She tapped my face ever so gently with her wand, and I could feel my nose go back to its Couterie form.

"Thank you, Galatea."

As she closed the door and put out the lights with a wave of her wand, Galatea whispered, "You will see that a lot of the old rules have fallen away. We thought we were protecting you all from favoritism. We thought we were making you equals. But depriving one another of connection just made us that much more vulnerable. We are so much stronger now."

I ran my hand over the quilt and finally crawled under the covers. It had been a very long day. I felt spent. I had received an unexpected gift, the return of my sisters and South. But it had come with a new crushing loss. Iolanta was gone again. This time for good.

Hecate flowed in through the window and curled up next to me on the bed.

"Hecate, you saw all this. You must have. Why didn't you tell me to look for them? Is this what life is now? Is this what it's always been?"

Was there no good without all this pain? Was there no gain without some new loss?

I reached for my anger again and quickly found it. It fit better than my sorrow for Iolanta and for South, which felt like an anvil sitting on my chest, and, left unchecked, would make me want to stay in this bed forever. So I laid my pain and South's and my sisters' where it belonged. At the feet of the Queen.

As I drifted off to sleep, Galatea's words stayed with me. All the rules were gone now . . .

CHAPTER 38

I awoke with a start in the middle of the night. There was a scratching sound coming from the fireplace of my room. Something or someone was coming down the chimney. I grabbed my wand from my nightstand, but I remained still as I watched a figure covered in soot land in the hearth.

With my other hand I grasped my pouch, but it was too late for Hecate to return to it. The ashes rose and flowed out the window. I was sure without looking that Hecate would be hovering just outside, ready to protect me.

Before me, the figure from the hearth shook itself, revealing a girl. Pale flesh and piercing blue eyes blinked out at me through the gray soot. By the startled look on her face, she had clearly not expected to be caught.

"Give me a reason not to scream," I demanded.

"I can give you thousands," she boasted. She opened a pouch of her own, reached in, and produced a sparkling diamond earring.

"You're a thief? Are you here to rob the house? Because I promise you, you chose the wrong one."

"I'm not here to rob the house. The house is mine. I'm Ella . . . Cinderella."

"You're the stepdaughter," I said, remembering what Bari said about her the day before.

"I am. Who the hells are you?"

"The niece. I'm Farrow. I am here for a visit."

Cinderella took a step back from me, eyes widening. "You're one of them."

Her tone told a story all its own. She knew what I was. What my sisters were. And she was afraid of us. But then why had she stayed with them?

"I don't understand. So you're a thief? Aren't you a member of a highborn family?"

"No. I don't steal, and I'm not rich. Not anymore. It's not what it looks like. I mean, it is what it looks like, but I didn't do it."

"Then who did?"

"I . . . We . . . were just . . . I wanted to see my friends. But it turns out they're stealing. I haven't seen them in months. They've changed."

"Changed how?"

"They take things . . . I was going to return this to its owner, but the guards raided the tavern and . . . Don't tell your aunt about this. Promise me. Please . . ."

I knew that the Hinter was changing for the worse—that people were growing more desperate every day. But I had never heard of the rich stealing from the rich before. I could see this was upsetting her conscience. I could see that she was telling the truth.

Suddenly Galatea rapped loudly on the door.

Cinderella flinched.

"Are you okay in there?" she asked.

"I'm fine, Auntie Gray. Just knocked something over," I said through the door.

When Galatea's footsteps died down, Cinderella whispered to me, "Thank you for not tattling on me."

"How did your friend even get that?" I asked, indicating the pouch.

"She helped a wonderful old lady across the street. And then another. Apparently, my friends have developed some new hobbies while I have been spending more time at home. I really am going to return it. Or you can have it if you want," she said, proffering the diamond to me.

"I won't tell your secret. But I have no use for that," I said, closing her palm on the diamond.

"I guess you don't need diamonds any more than your family does. Than any Entente does." She whispered the last, almost daring me.

Galatea had intimated that Ella knew what we were. But they hadn't mentioned her disdain for them. Her fear of them. She was not a fan of the Entente and yet she stayed with them. Had they spelled her to stay but not bothered to spell her to like them? It was strange.

"I'm not like them. Not in the way you think. I don't have any power."

She looked at me a long beat, as if she were trying to make up her mind about me.

"Good night, Farrow."

She shut the door quietly, and I could hear her bare feet tiptoeing through the hall and up the stairs to the attic.

I let the girl go. Because I believed her. And because I saw something in her eyes that was so sad and so desperate that it felt familiar. I only hoped I wouldn't regret my moment of charity.

I tried to fall asleep, but it did not work, and after a few hours of watching the moon through the window, I slipped out of the house and into the barn. There, I found Hecate watching over South.

"I'm sorry about Iolanta," I whispered to her.

Her ashes dissipated and then re-formed by my side.

CHAPTER 39

In the morning, I slipped back into my room and went to my closet to change into a fresh dress. I was startled when a flock of birds rushed through the open window of my room and stacked themselves on top of one another until they made a silhouette of Bari. In a blink they became flesh and Bari stood before me, not wearing a stitch of clothing.

She gave me a mischievous look, clearly proud of her magic feat.

"You've graduated to birds," I said to Bari, smiling back. Involuntarily, I flashed back to the day of the Burning and Bari's scorpions. Birds were much less scary.

"I still sometimes prefer my beetles . . . Our firsts stick with us, I guess," she mused as she walked over to the closet and grabbed a robe.

Bari stopped at the mirror and checked her own reflection. I wasn't sure if she was admiring herself or just making sure that all her flesh was in place.

Her features had grown sharper and more birdlike. She was beautiful, but that wasn't why I couldn't keep my eyes off her. Her movements were careful and precise, just as they had been when she was a child. Now, as she pulled the brush through her long, dark curls, I wondered how the intervening years had treated her. Was the Grays' the first door they'd knocked on or had there been years of scrounging and scavenging? Bari's impassive face did not betray any hint of what they had suffered through.

"Hey, look . . . ," she said. She took a knife off the table and in one swift move cut off her finger.

I gasped.

"Bari, what are you doing? Why would you do that?" I squealed and rushed toward her to help stop the blood that should have gushed from her finger.

But before I could get to her, a beetle crawled out of the space where her finger had been. And another and another, until the beetles made up the exact space and volume of the missing finger. Bari waved her wand with her other hand and the new finger was flesh again.

"When we were little, you pointed out the obvious flaw in my spell. That it left me vulnerable. I fixed it, Farrow," Bari said proudly.

Bari had turned her power on herself and perfected it. She could regenerate.

"That's amazing, Bari," I said, meaning it. "You've come such a long way."

She turned into a flock of birds again and flew in a flurry of feathers from one side of the room to the other—before returning to her human form beside me.

"So have you, Farrow."

"I have no magic."

"And yet you got within a hair of killing the Queen. And you were all alone."

"I had Hecate. And South."

"A pile of ashes is hardly—" She stopped herself at my sharp look.

It was true that Hecate was ash. But she was more than that.

"I'm sorry, Farrow. I didn't mean it. It's just that Galatea showed us what you went through. And I thought *our* years were harrowing . . ."

"But I am not like I was . . ."

She shrugged. "None of us are the same. But we are always sisters."

"Even if I am closer to human than Entente?"

"Bite your tongue. You will never be human," she said quickly.

"But what if Galatea doesn't find another way to bring my magic back?" I asked.

"Magic always finds a way. You'll adapt, like I did."

Bari looked down. One of the bugs that had escaped from her finger before was roaming around the floor now.

"You missed one," I said, expecting her to scoop up the bug and make it flesh again. Instead, Bari squashed it with her foot. She winced in pain as she did it. But she grinned.

I smiled at Bari. In her own way, this was her telling me that everything would be okay. I just wished I could believe her.

I left Bari, feeling a little lighter, and went outside to see South. When I entered the barn and climbed to the loft, I saw Cinderella hunched over him. In her hand was a cup. She was dressed in a servant's uniform.

"Get away from him," I commanded.

Galatea's spell was supposed to block humans from seeing South. Had it failed? But then I remembered how specific spells had to be. Cinderella was a member of the household. That was why she could see him.

She looked at me sharply.

"I heard him screaming. This is just water. What's wrong with him? Why is he out here? Who is he?"

"He's South . . . He's my . . . We grew up together. He has a condition. He is better away from people."

Cinderella and I descended the ladder. "It's more than just a fever, isn't it? It's magic? Did Amantha do it? Or was it Bari? Bari's always threatening to turn me into a fly."

Cinderella had seen South's wings. They must have burst through his shirt in his sleep.

"They didn't make him like this," I said, my heart flooding with guilt.

"Who did, then? Did Galatea? Did you?" she asked pointedly.

"I already told you, I don't have an ounce of magic," I hedged, which increased my guilt exponentially.

"Then what happened to him?" she insisted.

"He was touched by magic a long time ago," I hedged again.

It was enough that Cinderella had seen South's wings. There was no reason to tell her that she was harboring not just any Entente, but a Fate.

Before I could say more, South screamed again.

"It's okay, South . . . ," I whispered.

He turned over toward the wall and began to snore.

"Your voice calmed him," she marveled.

"What's with the uniform? Are you planning another heist?" I asked quietly, wanting to change the subject.

"They make me wear it. All our servants are gone. I will not allow my home to be a sty," she claimed proudly. But again her voice told another story as the words came out shakily. My sisters could banish dirt with a wave of their wands, and yet they had made her their servant instead of their sister.

"I don't understand why you stay here," I said. "Why are you helping us?"

"Because this is my home. It's where all my memories of my parents are. I'm helping because he's hurt. And my father taught me that we help the hurt, no matter who they are. No matter what the risk. He's gone, but I still live by that."

"Even when the Entente, when Galatea has made you essentially a servant in your own home?" I blurted. The uniform and the teasing did not fit with what the Entente were supposed to be. Amantha and Bari should have left their teasing days behind, and Galatea should have repaid the Grays' kindness by treating Cinderella as a sister.

"That's why I have to. I will not let them change who I am. What I believe is right. They are wrong but not because they are Entente. But because of the choices they have made. Because they did not return the kindness that my family gave to them . . ."

"That is noble of you. Maybe more noble than we deserve. For what it's worth, I am sorry for your loss," I said, but as her eyes clouded over, I couldn't help but wonder if there was more to the story and more to Cinderella.

South moaned again.

"I'll get him some mangal root. But I think he might need something stronger. I'll come back with more food and more medicine," she said, and she began to make her way to the barn door. I stopped her.

"Ella, can I ask you something else?"

She shrugged.

"The name . . . why do you call yourself the nickname they gave you? I don't understand."

"It's how they see me. It's who I am as long as I am under this roof."

"What do you want me to call you?"

She paused a minute, surprised as if no one had asked her that in a long time.

"Cinderella. For now. Perhaps if I ever become Lady Gray as my father once intended, I will be Ella again, but I think not. I think even then I will keep it. You can't make what's happened to you, unhappen . . . so maybe I am Cinderella now and until my Ever After . . ."

This I understood. I touched my nose. I had chosen to keep it because it was a reminder of all I had been through to get here. Cinderella's name seemingly was the same thing. A scar never belongs to the one who makes it. It belongs to the one who is scarred. And at some point, the scar becomes part of you. The nose was mine. The name was hers.

'Cinderella, it is, then . . . ," I said finally.

When she left, I climbed back up to South. He was curled into a ball. Even though there was no one else in sight, he still felt the pain of so many Presents. I didn't know what the radius was on his power, but if it was anything like Iolanta's, we were still too close to people.

"I know who I am now. I know who my mother was. She gave me her gift. I am more whole than I've ever been. But she's gone . . . ," South said as he covered his face with his hands. "We aren't alone. The others, they're all around us."

"Shh . . . ," I whispered.

That's an understatement, I thought.

"There are people here," he announced suddenly.

I raced to the window of the barn. I didn't see anything but the house in the distance. There was no sign of the Queen's guard on the horizon. All I could hear was the sound of the horse neighing in the stable below us.

"There is no one else here. Do you sense them coming, South?" I asked, thinking of the guards.

"No, they're here," he said emphatically, and he pointed to the rafters.

There was nothing there but a few birds, cooing and rustling.

"South, you need to rest."

"They're gentle, though. They mean us no harm," he said. He pointed to a mouse in the corner of the loft and seemed to strike up a one-sided conversation with it.

"I know, it's hard . . . But I hear you," he reasoned. The mouse perked up its nose probably looking for food, not comfort.

I sighed, hating that we were sharing a space with vermin. But hating even more that South was so very far from okay.

CHAPTER 40

Before dinner, Bari came to my room to catch me up on the rest of my sisters. She took a seat on the floor and patted the ground beside her. I sat as she opened her palm and released a swarm of beetles, which re-formed on the rug as a map of the Queendoms. As she pointed to each location, she told me a fact or two about each sister. But I could tell she was holding back. I may have known now where each sister lived and what her hiding place was, but there was so much I didn't know. And I could barely keep it all straight. There was a commonality shared by their hiding places, though. They were all close to power. Maybe too close.

"So Odette is the Queen of Doyenne's chef, and Sistine is the Queen of Vignon's mistress of music . . ."

"And Em is the creature that haunts the Sixth Queendom—"

"What do you mean about Em?"

"She's created the most wonderful ruse with magic. She appeared as a reptilian monster in the loch. It terrified the Queendom. They stay away from the loch and she's safe there . . ."

I know we were all left to our own devices, but terrifying a whole Queendom did not exactly sound "wonderful." Still, who was I to judge?

"We all have found our own ways to hide," Bari concluded. She studied my face like she used to when she was waiting for me to agree with her.

"Is that all we're doing? Because it looks like we are awfully close to power . . . It seems dangerous . . . and the people of the Sixth Queendom never hurt us. They had nothing to do with the Burning. Is it fair to them?" I asked hesitantly. I didn't add that it also seemed cruel.

"Fair? The Sixth Queendom pledged its allegiance to Magrit and the Hinter. And almost every other Queendom has followed suit."

"They had no choice. If they didn't fall in line, Magrit would have slaughtered them all."

"They had a choice, and they choose poorly. If the other Queendoms had stood by their Entente we could have built an army together to overcome Magrit. But they did not. They have not. Each Queendom one by one has given up without so much as a fight. It's as if our devotion and sacrifice all those years mattered not at all."

"So now we punish them?"

"No, now we take the place that we should always have had."

"And what place is that?" I asked. I felt the floor beneath me sway as if I were standing on a ship and not in my room. It wasn't magic. It was Bari's new worldview. I understood vengeance. I understood punishment. But I had never once in all those years longed for power over anyone.

"We are the power. When are you going to get that?" She said it with a flare of emotion, which was punctuated by the beetles dispersing through the air and returning to become part of her hand.

"Bari?"

"It's time for dinner. I'm ravenous."

"Okay, but this conversation isn't over," I said, getting to my feet.

As we arrived at the table, Cinderella was putting down a place setting for me. She stayed on her feet, serving, while we ate. Cinderella had called this her home. But they had made her their servant in it. She did not even have a seat at her own table. I thought of how I had felt when I saw what the soldiers had done to the Reverie—trampling on what had once been our home. Were my sisters not doing the same thing now? And hadn't the Grays been nothing but kind to my sisters, taking them in when they were most vulnerable, at great personal risk?

And now, to add insult to injury, I was struck by how rude my sisters were to her. Everything was too hot or too cold or too salty or too bland. It was as if she could do nothing right. It was as if she were the stand-in for every human they thought had hurt them. For the first time in my life, I felt embarrassed for them. And I felt confused by them.

I watched in horror as Cinderella's body tensed in response to every barb and complaint. Then she snapped into compliance and action.

"But of course, dearest Stepmother. Anything for you and yours," she said with a hasty bow.

Her eyes were downcast, and I could feel her fear. But she obeyed as fast as her tiny feet could carry her.

When Cinderella left the room, Galatea spoke freely.

"Humans are so tedious." She looked off into the distance like she did when she was looking into the Past. "Hecate wouldn't listen. There were so many things we did to serve them instead of protecting our own. And look where it's left us."

I thought of my childhood meals around the Entente's table. Odette and some of the other sisters would prepare daily feasts that were beyond human imagination. I indicated the spread in front of us.

"You could do all this with magic. Why keep Cinderella on? You could send her away to school or set her up somewhere else."

"She is the perfect cover for us. To the outside world I am the benevolent widow of Lord Gray. No one looks at us as long as it seems like I am continuing his legacy. She is part of that."

"One glance at that girl and you can see the fear painted all over her . . . Other people might see that too," I commented. "I learned from the Couterie that sometimes you get more with a kiss than with a slap. With a kiss, someone will give you the keys to everything—even their heart. With a slap, you might possibly end up with only a bite."

"In my experience, humans bite either way. It's their nature. You will never truly have their loyalty," Bari said sharply, weighing in.

"The girl is harmless enough. Her thoughts are so banal that I can't even bear to look into her head anymore. And I cast a spell that won't allow her to discuss anything outside the grounds of the manor," Galatea replied. "As for the food, I think you are right that we can improve on it." She flashed her wand over the food.

"Galatea, that's not what I meant," I protested.

She motioned for me to eat.

Pouting, I took a bite. She'd transformed the tastes to those I hadn't had since we all sat around the long stone table in the Reverie. Food that changed with every bite. Potatoes that were mashed, souffléed, and then in a pie. Meat that went from fish to steak to chicken. And flavors unique to the Reverie's own garden that would have brought tears if the Entente allowed themselves to cry.

"This tastes like Odette's . . . ," I whispered.

"It's her spell, but I don't quite do it justice."

Bari took the hint and raised a glass. "Hey, this is supposed to be a celebration. I don't think we should spend another minute discussing such unpleasantness. It's not every day our sister and brother return from the dead." Then she raised the glass higher, in the direction of the barn.

"Here, here," Amantha joined in.

Galatea raised her glass too.

And finally I raised mine. But I put it down before I could clink glasses.

Of course they had been changed by the last few years. So had I. But if the years had taught me anything, it was that the old way of doing things had left us vulnerable. I wasn't ready to celebrate yet. And as the minutes ticked by at the manor, what I witnessed from my sisters continued to gnaw at me. We had all calloused over distinctly from the wounds suffered that day and every day after. Perhaps what I had witnessed with Cinderella was an anomaly, no matter how routine their cruelty seemed just then.

But around the edges of me there was a buzzing like one of Bari's winged friends. As much as I wanted it not to be the case, my sisters were strangers to me. Only time together could remedy that, and hopefully with time would come understanding. For the life of me, I couldn't make sense of them now.

Amantha pulled out her wand. "Is it the food? I can fix that."

I shook my head. "The only remedy I need is the truth. I have so many questions about me and South . . . about the Entente," I said hesitantly. "Since I'm Hecate's daughter, will I become a Fate? Who is my father? Was he human? Who is South's? And why hasn't he shown any signs of magic if he was Iolanta's son all along?"

All the questions about the unknown I'd been holding back came spilling out at once.

Galatea took a deep breath, knowing the significance of what she was about to say. "I'm afraid the story of your father died with Hecate."

"But how is that possible? You can see every Past."

"We Fates honor one another's privacy, and we shield one another from seeing what we don't want anyone to see. I looked once and all I got was a glimpse," she explained.

She tapped my forehead with her wand. I had the fuzzy image of a man's face leaning in to kiss Hecate's. I could see his lips and brown eyes and the brim of his hat. He was probably a gentleman. He removed the hat as their lips met. The vision was accompanied by a blush of emotion, a heady feeling of happiness that seemed to belong to the two of them.

When she took the wand away, Galatea continued. "We were instructed not to fall in love. But we also had to keep the Entente alive. We spun the wand, and some of us were chosen to carry on the line. You and South were the results of that. As to whether you'll be a Fate, I cannot say. I can only see your Past."

I sighed with frustration. What good was Galatea's gift if it couldn't tell me more than this? I wished that Hecate had shown Galatea my Future.

"And South? What do you know about him that you haven't told us?" I asked, hoping she knew more, for his sake.

"There are two sides to his magic. One side is from Iolanta. The rest comes from his father. She believed he was a Rook."

"She met a Rook?" Bari asked in utter disbelief. Amantha perked up too.

"In the flesh," she said matter-of-factly as Bari, Amantha, and I froze, eager to hear more. Our forks hung in the air.

The Rooks had always been a joke, a fairy tale, never real to us. And now she was telling a new story. One that meant that South was half Rook.

"I myself have never met one, but their magic works differently than ours does. It's not tied to Fate or destiny. It's emotional and temperamental and unpredictable. It doesn't manifest itself until a boy comes of age. There is no way of knowing the result of two magic forces comingling. Perhaps his Rook blood will save him and keep him on our side of sanity. The decision to keep the Rooks and Entente separate was part of a covenant made by our ancestors. There is a reason that the Rooks and the Entente chose to stay six Queendoms apart all those years ago. To keep the balance of magic. But perhaps in South, he is the balance."

South's best hope was that the chaotic Rook magic would balance out all his encompassing Presents? A part of me sank for him even further. Another part of me rose in hope, but I wondered if the hope was real or a fairy tale I needed to make me feel less scared for South.

"Do you really think so?" I asked.

"South is unlike anything that has ever been, Farrow."

"Then how could you treat him as an orphan?"

"There had never been a boy born to an Entente until South," she continued. "And when we saw that he had no magic yet . . . we decided to raise him as a human. We thought it would be confusing for him and for all of you to reveal his Entente lineage."

"So you denied him the truth?" I accused.

"We thought we would be there when and if he ever got his

magic. And if he never got it, he would never know what he was missing."

"But he missed so much more. Knowing that he was part of us . . ."

Galatea nodded, her face downturned with apparent regret. "We chose wrong. We wanted to spare him any pain. Iolanta especially."

I hurt for Iolanta. I wondered if her inability to shut out all the Presents had to do with the fact that she had not dealt with the most important Present of all: the fact that South was hers.

I also hurt for South. His whole life would have been so very different if he'd known who he really was. He would have known that he belonged with us.

"Amantha, Bari, surely you must have these questions too . . . ," I added.

They looked at each other. Were they examining their faces for similarities to Galatea's? Was Amantha's nose Galatea's? Were Bari's eyes?

Was Galatea their mother? She'd always kept them close. They had to want to know. If the old rules really were gone, why hold on to this one?

Bari spoke first. "I have all I need in the Entente."

"All the answers we need will be given to us in due time. For now, we cannot have our hearts clouded by unnecessary entanglements. We know what we need to know. We are sisters. Nothing else matters," Amantha seconded, joining in her folly and raising her glass again.

"Tonight we celebrate. Tomorrow we begin rooting out the Queen and destroying her," Galatea announced.

"Can I help?"

Galatea's face dropped. "Why don't you concentrate on taking care of South for now?"

"I can't help because I don't have magic," I said, realizing and feeling left out all at once.

Galatea didn't deny it.

"We will figure out a way to get your magic back," she said. "You just have to be patient. After all, we waited years to reunite. What's a little longer?"

After dinner I went to South. He was now sleeping fitfully. I thought I heard him murmur the word "father." I sat down at a distance, making a place for myself on a bale of hay. I would be there when he woke. But the temperature in the barn had dropped and I had to get South another blanket from upstairs.

When I got there, Cinderella was outside my door, her hands full of linens.

"Cinderella, I am so sorry for their behavior back there . . . ," I began.

"Would you like the sheets turned down?" she said over me. She returned my gaze, clearly not believing me.

"They weren't always this way," I added. But even as I said it, I wondered if I was telling the truth. "Something happened to us. And we were separated. We have all dealt with it very differently."

Cinderella put her chin up. "Something happened to me too. *Your sisters* happened to me. I have never behaved like that to another person. And I never would."

"Cinderella—" I started to speak again, trying and failing to find the words to mount a defense for my family.

She cut me off, suddenly cold. "Miss Farrow, do you want me to turn down your bed now? Or I can come back and do it later."

"Cinderella, that isn't necessary." I felt wounded by her formality.

I wanted to break through it, but she was looking at me like I was a stranger. No, worse. She was looking at me like I was a witch.

"I know that they have behaved terribly. But I am the same person you met last night," I said finally.

"I hope so. But my history with your family has always told a different story," she said dismissively, curtsying before making her exit.

CHAPTER 41

Half Rook, half Entente, huh?" I whispered as I leaned over South just as the sun began to dawn, resisting the urge to kiss his cheek. "You just look like South to me."

South turned over and began to snore softly in response, as if unconsciously agreeing with me.

"So much is happening, and I think you can feel every minute of it. I wish you couldn't. I wish you could just rest. And at the exact same time, I want to shake you awake so you could help me figure it all out. Pretty selfish, huh?"

I adjusted his covers one last time and began walking toward the door, when I heard a girl's voice in my head as plain as if it were my own thoughts. But it wasn't my voice; it was someone else's. And it was so very mad. *I wish that they had never come here. I wish . . . I wish . . . I wish . . .*, the voice insisted.

The voice was familiar. It was Cinderella's.

I started for her room when I heard the sound of someone working in the kitchen. I opened the door and there she was. She was kneading honeybread over one of the oaken countertops with angry vigor. But she was silent, and the voice in my head was quiet. I must have imagined it. Or dreamt it. There was no way Cinderella would have dared express her displeasure with my sisters at the top of her lungs while they slept upstairs.

Just as I entered, the sun shone through the windows of the kitchen.

I could feel the suspicion radiating off her. It was evident in every muscle of her lithe frame—her face was purposely blank, but her muscles were tense and her moves jerky as she punished the dough with her hands, forcing it into submission. I thought I understood what she was doing. The dough was something she could control. Unlike everything else under this roof.

"What did that dough ever do to you?" I asked, trying to make light of it.

"I don't know. Maybe you should ask your sisters?" she bit back.

"They used to be different, I promise you," I countered emphatically.

"I didn't ask any questions about how your friend got hurt. But I don't need you to make a fool of me. I don't deserve that."

"So, it's really just you here?" I asked. "My old place had a full staff and it was only half the size of this house."

Cinderella was charged with doing all the cooking and cleaning for Galatea and her two "stepsisters," which I knew must be difficult.

"Just me and my pet mouse, Perdi. The staff wanted to stay. But between my stepmother and stepsisters, there were so many new demands. They left in the middle of the night."

"All of them?"

I wondered if Bari and Galatea had cast a spell that made them want to go. Or if it was just their pure disdain that had chased them away. Regardless, it made sense that my sisters wanted the smallest number of human eyes on them. It decreased their chances of being detected.

"I think they couldn't bear being here without my parents. I can barely bear it myself. But this is my home."

I wish the dishes were clean so I didn't have to stand here with her while she defends them, Cinderella's voice said, but her mouth was not moving. Her voice was in my head again. But how?

"Can you say that again?" I demanded, holding my ears.

"Say what?" she said, blinking up at me innocently.

"The part about the dishes," I demanded.

"I didn't say anything."

I wish I knew what was wrong with me. Shame on me for thinking she's different from the rest. I wish we had never met.

"You want to know what's wrong with you and if I am different from the rest. You wish I'd never come here," I said, quoting her own thoughts back to her.

"Stop doing that. Stop making fun of me on top of everything else," she said, stepping back from the dough and taking up a broom.

"That's not what I'm doing. I promise. I'm not like them. Just tell me if you were thinking what I said," I demanded, needing to know.

Cinderella put down the broom and looked squarely at me.

"I hate it here. I wish I could make everything stop. I wish I never had to touch another dish again."

Just as she finished speaking, porcelain began hurtling toward us. I pulled Cinderella to the ground. The dishes had exploded.

"What in the hells, Farrow?" she said underneath me.

For a split second I thought Cinderella had been keeping something from me—that she had magic all along.

But then I realized it—I had granted her wish.

CHAPTER 42

I think my power is back," I blurted. Galatea's spell had worked, after all. My magic had been late once again. This time it came with the rise of the sun. Why it took so long I did not yet know. I barely cared. All that mattered was that what was lost had been found. I was fully Entente again.

"You said you didn't have any. You said you weren't Entente," Cinderella said, sounding wounded.

For a second I had forgotten her. I refocused on her now as she sat there, clearly having the complete opposite reaction to my gift's return. She assumed I'd had it all along.

"I am. I lied. But I'm telling the truth now."

Cinderella got up and recoiled from me. "You're the same as Galatea and Amantha and Bari . . . ," she said in an angry whisper.

"I'm not . . . I promise you. Just let me explain," I said.

But Cinderella was already back at her broom. She shoved it across the floor, making a din as it swept the porcelain.

"What are you doing?" I asked, confused.

"I'm cleaning up . . . Galatea and the others will kill me if they see the kitchen."

Please let them not see it like this, I heard Cinderella think.

I could feel her fear of my sisters and her desire to put the room right again.

I concentrated on the shards of china. And as I did, they rose in the air. The pieces came back together and became whole. A second later they floated back to their rightful places in the cabinets. The dish Cinderella had been holding floated down in front of her and rested on the countertop.

I could control it. The magic. I looked at Cinderella. Instead of sharing my sense of wonder at what I had just done, I felt her fear cement.

"You're just like them," she said, her voice cold. Cinderella considered a beat, her bottom lip trembling.

She picked up the dish from the counter and inspected it as she spoke.

"It's whole again. If only you could do that to my parents," she said, her voice full of pain and something else I couldn't place.

She put the dish down and returned to the dough she had made for the honeybread. I could feel her frustration rising. Her fear of my sisters had robbed her of the ability to give in to her desire to stomp out of the room.

I wish I didn't have to do this, so I could get away from you.

I closed my eyes and concentrated on what Cinderella wanted. Then I opened my eyes to take the rolling pin from her hand. The pin began rolling the dough on its own. It rose into the air as the stove door opened. The dough placed itself on the oven rack.

Cinderella watched in wonder for a few seconds, and then walked away without saying a word.

CHAPTER 43

I had my magic back. I wanted, needed, to share it with someone who might actually be excited about it. South was still sleeping. I had to tell someone who would understand. Someone who loved magic more than anyone else in all the Queendom: Bari.

And with every step toward Bari's room, I began to hear other voices in my head . . . other wishes . . .

From what I could gather, they were Cinderella's neighbors. The Harts were a seemingly loving couple on the farm that shared a border with Cinderella's property. But their wishes told another story. They were not as loud as Cinderella's. They were whispers. Luckily, the Gray manor was miles away from the nearest city. Unfortunately for the Harts, I was not quite sure if they were going to have a happily ever after.

A voice sharp and screeching wished, *I wish that my husband would just die.*

A male almost simultaneously wished, *I wish she could love me again.* And when I closed my eyes, I could see them preparing for a morning ride into the city. They both had smiles plastered on their faces as he helped her into their carriage.

As the sound of hooves receded, I opened my eyes and proceeded to Bari's room.

The door was ajar. I knocked and entered, then stopped in the doorway, surprised: it looked identical to the room we had shared back at the Entente. There was my pink bedspread and her yellow one. And the pink-and-yellow wallpaper that glittered with actual magic. She'd re-created it with an illusion. It was a sentimental feat. Despite her bravado, she missed our old home just as much as I did.

"Bari..."

But I suddenly couldn't focus on the room. I was confronted with something unexpected. Bari was sitting in front of our old dressing table. She was looking at her beautiful face, only, half of it was missing and there was a jagged, ugly scar that made a red, angry jigsaw of a line, cutting from the center of her forehead, down the left side of her nose, and traversing her lips. She tapped her wand in the space where her cheek and jaw should have been, and, in its place, hundreds upon hundreds of black beetles began to fill it. They climbed over each other, directed apparently by Bari's wand to mirror the shape of her existing cheek, jaw, and chin.

Finally, her eyes lit upon me in the reflection and she addressed me.

"Oh, hello, Farrow..."

"I'm sorry... I..."

"Don't be," she interrupted without an ounce of self-consciousness. "Come on in. I took the liberty of re-creating our old room." She waved her arm to reveal that the room was very different underneath. It was rustic and charming in shades of blues and grays. Then, she waved it back. Our old room returned, but I no longer felt the comfort it had given me. All I could see was Bari's face.

"Your face . . . the scar . . . What happened?" I asked, the words coming out in a rush. I put a hand over my mouth, realizing how insensitive every word I had uttered was.

"The explosion in the square after Hecate was burned," Bari said.

"I don't understand. Galatea said she whisked everyone away."

"She did, but she was a second too late. I don't fault her. She didn't have the power of foresight. We're lucky to be alive at all."

I felt tears welling up in me and I blinked hard to fight them, thinking of little Bari realizing she was alive but part of her was gone.

"You always were squeamish for an Entente," she said ruefully. Bari's eyes had no trace of hurt in them. Just as when she was small, her beauty held no interest for her. Her scar was just more proof of the Entente's power and ability to survive.

I had stared too long. I feigned a sudden interest in our old wallpaper.

"I'm not— All that matters is that you're okay. I'm so glad you're okay."

Hecate's ashes rustled in the pouch around my neck.

"I'm more than okay. I'm more, Farrow . . ."

I nodded, forced a smile, and felt the tears recede. We could never be the same Entente, but Bari had just reminded me what it meant to be one. She had taken me back to our childhood room in more ways than one.

"I wasn't the only one the explosion touched," she continued.

I felt my confusion return. I had seen all the other Entente, and I had seen Galatea's memory of the day. If the other Entente had scars, they were hiding them too.

"Who else was hurt?" I asked, feeling gutted all over again for what had happened to us that day.

"Amantha," she said after a pause. "Amantha was blown up while she was traveling from one spot in the square to another."

"Are you saying that Amantha is dead? That she's a ghost?" I demanded, remembering how Amantha had appeared by her side when she was turning that soldier into beetles.

"Amantha isn't a ghost."

I waited for more of an explanation.

"She's Entente, but"—Bari paused dramatically before continuing—"Amantha's physical body expired in the fire. Her essence stayed with us. Galatea had given her a kiss of protection."

"Just like she gave Hecate . . . ," I said, understanding.

"So when the dust settled, Amantha reappeared. But she wasn't the same. Galatea saved her from the Ever After. But Amantha's body is gone. She can't stay put for more than a few hours at a time. She's mostly wind and magic. But then, she always was." Bari said the last part lightly, as if it were no great loss for Amantha to have lost her body.

"She was torn apart by Iolanta's Black Fire, but she can still come together using her magic. Poor Amantha," I said.

I digested this: Amantha was a scar. There was nothing left of her. Her pieces never came together again, except under the power of magic.

I tried to process what Bari was telling me and what I was seeing with my own eyes. Bari's wound looked angry even though it was a decade old. Why hadn't she healed herself?

"Why can't you heal with magic?" I asked finally.

"The explosion was Iolanta's magical Black Fire. And because at that moment she was at her most powerful, it has lasted that much longer."

I tried to reconcile this information as she continued. The

Entente had been creating moments of magic for years, the effects of which changed the course of humankind, but the magic itself was ephemeral. It lasted only so long. The spells that warded the Reverie and decorated it were renewed every moonrise. Love spells were not only forbidden; they were impractical as well. They, too, had to be renewed every night.

"Don't give my face another thought. I can hide it. And I do when there is a risk of me being seen by them. But I don't want to. I want to remember. I am not ashamed of my scars. *They* should be."

"Who?"

"All those who watched as the Entente burned."

I gulped, aware that whatever I said in the next moment mattered. I didn't have any scars, at least none that could be seen on the outside. And I didn't want to hurt Bari any more than she had been already. But at the same time, I didn't believe all of Hinter was responsible for the Queen's actions. I didn't think I ever really had.

"I hate that this happened to you."

"It didn't just *happen*. The humans put it in motion."

In this moment, I couldn't tell if it was better to have stayed with the Entente or to have been left behind. In all these years with all these scars—the Entente had twisted into something new.

"We spent a lifetime serving humans, and we paid with our flesh. It's their turn to pay," Bari vowed. "If the humans we served had stood between us and the soldiers, Hecate would be flesh; Amantha would be whole. We would still have our innocence. You would still have your magic."

Her words struck a pang inside me. Our separation, our pain, our loss would not have happened if humans had stopped the Queen that day. I felt rage fill me. They had taken so much from us.

Hecate. Iolanta. Amantha's body. Bari's face. We couldn't let them take any more.

"You're right."

I took a beat.

"Galatea said that she had a plan to take down the Queen, but she still hasn't told me the details. What is she doing? What are our sisters doing?"

"We all have a part to play, Farrow. Galatea will tell you yours in due time. Just trust her, and trust Fate."

She reached for my hand and squeezed it.

CHAPTER 44

I might as well have been walking through a swarm of Bari's beetles when I walked to South's barn room. I was abuzz with anger for the pain that had been dealt to my Entente that I never even imagined. Bari's face, Amantha's body . . . all those years apart . . . and for what? Human greed? Human whim? And beneath all my emotions and all my questions I could still hear the whisper of wishes.

I paused outside South's loft and tried to calm myself before knocking on the door and slipping inside.

"You're up?" I said when I saw him. He was standing at the window, staring out.

"I felt like you needed me."

"You heard what Bari told me," I assessed.

He nodded.

My heart ached suddenly. South was worried about me when he was the one who just found out about his past.

"You shouldn't be worried about comforting me, South. What Galatea said last night . . . your father . . . your power . . . the Fates keeping you from knowing who you really were."

It all seemed so big, so overwhelming, the enormity of all those revelations and the enormity of all the Presents crushing in on him at once. But maybe Galatea was right—maybe South was finding his balance. His peace.

"It's better to know than not to know. All that time I thought I wasn't special . . . and all that time you thought your magic was gone . . ." His voice was light, but his lids were heavy with thought.

"And it turns out we were both wrong . . . Your magic is back." South was reading me again.

"It turns out you are very, very special," I said with a smile.

He smiled back.

"And I am only half as special as I thought I was," I quipped, but there was more bitterness there than I had intended for him to see.

"That's not true," he said protectively.

"It's not the same as before. My power is limited. And passive."

"Passive?"

"I can't make magic for myself. I can only do it for others."

As I spoke, I got more flashes of wishes. It was as if the radius of my power was expanding by the minute. I could hear them, but I was careful not to grant any of them.

"I've never heard of that."

"I'm going crazy trying to figure it out. But what matters is that you look rested. At peace. I'm glad."

"It's funny. This place must look so peaceful to you, but it's a roaring cacophony to me," he said.

"Actually, it's not quiet at all. I can hear things too—not like you—but I hear things—wishes—all the same," I said finally. It felt good to tell the one person who would actually understand.

"What do you mean?" he said, looking at me sharply.

"Cinderella wishes that the Entente never came here. The pig farmer wishes he could take a nap . . . There is a couple down the way who are so in love, they wish that they'd die on the very same day . . . It's so romantic . . . and terrifying. Not the couple . . . but having it back . . . but not all the way back . . . It's been so long and now I've lived more of my life without magic than with it. Other Entente are missing so much more. I should be grateful," I said, thinking about Amantha.

"You should be what you are . . . ," South said, clearly holding back.

What he didn't say was that he knew how I felt right now: Scared I wouldn't get my gift all the way back. Scared I couldn't handle the gift I had. I appreciated that he didn't say the quiet part out loud.

"There's no such thing as half magic, Farrow. There's what you do with it. We will figure it out together."

I nodded, wanting to believe him.

"Can you do me a favor?" I asked, inspiration hitting me. I had only thought of myself when my gift returned.

"Anything," he said.

"Can you wish us someplace?" I asked.

He was smiling at me, happy that I had gotten my magic back if only in part.

"Where?"

"The Reverie."

"That's a terrible idea. It's too dangerous."

"I just need a few minutes. Please, South."

He looked at me a long beat, and I knew that I had him.

He closed his eyes and concentrated. *I wish Farrow wouldn't be so impulsive*, he thought.

Take us to where it all began,
Where South got his wings and he held my hand.

"I wish I were back in the Reverie with Farrow," he said out loud.

The air picked up in the room with such a force that we were thrown together. South took my hand, and a few seconds later we were standing on the grass.

"What are we doing here, Farrow?" South asked, blinking hard at me.

I could tell that he was trying to use his gift on me, to read my Present, but it wasn't working.

"I want to undo what I did to you all those years ago if you'll let me."

Surprise filled his face.

"My wings . . ."

"I know you have your own magic now. But I would be honored if you would let me fix what I did then. It is my greatest regret."

"You still don't understand . . . I want to keep them."

"Why?"

"After everything that happened, after I thought that the Entente were dead, I didn't want the wings gone anymore. I didn't think of them as scars. They were part of me. They were proof that the Entente were real. That I was one of them. All these years I wasn't hating them; I loved them. I was waiting for the day when they would heal. When I could do this."

He unbuttoned his shirt. As it dropped to the ground and the sunlight hit his shoulders and chest, I was aware more than ever how much time had passed since we were children. South's shoulders were broad. The musculature of his chest had developed from his years in the army. His body was a thing of beauty.

It was strange seeing him that way. Half dressed. And all grown up. I felt my heart quicken. I reminded myself that this was still

South—the kid who once annoyed me more than anyone under the sun. And now he was one of the most beautiful things under it to me. Maybe he'd always been. But I had been too young and misguided to see.

His wings unfurled, the span creating a shadow over us. He flapped them, creating a draft. Once. Twice. And then he began to lift off the ground. His wings continued to flap as he hovered in the air in front of me.

South rose a few more inches off the ground. He was flying.

I smiled up at him, feeling a little lighter myself.

When he touched down, his wings folded back behind him and he took a step toward me.

Before I could react, he reached for me. He ran his fingers through my hair, his hand cupping my face.

"South, you aren't supposed to touch me," I said in a whisper.

"I don't care . . . I forgive you, Farrow. You have to forgive yourself."

I blinked up at him.

And South leaned in. I closed my eyes, anticipating his lips meeting mine.

"Farrow," he said urgently.

"Yes, South," I said.

"Farrow, we have to go."

I opened my eyes, trying to shake off the fluster of emotion.

"They're coming. I can feel them."

"Who's coming?"

"Magrit's men."

There was the sound of boots against the ground on the path where the Veil used to be.

"Wish us back to the manor," I demanded.

"I have a better idea."

He put his arms around me, and his wings began to flap. This time we lifted off the ground. I looked down as the earth receded.

"South, this is a terrible idea. The Presents . . ."

"It's better up here," he exclaimed.

And in fact, he looked more serene than I had seen him since we'd reunited.

We were like that for a while—him flying over the dark forest with me in his arms. The sensation was like nothing I'd ever felt before. I could count on one hand the times I could remember being held in my life. And I had never been held by South. And I had never been held while flying through the air. Being up there in his arms felt at once unnatural and at the same time like this was exactly where I was supposed to be.

"We should keep going," I urged when he slowed down, making us hover in midair over the Dark Wood.

"Look, the guard is miles behind us. They can't catch us."

He was right. I followed his sight line. We couldn't even see them in the woods below. And if we could, they would be tiny specks.

"Look," he said again. "It's all different up here."

The Queendom was beautiful. I took in the forest . . . the edge of the Reverie . . . even the Queen's Black Glass palace . . . and the Gray mansion ahead of us. Everything looked miniature and more perfect from this vantage point.

He didn't have to say it. I felt it too. For a moment we were free. Free of our fears. Free of our sisters. Free of our vengeance.

"I could stay up here forever. Maybe I will," he said.

"South," I warned lightly.

He sighed, and I could see the weight of the Presents return to his visage as we got closer to the ground. He landed near the manor and finally released me.

I stepped away from him.

"You were right. It was too much of a risk to go back there," I said, a little out of breath.

"I think it was worth it." He didn't break eye contact for a long moment as if he wanted me to be sure. To know that he meant *I* was worth the risk.

"I want to show you something," he said, leading me inside the barn.

"Okay," I said, following him inside. There was a drawing on the wall. It was a golden palace. "What is this?" I asked.

"The Rookery."

I shook my head. He wasn't following Iolanta's orders. He was still letting Presents in.

"I couldn't help it. I saw something. Or rather, someone. Lots of someones . . ."

"South, what are you talking about?"

Was this like the animals he was talking to in the barn?

"I've been sifting through everything, and I think that Iolanta is right. There's magic at the edge of the Thirteenth Queendom."

"Magic?"

As I said the word, I realized where he was heading.

"Different from ours, and some of it is in me . . . Iolanta said my father is a Rook. Galatea, too. If we go, maybe we can find them. Maybe they can help us."

I had been wrong about South's demeanor. I had mistaken his plotting for peace. He wasn't accepting what the Entente had hidden from him; he was preparing to hunt down his other family himself.

"Can we trust them? When we were small, the sisters said they were tricksters. And Galatea also implied at dinner that the Rooks deal in chaos."

"Galatea has said a lot of things we now know aren't true. We have to try."

"The Rookery is Queendoms away, and for all we know they've already been wiped out by Magrit. And who's to say they aren't just as full of conflict as the Entente are? Just because the Rooks have magic, doesn't make them good. And even if they are good, it might not make them want to help us."

"You're right: we don't know anything about them. But I know what I feel, and there isn't a Present I can reach with my mind that says they want to hurt us. I'd travel to the edge of the Queendoms for you in a heartbeat, Farrow," he said.

His cheeks went red a second after he'd said it. He busied himself with taking his wand out of his pocket.

I could see in South's face how much he believed in the Rooks. But he had also just lost a part of himself in Iolanta and wanted desperately to find himself in the Rookery.

"Iolanta agrees with me."

"Iolanta?" I said, concern rising.

"It's in her book." He went to his nightstand and pulled out a book that Galatea had given him. He flipped through pages of spells. There was a drawing that matched the one he'd made on the wall.

"I want to go there," he said.

"Of course you do, South. After the Burning I had the same instinct . . . I wanted to go there myself. And that was before we knew that you were part of them. But we can't . . . not now."

South looked uncertain for a beat. He wanted this. Not just to save us but to fill the hole that Iolanta's death and the knowledge that she was his mother had opened in him. I hated quelling that need. But I had to make him see that he had to wait.

"South, I know it's not fair to ask you to wait . . . and I wouldn't ask if I didn't think that the Entente weren't on the precipice of danger . . . I don't know what they are planning, but I can feel it, South."

South put his chin up, taking in what I said.

"I understand . . . I can feel it too.

"But . . . after Magrit is dead, I want to meet them." The air began to flicker around him.

"Then I want to meet them with you," I vowed.

"You would do that?" he dared to ask.

"Wherever you need to go, I'll go with you." I squeezed his hand in answer and he smiled at me.

CHAPTER 45

I left South's barn and went back to my room. I released Hecate.

I needed to try out my magic again now. Hecate curled up on the bed, watching.

I closed my eyes. "*Bring the light; show my might*," I chanted.

When I opened my eyes again, the tip of my wand was unlit. I sighed, knowing I had been changed forever. Again.

Galatea knocked on the door and entered.

"Still trying, Farrow?" she said, looking down at my wand and sounding impressed by my persistence.

I turned to her and wondered if she was looking into my recent Past.

"More than trying, I see. If only there were really a correlation between how tightly you squeezed your eyes shut and what your wand did," she added lightly.

It was something I thought she might have said to us as kids in the Reverie. But Galatea would know that for sure, because she knew every moment of her own Past and could see every moment of everyone else's when she focused, unless someone or something was blocking her—like Hecate's spell.

"Can you see my Past now?"

She shook her head. "Only glimmers."

What had happened in the kitchen . . . What had happened with South . . . I could not seem to replicate it no matter how hard I tried.

Despite what Cinderella had said and thought, I still needed to understand my magic. I needed to know about myself.

"Galatea, I think . . . I know how the unbinding worked—or half worked . . . I just don't know how to replicate it on my own," I said. "It only works for others." My words were a jumble. "Is there such a thing as a half spell? I can hear what people want—their deepest desires and their fleeting ones. And sometimes I can grant them . . ."

Galatea cocked her head as if I were a spell that she hadn't figured out. "Come, let's see what's going on inside you." She motioned to the next room.

She pulled out her wand and put it to my temple when we got to the sitting room.

"I don't know. I think it's something else. I still can't read you."

And I couldn't read her thoughts either, not like I had Cinderella's. I pulled out my own wand and tapped it against her temple. When I looked into her, all I saw was her mind room—the quiet place she had built to keep from feeling too much. Nothing could get in or out unless she let it.

Iolanta had tried and failed to do the same inside her. She had never managed it. And then came Magrit and the years of torture. It wasn't fair, but some part of me wondered if I would end up like her or South.

It wasn't the same as South and the onset of his powers. Was it? Iolanta couldn't have possibly given her power to both of us.

"I think the reason your power is only halfway back is because

Hecate is halfway between worlds." Galatea looked at me a long beat after removing her wand.

"Am I like South?"

"No, this isn't at all like South," she said, sounding certain.

"How do you know?"

"Think about it—South's reach is across Queendoms. Yours seems more immediate. How far can you hear?" she asked.

I thought about it, realizing I had heard only the thoughts of Cinderella and South and a few of the people in the neighboring homes.

"And you are not hearing their every thought or their every Present? You're just hearing their deepest desires? Their wishes, per se."

"Yes. Then if I'm not a Fate, what am I?" I asked.

"Something new. Something Hecate made." Galatea tapped my temple one last time. "When I look inside you, I can see only flashes."

"I can't read you either."

"You shouldn't be able to read me . . . ," she began. "It's what I've been teaching South. You have to make a place for yourself where you are happy—where you are safe. Where no one can touch you. For South, it's a memory of you two together. For me, it's a Future where all my sisters are together."

She tapped her temple and then mine again. Her mind room got bigger, and suddenly, Freya, Tere, Amantha, me, all the other sisters, and South filled the space. We all looked older, and the blank space transformed itself into the drawing room of the Reverie.

"You created this Fate?" I asked, surprised. She was a Fate of the Past. How could she have this vision of the Future?

"It's an illusion. Like the Reverie. It's only in my head. A place in my mind I can go to when I don't want anyone inside it," she explained.

I nodded, wondering if I could perform the same trick. My mind went to the prince automatically. The two of us standing in the palace, his hand in mine. I blinked hard, willing the image away.

"But that doesn't explain why I can't see what you're thinking... what you're feeling. Why, even before the unbinding, I only got flashes of your Past. It's as if Hecate did more than bind your magic. She shielded your mind from our magic."

"But why would she do that?" I asked, my mind reflexively remembering what Cinderella had said in the kitchen.

"We will figure it out." Galatea smiled. She called for Bari and Amantha, who appeared almost instantly.

"We're going to shield Farrow's new magic. We need everyone," she ordered.

Bari flashed a grin and Amantha winked at me before they disappeared again.

When we arrived in the barn, South was awake and drawing on one of the walls.

"South? I thought you were feeling better," I asked. I thought he was, but the sight of him scribbling made me think he'd had a setback.

He gave me a pointed looked of reassurance.

"I am. Don't worry, Farrow," he said just as the others arrived, filling the barn.

I was with my sisters again. They each had a story, and I had gotten bits and pieces from Bari, Amantha, and Galatea. But there was so much missing. And there was never enough time.

Galatea put a hand on my shoulder. "I know you're in a hurry. But we have time. And when this is over there will be nothing but time for you to get to know your sisters. For you to get your magic back."

I nodded.

"We are here to shield you, but there is something you should see . . . ," Galatea continued.

"Sisters, show yourselves . . ."

Perpetua, who now lived in the Malle, the Second Queendom, cleared her throat and began to grow. Within seconds, her head was grazing the ceiling. From the Third Queendom, Tork's Blenheim, Effie made her face contort with bearlike fur and her incisors peek out from behind her lips. Em, from the Sixth Queendom, Mettlebrau, was a shape-shifter too. But her tufts of fur were more wolflike. Tere balanced a tiny cloud in the palm of her hand. Xtina, a ball of fire. Freya from Lasse was forever seventeen . . .

"Was this from the Burning?" I asked Perpetua, my sister who was now a giantess.

"No, I did it to myself."

"Why? How?"

"Galatea says we have the right to test our powers."

"No matter the result?" I wondered. We had always been taught moderation. And to know what we were doing before we turned the wand on ourselves. What was this? Every encounter with my sisters showed me how much my sisters had further abandoned all the old teachings. And every encounter made me wonder if this was a good thing or a bad one.

Not everyone's powers could be seen. Odette now lived in the Fifth Queendom, Doyenne, and her specialty was still magical food. Sistine, from the swamplands of the Seventh Queendom, Vignon, could hum and make you feel things.

Galatea gently got to the point. "Your sisters learned how

to work their magic. There are no mistakes. There are only opportunities."

Then she began the spell.

Keep us hidden
From those who aren't true.
Keep our magic in the dark
To make its mark—

As my sisters chanted, I felt their power course through me.

I pushed aside my worry about the rules. There was no turning back; what was done was done. And I grasped hold of the idea, the hope that Galatea was giving me. I would make the most of my gift just as my sisters had. I didn't feel any different after the spell—but I hoped that it had protected me as Galatea had promised. I had begun the day flying and in a way I was flying still.

CHAPTER 46

"Wake up, sleepyhead. We have to go now," Bari said.

"Where? What are you talking about?"

"Horatia needs us. Our sister is in trouble."

I ordered Amantha to make a wish directing us where to go. And in a blink of my magic we were in the Brume, the Fourth Queendom. Queen Daria had laid down her arms and given up magic without the guards raising a single sword against her. It was just as dangerous a land for the Entente as the Hinter was.

We are too close to the palace. We are too close to one another, I thought as we walked through the streets like tourists. We stopped in front of a store.

"I don't understand what we are doing here. What is this place?"

Bari put a finger to her lips. "You trust me, don't you?" she whispered. Everything was out of sorts. But she was still Bari and there was a part of me that had missed being at her heels, even if it meant being in her shadow. I nodded, and we stepped inside after Bari used her magic to unlock the door.

It looked like a dress shop. There were beautiful fabrics and dresses in every style. There were no customers. It was quiet. We moved through to the back of the shop and Bari knocked on the wall. The wall slipped open, and we stepped through.

It took me a second to take it all in. There were walls of bottles filled with cloudy liquids. There was a table in the center of the room with a glass globe on it. There were cards on the table with drawings on them. There was a teacup, empty except for leaves settled at the bottom. And on the ground next to the table was a woman lying still as the dead at Horatia's feet.

There was a whimpering sound behind us. We turned around and saw another of our sisters, Ocenth, who looked ready to cry.

Bari gave her a stern look. "Tears will not fix this." She returned her attention to Horatia.

"Silly humans. They never can stop themselves from touching every single thing," Horatia quipped as she nervously grabbed one of her curls and began twisting it. For all her bravado, she knew she was in trouble.

"Is she . . . ?" I began.

"Just sleeping. She touched the spindle."

Behind her was a spindle made of gorgeous blond wood. I recognized it as the same kind that some of our wands were made of. My brain belatedly began to put the pieces together. On the table the tea leaves in the cup seemed to be moving, forming a face. The bottles . . . the wands . . . the globe . . . the tea leaves . . .

"You're running a magic shop right under Queen Daria's nose?" I exclaimed. "You can't trust humans to keep your secret!"

"We need to keep magic alive in the Queendoms," Ocenth explained, finally speaking and wiping her eyes.

"We're creating goodwill. The humans that come here walk away with their Futures foretold, their questions about their petty existences answered. Their crops heartier. We use small magic, and they are oh so grateful. We give magic a good name. And we need to practice. We need to know them if we ever want to . . . ," Horatia countered, defensively.

"Want to what?" I asked, feeling unsettled. It seemed like way too much of a risk for sharpening our craft.

"Want to . . . live with them," she said, almost too quickly.

"Now is not the time to argue ethics." Bari interrupted us, her hand on the woman's wrist. "We need to wake her."

"We need a Fate. We should get Galatea," I said, focusing again on the woman on the ground.

"I tried to reach her already."

"There is another Fate we can ask," Horatia offered.

"But he's not ready," Bari said, shaking her head.

"What else can we do . . . ?" Horatia conceded, looking to Bari for another idea.

"South, I need you," I whispered. I had told him not to listen to my thoughts anymore, but my guess was that he could still hear me.

I looked around, and then back down at the woman's unconscious body.

I got closer and took her hand in mine. My instinct was to try a spell even though I knew it wouldn't—couldn't—work.

"What did she come in for?"

"We didn't get that far. But it's always either love, coin, or health."

I was struck that Horatia could be so cavalier at a moment like this. I was comforted by another nervous twirl of her hair.

Bari, on the other hand, was focused. She knelt down beside me too.

"Who is she?" she demanded.

"A noblewoman named Sandrine. People are going to miss her soon," Horatia replied.

I concentrated on Sandrine. I could hear her heart faintly beating, but I could also hear something else—what she wanted.

I want to find her . . . Where is she?

As I heard Sandrine's wish, I got a flash of who she was looking for: one of the girls in the square.

"Hand me her bag."

Inside was a cameo of a girl with brown hair. As I held it in my hands, I got a flash of where she was.

I tapped my wand to Sandrine's forehead. I showed her what I was seeing: a group of soldiers accompanied by a hooded figure. My guess was that it was the Queen's Witch Finder, whose face no one had ever seen. He and his men walked toward one of the Queendom's many academies, just as I had seen a Witch Finder walk out of the Couterie over a year ago.

My vision flashed to the exterior of the school in town. It then flashed again on a pretty girl with brown curls that framed her face. She looked up from her notebook as if she had just come up with something brilliant. There was a crash, and a group of soldiers came through the academy doors. The kids scattered.

The girl I had focused on ran. I flashed again. She was in the Dark Wood, alongside her classmates. She was safe. Horatia wasn't completely right about what humans wanted. There was something else that they wanted just as much as we did: family.

"It's Sandrine's daughter."

I closed my eyes and tried to share what I had seen with Sandrine.

I looked down at the poor woman again. Her eyes fluttered open.

The air flickered around me. South was beside me.

"You needed me?"

"You're late," I said, half joking, half relieved.

He gave me a small smile as he took in the scene.

Sandrine, waking with heavy eyelids, looked at South with confusion.

"You were not there a second ago. What's happening?" she asked blearily. "Is what I saw real?"

"I think so."

Horatia leaned in. "Miss, are you okay?"

"I'm better than okay. Thank you so much," she said, getting to her feet and rushing out of the open doorway.

"What did you do, Farrow?" Bari asked,

"I granted her wish."

I looked beside me at Hecate's ashes, which had siphoned themselves out of the pouch and were leaning in and watching our every move. If I didn't know better, I could have sworn my mother was a little proud of me. I had my mother's approval, but I couldn't help looking to Bari to see if she approved too. For the first time in our lives, I had done something that Bari couldn't.

"Are you a healer now?" Horatia wanted to know. Healing was a rare gift, usually requiring more than one Entente, and even then it was not always possible.

"I thought your power was gone . . . ," Ocenth marveled.

"It's back. But it's different than ours. How did you do it, Farrow?" Bari asked as the others peppered me with questions.

My eyes were on her as I explained. "There was a cameo of a girl. As I held it in my hands, I got a flash of where she was. It was Sandrine's daughter. She ran off in one of the raids. Sandrine wanted to know that she was safe," I said to the others.

Bari *was* impressed. She followed my explanation with animated interest. "And you showed her with your wand . . ."

"I think so."

"When I was little, I used to throw out my wands and carve new ones for my new skills. It was such folly. It turns out that perhaps broken things are stronger than we imagined. Look at Farrow—even she doubted herself because her powers were gone—but power always finds a way. It may just be different than you think. It may be better . . . ," Bari mused.

Before I could answer, South spoke. "I agree—all hail Farrow's new gift. But why was her gift needed? How did that woman end up on the floor in the first place? That spindle—what is it really for?"

"A spindle spins thread," Horatia deadpanned.

"But this one does something more, doesn't it? Why did you spell it?" South pressed.

The irony had not escaped me either. Horatia could spin a dress with a single thought, but here she was with a spindle that could render someone unconscious with a single prick of their finger.

Behind Horatia there was a shadow. It grew and grew into something bigger. It looked almost like a dragon. I blinked hard and the shadow returned to the shape of a girl. I must have imagined it, but had I?

Horatia gave me a knowing gaze. "We are so much more powerful now . . . ," she began.

"Horatia," Bari said, not gently, as if to warn her off from what she was saying.

"Because of this place. Because you practice on humans," South countered.

"Because we are free of all the old rules," Horatia carried on, ignoring Bari.

But Bari took a gentler, more effective tack. She focused on Hecate's ashes, which were still at my side. "The day of the Burning our servitude to the humans ended. Our unfortunate covenant with them burned in the fire along with your flesh. What happened to you, Hecate, should not have had to happen for us to be free of human rule. We are not there yet, but we are closer."

Horatia and Ocenth looked to Hecate and nodded, their faces full of sympathy. I felt it too. Despite my reservations about my sisters, seeing them bond with Hecate erased some of my doubts. They were still my sisters. Hecate's ashes returned to me and the pouch. But South was still on a single track.

"You still haven't explained the spindle," he said.

"It protects our Future. That's all you need to know," Bari countered firmly.

Everything my sisters were saying made sense. But something inside me was shifting, questioning. Something was unsettled, and I couldn't push it down as much as I wanted to.

"Farrow?" Horatia prompted. "Where did you go?"

"Sorry, I'm right here." I smiled wide and squeezed her shoulder, giving in to the part of myself that was just happy to see her and Bari in the same room with me after all these years. No matter that the room was a secret magic shop and not the Reverie. No matter that something had changed in all of us since we were girls together. Something sad and dark. But what mattered was that we were here.

A few seconds later Bari and South took my hands, and we landed back in South's barn.

"You have to know everything we do keeps us all safe. You will know everything in time. I promise," Bari said to both of us.

"Okay," I said, relenting.

"I'm famished. Are you coming?" Bari proffered, already heading for the door.

"In a minute," I said, catching a look from South. He had something he wasn't saying.

"Well, hurry. We had Cinderella pick apples from the Dark Wood for a tart," she added as she exited. As she left, I felt the gravity of her. Some part of me was still caught up in her wake.

"Cinderella!" I could hear Bari call a couple of seconds later, her voice full of impatience as she pushed open the door to the mansion.

"What?" I demanded from South, sensing his disapproval.

"You still look at her like you did when we were young."

"What's wrong with that?"

"You look at her like she's got all the power. But the truth is, growing up back then, you had more magic than she did. You just didn't know it yet."

"That's not true. She was already on her way to turning herself into a flock of birds."

"She can make birds that last a few hours, and you gave me wings that I have to this day."

I knew what he was getting at, but I resisted.

"It was a fluke. It's not a competition, South. We aren't kids anymore." What I said felt like a lie. At this moment, standing here with South, but knowing that Bari was waiting for me back in the house, took me back to the Entente of our youth.

"I was never competing. I just wanted to belong."

I felt my guilt punch me in the gut. I had been so focused on me and what I didn't have, I had not thought about what South had lost—Iolanta. We'd been broken in the same ways. We'd lost our mothers. We'd lived without magic, only to have it thrust upon us. But I had years of dealing with the loss of Hecate, and in some ways, I hadn't lost her at all. And South had discovered and lost his mother and found his magic in the same night.

"South . . . ," I began.

"No more guilt, Farrow."

I stifled it. "You said you were happy for us to all be back together."

"I am."

"Then what's the problem?" I pressed. "Do you see something in their Presents that scares you?"

"I don't see anything. That's the problem. Why are they all being so careful to block me?"

"Maybe because you spent more of your life as human than Entente?"

"Ouch," he said, pantomiming a wound to his heart.

"I didn't mean it like that, South."

"I know," he said.

But the look on his face told me that my words had hurt him all the same.

CHAPTER 47

I got halfway to my room before I turned to look back at the barn. Every step away from South felt like there was a bigger chasm opening up between us, and I couldn't bear it. South was . . . South . . .

I couldn't leave things the way they were. I retraced my steps, and when I reached the barn, South was waiting for me with open arms.

"South, I'm sorry. I didn't mean . . . ," I said as I ran into them. It was too hard to say the rest out loud, but I knew he could feel everything I was thinking. *Have you ever wanted something so much that you ignore everything that is wrong in hopes that enough time can make it right? Bari was right. You don't throw out a wand because you think you can get a better one. And you don't throw out one that was broken. I'm not ready to throw out my sisters—I just have to find a way to make them better. But you aren't wrong either. There is a chance that our sisters are very, very broken.*

"I know . . . I can't be mad at you either." South put his arms around me. I looked up at him. At his eyes, his lips.

I wondered what it would be like to kiss him again. Our first kiss had been a diversion for the guards. I wondered what it would be like to kiss him with intention. I wondered if I could forget about all the bad things in all the Queendoms for a few seconds. All the bad things in our own Entente. I pulled back, realizing what might make me feel better wasn't fair to South or his heart.

He leaned in and kissed me. His kiss was soft and sweet and something else. It was magical. When his lips met mine, I could feel what he felt for me. A heady rush of passion and understanding. He knew me because of our entwined histories, because of all the moments we'd shared. He knew my secrets and pain, my heart and soul, my flaws and strengths, and he loved me for all of it. He loved the selfish Entente who gave him wings, the vengeful magicless Couterie, and now the tortured half-magical girl who stood before him. Before we parted, I felt love all around us from hundreds of Presents—young love and old, chaste and passionate, and everything in between, from first blush to last, all at once. It was a kiss like no other. Intimate and part of everything all at once.

"Is that what you feel all the time?" I asked. The rush of emotion and Presents receded like water after a tide breaks and I was left on the shore, exhausted but tempted to run back in. I stopped myself. I put my hand against his chest. I could feel his heart beating faster, stronger, just for me.

"It's how I feel when I'm with you . . ."

Regret washed over me. I felt as if I had taken advantage of his feelings for my comfort.

"Don't . . . ," he said with a slow, sad smile. "I know your heart and I know it isn't in the same place as mine."

"Then why?" I asked.

"Because when I kissed you, there were only happy Presents. Because maybe I needed to forget everything for a minute too . . ."

But wasn't I one of the things that he wanted to forget? I wondered in my head.

"Don't you know, Farrow? You are the one thing in all the Queendoms that I want to remember," he said firmly before he walked away.

My fingers went to my lips where he'd kissed them. He had not erased the prince or the trouble we were in. But South had made his mark on me. I would never forget that kiss.

CHAPTER 48

The next morning, I took a walk to clear my head and test out my new power. But mostly to push away thoughts of South's kiss. Would that kiss be in the way of everything between us until Ever After, or could we go on as if it had never happened? Did I want it to be as if it had never happened?

Before I could answer myself, I heard someone thinking in the barn. The voice sounded gruffer and older than South.

I want to be myself again.

I want my life back.

As I got closer, I wondered if the sisters were keeping someone in the barn against their will. I shook it off; I was letting Cinderella's words get to me. I was far from in control of my new power yet. I was probably just hearing something from the next house over.

But the wish was closer and insistent. I could feel the wisher's longing through the door of the barn. It felt as real as South's heartbeat when I'd laid my hand on his chest.

I inhaled sharply and pushed the door open.

A relieved laugh escaped my lips as I took in the barn. South wasn't there. There was no one inside except a horse.

It was standing in the center of the barn.

"Easy, buddy," I said.

But the horse's nostrils flared, and I heard the wish again.

Please let me be me.

I studied the horse another beat. Its eyes were a shocking shade of blue that I had never seen on a horse before.

Please let me be me.

The wish repeated.

I looked at the horse's eyes again. They seemed almost... human.

Bari had boasted that I had no idea how far she had come with her magic. South had said that we were not alone in the barn. He had been talking to the animals. But what if they weren't animals?

"You're in there, aren't you?" I asked.

I took a step closer.

I thought I saw the edges of the horse blur for a second.

I thought about the mouse we'd seen in the barn. And the strange birds.

I thought about Bari.

What had she done?

The horse made a guttural sound and began to charge toward me. I turned to run, but as I did, the ashes from around my neck burst through the pouch and momentarily stunned the horse.

I lost my balance and fell facedown in the dirt.

"Thank you, Hecate," I blurted as I got to my knees.

But the horse wasn't done. It charged through the ashes, aiming right at me. I rolled over just in time, but the horse remained undaunted. It came at me again, rearing up on its hind legs and preparing to stampede.

"Fessie, no!" Cinderella's voice cried out—and the horse turned his head to look at her.

In all the commotion, I hadn't seen or heard her enter the barn.

"Fessie!" she yelled again, and he put his hooves down.

He neighed obediently, as if waiting for her to come to his side.

"Farrow is nice. Do not do that again," Cinderella said gently as she tiptoed next to the beast and cooed in his ear. "You okay?" she asked without looking at me.

I got to my feet. Behind her I could see my mother's ashes re-form into her silhouette. I shook my head at them, willing the ashes to dissipate, but Cinderella, oblivious, assumed the gesture was for her.

"Did he hurt you?"

"I'm okay," I said as I smoothed out my dress. My mother's ashes separated and floated up toward the ceiling.

Cinderella glanced behind her as if she had felt my mother's presence, but she didn't look up to where the ashes had formed a cloud. I breathed a sigh of relief. I could feel my heart rapping at my rib cage. I willed myself to calm down. I had narrowly missed a trampling and the discovery of my mother's ashes by a human all in just a few minutes.

"What is wrong with that horse?" I asked as she petted him gently.

"Fester's been like this since he showed up. He's a one-girl horse. He won't let anyone else ride him or get near him but me."

"Showed up?"

"He was grazing outside the house one day. No one came to claim him."

"When was it?" I asked again.

"I don't know. Sometime after the servants left. I remember being scared that Galatea wouldn't let me have him because there was no coachman anymore. I promised to take care of him myself. Why does it matter?"

"No matter. Just curious."

But it did matter. What I was thinking was too horrible to voice. It meant that my sisters had crossed a line I had never imagined.

I pulled out my wand.

"What are you doing, Farrow?" she asked.

The horse neighed nervously.

I thought about what had happened with the dishes. I thought about what Iolanta had said about my gift. What if I could replicate what I had done in the kitchen? What if . . . ?

"Tell him to concentrate on what he wants most in the world."

Cinderella spoke softly into Fessie's ear.

I want to be myself again, he wished.

I raised my wand and whispered:

Make him as he was before
The sisters darkened the barn door.

There was an interminable pause, and then I heard it—the cracking and repairing of bone. Then Fessie moaned in what sounded like enormous pain. Cinderella gasped.

The horse fell to the ground and began to convulse.

"What did you do to him?" she asked protectively.

"I think, I hope . . . I granted his wish," I said.

We watched as his hair disappeared, revealing pink skin, and his torso collapsed into itself and re-formed into a man's chest. His head was the last thing to transform, and for a few seconds it looked like a flesh-covered horse head on top of a man's body. A few more seconds ticked by and his visage finally changed. The nostrils shrank. The nose retracted and the sad blue eyes became more almond shaped. The large horse grin was gone and, in its stead, there were full human lips.

He reached for his own face, touching it as if to confirm that it was really there.

Finally he spoke and his first word was "Ella."

Cinderella put a blanket around the man. She sat down beside him, hugging him. "Hodder, it's you! You've been here the whole time?"

Over Hodder's shoulder, Cinderella mouthed, *Thank you.*

I felt a surge of warmth in my chest. I had reunited them. My magic was back, and I had accomplished something good with it.

Hodder turned around, his eyes full of suspicion, but his attention went back to Cinderella.

"What happened the day you disappeared?" I asked, wanting confirmation and not wanting it at the same time.

"One minute I was standing outside the barn. The next I was inside the stall like that . . . ," he said, shuddering, as if the memory of it all still hurt him.

"I am sorry this happened to you . . . ," I began.

"It was awful," he said. There was a slight neighing sound beneath his words.

"Can you remember . . . ? Was anyone around when you transformed? Do you know who did this to you?" Cinderella pressed, clearly thinking of Galatea and my sisters.

"I tried to leave. I got to the edge of the estate. But then *poof,* I was back here . . . Every time . . . *poof,*" he said, lost in thought.

"Fessie . . . Hodder . . . Did you see anyone before you *poofed*?"

"I never saw anyone, but I know who did this to me . . . Those witches . . ."

"Who?" I asked, wanting the answer to be something other than what I knew was coming.

"The wicked stepmother and her daughters."

Galatea, Amantha, and Bari . . . My stomach sank; his explanation made sense. And there wasn't another I could think of. Bari had done this.

He paused, his voice suddenly filled with suspicion. "Who are you?"

"Hodder's a little confused," Cinderella said. "He was our cook. I bet he misses the kitchen."

"I am Farrow," I offered.

"Farrow's going to stay with you while I get you some clothes and food."

He nodded, and Cinderella raced out of the barn. She squeezed my shoulder, in what I assumed was gratitude, as she passed.

As soon as she had gone, Hodder ran at full speed out of the barn and down the path, away from the house.

"Hodder, no . . . ," I protested. But after running a few steps after him, I realized I would only scare him further.

When Cinderella returned with a plate of food and water, she was incredulous to find Hodder missing. "What happened to him? Did you turn him back into a horse?"

"He ran off," I explained.

"Because he was afraid of you. You are Entente."

"I am Entente, but up until a few days ago I didn't have any magic. That part was true."

She turned for the door.

"Where are you going?" I asked.

"To look for Hodder," she said. "Are you coming?"

I felt some part of me lift as I got up to join her. I had resisted befriending humans since the day of the Burning. So why did it matter so much to me that Cinderella trust me? Perhaps all the years living among them had worn me down. Perhaps seeing Tork's and the prince's kindness had shifted something in me. Or perhaps seeing my sisters' misuse of her and now this poor man made me want to do something to counter it. I couldn't pinpoint it. But it almost felt as if, for the first time, my sisters were on the wrong side of Fate and I had to do something to tip the scales back in the right direction.

We spent the next few hours looking for the man in the blanket but came up empty.

"He'll come back," I said finally.

"How can we know that?"

"I think the spell my family cast keeps all of you from leaving. He said that he tried to leave but he ended up back in the barn. I think it's the same for him now. He'll be back by morning."

She sat down on a nearby rock, exhausted.

"I'm sorry that my family did this to yours."

"I can see that, but that doesn't really help me or Hodder, does it?"

"No, it doesn't."

CHAPTER 49

In the morning, I came down to the kitchen to find Cinderella petting Fessie through the window. Hodder was back in his horse form.

"What happened to you?" I asked in a whisper.

Fessie neighed, and I could hear his human thoughts again.

I wish your spell had worked. I only got as far as the edge of the Dark Wood before I changed back into this monstrosity.

"Moonrise. It expired at moonrise," I said, realizing.

"Then cast it again," Cinderella demanded, clearly feeling for him.

I wanted to. I could see the anguish in his eyes at being stuck inside this horse body.

"I can, but . . . I'm so sorry, Fessie. My magic isn't as strong as theirs. I can give you only a few hours."

His eyes narrowed on me, seemingly unconvinced of my intention to help. He pawed the ground angrily.

I wish I could believe you.

Cinderella petted him on the head reflexively and cooed at him reassuringly. "I promise you that Farrow only has the best of intentions for all of us. She's a friend to humans."

I stopped in my tracks at Cinderella calling me a friend. My eyes met hers.

"Well, she's a friend to me. We can trust her," she added with a small smile.

Fessie nodded.

"You'll have to hide, but I promise I can give you some time each day as you until I can make it right permanently. Okay?"

Cinderella stepped in my way. "What are you going to do? You can't confront them. You don't know what they'll do to any of us," she said. Her voice was certain, and fear filled her eyes.

"I promise, I'll find a way," I said.

I meant the promise, but I had no idea how to keep it. My sisters were stronger than I was. And they were not restricted by wishes. But even as my head scrambled for a way to make good on the promise I just made, I felt a sense of vertigo, as if my very center had been knocked off its axis. My sisters had done a thing for which I could not make any excuse. My loyalty to the Entente, which I thought was unwavering, was now on shaky ground and I felt untethered from all that I had long believed.

The former cook sat disoriented for a full half hour before he spoke.

His voice still cracked and half neighed. I wondered aloud if Hodder had been cognizant of who he was in horse form, and sadly the answer was yes.

"It was a nightmare. One from which I could not wake. The stables. The filth. The hay . . ." He spit on the floor when he said the last, as if he were still tasting it. He then looked to the ground in shock. "I apologize. My manners are not quite back yet."

Cinderella patted him on the back. "You should not be the one to apologize," she said pointedly.

"She's right. You didn't cause this."

Hodder took a long look at me and squinted as if he were trying to figure me out. "I'm not the only one. What about the rest of us?" he asked.

"Us?" I asked.

He looked around at the birds on the rafters, the mouse in the hay corner, and the squirrel in the doorway. "The other servants."

I felt my stomach sink.

I remembered what Cinderella had said about the servants sneaking off in the night. But they had never left. And I remembered, too, when South had been so very certain there were other Presents in the barn. There were. South would feel terrible when he found out that he had not been able to discern the plight of the servants who were right under his barn roof. Whatever spell my sisters had cast around them had somehow mostly blocked them from him. He'd been able to hear whispers from the servants but nothing more. And in his confused state, he had not understood that the animals that shared the barn with him had been touched by magic.

"There was a full staff—a cook, a maid, a butler, and two footmen. They all disappeared before me. But I know now they are all still here," Hodder revealed with a still-shaky voice.

"I can help them," I offered. I pulled my wand out of my pocket.

Cinderella collected a mouse, a red bird, and a squirrel and deposited the animals into the center of the barn.

I listened to their wishes and made them come true.

Renell, the mouse, had been a footman before his transformation. He was not much older than Cinderella and me. Jacques, the butler turned red bird, was older and had a shock of red hair. Wendell, the stableman turned squirrel, was short, round, and bald.

Jacques sniffed the air with a twitching nose while Cinderella explained to them what had happened.

All the "animals" were thrilled to be human again and surprisingly willing to believe Cinderella because her kindness knew no bounds in whatever form they were in. I wasn't sure I would feel as accommodating if I'd spent so much time as a bird. But their loyalty to her was a testament to her kind heart.

This was a good start. But I wanted to test my power away from my sisters. I needed to be around people and their wishes. And even as my power had increased by the hour, it seemed to have limits. There wasn't a soul within range of my power whose wishes I hadn't already read.

The carriage and horses were very much not available, and a shortcut would be extremely helpful. If I could get to town with a new face, then I would see what exactly my magic and I were capable of. And for that, I needed a wish. I could have asked South. But after our last encounter, I could not bring myself to approach him.

"I'm asking you to trust me, Cinderella," I said when we were walking back to the house from the barn.

"You have no right to ask that," she said automatically, with a pointed look at Hodder.

"I know, but I need to figure out what I can do. Do you understand?"

"I will help you, but only because you helped the staff," she said out loud.

"I need you to wish for me to look like someone else. Someplace else. And I need you to wish me back by sunrise."

"What do you mean?" she asked.

I explained how my magic worked. And how it didn't.

Cinderella took it in, blinking hard. "So, when I wished the kitchen to be clean, you could hear it. And when you heard Fessie's wish to be human again . . ."

"I granted it. But I can't make anything happen for myself."

"The irony. An Entente who can't use magic for herself," she assessed.

I nodded.

"Any chance your sisters could catch the same malady?" she said lightly.

"It seems I am one of a kind."

"So what do I have to do?" she asked after a pause. I felt a rush of relief that she had agreed so readily, given all that my sisters had put her through.

"Imagine a face that isn't your own. And then imagine you want it to be mine."

She closed her eyes.

I could see what she was seeing. The face was beautiful and somehow familiar. Young, but older than we were, with a big smile and wide-set green eyes. Brown ringlets surrounded the pretty face. The eyes twinkled with kind mischief.

I tapped my wand to her temple and then to my own. I felt my face contort, and I walked over to the mirror just as the hair on my head transformed into the ringlets from my vision. I was the mirror image of what I had seen in Cinderella's mind.

"Who is she?" I asked.

Cinderella began to tear up.

"Relax, Cinderella. It's just magic," I said, but I knew it was more than that, judging by her emotional reaction.

"No, it's the face. I didn't mean to think of her. But I guess she's always the first person I see."

"Who?"

"It's my mother when she was young . . ." Cinderella trailed off.

Why would she give me her mother's face? I wondered.

"I guess some part of me just wanted . . . wanted to see her again," she explained, her voice breaking. Her love for her mother was so palpable, it struck a chord inside me.

"Oh, Cinderella, we can change it. Just think of someone else," I volunteered quickly. I still had Hecate's ashes. Cinderella didn't even have that.

"No, it's the perfect disguise. My mother did not leave the estate much. She was very private. No one will recognize you."

"Thank you, Cinderella," I said.

She sniffled and straightened up. "Where do you want to go?"

"To town and back," I said, glancing at the clock. I needed to return before the sisters.

"Be careful, Farrow," Cinderella said as the new image formed in Cinderella's brain just as I blinked away to it.

It took me a few seconds to recognize the neighborhood. I'd been here before. I was next to a meetinghouse near the Couterie.

I let out a relieved sigh. I wasn't sure if any of my spells would actually work. But it was time to find out.

CHAPTER 50

To my great surprise, my face—my real face—was staring back at me from the door of a tavern. It was a drawing, but the features were unmistakably mine. Beneath it in script there was the word *WANTED.*

And beneath that was another solicitation with a likeness of South and the same offer of a reward. *DEAD OR ALIVE!* Among a plethora of drawings of thieves, South and I stood out on notices for *treason.*

I cursed under my breath and heard a low whistle that I recognized immediately.

"Man, would I love to get my hands on one of those . . ."

"Pardon me?" I said, but I knew the voice before I turned around.

I almost cursed again. Wasn't there enough danger already? Did I really have to invite it in? Did I really have to walk right up and stand beside it?

I turned slowly and faced Tork. He was dressed even finer than usual, but he was the worse for wear. There were circles under his eyes, and his brownish-blond hair seemed lackluster. His handsome face wore an uncustomary frown. Obviously, after my attempt on the Queen, Linea and the rest of the Couterie would be livid, but somehow I had not imagined that would include Tork. Perhaps there was some other reason for his unhappy face.

He shot me one of his dimpled smiles the second he saw that I was looking at him.

"If I could nab one of those criminals, all my problems would be solved."

"You don't look like you are wanting for many comforts," I quipped back.

He raised one of his eyebrows, scrutinizing me for a beat.

"You'd be surprised," he said with a wink.

I wish enough drink to forget. But there isn't enough in all the Hinter, he thought.

Tork held the door for me and, after I walked through, he followed me inside. I considered making a hasty exit. I was supposed to be testing my power, but it was too dangerous to do it on someone I knew. Still, I couldn't help myself. I wanted to know what was wrong with Tork. As we made our way farther into the bar, I could hear the wishes of the other patrons, which seemed to be louder than even his own.

I wish to sleep.

I wish to leave.

I wish I had more money.

I wish to work.

I closed my eyes. I had to resist granting the small wishes to quiet them in my head. Because if I did so, I could be discovered.

"Hey, are you all right?" Tork asked gently.

"I'm fine," I said as I opened my eyes and refocused on Tork.

I realized that my curiosity had led me into another mistake. Perhaps there were too many people and too many wants. I spotted a corner table and made a beeline for it. There, I could listen to Tork's thoughts while I pretended to dine. Cinderella had given me a few of her precious coins from her stash back at the manse. I felt guilty using them, but it would have looked strange if I had only gotten a glass of water at a tavern. To my surprise, Tork sat across from me. He looked around for the waiter with a hint of desperation, which he never would have displayed back at the Couterie.

I wish I could stop thinking about her.

"My manners! Do you mind if I sit . . . ?" he began.

I knew what—or rather, who—he was thinking about. Lavendra. Always Lavendra. I felt a wave of guilt for my part in his plight. I remembered I wasn't wearing my own face. My apology would not only be confusing; it could be dangerous as well. I nodded.

"I hate eating alone," he said.

"So really, what would you use it for?" I asked, circling back to our initial conversation.

"What, the reward?" He laughed. "I was just jesting. I'm Couterie. I have everything, but one can never have enough of the finer things," he retorted lightly.

I could still hear his heart above the din of all the other wants.

Money can't solve what I did, but maybe it could take me to where she is. I want to know where she is. I want to go to where she is. I want to find her. I want to turn back the clock. I want to do it all differently. I want the moment back. The moment where I screwed it all up.

As my head filled with his wishes, I closed my eyes and grabbed the wand that was in my pocket. I held it tightly and whispered an incantation beneath my breath.

I could hear Tork reacting. "Mademoiselle, are you okay?"

But I continued.

Now that my magic has come to light,
Help me put this right.
Let me find what he's lost and put true love back on course.

The image of Lavendra filled my vision, and at the exact same moment I knew where she was and everything that Tork had wanted to know. I opened my eyes and spoke to him.

"What if I told you that she made it to the Thirteenth Queendom? She's working as a nanny in a manor. The family's name is Lemarc. And no, she has not found another love."

Tork looked at me with surprise, but he quickly chased it with suspicion.

"What do you mean? What are you talking about?"

"Lavendra. I'm telling you where she is. How she is."

He gasped. "How did you know I wanted to see her? Who are you? What are you?" he demanded.

I could see his eyes narrow and his lips purse.

"I'm a witch, but one you can trust."

"Entente?" he whispered.

I respected that he would never use the word "witch," even though I just had.

I took Tork in. In some ways he was my first and only human friend. He'd shared his deepest secret with me. He'd tried to help me with the prince. And how had I repaid him? I'd endangered the Couterie and his station. I'd never shared my real truth with him. Sitting before him now, I felt like I needed to tell him. And knowing him as I hoped I did, I decided it was time.

"One that you know. It's me, Farrow," I whispered.

"This is a test, a trick . . . Did Madame Linea put you up to this?" he said accusingly.

"No one. I'm risking everything telling you this in public," I countered in a whisper.

"I will not be ridiculed!" Tork began to stand up.

The woman behind the bar looked at him sharply. Some of the other patrons began to turn toward us too. I had to make him stop.

" 'I would forgo today if we could have forever.' " I repeated the line that he had composed to Lavendra when he wanted to ask her to be Shadows together.

His eyes widened in recognition.

"We don't want trouble here, sir," the bartender said from behind the bar.

"Neither do I. My friend and I were just remembering old times," Tork said, and he sat back down.

"Apparently, we have a lot to catch up on," he added. "How did you do this? No paint can do that. It's really you, isn't it? But how? There's no such thing as Entente anymore . . ."

"Rumors of our demise were apparently greatly exaggerated . . . I am sorry I couldn't tell you—but my secret was life and death."

He shook his head like he always did when he was processing something.

"I'm risking everything to tell you this, Tork. One scream from you and my life is over."

"I still could scream. You lied to me for years . . . about who you were . . . and then for months about what you planned."

"But you won't, because you are a lot of things, Tork, but cruel isn't one of them," I whispered.

"A lot has happened, Farrow . . . How do you know that I haven't changed?"

"Because 'there isn't enough time in all the Queendoms to change the heart,'" I said, using his words against him again.

"Why now? Why not tell me when you were at the Couterie? I shared everything with you."

"I wanted to. But I was scared of being found out."

"And now? Why now? Why here? You escaped the Queen. They're saying you tried to kill her . . . I didn't want to believe that was true . . . But you are wearing someone else's face. That's magic. You have magic . . . Tell me what's true . . ."

"You're right I have magic—and the rest is a much longer story."

"I have time. I'm all ears."

"She took someone from me . . . my . . . mother. And everything I've done from the second she died was to punish her for that."

Tork's stern face melted a little. He and his twin brother had lost their mother in childbirth. The idea of the Queen taking mine seemingly struck a chord in him.

"You could have told me. I have no love lost for the Queen. Who knows? I could have helped you . . ."

"I couldn't ask you. I couldn't risk you . . . Tork, I should have left today when I saw you without you ever recognizing me. But when I saw you, I knew I couldn't stay in the shadows forever. I owed you that. I owed both you and Lavendra."

A crease formed in the center of his forehead.

"Lavendra? What are you talking about?"

"You and Lavendra deserve your Ever After. Especially since I'm the one who altered your Fate. If you want to scream now, go ahead and scream. I'll understand, but please let me show you something first."

"Why should I? Considering what you are . . ."

"What I am is your friend."

Even though we were in public, even though it was risky, I slipped my wand into my hand and covered it with my sleeve. I reached for him and tapped the wand against his cheek. To outsiders, it would hopefully look like an intimate moment, not a magical one.

Tork began to protest, but after a few seconds, I could see a vision of what he wanted most: Lavendra. And then I concentrated on her. What did she want most? What did she desire?

I tapped the wand against his temple like I had seen Hecate do to Magrit years ago. And like I had done to Sandrine. I wasn't sure if it would work at a distance, after failing to reach any wishes past the vicinity of the Grays' manor. But now I had Tork's wish to hopefully traverse the distance.

"Lavendra?" he whispered.

He could see her. He was sharing my vision. When I opened my eyes, Tork's cheeks had found some color. It was as if the sight of her had brought him back to life.

"Thank you for showing me that she's okay, even though you are only doing it to assuage your own guilt. You really are Entente. That's what you do, right? Mess with people's fates without their permission," he accused.

"I'm doing it so you can take Fate into your own hands. I can see what I've always seen even without magic. Your deepest desire is to be with Lavendra. And it's hers as well. To this day."

I saw his expression shift to disbelief mingled with hope. "It can't be. She couldn't really return my feelings . . ."

I put the wand up again. In the next vision, the image changed. Tork crossed the room to join Lavendra in the sitting room at the manor. She looked up, surprised. And then she smiled.

I removed the wand. "That's Lavendra's wish, not yours."

"I don't want to see any more," he said a little too loudly, finally seeing that his love was requited after all.

All the eyes in the room turned our way again. I slid my wand into my sleeve, but the murmur of voices and the continued stolen glances made me wonder if I had been seen.

"I have to go."

Tork stood with me protectively. "You're right."

"I am?" I said, blinking hard, surprised at the ease with which he accepted me with a different face and my meddling in his life.

"The thing is, it didn't matter what you did. We would have ended up in the same place anyway. Apart. And not because of you. Because of me. Because I wasn't even brave enough to tell her how I really felt about her . . . You know me, Farrow. This is who I am. I would have broken both our hearts eventually without your interference. I couldn't have run away. I couldn't have lived without all this."

"It's not who you have to be. Tork, if a little girl can go from witch to Shadow to Couterie and back again, you can cross Queendoms to be the man I know you want to be," I declared.

I kissed him on the cheek, hoping that my words hit their mark.

He shook his head again. "I wish I had the strength, Farrow . . ."

I was tempted to grant his wish, to give their love the engine it needed with a wave of my wand. But I did not. I had meddled enough. The next step, if he ever took it, had to be entirely up to him.

"You should go, Farrow. There's an exit in the back," he said with sudden urgency, which he chased with a mischievous smile.

A smile I had missed. He was the first human I'd willingly told my secret to.

As I made it through the crowd, I felt all the eyes in the room turn toward the guard standing in the doorway.

It's nothing, I thought, willing it to be so.

I mouthed a thank-you and began making my way to the rear of the room.

When I looked back, I saw Tork raise his glass.

"Another round, on me . . . Or rather, on Queen Papillion!" he announced.

A cheer went up and all eyes went in his direction.

I slipped through the back room of the pub, past a barback who was busy cleaning glasses. I spotted the exit and opened the door. I pulled my hood tighter around my face and went out into the cold air. I breathed a sigh of relief and then pulled out my wand and whispered:

Return me from whence I came,
Honor the wish in Cinderella's name . . .

I waited.

But nothing happened. I was still standing in the exact same place, only voices and footsteps and wishes were growing louder.

The first soldier turned the corner and pointed at me.

"Halt there, witch!" the guard said.

I froze. Back in the tavern, somehow they knew it was magic. Somehow they knew the magic was from me. I thought I'd been careful. But someone must have seen. I had no choice. I had to run.

I ran as fast as I could, but I could feel the soldiers gaining on me. When I rounded the next corner, I saw a boy in a hood leaning against a building with a rucksack looped around him. He noticed the soldiers and offered his hand.

"Come with me," he said.

I took his hand and followed him as he began zigging and zagging through the network of streets. I found myself in a neighborhood that I rarely frequented on my walks from the Couterie. This part of Vessie, the Hinter's capital city, was in disrepair. Paint was peeling. Steps were broken. There was no Black Glass in sight. The Queen had clearly not gotten to rebuilding this part of town yet.

"I think we're safe now. I think we can slow down," I said to my hooded companion.

"That guard is relentless," the stranger countered, and pulled me along for another couple of streets before we ducked inside an alleyway—that turned out to be a dead end.

I suddenly wondered if I had miscalculated. Had I left one danger for another? I did not know my savior. Perhaps he wasn't one.

"In here," he said, pointing to a hidden door.

I hesitated. "I can make my own way from here, kind sir," I said with a bow.

But the sound of boots on the ground came from the next street over.

"On second thought," I said.

He gave me a coy smile and extended a hand to help me inside. I ignored it and instantly regretted it as I felt myself falling rear first in the dark. I landed with a thump on the ground. A few seconds later the boy landed beside me.

"Are you all right?" he asked, helping me to my feet.

As he fumbled in the dark, I could hear him cursing under his breath and I could hear what he wanted most: light, and for them not to find us.

I made a decision. I didn't know if I could grant a wish that affected multiple people, so wishing they wouldn't find us didn't seem feasible. But the other wish . . . He already knew I was running from the guards, so I extended my wand and granted his wish for light. The wand lit up and cast light around the room. The boy laughed in wonder and removed his hood.

It was Mather. Prince Mather had saved me.

It took me a second to remember that he wasn't looking at my face. He was looking at the one I had made this morning: Cinderella's mother's.

"Yes," I said finally as I heard the footsteps pick up behind me.

He led me down one hallway and then another. And finally we ducked into a dark room.

"Don't be nervous," he said. "We're safe now." He released my hand and gave me the strangest look, bordering on recognition.

I knew I must be imagining it.

"What is this place?"

"My mother thinks the secret to saving her throne is here," he said, not really answering my question. He was too busy staring at me.

"You really are one of them?" he asked. "I wasn't sure, but when I saw the wand and the guards . . ."

"You saw the wand? And you still helped me."

"She has killed so many innocents. I try to help where I can."

"But I am not innocent to you. I have magic."

"You misunderstand me. You are just as innocent."

I've scared her. She wants to go. I pray I can keep her safe. I don't want what happened to the others to happen to her.

I could hear his heart. He was telling the truth.

"They'll go house to house. But Mother insists on a late-night briefing at midnight. We should wait till then," he said firmly.

I could have him wish me home. But then I would be telling him where my sisters were. Then he could find me again.

Suddenly, the prospect of another moment with Mather began to feel untenable. I wanted to be with him and I wanted to be away from him all at once. I was uncomfortable feeling so much of something other than rage and vengeance, but my heart seemed not to know that. It was beating double time.

I pushed the thought aside. It was one night. And I had been trying to kill him. Everything had been heightened and was still heightened now. I recalled the Ana and what it said about his escaping the palace. Was this where he went when he left? My fingers went to Hecate's pouch for assurance. What were the chances that I would see Tork and the prince in a matter of hours? I had given up on Fate the day I'd lost Hecate. But everything that had happened since the night of the Becoming . . . finding South, Iolanta, my sisters . . . getting this new, strange power. I wondered if perhaps Fate had not given up on me.

"What is this place?" I asked again, taking in the acrid smell as we walked into another cavernous room.

"It's where she makes it," he said matter-of-factly.

"What?"

"The Black Glass," he said, and as he did, I took in what it was—a Black Glass factory. There was a huge vat of black sand that extended all the way up to the ceiling—it funneled down like the top of an hourglass into a long chute. The chute led into another vat, but this one was sitting on top of a flame. Red-hot glass poured out of the vat to another long chute. This one had holes in it that poured into molds. The molds were shaped into bricks.

"She thinks if she covers the whole Queendom with it, she'll be safe. This is a new recipe, a version she says will help her hunt Entente."

I gasped and stepped back from the glass. I couldn't let the prince see what I saw: my real reflection in the Black Glass.

He suddenly realized what he'd done.

"It didn't hurt you, did it?" He put a hand on my shoulder, looking at me, concerned.

"No, I am not affected at all," I murmured. But I was affected by Mather's hand on my arm. I felt my heart double its pace again.

I looked away from his intense stare.

"Good. I wouldn't want anything to happen to you," he whispered. "Also, I don't think it really works. She's just using it as an excuse to burn girls and scare the people into submission."

"How's that?"

"Depends on the day. She has a Witch Finder, a gruesome hooded truth tester. People say he filled a girl's pockets with Black Glass and sent her into the river. If she floated up, she was a witch. If she stayed down, she'd passed the test. The girl passed the test, but by the time the guards got to her, she had already drowned."

"It would be clever if it weren't maniacal," I said, remembering the Challenge between me and Lavendra. She did not kill either Lavendra or me, but then, like now, the Queen enjoyed playing with life and death.

Suddenly one of the vats in the corner began to tip over and liquid glass poured down a chute toward another vat. My head began to hurt from the fumes. The pain was piercing and left me breathless for a couple of seconds.

"What is that?"

"Don't worry, no one's here. When the vat fills, it turns over automatically."

I took a step backward, needing to put distance between myself and the acrid, dangerous glass. I turned from the prince. I could feel my face, my real face, return and then be replaced by the disguise again. It was too soon for the spell to fade; it must be the Black Glass.

"Hey, are you okay?" he asked.

I felt better once I'd walked a few paces away from the heat of the glowing glass.

"Miss?" he asked again.

"I'm fine," I said, remembering him. I knocked something over. It was the prince's bag, which he'd slung over his shoulder when we'd run.

"Just leave it," he said quickly.

I moved to pick it up, and the prince whispered in protest, "No, don't."

But it was too late. A bottle dropped out and onto the floor, crashing into pieces. I was surprised by the smell of accelerant.

I tried to make sense of why the prince would have it. Was he going to set something on fire?

"What are you doing here, Your Highness? How did you know about this place really?"

"My mother plans on using this glass to continue her pursuit of the Entente. Until tonight, I thought you were gone."

"Then why do this? You were going to burn this place to the ground? You were going to risk your life for the Entente?" I asked, but I already knew the answer.

I wish I could kill my mother. But I can't, so I have to stop her. I can't let her kill another soul. Entente or human.

"A lot of girls have died in the name of the Entente. In the name of her war on magic. I can't stop her until I can sit on the throne myself. But I can slow her down. I thought about running away, but a friend told me to fight," he admitted.

"A friend?"

"I don't know what she was really. She's gone. But what she said stayed with me. I can't sit by anymore, and I can't run away." He ran his hand through his hair as he said this. There was a faraway look in his eyes as if a part of him was in that moment. And it was. I could still hear what he was thinking about his Couterie. About me.

I wish I could see her again. I wish I could talk to her. I wish I could ask her what really happened that night. I wish she had not run away.

"So when you saved me today, I ruined your plans?"

"Helping you today makes me know that maybe what I'm doing isn't in vain," he said with fresh certainty.

He had no idea it was me, Farrow, who he was saving, but I felt my cheeks warm all the same. And I felt my heart pick up its pace yet again.

It wasn't supposed to matter. But I cared that the night had meant something to him. And that *I* mattered to him. We never Became. But it seemed we were both changed by the hours we'd spent alone together.

"No need to be nervous. We're safe here . . . ," he said, a quizzical smile on his face.

Suddenly whatever he was thinking was drowned out by a soldier's thoughts a few blocks away.

I wish I could find her. Where did she go? We can't go back empty-handed.

"I'm not nervous," I said.

"Tell that to your fingers," Mather said, still smiling.

I looked down. I was tapping my fingers against my wand. I stopped.

"Well, I guess I'm a little nervous," I admitted.

"But that's not all you are," he said.

"Pardon?" I said.

Before I could concentrate and look inside his wishes, they were drowned out by the sound of the soldiers changing course. They were coming nearer. I put my finger to my lips, and Mather silently steered me out of the way of the windows. He pressed me against the wall just in time, as the guard came into view through the panes of glass.

I wish we could find her already so we could get back to the palace. I wish we were anywhere but here. I wish I was eating. I wish I was with my wife. I wish all witches would die.

I gasped at the last. I knew that some humans hated us, but it was different hearing it, feeling it, directly from their hearts.

The prince looked at me, concerned, and put a finger in front of his lips to remind me to be quiet. I could feel how concerned he was for me, and I marveled at how much he was risking for a stranger—and a witch.

I had made the right choice in choosing not to kill him. He would be a good king.

"I think we have to stay till midnight," he whispered. He was close enough for me to feel the warmth of his breath.

My sisters would be worried. And they would be suspicious. What if they came looking for me? Worse than that, what if Galatea looked in my immediate Past and saw the prince with me?

I had spared him. Had I now, just by being here, put him back in harm's way?

"She won't hurt me," he said boldly.

I realized then that he was worried about me. Not himself.

This was a new Mather. He had been teetering on the edge of action for years, but after our night together he had begun putting his principles in motion. Looking at his profile, feeling the warmth of his arm against mine, I wondered what another night would mean to him and to me, even though he didn't know who I really was.

"You know, our throne wasn't always tyranny," Mather said. "My grandmother Meena wasn't like that. At least, I don't think she was. I don't know if I really remember her that way or if it's something I just made up."

"What?"

"Her kindness."

"I never met her, but she was always a friend to the Entente. My sisters spoke so highly of her."

He seemed heartened by this, and he continued. "I picked the room I have at the palace for a reason."

To get away from your maniacal mother, I thought.

"It has a secret passageway."

"You had it built?" I wondered.

"My grandmother did. She used to sneak out at night and mingle with the people."

"Wasn't she recognized?"

"She wore a disguise. She took me with her sometimes. I thought it was a game at first. But she told me that it was more. It was a duty. 'We do not rule. We help. These are our people,' she'd say.

"When I started sneaking out, I didn't do what she did. I just wanted to enjoy a night or two without anyone knowing who I was."

"So, what changed? When did you start doing this?"

"I'm ashamed I didn't do it sooner. When I saw the people, I saw their freedom, which I envied. I didn't see the rest. How many people were hurting. How many people were afraid. And all because of the Crown. All because of my mother."

"Did your mother ever go with Meena to see the people?"

"My grandmother said Mother came sometimes, but her heart wasn't in it."

"Was she always like this?" I asked, surprising myself by the question. I didn't want to hear an excuse for how Magrit was the way she was. Knowing would not bring Hecate back. But I paused; maybe knowing her better might tell me how to kill her.

Just as he opened his mouth to say something, light began to pour in through the windows. We could hear the guards getting closer again.

"Whatever happens, stay behind me. I'll handle it."

I could hear his wish. He was wishing me safe.

If I granted it, I perhaps could be home in seconds. But at the same time, I would be revealing the secrets of my magic. It was enough that he knew I was Entente.

"They're heading back toward the palace. This is our window to escape. I'll get them to go. You stay here," he whispered, his lips accidentally grazing my ear.

The sensation sent an involuntary shiver down my spine.

"Thank you," I whispered back, meaning it. It was nonsensical, but I didn't like watching him leave.

A few minutes later, I began the long way home. I had to walk. There was no wish to take me.

CHAPTER 51

All the way home, my head was full of the prince. When I got to the front door of Cinderella's house, I looked behind me. I could see smoke rising from town, and then there was an explosion of fire crystals in the sky over the factory. The prince had made his point.

My heart beat faster in my chest. I told myself it was the effect of the explosion, not the prince. My heart was the most honest part of me.

I realized that I had worried in vain. The house was dark, and no one was stirring. My sisters were still asleep in their beds, no doubt waiting for Cinderella to wake them with breakfast. South snored softly in the barn. I wasn't sure if his sleep was real or had been induced by Galatea. I hoped it was the former.

When I got back to my room, I was surprised to hear the telltale rustling in the chimney, which could only mean one thing.

"Cinderella?" I whispered as she tumbled into the room, covered in ash.

It appeared we had both been out late.

"You know, you really should wish for me to clean the chimney," I suggested, reaching for my wand.

"Did it . . . are you okay?" she whispered.

I couldn't keep everything in. I let the whole story out of me. Every moment I had spent with the prince. His noble attempts to destroy all the Black Glass. And in doing so, I realized something.

I remembered how my disguise shifted away for a few seconds when I was close to the hot glass in the factory. I recalled in vivid horror the moment that Iolanta was struck by the arrow the day of the Becoming. She'd put up a fight and pushed the Black Fire through the hallway. The arrow must have gone through that fire. When the Black Glass was hot, it was deadly. Otherwise Iolanta would have done what she and the other Soeurs had done before: heal herself.

"That's it! Of course that's it. The Black Glass was hot. That's when it affects us," I whispered. The discovery had come too late for Iolanta. If only I had figured it out sooner. Perhaps my sisters could have reversed the damage with a different spell. If only, if only, if only . . .

"What on earth are you talking about?" Cinderella asked.

"Nothing! Never mind. It doesn't matter." But it did. How had the Queen figured out the secret of the Black Glass? Had Fate suddenly chosen her side over the Entente's? Or did she not even know what she had?

The morning light shifted into my window, illuminating Cinderella's face. There were tears running down her ash-covered cheeks.

I realized I had been insensitive. I should never have worn her mother's face, no matter what she said.

"Is it the face? I am so sorry; I shouldn't have borrowed it," I began.

"It's not the face."

"Then what? I can see that you're upset. What happened?" Had her friends gone on a looting spree again?

"The guards took my friend Maggie."

"For stealing?" I assumed. I was in no position to admonish her for the company she kept. She was clearly lonely.

"For being a witch. I have to do something. They think that she's Entente. I've known her my whole life. She's not the least bit magical."

"I'm sorry," I said again, and I meant it.

"What if they burn her or drown her? I have to do something. When we saw the guards coming, we ran. We all ran. But we realized too late that they'd snatched Maggie up."

"Did you see him?"

"Who?"

"The Witch Finder."

"All the soldiers looked the same. If he or she was there, there was no way of knowing.

I cursed the Witch Finder under my breath. Cinderella continued, defending her need to act.

"You don't understand how urgent this is. The guards took my friend Rebecca a few years ago. She found her way back to us. But she hasn't been the same since. That—or worse—can't happen to Maggie. I know one of the dungeon guards . . . I think he can get me in . . . I just have to figure a way out . . ."

"Wish it so. Just like you wished me to town. Wish her here," I offered with a confidence I did not entirely feel. Her eyes widened with hope.

She closed her eyes, *Please bring Maggie back to me.*

I closed my eyes too. I concentrated as hard as I could, but I did not see the girl. I could not find her. I could not bring her home.

I opened them.

"I am sorry, Cinderella."

"You tried. Now it's my turn."

I was surprised. Cinderella was human. But she was willing to risk herself for someone else. Did she really think that she was going to storm the palace? *One girl, all alone,* I thought. But wasn't that what I was going to do before I got reunited with the Entente? Who was I to dissuade her? Still, patience had served me well. Perhaps it would do the same for Cinderella.

"Haste is not your friend. Give it today." I thought about what the prince had told me about the girl the Queen had drowned. "The Queen believes that no death goes forth without gain."

"What do you mean?" Cinderella asked.

"Magrit wants a show. That way, she gets more out of it. She gets the fear out of everyone who sees it. Or she gets the fear out of all of you. I think your friend will be home by dinner."

I would somehow make it so.

Cinderella rocked back on her heels, absorbing my advice.

"Give it today," I repeated.

"Cinderella. Promise me. I'll keep you safe. If they don't let her out by tomorrow morning, I'll help you myself. You have a full day of chores. Galatea won't notice that you're gone at night, but she certainly will notice if her eggs aren't perfectly herbed in a few minutes."

"I don't care about her eggs. I care about Maggie."

"Just one day," I persisted.

"What if she dies today?"

"I promise you she won't."

"Don't make promises you can't keep," Cinderella said.

"I never do."

"Ella!" Galatea squawked from down the hall.

Cinderella moved for the door.

"Wait," I said. "Wish yourself clean," I ordered gently.

I tapped my wand on the hem of her soot-covered dress and Cinderella was perfection again. She tottered off.

I slipped out of the room and made a beeline for the barn and South. A plan that involved today, despite what I'd told Cinderella, bloomed in my mind. But seeing him, I realized we hadn't seen each other since the kiss and so much had happened since then—the animals, the prince, and now this . . .

South looked up, not at all surprised when I entered. He was already pulling on his jacket. He knew I needed his help.

"South . . ."

"I was just about to come and tell you about the Reverie. I went last night to see if Iolanta's walls had any more clues about the Rooks . . ."

"And did they?"

"It can wait. Those girls can't."

I nodded and reached for his hand, ready to travel.

My plan had to work. Our Fates depended on it.

CHAPTER 52

We used South's power of the Present to locate Maggie, and his wish brought us to an alleyway near the square. South tapped my face with his wand and then his own. He tapped my dress, and it became a soldier's uniform.

The Queen had upgraded the theater, and there was an audience. Three girls stood in front of three tanks of water. It was just as the prince had described it, only that much worse. She had made trying witches into a performance for the people's enjoyment and terror.

Maybe this was a mistake, I thought. It was so public. My magic was only half back and unlike any other Entente's, and South's was so new and painful to him still. There were too many people.

I had been to the square before when there was a burning, making sure that Magrit had not indeed found one of us, even though I had been so sure then that the rest of the Entente were dead. But I had always turned back and rushed home to the Couterie before the pyre was struck with flame.

"Trust your first instinct, Farrow," South said softly, reading me.

I lifted up my chin and focused on the girls. I hoped South and Cinderella were both right.

South indicated in a whisper, "Maggie's on the right." He knew from his vision of her.

We both looked on in silence. South's wings twitched beneath his jacket. I tapped my fingers along the wand in my pocket.

"We have to release all of them," South whispered again, his voice full of emotion.

He was still in my head, even if he was trying not to be. He knew I thought about just saving Maggie alone before I thought of saving the other girls.

"If we do, the Queen's guards will redouble their efforts to find the Entente."

"That's him. The Witch Finder," South said.

The man was wearing a mask. He was looking at the row of girls.

"We have to save them all," South said without pause. His body went even more rigid. His features tensed too. He was in soldier mode.

He was right, of course. But releasing one girl would spark some embers of suspicion; releasing them all might be a fire we could not put out.

"If we do this, we prove that magic exists in the Present."

"That ship sailed long ago," South said. "Iolanta already did that back at the palace."

"But this is a little more public than that." After breaking Iolanta out of the palace, the Entente were more real than ever to the guards and the royals. But we were still just a story to the people, except for those who had witnessed the Burning all those years ago.

"We can't let these girls die. Especially not in the name of magic."

I was on a dangerous road. Before, all paths led to vengeance. Now, South threatened to drag me back to the Past when the

Entente believed in humans. When we wanted nothing more than to please them, only to be rewarded with ashes.

The Witch Finder made each girl step forward. He filled their pockets with Black Glass.

I stared a second more at the girls' scared faces. I thought of Hecate's when she'd stood on the pyre in the square once upon a time.

"Look at them; think of how Hecate felt—being there when she had done nothing wrong."

I didn't respond, though his words cut to the quick. South grew quiet beside me, but there was tension in his stillness. He was a coiled spring, ready to attack. He was going to try and save the girls with or without me. He wasn't judging me; he was trying to pull me back to those old lessons from the Fates. The ones that said we should help humans, even when they never helped us.

Finally I said, "I am going to regret this."

He hesitated.

"Is it too much, all the Presents?" I asked.

South shook his head.

"Liar."

"There's no time for hesitation," he said, more to himself than to me, but his wand shook when he raised it.

The Witch Finder said, "If you float, you are a witch. If you don't, you're true."

A soldier behind him laughed and added, "True and blue."

The girls shivered in fear. But one, a tiny brunette with curly hair, spat at the soldiers.

And then they were in the water.

"On three. I'll hold back the soldiers and you get the girls. I'll wish them safe," South added.

I could hear the girls' wishes over South's. They wished for air. They wished for their mothers, and finally they wished for it all to stop. And when they did, I got an idea.

Hecate's words came back to me: *With enough will and enough magic, anything is possible.* The words were no longer my own. They belonged to the wisher, but the result just might be the same.

South had begun counting.

"One, two . . ." When he reached three, I closed my eyes, grabbed his hand, and granted the girls' wishes. And when I opened my eyes again, everything and everyone was still, except South and me.

"Farrow. How did you . . . ?"

"I granted their wishes," I explained as South looked around, taking in the still town. "For it to all stop. We have to hurry. I don't know how long I can hold this."

Time stopped for me as it had for Hecate in the palace all those years ago. Every person had stopped moving mid-action. The Witch Finder's mouth was open in a threat. The guards' mouths were open in apparent laughter. The crowd was stuck in fear and awe of the spectacle, and the girls in the tank were frozen in agony. But after a couple of seconds ticked by, bubbles began to float up from their mouths and noses. I had given them breath just as they'd wished for.

"Help me get the girls out of the tanks," I ordered.

"Hold on to me," South said. He flew us to the tanks and set me down beside them. We pulled each girl out and laid them on the ground. They still appeared unconscious. They were blue and ashen from the water. Looking at their still forms, I felt the panic begin to rise in me. What if they didn't wake? But we had to move them before we could wake them or the Witch Finder would make sure they never woke at all.

"We have to get them away from here."

"Take their hands," South ordered.

And I complied.

He closed his eyes, whispered a travel spell, and we were suddenly on the edge of the Dark Wood. The girls coughed themselves awake.

The girl who had spat spoke first. "We're alive. How did we survive? What happened?" she asked.

"There isn't much time. You have to go, and you cannot return until the Queen is dead. Do you understand?" I demanded.

"Are you Entente?"

"Who we are doesn't matter. Who they think you are does. You will now be hunted as if you are Entente. I am sorry for that. But there was no other way."

South was gentler when he spoke to them. "She speaks the truth. You can never come back here. At least not until the Queen is gone."

The girls nodded. Another one of them spoke.

"We were told that you wanted to hurt us. But that's just another of the Queen's lies, isn't it?"

South stepped in. "The Entente have always loved and will always love the people."

"I'm Portia. Who are you?" she said, and she offered her hand in thanks.

Maggie and the other girl echoed their thanks.

"I'm—" I stopped short of telling her my name. "I am happy to have helped."

South and I equipped them with new faces that would hopefully last till moonrise. Tucked in their pockets was some honeybread and cheese, and South handed Maggie a tiny, lighted, and enchanted compass that would guide their path. Then they made their way farther into the Dark Wood in the direction of the Thirteenth Queendom.

South turned to me after they had all disappeared. He said in wonder, "Did you know that you could do that?"

"Which part?"

"The part where you put the whole Queendom, maybe the whole world, to sleep. How on earth did you do that?"

"It wasn't to sleep exactly. I would say, more like frozen in time . . . ," I countered.

"Farrow . . ."

"Okay, I didn't think it would work, but I had to try. I thought of Hecate on the pyre. I did what I wished I could have then. I stopped the world just long enough to save them. At least I could save *them*."

South's eyes filled with emotion. I wasn't sure if he was thinking of Iolanta or Hecate or both.

"Maybe that's the beauty of your gift. Galatea can't see you grant a wish," he said with a rueful grin.

"Or maybe Galatea will be waiting to drown us herself when we get back to the manor," I quipped. But I was smiling too when I said it.

When we got back to the barn, South and I stood close together, our hearts and minds pulsing with the nervous beat of what we had just done.

"We really rescued them . . . ," I said, marveling at how we'd saved the girls.

"You did it—I wonder what else you can do," he said brightly. But then South's face fell. "There's something I should have told you back there . . . ," he began haltingly.

"What?"

"There is no such thing as a Witch Finder."

"What do you mean? I saw him with my own eyes."

"It was the Queen's idea. She wanted to keep magic alive, since all the Entente were supposed to be dead."

It was as brilliant as it was demented. Queen Magrit had used the Entente as the excuse and a common enemy that the other Queendoms needed to rally against. And with the Entente presumably extinguished, she had to continue finding more of us.

"So she made up a magical detector?"

"No, I think there is a real one. But she uses a decoy to keep him or her safe. They pass the honor to each of the guards. They round people up and find magic all over the Queendoms."

"How do you know this? Could you see the real Witch Finder's Present?"

"Wherever the real Witch Finder is, he or she is cloaked in magic."

"Then how do you know about the decoys?"

"Because I was a guard," he said.

South had told me that he was more mascot than soldier. I had been prepared to do horrible things to get to the Queen. Had South had a similar dilemma?

"South, if you did things as a soldier . . . All that matters is that we ended up together. Whatever we had to do to get here, we had to do. Everything we did brought us here. Brought us back to each other so that we can defeat Magrit together."

"I never hurt anyone. But I had heard rumors about what the Witch Finder did. Today I saw the truth."

"You saved those girls today."

"What about the ones I didn't?"

"When the Queen is gone, you'll be saving all of us."

South put his chin up. "We're really going to get her finally."

I nodded.

He smiled down at me. His wing created shade that somehow felt comforting to me.

"I feel like we've already won. We have each other back. There's part of me that doesn't want to risk it," South said. "When we go after her, what if we lose what we've found?"

I shook my head and recoiled from him. "As long as she's alive, Magrit will come for us. As long as she's alive, we don't have peace. And neither does Hecate."

South opened his mouth to take the words back. But before he could, we heard a loud squawking sound coming from inside the manor.

What now?

CHAPTER 53

I raced inside to find Amantha holding one of the Queen's crows under her arm. She was wresting something out of its mouth. The squeals belonged to Amantha, who didn't like how the crow resisted. Next to her was Bari, who was trying to conceal her amusement.

"It tried to deliver a message to Cinderella," Amantha said, annoyed and out of breath as she wrangled the crow.

"Cinderella *is* technically the only true lady of the house," I said, suddenly feeling protective of her, knowing how close her friend had come to death.

"You know how they say 'absence reminds the heart of what it is missing'? It appears that is not always the case," Amantha said with a smirk, looking directly at me.

"I missed you too, Amantha," I retorted. And I kissed her on the cheek.

When I pulled back from her, I saw that her cheeks were red. There had been little place for emotion in the Entente, but in the years of pretending to be human, my sisters had started to act a bit like them despite themselves.

I petted the bird in her arms, and it dropped the scroll before me.

"I thought Bari was the only one who had a way with beasts," Amantha said, almost accusingly.

"Like I told you, sometimes you get more with a kiss. I think it applies to animals too. And to Amantha . . . ," I said lightly.

"You will never truly have an animal's loyalty," Bari said sharply, weighing in. "It's their nature."

I was almost certain she was talking about humans.

I took both of them in for a long beat. Bari wasn't saying anything I hadn't thought about for most of my life, and still I bristled. I shook it off. We'd just been away from each other for too long. It would take some time before we found our rhythm. It would take some time before we were whole again.

My sisters weren't the same, and neither was I. But maybe if we kept playing our parts, the lighthearted bits would outweigh the rest.

Still, my heart hurt. The pretense hurt. All I wanted was for us to be what we once were. What if we never were again?

I reached for the scroll, but Bari, ever the animal savant, clucked her tongue and the crow dutifully picked up the scroll again and flew to her waiting arm. She held her palm out in front of the bird, and it deposited the scroll in her hand.

"Not fair," Amantha said, eyes flashing at Bari now.

She disappeared, and I felt a rush of wind as the paper left Bari's not-quite-clenched-enough fist. Amantha reappeared on the other side of the room. She hadn't really disappeared, I realized. She'd just moved really fast—faster than the speed of sight.

When she stopped, I could see her chest moving up and down from effort. Amantha began to unfurl the paper, which folded itself up again.

We all reacted with wonder as it took the form of a paper bird and floated out of Amantha's hand. We followed the paper bird into the living room, where Galatea sat waiting to receive it.

"There's going to be a ball, and we're all invited," she announced with a flourish. She unfurled it and showed us the contents without having to read the paper itself.

Galatea already knew what had happened—the second after it had happened—and she watched the Queen's every move. So, naturally, she knew that the invitation was here. She clapped her hands to get our attention.

"Apparently, the Resistance made a move. The Queen is up in arms. Some poor wenches escaped the Testing. There was an explosion at a factory in town. Perhaps the guard is losing its touch . . . The Resistance scared the Queen enough to move up the ball. Everything is as it should be. This is it—the moment we've been waiting for. Our chance to take the throne. Praise the Fates. Our plan goes into motion at the ball."

"Praise the Fates," my sisters echoed. But I did not join them, because I realized what Galatea was saying.

Amantha shot me a look, which Galatea caught.

"Girls, we have no time for squabbling. There's not a moment to waste. We have a ball to get ready for. Ella! Ella!" Galatea screamed.

"The prince is getting ready to find a bride," I surmised.

While my sisters were busy choosing their gowns for the ball, Cinderella and I snuck into the barn to transform the animals, later than usual. On the way, I told her about Maggie. Cinderella stopped on the path and wrapped her arms around me.

"Thank you for saving my friend."

"I can't tell you where she is. But she is safe," I whispered.

When we got inside the barn, all the "animals" were there, eagerly and still sometimes angrily awaiting their transformations.

"We are so sorry we are late," I said as Fessie greeted us with a not-so-happy swish of his tail.

I took a deep breath and focused on each of the servants. Every time I raised my wand, I felt their pain, their relief, and their confusion. Their gratitude was very rare. They blamed me, even as they stood still and let me make them temporarily themselves again.

"I will find a way to counteract the spells that bind you, but in the meantime, I can give you until moonrise," I promised Hodder.

He cursed at me under his breath every time I transformed him. But he was always the first at my feet every morning, ready to be transformed.

"I will find a way to make the change permanent," I vowed.

The red bird, Jacques, looked at me and squawked, "I can think of a way."

"What's that?" I asked.

"We kill all the witches." He scowled at me.

"He doesn't mean that," Cinderella said quickly.

I raised my wand defensively.

"Yes, he does," Hodder said, his arms akimbo, reminding me of his long horse legs.

"I will handle my sisters," I said firmly.

Hodder backed down, his arms resting again by his sides.

The staff was not happy with their confinement, but Cinderella did her best to make them comfortable. She brought them food and clothes. And Cinderella had wished for a tub that replenished itself after every user so we could give them as much comfort as possible.

I worried about Galatea sensing their Pasts and realizing where they were hiding. But she had focused her gift outside the manor house and never within it. She trusted her sisters, and she found Cinderella and the "animals" too inconsequential to examine their Pasts. For now, they seemed safe.

"Thank you," I told Cinderella as we snuck back into the house.

"I was helping my friends."

"But earlier you helped me. I owe you a giant wish with a bow on top."

Cinderella smiled. And when her hand brushed mine, I got a flash of her.

I hope that it will all turn out as planned . . .

She was standing before a room of townspeople. What was she doing there? What were they all doing there?

"I think it's time for us to act. The witches are planning something. The Queen's evil is escalating," Cinderella said, her voice quavering as she looked at the waiting faces of the crowd. So this was where she'd been going.

The baker girl who I recognized from years of honeybread runs at the Couterie spoke up first.

"But what if we just let them cannibalize one another?"

"We are the ones who are getting hurt."

"It's time to act."

And then all at once they lifted their hands and put on masks. The masks were gorgeously crafted. Each was uniquely stunning in different colors and covered in lace and pearls, and each was fit for a costumed ball—the kind where a prince could pick his future Queen, and the kind where a fledging resistance could do something to become a full-fledged one . . .

“Are you all right?” Cinderella asked, taking me out of my vision.

“I’m fine. Just tired,” I lied.

Had I been wrong about her all along? I had been so concerned about earning Cinderella’s trust; had I missed something fundamental about her? I had risked my life and my sisters’ lives saving her friend. What if she just couldn’t forgive the Entente? After all, why should she? My sisters had treated her terribly.

Another reality slammed into me as I headed back to my room. Cinderella and her resistance were our legacy. They were what we left behind when we couldn’t take care of the Queendoms any longer. The only question now: Would they be a hindrance to what I had to do?

CHAPTER 54

I have neglected you, Farrow, for far too long," Galatea said, waking me before the sunrise could. She was sitting beside my bed.

Had she found me out? All the things I had not told her. The questions that were growing in my heart about my sisters. Had she figured out how to read my Past fully?

"What do you mean, Galatea? You have been nothing but welcoming to me."

"I have left you to your own devices. That is not a mistake I would have made were Hecate and Iolanta here with me."

"I have managed," I offered up. The mention of Iolanta and Hecate softened me toward her. If she was thinking of them, then perhaps she was thinking of what they would have wanted her to do. Perhaps there was still hope for her to right her course.

"I want more than for you to manage. I know it is hard for you, dealing with your half magic. Finding us so much changed . . ."

"You are different than I remember. But I suppose I am too."

"I know you have more questions than I have answered. I can at least help you with this one. About how we have changed. I don't carry the Pasts in the same way."

"What do you mean?"

"Before, I felt all their anguish," Galatea said. "I felt their darkness, their sadness, their meanness . . ."

"And you don't anymore?"

"I still feel the emotion of it all. But I feel no pity for their misery. I relish in it."

She looked at me a long beat, taking in my disapproval.

"That goes against everything you ever taught us. Everything we believed." Galatea had been the Entente who objected to the use of even the smallest amount of pain to turn Fate. What would she be okay with now? "Don't you want your empathy back?"

"I feel better without it. I feel stronger. I feel limitless. And I want you to feel that too."

"I don't think I will ever get there," I said, not entirely sure I wanted to.

"I told you once that that there was a time that I wished I had as much power as my sisters. When Iolanta seemed to be the strongest of us. I never fathomed that I would be the only one of us left," she began. "I mean, in this form," she added, for Hecate's benefit and for mine. "I know that it seems like you will never get it all back. But like I told you when you were small, it takes only a tiny touch of magic to turn Fate. And you have that at your disposal already. Let's see if we can get you a little more of it."

In an instant, she grabbed my hand and we went back to the Reverie.

I felt a flood of emotion as my sisters appeared one after another in the courtyard.

They raised their wands and chanted, trying to remove the rest of Hecate's binding spell. But when the words were spent, I was unchanged. I raised my wand and tried to make rain. And there was not a single drop from the sky.

Galatea nodded at Tere to make a wish for rain. I raised my wand again, and the sky opened up.

My sisters hugged me goodbye before traveling away.

"Half magic is better than no magic at all," Tere whispered, vanishing into the blur.

When we returned to Cinderella's house, Galatea followed me back to my room. She paced away from me.

I assumed that she was disappointed in me.

"I am sorry that I have failed," I said.

Galatea took my hands in hers.

"You have not failed. None of this is your fault. You have withstood so much—and all alone."

"Not alone. I had Hecate."

"Yes, you did. But you did not have us or magic. I am nothing but proud of you, Farrow."

But I read her face and knew there was more.

"Then what is it?"

"I'm sorry, but you can't come with us to the ball," Galatea said gently.

"What do you mean I can't come with you? That's where you're enacting your plan against Magrit," I protested.

Was I to be punished on top of already losing my gift?

"I know how much this means to you. But it's too dangerous."

"Why?"

"Because we can't be sure we can protect you. However the Queen is discerning magic, she could still find yours."

I took this in.

"But what about the cloaking spell? You cloaked South. You could do the same for me."

"We cannot be sure of magic we do not fully understand. Magic of the like we have not seen before. And we cannot take the risk. Your magic isn't the same as ours; not yet."

"You mean I'm not Entente anymore," I said, feeling hurt.

"You are always, always Entente. Never forget that," Galatea said firmly. "I'm sorry, Farrow. I know you want to see the Queen's downfall. But this is only the first step of many."

"What do you mean? What other steps could there possibly be?" I asked, confused. Wasn't this what we'd been waiting for since Magrit took Hecate from us?

"I promise she will die when the time is right. And if you want, you can even light the match. But for now, I need a little more patience from you, Farrow."

CHAPTER 55

That night, I skipped sitting with my sisters and chose to be alone with Hecate instead.

She sat in the corner, seemingly focused on me.

"We have our family back, Hecate," I said firmly, trying to shut out my growing doubts. I echoed what South had said to me.

I did not mean to sleep. I had so much to figure out. But at some point I must have drifted off. A scream pierced the air—I knew not where from. I ran down to South's barn, concerned he had again woken from his slumber in the face of a flood of Presents. But South was sleeping peacefully. I blushed as I caught the smile on his face. I knew that while he slept, he was still in the moment that he had shared with me.

I headed back to my room, wondering if the scream had just been in my head. But as I continued through the hall, there was a whimper from Cinderella's room. The scream had to have belonged to her.

When I pushed the door open, she was sitting in the center of her floor surrounded by shreds of voluminous blush-colored fabric. Next to her was a corset once covered in pearls, but someone had smashed each pearl individually. Cinderella ran her fingers over the garment in disbelief.

"They found it. They ruined it," she said haltingly, between tears.

"Who?" I asked, but I already knew the answer. She meant my sisters.

I heard the distinct flapping of wings. Bari and Amantha appeared together in the doorway. I hadn't heard footsteps. They weren't even bothering to use the stairs anymore.

Galatea was right behind them.

"What's all the fuss?" she asked.

"My dress. It's ruined. You did it," Cinderella said, pointing at her stepsisters.

"That's ridiculous. The dress was clearly wrecked by vermin. You should do a better job at keeping this place clean," Galatea returned with disdain.

"Perhaps that mouse of yours got out of its cage again," Bari offered. Her voice was cold and unfeeling, even though I knew for a fact that Bari preferred four-legged creatures to human ones.

Cinderella put a hand over her mouth and raced to her pet's cage, which was empty.

"What did you do with Perdi?" Cinderella demanded, looking at Bari.

She couldn't have known about Bari's predilection for all things that crawled, but she did seem to know that Bari's hands were all over this.

"Wouldn't you like to know?" Bari laughed.

"Now clean this up," Galatea said before turning around.

The sisters followed her. Bari looked at me as if to say that I should come with, but I stayed put.

Cinderella dropped to her knees and began looking for the mouse.

"I'm sure that Perdi will come back," I offered. Then I added, hoping to comfort her, "Bari loves animals. She would never hurt one."

"I hope so," Cinderella said, sitting back on the floor.

"What was the dress for?" I asked, but I could already hear it.

I wish to go to the ball.

"It's stupid."

There was absolutely nothing stupid about the gorgeous fabric that had been shredded to pieces. It was as if part of Cinderella had been shredded too. All the cheer that she had somehow managed to summon up each day might as well have been lying on the ground in pieces. Her face had fallen, and her eyes looked as hollow as if she had seen Amantha's disappearing and reappearing act.

"I can see that it was beautiful. You wanted to go to the ball," I said. I hadn't needed to hear her thoughts to know that I was right.

"I don't want to marry the prince or anything. I think the whole idea of having us all parade around like mutton and wait for him to choose one of us is ridiculous," she said quickly.

"Then why?"

"I just want one night away from all this. One night where I can pretend, you know. Just be with my friends the way we used to be—not in the shadows but in the light. To dress up and dance and just be . . . you know?"

Cinderella was using this to cover whatever it was she was planning in the vision I'd had of her.

Cinderella sighed heavily. "Like I said, it's ridiculous for me to dream of a stupid ball."

"It's not. It's human to want things. It's human to want friends and companionship. I'm sorry my sisters have stood in your way."

"You believe me?"

"I've known them a really long time. And I think I know you. That dress didn't tear itself apart. Not without some help, anyway." I drew my wand. "Save all the pieces. I will put it back together. They will be none the wiser. Just wish for it."

Cinderella smiled up at me warmly. For a split second I thought that maybe, just maybe, she could trust me enough to tell me what was really going on. But I knew that something else was happening. I just didn't know what. Maybe if I played along long enough, I could see what she was planning to do at the ball.

"Thank you. Now I owe you one," Cinderella said.

But as she spoke, I could hear her heart's desire.

I want to believe her. I want to trust her. But she's what they are. And they killed my father. And my mother.

"What do you mean, 'they killed them'?" I demanded. Bari had told me that they had fallen ill. And Cinderella had never said anything different. This couldn't be . . .

"Stop doing that! Get out of my head. My thoughts are mine."

"Just tell me what my family did. Tell me so I can help you. I want to help you. I want to know."

Cinderella studied me, her bottom lip trembling.

"What do you think that Galatea did?" I pressed.

"My parents took them in, and within weeks my mother was dead. Galatea became my stepmother, and my father was dead before we finished all the cake in the icebox."

"But that doesn't mean my family killed them," I said. However, looking at her face, I could see that it did.

Under Magrit's rule, many of the Queendom's noblemen had disappeared or died under mysterious circumstances. I had heard of a few instances at the Couterie. A few Couterie had lost those they were meant for, and they were reassigned to the heirs. Wasn't it possible that the Queen was responsible for this and not the Entente? I needed that to be the answer and not what Cinderella was thinking.

"How do you know it was the Entente's fault and not the Queen's?" I said, trying to change her mind.

"The Queen can't conjure a plague or make people stop breathing just by willing it."

"People get sick all the time. Under Magrit, doctors are scarce. There is more disease. We are not at fault for that."

"My father fell in love with Galatea the morning after his wife died. It didn't make sense. He loved my mother more than life itself. He didn't fall for Galatea. It was a spell. She stole his heart. I know it."

"Love spells aren't possible," I blurted. But I knew better. They just weren't done because they weren't practical. They had to be refreshed nightly. And then there was the matter of consent. No one should want a heart that isn't given freely.

"But wings are? And people who turn into horses? Think about it, Farrow. You keep talking about what magic can't do. But look around. Everything you'd told me about the Entente—this code that you talk about. They stopped using it long ago. Maybe when they killed my parents, maybe even before. If I didn't know better, I wouldn't even guess they were in the same family as you. I don't want to leave the Future of Hinter up to the Entente. My friends and I have our own plans."

I shook my head. What Cinderella was saying about my family couldn't be true. She was human, I reminded myself. And no matter how much I felt a connection to her, she wasn't my sister. And I wasn't hers.

I had saved her friend, but there was no reason for me to expect her loyalty in return. They were not just thieves. They were the Resistance, and clearly Cinderella was part of it. But I couldn't blame her. We had pushed her to this.

CHAPTER 56

Everyone has a secret. Everyone lies, I thought, walking away from Cinderella's room and into Bari's.

Some lies were more worthy than others. Cinderella's secret was a noble one. But the Entente, as much as I wanted to deny it . . . their secrets went beyond plans for justified vengeance. They meant to hurt the innocent or rule them or both. I had been so glad to have my family back, I didn't look at who the Entente were. I'd ignored every anomaly because I didn't want to see what they had become. I had tried to push down my objections to how Galatea, Amantha, and Bari treated Cinderella, to how my other sisters manipulated humans in every Queendom for their own survival. But to take lives of innocents, to take the lives of those who actually sheltered her—Galatea had not just thrown out the rules of what it meant to be Entente; she had also thrown away everything we were supposed to be.

This was not what we had been taught. Never cruelty. Never interfere with what was to be. Only serve and keep the balance. We were done serving. But I still believed in the rest. Even if they did not anymore.

I wondered what it would have been like if we had all stayed together. If the Queen hadn't torn us apart. Would Bari and Amantha still have turned out this way?

"Bari, this isn't who we are," I implored. "This isn't what the Entente were meant to be. I think Galatea killed Cinderella's parents."

"She didn't."

"How do you know?"

Bari looked down at the ground like the answer might be found there. And then she looked up at me. As she did, I felt my heart catch.

"Because I did."

The earth beneath my feet remained still, but I felt myself wobble. It wasn't possible.

"We don't kill innocents," I reminded her.

"None of them are innocent. We were unprepared the day of the Burning. But we will never be unprepared again. And we will never lose another sister."

Bari looked at me a long beat.

"I did what the Entente have done for years. Only I did it for our kind and not theirs. I serve the Entente. I bow down to no human, or Queen or king for that matter. Don't you want justice for your mother and for the Entente? So do we . . ."

"I was going to kill Queen Magrit. I could still do it, but only her."

"Galatea, Amantha, and the rest of our sisters are planning to take over the Queendoms. What happened that day in the square is larger than Magrit. It's as big as every person who stood by and didn't stop it and every person who allowed us to be persecuted all over the lands."

"People got scared. And with good reason. Queen Magrit has persecuted humans too."

"The humans have proven that they can't handle power. And they are never going to leave us alone. They will never accept us. They will always be threatened by us. Because we have magic, and they don't. We will take their Queendom one nobleman and royal at a time, and they'll never even know that they lost the war."

I looked at my oldest friend. She thought she had figured it all out.

"Oh, Bari," I whispered.

"Oh, Farrow," she parroted back at me.

Bari was a killer. And not in self-defense. She was my first friend. She was my sister. My heart hurt as the reality set in.

"Why not spell them, control them? The Grays were kind to you—they hid you; they saved you. Why did you have to kill them when they took you in?"

"If you kept a scorpion as a pet for long enough, it would bite you eventually no matter how good you were to it."

"Are we the scorpions or are the humans in your analogy?"

"What if we both are? What if this is just where we end up? One eating the other eventually . . . I'd frankly prefer to do the eating."

I was struck mute by her cruelty for a moment, but she continued.

"The Grays' will and their love were strong . . . The spell kept breaking . . . We had no choice."

"What if you are wrong about the humans? There is good in them," I returned.

I thought of the prince. I thought of Cinderella. And I thought of Tork.

"Are you willing to bet all our lives on the humans? Because I'm not," Bari said.

I wanted to show her she was wrong. I wanted her to take it back. But the only one wishing in this room was me, and I wasn't able to grant my own wishes.

"This has never been our way," I said firmly.

"Our way didn't work. If it had been left to the old ways, we would all be dead."

"There's a difference between choosing *us* and killing *them*," I countered.

"Is there?" she asked. "We've put an Entente in every Queendom to take control from the inside. We're not just hiding. We're taking over."

"What do you mean 'take control'? And what is your plan for Magrit?"

Bari laughed. "We will gain our influence back over every Queendom one way or another. Starting with Magrit."

"And the prince?"

"It's simple, really. The prince will fall in love with me at the Royal Ball. Our magic can't make the heart want something it doesn't want, of course. So when the prince sees me, he will see the face of the girl he loves: you."

Bari thought the prince loved me. Their entire plan turned on an idea that I had never let myself entertain. Could Mather really love me? We had only met three times, and one of which I was wearing another face. Had I really made that much of an impression on his heart? A part of me whispered "yes," remembering the electricity of our every moment together. Another whispered "never" because it could not be. He was the son of our enemy. His royal blood was never meant to mix with mine. Still, another screamed inside in protest. Whatever we were or weren't to each other, I did not want Bari to use it to twist his heart to her will. And I could not bear the thought of her borrowing my face to do it.

"There will be fire crystals at midnight. The entire ball will spill out into the courtyard. I will plant a kiss on him, and the rest is Happily Ever After. For us, anyway.

"After we're married, the Queen and the prince will have an unfortunate accident. I will become Queen, and I will be loved by all the Queendoms. You see, Farrow, revenge is not always a single strike. Sometimes it's a series of them. And we are striking at the heart of humanity. They will submit or they will die."

"The prince isn't like his mother," I said with more emotion than I meant to betray. "I know him."

Bari studied me for a beat, clearly reacting to my impassioned tone. "He's human. He will disappoint you in the end. And we will pay the price for it."

I remained silent, taking Bari in. There was no talking her out of her belief about the prince or the rest of their plans.

The only way I could save the prince was if I did it myself.

CHAPTER 57

What are you doing here?" I asked when I got to my room after leaving Bari's.

Amantha was standing in front of Hecate in the center of the floor. Amantha's wand was drawn. She flickered in and out of sight, finally settling in the chair by the window. Her wand was now put away.

Hecate broke into pieces and re-formed behind me as if she needed my protection.

"I know things. I see things, even though no one thinks I do. It's the beauty of being a ghost," Amantha said, not answering my question.

"What do you know?" I asked, feeling trepidation rising.

"Bari and I are sisters by blood. I overheard Hecate and Galatea talking about it once. I don't know about our father. I don't even know if we have the same one."

"What else have you seen?"

Had she seen me plotting against them? I held my tongue. The less I said, the more she would talk.

"I used to be so jealous that you shared a room with Bari when we were small, but then I really missed you when you were gone."

Was that guilt? Was Amantha even capable of guilt? I had thought of her as seven years old, even after all these years, and her behavior since we had been reunited had not necessarily improved upon that image. But perhaps Amantha had more dimension than I had given credit for.

"The way your face used to scrunch up when you failed at a spell. You still do that," she added.

"I missed you too, Amantha."

"Bari was always your favorite," she countered.

It was true, but I didn't want to raise her ire.

"It's okay. She was mine too," she said.

"But we're all grown up now. I'd like us to be closer this time around. I have so many regrets about the past. I know we were children, but what we did back then . . . South . . . the wings . . ."

"I suppose it serves us right. South winds up being the handsome flying guy while I am a ghost, you're a half witch, and Bari has half a face. If I didn't know better, I would think that we were being punished."

"From everything we know, it doesn't work like that."

"Galatea is abandoning everything she taught us to enact vengeance," Amantha said. "What do you think happens after that? Was this fated too?"

"I don't know," I said.

It was strange. This felt like the first real conversation I had ever had with Amantha.

"Amantha, I really do mean it. I do wish that we could fix what we did . . ."

"I didn't come to see the Past. I came to see the Future . . . I came to see Hecate."

"Why?" Did my sister have some plan involving Hecate? Were

they somehow going to use her in their plot against the prince? I didn't understand.

"I need to know what she knows about Ever After."

I stopped short. I was not expecting this.

Amantha's smile dropped. She looked more vulnerable and open than I'd ever seen her.

I couldn't help it. I wanted to reach out to her, but I didn't want to break the moment. Which felt as fragile as she did at this second.

"I want to see if maybe I could communicate with her. She's half in this world and half in the next, like me. But she wasn't very forthcoming. She isn't much of a talker."

Amantha's smile was wan, but emotion was stirring underneath.

"I'm sorry—she is never very forthcoming. That doesn't mean that she doesn't . . ."

"It doesn't mean that she does either," Amantha said matter-of-factly.

"Oh, Amantha," I said, feeling so much for her. Bari had told me about her corporeal loss, but seeing and feeling her pain up close was something else. Suddenly, I could see her expression darken. Before she spoke, I knew I'd made a mistake. Amantha did not want my sympathy.

"I don't want or need pity. I may be half in this world and half in the next, but I am all Entente. I can't say the same about you."

With that, Amantha disappeared.

"Oh, Amantha," I whispered after her. Her words had meant to sting, but they didn't. Instead, they churned me into worry. I did not feel the insult, but I did feel the fear. What if she saw something of our plans? I hoped that she had found enough satisfaction in that moment not to look any further.

A few minutes later South knocked on my door.

"Shh . . . ," I said, ushering him inside. "How much of that did you hear?" I asked as he stepped into the room.

"All of it."

"Do you think she spelled the room? Is there such a thing as a listening spell?"

"You okay?"

"What if she's been spying on us?"

Hecate settled in beside me as if to say that she was more trusting of Amantha's intentions.

"I agree with Hecate. I think she was genuine or at least as much so as she can be. And I also think she likes scaring you. She always has."

I felt a little bit of relief as I took in South's look of unconcern regarding Amantha's unwelcome visit. In the maelstrom of secrets and doubts and loss and discovery, South had become my safe place. His calm became mine, and I found myself breathing easier just because he was there. It didn't seem quite fair that I relied on him for comfort, knowing of his feelings for me and knowing the weight he bore from all the Presents pressing down on him.

"I hope you're right."

Hecate took her leave of us, choosing now to slip under the door. I wondered if she went to check on Amantha.

"Do you ever feel anything from Hecate? Amantha claimed that was why she was here."

His face turned serious. "I don't . . . but that doesn't mean that there isn't anything there. When I look at Galatea, I see only what she wants me to see. Perhaps Hecate is the same. I think you need to make your own mind palace."

"Why?" I said. "Has something else happened?"

"No, but something could."

"And you think I need to protect myself from my sisters? Galatea already said she can't read me. Why do I need any more protection?"

"That may be true, but what if it's not always true? I think you should practice. I think you should be ready for anything that is to come."

"You're scaring me a little, South," I said.

"I think it's good to be scared. We weren't at all scared when we were young and look what happened to us."

I took this in.

"I'll work on the mind palace. But even though we weren't scared as children, we were alone. I had Hecate but . . . Now that I have you and Cinderella, I don't feel so alone."

CHAPTER 58

You've come around just in time. I hate being at odds with you, Farrow," Bari said when I knocked on her door a couple of days later.

"In time for what?" I said.

Just like when we were small, Bari was quick to believe that I would follow her anywhere. Whether it was in teasing South then or killing the prince now.

"One last spell before the ball tonight," she announced gleefully.

"I thought you were just going to change your face," I said, trying and failing to keep the flatness out of my voice.

"The prince isn't just in love with your face; it's the way you move, breathe, think. I have to be indiscernible. And even that won't be enough."

"What do you mean?"

"We need you for the spell, Farrow."

"What do you mean?" I asked again, but I already knew. Bari would go to the ball disguised as me. When the prince looked upon her, he would see me. Their plan was not that different from my own. That was the irony. My plan was to make Cinderella look like me when the prince saw her. The difference was that at the end of my plan, his heart would be broken but still beating.

"I can't go, but you can go wearing my face. She was my mother, Bari."

"I know. It should be you. But I promise you, I will do your face justice. I will get justice for you wearing it," she said firmly.

But as she spoke, I felt a chill listening to her words. I believed she meant them. But our ideas about justice did not line up anymore. She was going to use my face to kill an innocent—to kill Mather.

A few minutes later I was with my sisters in the dining room of the manor.

I looked around—Galatea and Amantha were not there, but the rest of my sisters were. South was missing too.

We sat in a circle, where a teapot floated around the room, serving everyone.

Each of them displayed their gifts almost unconsciously. Or maybe consciously. Maybe they were just glad to be in a safe space where they could let down their hair and magic.

Horatia and Ocenth were changing their faces with their wands.

"What do you think of my hair? Be honest."

"It does not go with your face. Not everyone can pull off bangs, Horatia," Ocenth said with a giggle. She waved her wand in front of Horatia's face, and her features changed again, with rounder cheeks and bigger eyes. This face matched the bangs better.

"How about this one?" she asked without missing a beat.

Horatia clapped when she noticed me. "Sisters, let's raise a cup to our hero, Farrow. She lifted the spell with a wish when we were in the magic shop. I've never seen anything like it."

Ocenth added, "She was like a magical detective. She figured out what that poor woman's problem was and woke her with a wish!"

I was met with proud glances around the table, and the girls grabbed their floating cups to raise them in my direction.

If I wasn't horrified by what I knew now, I would have been so very flattered having my sisters praise my magic. But instead I had to maintain my calm.

Bari beamed too. She didn't begrudge my success; she seemed relieved by it.

Looking at the floating teapot, I couldn't help but marvel at how my sisters all performed magic with ease. Despite the circumstances, I was filled with a sense of wonder at how far their magic had come. If I had grown up with them and with my magic, that could have been me floating the tea or changing my face at will. Instead, I clasped my hands in my lap, waiting for someone to have a wish so I could grant it. But there would be no wishes here that they couldn't grant with their own wands before I could even raise my own.

I had always thought my sisters were miles ahead of me in magic, at least until the day I gave South his wings. I still wasn't the same as they were. Maybe I never would be again. But I was here. And so were they. That was something. That used to be everything. But it wasn't enough. I knew things now that I could not unknow.

Xtina lit the candles without the power of her wand. She used her hand.

Tere created a tiny tornado and blew them out with a wave of her wand. "We should wait for the others."

My gaze followed her little tornado until it disappeared out the window, and then I looked back at my sisters. While Freya was exactly the same, I couldn't stop looking at Perpetua, who was now another two or three heads taller than she had been a few seconds before.

"I don't mean to stare, Perpetua, but did you just grow again?"

"I don't mind . . . ," she said proudly. "I have been growing since the day of the Burning. But when I am around humans, I have to hide it."

She tapped her wand against her chest. She frowned in apparent pain as she sank down to my height.

"It hurts?"

She nodded, tapping the wand again and returning to her real height.

I spotted a plate of Odette's cookies in the center of the table and reached for one. As good as Galatea's dinners had been, it could not compare to Odette's otherworldly cuisines.

The treat was a full-course breakfast all in one bite: first juice and coffee, then pancakes and sausage, then eggs, and ending with dragon fruit.

I closed my eyes and let myself savor the taste.

"I have missed that," I moaned.

I reached for another cookie and bit into it just as Odette raised a hand to stop me.

"Oh no, not that one," she said.

But I swallowed it, believing she was teasing.

This one tasted like a flight of desserts: first sherbet, then pie, then chocolate—but it was chased by a bitter aftertaste. The bitterness grew, and I reached for a glass of water. But before I could take a sip, I had a sudden flash of the Burning and Hecate on the pyre, and tears began flowing down my cheeks.

"What is wrong with me?" I whispered, confused.

"It's not you. It's the cookie. Odette can make you feel any emotion with one bite," Bari explained.

"Why would you make that?" I asked, turning to Odette.

"It's a new recipe. And possibly a new weapon. I can make anyone feel anything with a single bite. For a while, anyway."

I dried my eyes. The sting of being mad at her for the manipulation of my feelings was replaced with wanting to know more about the spell.

"You okay, Farrow?" Perpetua demanded.

"Of course she's not okay. I gave her the saddest moment of her life on a platter . . . Here, have a happy one," Odette offered, shoving another cookie into my hand.

I took a bite. This one tasted like chocolate with an aftertaste that was way sweeter. It felt like kisses . . . specifically, those I'd shared with the prince.

My eyes fluttered and my cheeks warmed.

One of my other sisters, Sistine, suddenly began humming—and I felt myself compelled to my feet.

"Sistine," Bari admonished.

But Sistine hummed louder and the other girls were all pulled to their feet.

"You're making us dance?" I laughed and smiled as I gave in to the rhythm.

As my sisters danced beside me, I realized how much I had missed all this: the music and the magic. But my family was all here now. The dance was tinged by what I knew I was going to do in a few hours. They would consider it a betrayal. But I considered it a chance to save us all. Save them from themselves. Save our Future as the Entente. They might never forgive me. But I would rather live with that than a Future with my sisters' hands soaked in innocent blood.

Galatea appeared with Amantha and South alongside her.

"What is going on here?" Galatea demanded as Sistine immediately stopped humming and our feet stopped moving.

"Sorry, Galatea. It's just that Farrow's missed so much," Bari explained, taking a step forward.

Despite the fact that she was the youngest, save me and South, Bari was clearly the leader.

"Well, she's here now. There will be plenty of time for us in the Future, praise Fate."

"Praise Fate," everyone echoed as we returned to our seats and recomposed ourselves.

"Now, girls. Tell me of your progress."

Galatea went around the table, and each girl gave a cryptic line that made sense to everyone else, but not to me.

Xtina relit the flames on the candles around us and piped up, eager with her update. "Blenheim . . ."

I remembered that was Tork's land. I wondered if he'd gone back there after our encounter or if he had followed my advice and his heart to Lavendra.

"Blenheim burns," Xtina said dramatically. "Well, part of it anyway. I took out the northernmost plains and drove the people closer to the palace just like you wanted, sister."

"Any casualties? We do not need the attention."

"I was careful . . . ," Xtina said haltingly.

"Remember, magic doesn't control you. You control magic," Galatea said.

I wondered about her comment. Clearly, there must have been a time when Xtina had lost control of her magic and the results had been unfortunate.

Next to her, Em made a guttural sound that did not sound Entente or human. It sounded almost like a wolf.

"Em, you can be yourself here."

Her cheeks warmed with embarrassment. She nodded, and tufts of gray fur began growing on all her exposed skin. Within seconds she was covered. But her eyes still screamed Em.

"I want you all to be yourselves when we are together. Farrow, I'm afraid everyone is shy because of our long separation."

Within seconds, with her permission, a few more of my sisters had transformed. Almost all had scars. And from what I gathered from their reports, they all had used those scars to their magical advantages.

"But you see, there is nothing to be ashamed of," Galatea said. "Every one of us who was broken has been restored in other ways. We are stronger than ever. And now we have our Farrow and South back. We are complete."

The reports about each of the Thirteen Queendoms continued. Each sounded more ominous than the last. We were not hiding; we were lying in wait.

Tere had driven the people of Hesperoux underground and had infiltrated the Eighth Queendom. She hid among them, pretending to be the victim of the strange climate change. No one had yet reached Nimolet, the Eleventh Queendom, or the Quillory, the Thirteenth and the rumored land of the Rookery, the latter because of an apparent treaty with the Rooks. The former because Nimolet was rumored to have an army of Witch Finders, and a plan had not yet been hatched to infiltrate either land.

Horatia was last to tell of her progress. I perked up, knowing that I would undoubtedly be mentioned because of my show of magic at the shop.

"The girl grows. The world turns. There is nothing new under the sun."

I had no idea what she meant about "the girl," but I knew the last part was a lie. And apparently so did Galatea.

"Should I ask Bari, South, and Amantha the same question?"

Horatia blushed and twirled her hair. "I had a slight mishap with the spindle. But it won't happen again."

Galatea lifted her chin and continued.

This wasn't a tea party. It was a war room. And my sisters weren't just my sisters anymore. They were an army. And they had their wands close to the Crowns of every single Queendom.

The truth was, I already knew this. I just didn't let myself know the heart of it. And I still couldn't make out the details. Even now.

"South and Farrow will not be raising their wands tonight. South, your time will come, once you are surer of your gifts. And, Farrow, just because you cannot come to the ball doesn't mean that you will not be contributing to the spell."

"Farrow, you were fated to be part of this. But any sacrifice must be given willingly," Amantha stated, suddenly appearing next to me.

Hiding my trepidation was harder than I thought.

"I don't understand."

"Hopefully Bari told you that the spell will work so much better if your contribution is of your own free will," Galatea began.

I was a little busy hearing about the murder of Cinderella's parents, I thought in protest. But I suddenly wondered what exactly they meant by "sacrifice."

Galatea raised her wand and my teacup turned into a pair of scissors in the blink of an eye.

"A lock of your hair is all the spell requires."

As I picked up the scissors, I felt an irrational sense of relief that hair was all that was required. But I remembered as my fingers tapped the blades that they were not cutting just my hair; they might as well have been slicing out a piece of my heart.

It was gone before it could hit the table. It reappeared on a plate before Galatea. The table and all the settings disappeared too. So did the ceiling above us.

Suddenly we were not in the dining room anymore. We were outside the manor with the moon overhead. Galatea had moved us with a wave of her wand. The plate with my hair and another were on two altars before us. We stood, and our chairs disappeared too.

"We all know that love spells are the most complicated of spells, and we have been taught not to cast them. But these are desperate times, and the prince is lucky that at this moment it is love and not death that he is to be cursed with."

I watched in horror and in wonder as the spell was cast. They were going to try and take the prince from me. Even though he wasn't mine to begin with. It wasn't that I didn't already know that this was their plan, but having to participate in the ritual knowing its intent made my stomach turn. And looking at my sisters' faces full of anticipation and glee... Seeing how incredibly powerful each of them was showed me what I was up against. Suddenly, I felt like I had when I was small. When it seemed like all my sisters outmatched me in magic. When being the youngest and least-accomplished Entente seemed to be my Past, Present, and Future. Then, I had shown myself to be powerful by accident in giving South wings. But we had been on the same side. Now, what if I wasn't up to the task? What if a piece of myself—my own hair—was what actually killed the boy I . . . the boy I did not want to kill.

The moon rose over the manor as each sister did her part. Every one of them formed a golden ball of light in her hand, but each one was filled with a different component of devotion.

My sisters spoke two by two or alone as their lights joined the others.

"Beauty . . . ," said Horatia and Ocenth.

"Strength . . . ," said Perpetua and Effie.

"Kindness . . . ," said Odette and Em.

"Rhythm . . . ," said Sistine and Tere.

"Forgiveness . . . ," said Selina and Xtina.

"Grace . . . ," said Freya.

"Humor . . . ," said Bari.

"Suspense . . . ," said Amantha.

"Surprise . . . ," said Galatea.

As the light glowed, Galatea continued:

Fill the places that he lacks;
Make him feel like she is unmatched.

"This spell will take his will and mend it to Bari's," Galatea explained to me.

Galatea produced a lock of hair that I would recognize anywhere. It was the prince's.

She placed it on the altar.

"Taken from the royal barber this morning."

The hair dissipated and became another globe of light. The light unfurled into strings. And the strings of light met in the air, intertwining. And as they danced around each other, they became a larger globe that spun in the air, then floated down in front of Bari.

The light became solid, a face she took in her palms and then put up to her own. The new face concealed hers. It was mine.

May the prince be unable to resist.
May you seal his fate with a kiss.

All the sisters echoed back Galatea's words.

"May the prince be unable to resist. May Bari seal his fate with a kiss," they repeated again.

Bari smiled a slow, mischievous smile. The spell was done.

"She's me," I whispered as I took in my own face. It wasn't a surprise, and yet it was. I had spent years at the Couterie looking at Lavendra's face, which nearly matched mine. But this sensation was different. My face would be a weapon wielded by Bari.

"She is a version of you, the perfect one that he has in his head and heart," Galatea explained.

I stopped short. The face was unblemished. The skin glowing, the eyes brighter. The smile knowing but mischievous. This was how he saw me. This was how I looked to the boy who loved me.

"Won't the Queen and the guards recognize the face of the Couterie who attacked the palace?" I asked, tearing myself away from the face and making myself look at Galatea. I thought I had found a flaw in their plan. Maybe one that could stop all this madness.

"No, they'll see Bari's face. Only he will see yours."

There was no flaw; they had thought of everything. When he saw her, it would be my face. But her magic would make her look like herself, Master Gray's stepdaughter, to the guards and the Queen.

"And when he kisses her, he will want to marry her, no matter what the Crown says. The kiss will seal the spell," she continued.

As she said the words, my heart betrayed me, screaming in my chest against the idea.

My sisters' satisfied faces mirrored Bari's. They were practically aglow in their pride. But for the first time in my life, I felt no pride in being Entente.

South was unreadable. He didn't cast a single objection. But he didn't lend his power to the spell per Galatea's instructions. I hoped he could read the true conflict in me. I needed him to know that I wanted no part of this.

I was beside myself. I had managed to make it through the ceremony. I was planning to betray them, yet I still felt the draw of being part of them.

But this wasn't a dare from our youth. This was a preamble to more than our vengeance on the Queen—this was the first step toward the prince's death and the Entente taking over the Queendoms.

I shoved aside whatever else I was feeling. I knew the human words for it—the jealousy of him being in someone else's arms.

But all that was eclipsed by something else: the idea of him not being here in the world at all. And the idea of my sisters killing an innocent.

My sisters were stronger than I was, no matter what South said. But Hecate's words from years ago rattled around in my consciousness. *With enough will and enough magic, anything is possible.* She had said that with an army of Entente at her back.

I would need an army of my own and someone else's wish.

PART IV
FATED

There is no such thing as bad or good magic.
There's what you can do and what you cannot.
—Farrow, Fairy Godmother

CHAPTER 59

I had to stop them. But I needed help. I needed South. I needed him to help me.

When we got back to the manor, I followed South to the barn. What I wanted to do came in pieces. *I have to save the prince but still give the Queen her due. I must stop my sisters but not reveal myself or them. I need a way to save them from themselves. A way to save the Hinter. A way to save all the Queendoms. A way to save the world.* But with my fractured magic, it would take more than my wand, more than myself. Now I just had to ask for help. But South of course would already know before I said a word.

"I know what the Entente are planning," he said, taking off his shirt suddenly. "I think the answer is you."

"What are you talking about? And what are you doing?" I demanded.

As he spoke, he extended his wings to their full span.

"You said it yourself. My wings shouldn't be here. But they are. Hecate shouldn't have survived death, but she did. What do these things have in common?"

"I don't know, magic?" I said, slightly distracted as I looked at South's muscles.

Was it possible that he had developed more of them despite barely leaving this room?

"You, Farrow. You," South said. "Galatea and Iolanta both said that great emotion can make magic last. Hecate loved you so much that when she gave you the kiss of protection, she did not leave you. She did not go into the Ever After. And you gave me my wings."

"I had no idea what I was doing. It wasn't supposed to happen."

"I was scared that day. And you were too. That fueled the spell. I wanted to have magic more than anything in the world. And Hecate wanted to stay with you more than anything. Farrow, maybe you have been granting wishes all along.

"You've proven that you can make magic last. You just have to do it again. We'll use their plan against them. You must get the prince out in the garden and kiss him first."

"South . . . ," I said, still unsure.

"Kiss the prince, grant the wish, and hope," South added.

CHAPTER 60

I left South in a daze. I could feel Hecate's ashes rustling in her pouch, and I released her.

"Hecate, it's worse than anything we imagined . . . Our sisters . . . they . . . have done the most awful things . . . and they are not finished."

As she stood before me, I realized there was something I needed to do before anything else.

"Hecate, I have to tell her. And she has to tell me. A truth for a truth."

Hecate stepped out of my way as if she was giving me permission.

I found Cinderella in her room curled up with a novel. She looked up from the book. I almost hated taking her away from whatever she was reading. In all the time I had been here, I had so rarely seen her in repose.

"I don't know why I read these things. I know the Queen is behind them. She's trying to make the prince into a hero." She laughed guiltily.

There had been years of romance novels written about all the Queens of the Queendoms, usually saving and falling for commoners, all designed to make the Queendoms fall more in love with their royals. I was sure there was not a single author writing one where the Prince fell for an Entente.

She put the romance down.

"What is it, Farrow?"

"I'm so sorry, Cinderella. You were right about my family. You were right about everything. Galatea, Amantha, and Bari have a plan that will end with the prince's death. I have to stop them."

"Okay, I'm in," she said without hesitation. "Maybe this will help. I've been carrying it around since my father gave it to me."

Cinderella reached into her pocket and retrieved something. She pressed a wand into my palm. I examined the hilt. The carving of South with his wings stared up at me. This was the wand I'd given away to the man with the horse by the Reverie so long ago. My heart sped up. It couldn't be.

"Where did you get that?" I demanded, not understanding.

"My father gave it to me. He said he thought he'd met the last of the Entente. I didn't notice before. But I see it now. That's South on the wand, isn't it?"

"Yes . . . it is . . ."

"I didn't notice it until I pulled it out to give it to you . . ."

"I gave your father that wand. But how can you have any faith in magic after what it's done to you?"

"It wasn't magic that killed my parents. It was a single witch. Not every person is evil because the Queen is evil. I have to believe that the same is true for the Entente."

I took a deep breath, and then made a decision. But there was something I needed to know first.

"You aren't just a thief, are you?"

"I'm not on the side of the Entente or the side of the Queen."

"What other side is there?" I asked.

"The side of the people. Not all of us want to serve her. Some of us want to be free."

"And how do you think you're going to accomplish that?"

Cinderella didn't have any magic. The Resistance's numbers seemed so few from the vision I had seen. And yet here she was, part of a ragtag army.

I continued, "When I got home after we saved Maggie, I got a flash of your wishes. I needed to know if you presented danger to my . . . to the Entente."

"They are the danger."

"That doesn't mean you aren't too. I saw you with a bunch of masked people. You aren't alone, and you aren't a thief. You are part of the Resistance."

"I wasn't. Not at first. And they weren't either. Then, they were just stealing to get the things that had become scarce under the Queen's rule. But they decided to do more, to use what they made to help the people. To fund taking down the Queen. They were just doing what they had to do to survive the Queen and the Entente. They were stuck in the middle."

"And now you're part of them."

"I guess I always was. Do you ever think of us, Farrow? What it's like for us, the people of the Hinter? We never asked for this war. We loved the story of the Entente. We loved the Queen. And now we're drafted into the army or we're left to starve, all because you can't keep the peace."

"What changed for you?"

"When my friend Rebecca was captured and released, she wasn't the same. I don't know what they did to her. She's quiet where she was loud, she's thin where she was soft, and she's empty where she was full."

"She's not empty—she's angry. Or at least that's how I was after the Burning."

"Like you and your sisters . . . ," Cinderella assessed.

"Why aren't you angrier? You've lost so much too."

"I am angry. I just thought that things would get better. I know now that I can't stand by. I have to do something. I have to help."

I understood. And some part of me was saddened by it, that she had been pushed far enough to be moved by vengeance. But I was heartened too because it meant humans could change. I just wasn't sure if this change was for the better. The girl before me had somehow managed to be so gentle and kind despite the abuse from my sisters. Had they now twisted her to the point of murder?

"So, what is your weapon of choice?" I asked. "Poison? Knives? Because I promise you, it is harder than you think to kill someone up close."

"Kill? We're going to rob the royals blind while they are at the ball. It's the perfect opportunity."

I felt myself flood with relief. The flash I had seen wasn't her planning a coup on the Entente.

Her face filled with surprise, then recrimination. Cinderella pressed, "Wait, what did you think I . . . we were capable of?"

I could see her confusion and her anger. But there was patience too. She was hoping that I would give her a reason to trust me, that I would give her a reason not to hate me.

"No matter," I said. "You are a far better being than me, Cinderella." I paused, then spoke again. "What if I told you I had a better idea? How would you like to go to the ball *and* save the Queendoms?"

"Yes, I would very much like that," she said, without missing a beat. "And so would my animal friends."

CHAPTER 61

Cinderella and I met in the barn.

I used my wand as each member of Cinderella's household wished for the role they were to play tonight. Hodder stayed in his horse form and Wendell changed from a squirrel to a matching white stallion. They would pull Cinderella's carriage.

Wendell neighed and tossed his tail. I could tell that he preferred this to his squirrel form.

The others tittered about, dressing the horses. Cinderella made a wish, and a beautiful coach laden with gold appeared.

"We still need a coachman," I said.

"We have one more friend to ask. I wish Perdi to be my coachwoman." Cinderella slipped the mouse out of her pocket. "She showed up this morning. Perhaps it's a sign that everything might end up Happily Ever After," Cinderella said with a smile.

I took Perdi's small, soft body in my hands and gently placed her on the floor.

"Hi, little Perdi, I am so sorry for your ordeal," I whispered. And then I began my spell.

Return Perdi to her previous life.
Make what my sisters did right.
Legs . . . arms . . . fingers . . . toes . . .
Bring this mouse back to its origins.
Give her arms and fingers and toes and everything that once was lost.

The mouse made a guttural sound. The flesh beneath her fur began to contort and expand. The tiny button nose stretched into a large one, and the tiny mouse ears popped out into larger-than-average human ones.

Cinderella let out a half laugh, half gasp. Within seconds the mouse stood on its hind legs. After a few more seconds, a naked elderly woman sat in the center of the barn. Cinderella raced to get her a couple of aprons and then covered her. But Perdi was too dazed to be shy about her lack of clothes.

"Oh my," Perdi said. Her voice was somewhere between a human voice and a mouse's squeak.

Renell, the footman, and Jacques were there too. One reached for a blanket to cover her and the other for a glass of water for her. They knew what it was to make this transition, and they sought to make her comfortable as quickly as they could.

"Welcome back, Perdi," Cinderella said sweetly.

As the others tended to her needs, I had to break the bad news.

"I hate to tell you this, but the magic is not going to last. I am not strong enough. You will turn back at midnight," I explained to all the animals as gently as I could. "I will find a more permanent solution. I promise. But there's something I need you to do tonight. For Cinderella. For all of us."

CHAPTER 62

Now it was Cinderella's turn. It was time to create the perfect dress for the ball. One that would distract the prince. One that she wished for with all her might.

Make Cinderella the belle of the ball.
Put the prince in her enthrall.
Make her and her dress the fairest of them all.
And when he sees the face of the one he loves,
Make him love her most of all,
So deeply that he will follow her every footfall.
But when the moon reaches its height,
Make it so that everything returns to as it was before tonight.

I thought of every detail as I designed the gown. As I waved my wand, white silk and lace encircled Cinderella, accentuating her every curve. I slightly tinted the fabric a shade of silver.

Cinderella watched the dress form itself, her eyes wide with delight.

"It looks just like my mother's!"

Cinderella gave me a quick hug, which I returned. Gazing down at my dress, she commented, "But you can't possibly wear that."

"Just wish me a disguise that no one can see through, and I'll do the rest," I said, raising my wand.

Cinderella frowned, unsure, and then closed her eyes, complying.

When I looked in the mirror, the face staring back at me was one I had not seen before. She had long brown hair with blondish streaks. Wide-set green eyes and a full lip. Her skin was paler than mine. Her cheeks higher.

"Who is she?" I asked, taking in the beauty of the face.

"Someone I made up. My father's eyes. My mother's nose and the baker's girl's cheekbones."

I felt myself smiling in wonder. Cinderella was a constant surprise.

"You keep thinking your magic has limits. But I think it can go as far as the imagination."

"You are quite the artist, Cinderella. It is a face that would stop anyone's heart."

"And if anyone sees the resemblance, they won't make sense of it. You can say you are a long-lost Gray from the Ninth Queendom."

"Are there any long-lost Grays in the Ninth Queendom?"

"If there were, I think they would have sought me out by now . . ."

I smoothed the pretty, pale-peach dress I wore, with its delicate raised floral pattern and crystal shoes, just like Cinderella's. I exhaled, suddenly nervous. Was it the corset or the prospect of seeing the prince again that took my breath away?

There was one last thing that I hadn't thought of. One last thing that I hadn't anticipated. How could I cast a protection spell when I could only grant wishes?

"You can do anything. All you need is a wish," Cinderella said.

"But not my own."

"That's why it was important to have friends," Cinderella offered.

Friends? Was that what we were? Was that why I had sought her out? Was it more than my guilt for what I first suspected and now confirmed my sisters had done to her? I was beginning to think it was.

I smiled at her and added, "You're going to have to memorize a spell."

CHAPTER 63

The royal palace was decorated in all its finest. There were chandeliers made of pearls and other precious stones. The floor itself was mirrored so dancers could see themselves while they moved. And the walls were mirrored too, but hand painted with scenes from Prince Mather's life. Even the Black Glass seemed to have taken on a special glow.

Our plan was in motion.

As I strode to the back of the ballroom, my mind flooded with an onslaught of wishes from the partygoers.

I wish he would look at me.

I wish I were taller.

I wish I were thinner.

I wish I had a better dress.

I wish I didn't have to be here.

I wish I were here with Aldopho.

I wish Frederika and I could be together.

I wish . . . I wish . . . I wish . . .

I rocked back on my heels as my brain flooded with all the wanting in the room. *This must be how South feels all the time*, I thought.

I spotted the Queen's receiving line before I spotted the Queen, and I ducked behind it pausing only to get a glimpse of her. Her throne sat on a raised dais a hundred feet from where I entered. Beneath the dais was her court of ladies, who looked up at her adoringly and hung on her every word.

I tried not to stare at her, but I couldn't help it. My instinct was to cross to the Queen and take her out with my knife. There was so much that was not assured about tonight. So many twists and turns could go wrong. I steeled myself. I had to trust in the magic, in South and Cinderella and Fate itself.

The ball was supposed to be for the prince, but like everything in the Queendom, it still revolved around her. There was a steady stream of guests all offering her presents. Beside her was a giant golden box, a present that Queen Jolie of the Sixth Queendom, Mettlebrau, had sent in her stead. From the whispers around me, I gathered that Queen Magrit planned on opening the box in the middle of the festivities.

I forced myself to move away from her and look for the prince and Cinderella. I took in the ball.

What the Queen lacked in magic, she made up with in manpower. Every person in the palace must have worked tirelessly to make the ball perfect. Uniformed men directed partygoers, circulated food, and refilled every glass before it was empty.

Meanwhile, every woman in the Queendom had the day off so they could properly prepare and enjoy the ball. Queen Magrit had decided Prince Mather should be married off immediately. After a Couterie attempting to murder her and freeing her pet Entente, the Queen was not going to wait for the prince to replace his Couterie. The likelihood of the prince choosing a commoner as his bride was next to none, but the Queen had ordered every woman in the land to attend as guests of the prince.

Most women didn't care about marrying the prince, but that did not stop them from wanting to see him and get a glimpse of the palace. They wanted to taste the Queen's food and see what she was wearing. They wanted a night out, just like Cinderella did.

There was a loud laugh from near the Queen, and I was drawn to her again.

The Queen was watching something intently. No, someone.

The prince. He was dressed in full uniform, complete with buttons and epaulets. His hair, which had been tousled when I'd met him, was now slicked down into submission except for one errant curl at his temple.

Despite my grand plans, despite the danger, part of me wanted to reach out and touch that curl and muss his hair. Part of me wanted that moment back when it was just me and him in his bedroom.

I shook the feeling off and turned to find myself face to bust with Madame Linea.

Did she recognize me? Had my magic held?

"Some party," she said, twirling her glass of champagne between her long fingers.

I nodded. There was no way that she could know who I was. I had a new face. But of all the humans in this room, she was the most likely to somehow guess.

"For a man who has every eligible woman in the Queendom lining up to meet him, the prince doesn't look at all happy," she assessed.

I looked at the prince again. She was right. I had only spent a dozen hours with him, but I remembered the forced smile he'd plastered on for his friends. It wasn't dissimilar to the one he was wearing now.

"You would almost think that his heart already belongs to another," she mused.

I bit my lip and scanned the ballroom, finally spotting my sisters. They had positioned themselves on the edge of the dance floor to be among the first to greet the prince once he began his receiving line.

I spotted the rest of the Couterie seated together across the ballroom. Sypress and Knola were dancing with each other, full of mirth, which could have been real or make-believe. Dinah was seated and knocking back a champagne flute. Holocene, my former Shadow, was taking in the ballroom in wonder. She was wearing a dress I had never seen before. It was white with blue trim, which accentuated her skin color. I couldn't help it. I wanted to know if she had met the prince yet.

I reminded myself that it was none of my concern whether they would have a Becoming. But seeing Holocene in her new finery affected me.

The crowd murmured and turned toward the stairs. I broke my gaze on Holocene and watched as Cinderella appeared. She whispered her name to the attendant who was charged with announcing every lady to the ball.

"Presenting Lady . . . ahem . . . Lady . . . Marrow."

I stifled a laugh. Cinderella somehow managed to keep her sense of humor in the middle of all this danger.

The ballroom seemed captivated as she descended the stairs—and the prince was not immune to her beauty or her presence either. I saw her face light up at the attention. After months of being in my sisters' shadows, of feeling unseen and uncared for, Cinderella was the center of attention.

The prince crossed the room and bent down before her. I felt my heart catch in my chest with unmistakable regret. I wanted to be the girl he kneeled for. I wanted my hand in his. I wanted him to glide me across the floor.

"Madame, you were saying?" I pressed, turning back to Madame Linea. "You think another has the prince's heart?"

"Someone I thought I knew," Linea said.

She stared at me as if she could see right through me. *Could she recognize me?* I wondered. I concentrated on her. Much to my relief her wishes were far from me. They were on the Queen.

Please let her not retaliate against me. I should have known something was wrong with the girl. Please don't let the rest of the Couterie pay for my mistakes.

I was surprised. I expected pure self-preservation from her. But she was thinking about the Couterie.

I did not want to see the Couterie shuttered, but the prince's idea to stop the practice of Becoming and maintain their roles as confidants and advisors made sense to me. But Madame Linea wasn't thinking of a new path for the Couterie. She was trying to save the old one. And knowing that she was dealing with such a volatile Queen, she was also worried about saving their necks.

"I should tell the Queen the lesson I failed to follow myself," she said suddenly.

"What's that?"

"Beware uninvited guests," she said.

I told myself again that there was no way for her to recognize me, that the Couterie's power was discernment, not magic. But that did not stop my heart from speeding its pace.

"Every eligible girl in the Queendoms is invited," I reminded her, trying to stay calm.

She laughed. "I know everyone of importance in all the

Queendoms. And a girl like that with a gown like that does not come out of nowhere."

I remembered I was wearing the dress and face of a stranger—and that Cinderella's face had barely been seen by anyone since her mother died. Not to mention the forgetting spell that my sisters had cast to make people forget her.

"But you do not know me . . . ," I blurted, not meaning to ask for trouble, but Linea's presence had rattled me.

"Don't I? Aren't you in Queen Marvel's court? You were at her Becoming soiree."

"Indeed. What a memory, Madame Linea," I said, knowing how she loved flattery. But I was focused on her dangerous mood too. Linea was rarely wrong about names and faces. Perhaps her focus on Cinderella had distracted her.

From what Tork told me about the Queen's actions after my night with the prince, the Queen's concern about strangers had nothing to do with the girl on the dance floor and everything to do with me and my breach of the palace. Linea was justifiably bitter. I had put her and the Couterie in danger. I wanted to tell Linea that I never wanted to hurt her or the Couterie. Becoming was the only way I could think of to get into the palace. But I stayed mum. Telling her meant giving myself up, and I couldn't count on her being forgiving.

"I should really warn the Queen," she said, still staring at Cinderella.

Fear cropped up in me. Could Linea ruin all our hard work with a word to the Queen? I had to say something. I had to change her mind.

But before I could speak, she sniffed. "I do want to see what trouble this girl stirs up, though. This party is an absolute bore."

Linea took a swig from her glass, temporarily drowning out my access to her wishes. She studied me for a moment. Her gaze suddenly cleared.

"May I offer some unsolicited advice? If you want to win the prince's heart, there is nothing more attractive to a man who has everything than the girl who offers nothing. Do not seek him and he will seek you."

"Who says I want the prince?" I said, keeping my tone light.

"I'd like to think I can still make a match," she said with a small, wan smile. Then she raised her glass to me and disappeared into the crowd.

"It's not you, it's her," said a man beside me.

When I heard his voice, I had to swallow his name before it spilled out of me. It was Hark. He cut a dashing figure in a pale-blue suit and wore an elaborate and appropriate dragon's mask. "Pardon?" I asked.

"It's a wonder she'd show her face here at all. Two Couterie missing in a year . . . What are the odds?" Hark said, even though I hadn't commented on Madame Linea out loud.

"I'm from the Ninth Queendom. We are not privy to all the gossip from the Hinter. We heard about a wayward Couterie who left the prince; surely there could not have been another . . . ?" I said, feigning ignorance.

"They called him Tork—Queen Papillion is livid. And poor Madame Linea believes the Couterie is done for. But as you can see, she is trying to put on a brave face."

Good for you, Tork, I thought. I felt a flood of joy for Tork and Lavendra. And as I scanned the room, I spotted Jacoby with the Couterie—awkward as ever but smiling broadly. He was there because Tork was not. The smile that threatened to overtake my lips was tempered by another thought that chased it.

"Would the Queen retaliate? Would she hurt the Couterie?" I asked.

"The other Queens would never allow that. And the Couterie know too much," Hark said confidently.

Tell that to the Entente, I thought. I smiled then, but underneath I was unnerved. I needed to get out to the garden to wait for Cinderella and Mather when she led him there. I glanced at the dance floor, trying to get a glimpse of the prince, who had taken Cinderella into his arms and begun a waltz.

"Am I boring you . . . ? All eyes on the prince—I know. But I must do my part and keep the dance floor from being empty," Hark said, bowing and proffering his hand to me.

"Still a flirt," I said.

"Pardon me. Have we met before, miss?" he asked with a twinkle in his eye.

I recovered. "Never, but I can tell that you have always been that way."

"I would say you were presumptuous if you weren't so accurate."

"I thought that only the prince was to dance with the ladies."

"You know how the Queen and the prince have a taster to make sure that their food is not poisoned?"

I took his hand. "So do I pass the taste test?" I quipped as he led me out onto the floor.

He laughed heartily and picked up our pace to match the tempo.

Suddenly, he stopped, and then he danced us over to the prince, who was still dancing with Cinderella.

"May I cut in?" Hark said, not really asking. "I'm sorry to interrupt, but it is the Queen's directive that the prince dance with every lady, and there are many more in line."

Prince Mather looked genuinely surprised by Hark's imprudence. He bowed in an apology to Cinderella.

"I'm sure this lovely maiden would like a moment of your time," Hark said, pushing me toward the prince.

The prince kissed Cinderella's hand. "I will find you again, mademoiselle."

Then he turned to Hark. "Hark, I'll find you and thrash you properly later," Mather promised.

But he still bowed before me, and I took his hand.

I reminded myself all that mattered was keeping the prince out of Bari and Amantha's grasp. If I had to spend all night with him, it was worth it to save him.

"There's no need to be nervous. I don't bite," he said as he glided me toward the center of the floor.

"What makes you think I'm nervous?" I asked.

"You're playing a symphony on my left hand."

"Forgive me. I've never danced with a prince before," I lied, quieting my fingers.

"Really?" he said, cocking his head. "You could have fooled me."

I forced a smile, knowing that I had to keep his attention for as long as possible. But I tried to keep an eye on Cinderella, who had been whisked away by Hark in the direction of the Queen's throne, which was empty at present.

Still locked in the prince's embrace, I considered what I could do without magic and without revealing myself. But Cinderella shot me a look, and then her eyes darted toward the balcony.

Farrow, I wish you could see what I am thinking. You can get the prince alone all by yourself. You don't need me for this.

She was right. The reason I had enlisted Cinderella wasn't for the safety of the plan. It was for the safety of my heart.

But the spell itself... I thought with a panic rising in me. Cinderella was supposed to say the words and seal it with a kiss and a wish.

Farrow, you can say the words. They're yours after all. When the clock begins to strike at twelve, I will wish and wish and wish. All you need do is grant and kiss.

It was not the plan. But it had to work. I stumbled into the prince on purpose, and he caught me around the waist.

"Mademoiselle, are you all right?" the prince asked, looking down at me.

"I feel a little faint. I think I need to get some air," I demurred, preparing to lead him to the garden, where I could use the spell. The clock was almost at midnight.

But suddenly I heard a new voice, which was louder than all the rest. It was Queen Magrit's.

"Who on earth is he dancing with?" she demanded.

The ballroom went quiet. The Queen strode to the center of the room.

It was time for me and Cinderella to leave, plan or no plan.

"I have to go," I said as his eyes found mine again.

"No one move," the Queen said, traversing the ballroom and commanding everyone's attention. But hers had already flickered elsewhere.

"It is time," she said, indicating Queen Jolie's mysterious present.

The room tittered with overly exaggerated applause from all the guests, but particularly those of the Queen's court, who were seated around her throne. They clapped as if their lives depended upon it, because, of course, theirs did. Two servants carried the box and set it before the Queen.

Magrit approached it.

The party that was supposed to be about her son was all about her.

She strutted around the box and ordered it opened.

"This is proof that we will soon be in control of all the Queendoms. This gift is only the beginning. We thank the Sixth Queendom in absentia."

The box was opened, and a feathered cape was lifted from it. Two of her men raised the cape over Queen Magrit's shoulders, and she twirled around.

Then I heard Cinderella's next wish . . . and I made the symbol for the Resistance appear on the box.

The Queen opened her mouth in horror. "What sorcery is this?"

The coat began to move.

I hid the smile from my lips as the fur revealed itself to be a coat full of mice.

The Queen shrieked and tried to rid herself of it.

Birds flew in through the open doors. And there was the sound of hooves against the ballroom floor. The horses outside had broken free of their carriages and made their way into the ballroom.

For a few mesmerizing seconds, everything froze as the mice and the other animals moved in sync, almost in a dance. They formed the sign of the Resistance again.

Everyone looked on in awe.

Then the animals began approaching the guests.

But they did so selectively, somehow finding the most privileged among them and ignoring the servants and the girls from town who'd just been hoping to get a glimpse of the prince.

The Queen screamed. "Don't you see? The Entente are here. Close all the doors! We will root them out."

But for the first time, perhaps since the Entente had defied her, so did the rest of Hinter. The guests began pouring out of the doors.

The prince seized my hand.

"Come with me," he said, pulling open the double doors toward the garden. "My mother won't bother us here."

But my mind was filled with worry for Cinderella, for South, and even for Galatea, Bari, and Amantha. None of us could be captured by Queen Magrit.

I had not completed my mission, but perhaps I'd caused enough chaos that my sisters would not complete theirs either. It was time to go home.

"I have to go home . . . ," I whispered.

But I spotted something behind him. Time had stopped for the people pouring out of the ball again. They were frozen in place through no magic of my own.

I heard South's voice in my head.

I can buy you a few minutes, nothing more.

I could see his winged figure atop one of the palace's battlements. South was here. He'd come to help us, despite my warning to the contrary.

"Thank you," I whispered out loud before I allowed the prince to lead me through the garden into the maze of fountains and shrubbery pruned to look like animals. We stopped in front of a bench next to two giant doves.

"Are you all right?" he asked.

"I'm fine. I just needed some air. Thank you for the rescue."

"It is you who rescued me . . . My mother wants me to pick a bride tonight, but I'm not ready. Perhaps I never will be," the prince said judiciously.

"Why?"

"My heart isn't healed yet. There was another girl who I felt something for. But . . ."

"But what?" I asked.

"She tried to assassinate my mother."

He clapped his hand over his mouth. "I don't know why I just told you that . . ."

It had to somehow be the spell. He'd probably tell his whole life story to any girl he danced with at this point.

"I'm glad you told me . . . I just wonder. How can you still care about her?"

"I know it sounds unbelievable. We spent only a few hours together. But for the first time in a long time, maybe ever, I felt understood."

I wish I could forget about her.

I wish I didn't remember everything about her.

I wish I didn't keep replaying every moment we spent together over and over in my head . . .

I wish I could just concentrate on what's in front of me.

I could hear his wishes, and I knew that I could grant them. I could set him free.

Instead, I admitted I was getting over someone too.

"Who is he?" the prince asked.

"He surprised me. I had an idea of who he was, and I was wrong. And when I saw him for who he really was, it changed how I saw the world and everyone in it."

"Love doesn't just change the heart. It can change the mind. That girl was the first person to make me feel understood. Until now. I feel like maybe you know me. And somehow I know you," he said.

"You don't know me . . ."

"Don't I?" he asked, his eyes fixed on mine.

The clock struck once, interrupting us. I didn't have any time left.

I couldn't see Cinderella, but I could hear her wishing.

I wish . . .

I turned to the prince as the second chime rang. "I have to go . . ."

"You have to stay," he answered, his hand on my waist.

I wish . . .

I felt a flash of unexpected emotion. Could he somehow see through to the real me? I was so aware of his touch. It affected me as no spell could ever do.

The clock struck again.

"I am not the answer to your broken heart, Prince."

I wish . . . that Farrow's spell is as true as her kiss.

The clock struck again and again and again until the very last chime. Time—which, I was sure, had never been a friend—was now the enemy.

I held my wand in my pocket, and I said the words out loud, praying that this complicated pretzel of wanting and granting and spelling and kissing resulted in no harm coming to the prince.

Keep your heart and crown your own
Until a worthy heart comes along.
Let no magic change your heart.
Let this kiss protect you from any harm
And keep you from the Entente's charms.

"What are you doing?" he demanded, confused.

"What I have to do to save you."

And then I leaned in and kissed him on the lips. I felt warmth wash over us, and when I opened my eyes, I could see a hazy glow around the prince.

His eyes fluttered open.

"I have to go," I said, and took off out of the garden and down the steps of the palace.

Cinderella met me at the bottom of the stairs. "What happened to you?" she deflected, looking down at my feet.

I had lost my shoe.

There was a noise above. It was the sound of footsteps. The prince was catching up to me.

"Make a wish to take us home . . . and be specific," I ordered Cinderella. "There's no time to get to the carriage."

Cinderella closed her eyes, and I waved my wand. In a blink we were standing in front of her mansion.

CHAPTER 64

We left them behind," Cinderella said breathlessly as we found ourselves in the barn. Her concern for Hodder, Wendell, and Perdi were her first thoughts after our narrow escape. I felt a pang of guilt for leaving them there.

"Wish them home," I said, fervently hoping that no harm befell them and that no one witnessed their transformation.

A few seconds and wishes later, Hodder, Perdi, and Wendell were back with us in their animal forms.

"Thank you," I whispered to them.

"I'm sorry." Cinderella purred apologies, nuzzling her head against the horse.

All the magic had worn off, but when I looked down at my feet the other glass shoe was still there. Had I blinked too fast? Was my power already fading? How was this shoe still here? And where was the other one?

Cinderella looked down as I took off the shoe and examined it.

She exclaimed, "Oh no!"

"Was it the wish? I wasn't specific enough," she supposed, blaming herself.

I shook my head—it wasn't the wish's fault. My dress had

transformed back into its original form. But the shoe remained. I wondered about its mate. I had left it on the stairs.

"Do you want me to wish the other one home?"

"And raise more suspicion . . . ? I think it's best we leave it alone."

Cinderella accepted this, but she wasn't ready to let it go.

"But that still doesn't explain how the shoe outlasted the spell. Mine are gone," she said, pointing down to her own shoes, which were indeed moccasins again.

"When magic lasts longer than its spell, it's usually because of intense emotion, or at least that's what I think happened with Hecate still being here as ash and with South's wings . . ."

"So that means . . . you love the prince."

"No . . . I . . ." I opened my mouth to protest, but I closed it again. It couldn't be.

I was Entente. We were not supposed to love. Especially not humans. *The old rules don't apply anymore.* Galatea's words came back to me. She was talking about revenge, not love. But that didn't mean they weren't true.

Cinderella was still blinking her big eyes at me, waiting for a response.

"Is there another explanation?"

"All my emotions were heightened. I am sure that fear could do the exact same thing."

"When you were in the prince's arms, you didn't look scared to me . . ."

"There is no room for love in this plot . . ."

"Tell that to your heart. And your shoe."

"We don't have time for this. You should go to your room. Get in your nightclothes. Galatea, Amantha, and Bari will be here momentarily," I ordered, and Cinderella dutifully raced off.

I was still thinking of the single shoe without a mate and Cinderella's belief that it was still here because of love.

When I opened the door, I found that the noise outside wasn't the arrival of my sisters. It was South. He was climbing the trellis outside that would lead to my bedroom.

"Farrow." He was calling up to the window.

"What the hells are you doing out there?" I asked.

South turned around, and I waved him in through the front door.

"They're not home yet. But you need to get to your room and get dressed for bed. Why didn't you blink yourself back into your room?"

"Galatea would see the Past. This way, without using my magic, there's a chance she wouldn't bother to look."

"How is it that I underestimated you all my life?" I asked.

"I have a way of sneaking up on people," he said with a smile.

"I told you to stay home."

"And if I had, you and Cinderella wouldn't be here now."

"We would have improvised," I defended, but I smiled at him. His distraction had helped us get away.

"I had to go. I needed to help you. I had to see for myself."

"See what?"

Just then I could hear the sound of my sisters arriving home. South slipped back up the stairs, and I braced myself.

"How was the ball?" I asked when Bari, Amantha, and Galatea actually got inside. They had taken their carriage instead of returning by magical means. I had slipped into one of the chairs in the sitting room and put the shoe in my pocket.

"Where is she? Ella, get down here!" Galatea screamed with a wild look on her face.

I rose, feigning innocence.

"Ella," she called again. She stared at me a beat. She drew her wand from her pocket. I wondered if she was preparing to look into my Past or Cinderella's.

I hoped that I had not miscalculated. I hoped that Galatea would not look into Cinderella's Past because she assumed that it was, as always, uneventful. Amantha and Bari comically fought to get through the door with their competing dresses. A frustrated Amantha disappeared and reappeared across the sitting room. This time she appeared with hibiscus nectar and glasses. Galatea, meanwhile, approached the stairs.

"Where is that girl?"

"It was a nightmare," Bari said dramatically, reaching for a glass.

"What happened?" I asked her.

The glass slipped to the ground with a crash as Amantha flickered beside her, still pouring where her glass should have been.

"There was another girl, and she hijacked the prince's attention all night," Bari continued, unbothered.

"Cinderella!" Amantha called, looking down at the spilled glass and champagne.

Cinderella appeared at the top of the stairs, stretching for effect.

"What do you need, Mother?" she asked.

"Never mind. I just wanted to see that you were here," Galatea said, looking relieved.

"Where else would I be?" Cinderella asked innocently.

"Don't be insolent, Ella. Back to bed," Galatea barked.

"Galatea, I need her to clean this up," Amantha protested.

Cinderella bowed and turned without making eye contact with me. When she disappeared into her room again, I had to hold in a sigh of relief.

But then Galatea returned her attention to me and my sisters.

"I need to think," Galatea said with a furrowed brow.

"We should run," Bari said in a whisper.

"Why would we run? You're scaring me. What happened at the ball?"

"You don't know?"

"How would I know?" I asked.

"I assumed that South would have told you every moment of the ball," Galatea said.

"He was sleeping. I couldn't wake him."

"It was awful. You should have been there. Maybe I could have wished her to implode, and you could have granted it," Bari said with a loud sigh.

Amantha laughed, but added, "Her dress was pretty magnificent though. So much so it made me positively angry."

"Who was she? I don't understand. Did the spell not work? Did he pick the princess of Garbon?"

"There was another girl. She called herself Marrow. What kind of insipid name is that? He danced every dance with her," Amantha said, despaired.

"Well, the Queen won't let that stand. Surely there will be another ball and you can reenact your plan there," I consoled.

"The people have fallen in love with the idea of a people's princess. And the Queen will have no choice but to go along with it. It is just as we planned, only some other girl enacted our plot."

"But who the hells was she?" I asked, pretending to match their fervor.

When Amantha gave me a sharp look, I wondered if I had overacted. But instead she just joined in. "If I didn't know better, I would think she had magic."

"And you couldn't use your magical wiles to split them up?"

"It was too much of a risk to use the spell more than once. If we couldn't get close enough, then it was not worth being exposed."

"There will be other chances."

"You don't understand. You were right—Magrit knew we were there—she could somehow sense magic. She stopped the ball and started searching every guest. My guess is she will start searching every house."

"But we're cloaked."

"We are, and we were tonight. But somehow she knew."

"The bigger question is, what are we going to do now?"

"She didn't identify us. I say we stay. We'll take another crack at the prince," Amantha said.

"She's never going to hold another ball. We'll be lucky if the prince ever leaves the palace again," Bari added with a sigh.

"Then we'll think of something else. There has to be another way, Galatea. If not the prince, then something else. We'll find it in time," I said gently.

Galatea sank into a chair, unsure.

We had come so close to what I wanted: a stop to all this. But at least the prince was safe tonight.

I returned to my room and placed the shoe on the bed. I released Hecate from the pouch. The shoe stared up at both of us.

"I know, I should throw it away, Hecate. I can't be in love—there's no place for love in all this. And of beings in all the Queendoms . . . how could it be him? Did you see all this, Hecate? Did you see him? Can you tell me what's going to happen with us—with my sisters?"

Hecate didn't respond. She just took a seat on the bed.

I slipped the shoe into a drawer and piled some underthings on top of it.

I knew I should smash it into a million pieces. But I couldn't bear it. I wanted to keep it, since I could not keep him. It was a souvenir—a memento of love that could not be.

Hecate curled up in her ash form beside me. It wasn't a "yes." But it was something. Hecate could not give me the answer I wanted—but she was giving me comfort. As she always had.

"Are you even a little proud of me?" I wanted and needed to know.

Everyone was still alive, and my sisters were none the wiser . . .

Hecate snuggled a little closer to me.

CHAPTER 65

The skies opened up, and it rained all night. The thunder and lightning had just subsided when there was a knock at the front door.

"Allow me," I said. Cinderella was pulling a loaf of our breakfast bread out of the oven, so I skipped past her to see who had come calling. Galatea's charms on the house had disguised my face before I opened the door.

It was Prince Mather. And he was dripping wet.

He was more disheveled and harried than I had ever seen him. He looked as if he hadn't slept. There was worry written across his handsome face. Something was very wrong. I reminded myself of my place, of my face, of my station. And I tried to do something that Lavendra had told me long ago . . . not to listen to my stupid, stupid heart. Because if I did, I wouldn't be talking politely to that prince. I would be kissing him.

"Your Highness, what brings you to our humble door?" I asked with a bow.

Mather stepped inside. He shut and locked the door behind him.

"Your Highness?" I asked as he turned to face me.

"There isn't time for any more lies. I know who you are. I know it was you in the alley. And it was you last night in my arms at the ball. It was always you. And I've come to warn you. You must run!"

He couldn't know. We had been so careful. How could he have seen through my disguise when my own Entente sisters had not? And the Queen . . . She wasn't supposed to hunt me down. We were hunting her.

"You're mistaken. I could not attend the ball."

I turned away from him, trying to push down the feelings and the fear rising to the surface. I wanted him to know me. But I couldn't tell him the truth.

"You have a tell, Farrow. No matter what face you are wearing."

"I don't know what you're talking about."

He took my right hand. "You just did it again."

I inhaled sharply. I had been tapping my fingers together where my wand was supposed to be.

"Prince Mather, I can explain. Just not here."

"My mother has your shoe. She has Hark going door to door with it, looking for its rightful owner. She claims it's the Queen's duty to find my bride. But from the look in her eye, I think she suspects that you had something to do with the Entente. She'll be here any minute."

Perhaps it was the mere mention of the Queen that caused Galatea to rush downstairs and through the doorway. She pushed poor Cinderella, bread and all, aside. I expected Amantha and Bari to be at her heels, but they probably were snoring through all the commotion.

"Your Highness! What a great honor it is to have you visit our humble abode. To what do we owe the pleasure?" Galatea asked.

"Love," Prince Mather answered finally for himself, and stepped closer to me.

My heart stopped. I wanted to get him as far away from Galatea, Amantha, and Bari as possible.

Galatea approached Mather, her eyes narrowing on him. "Love?" she asked, waiting for him to elaborate.

But there was no time to answer. We could see through the window that the royal carriage was arriving at just this moment. Hark hopped out. He was holding the crystal shoe on a blue-velvet pillow. Behind him gathered the Queen's personal guard and a half dozen of her soldiers.

Prince Mather's eyes met mine.

Galatea stepped in front of me protectively.

"Get your sisters," she commanded to me in a whisper.

"Madame Gray, you can't—" Mather started.

But Galatea ignored him, opening the door, smiling, as Hark's handsome form filled the doorframe.

"We seek the owner of this shoe, which was left on the palace steps last night. Its owner is to marry the prince. Every woman in the Queendom must try it on," Hark explained.

In another Present, I would cross to Prince Mather, let him slip the shoe on me, and wrap my arms around him. But in this one, all I wanted to do was grab his hand and escape together.

"We need to see all the ladies of the house," decreed Hark again.

Galatea curtsied and then let him in, along with a couple of royal footmen and a half-dozen soldiers. The rest waited outside. "But, of course. And how lucky we are to see the prince twice in as many days . . . Farrow, your manners: get your sisters!"

I didn't turn around. I could already hear Bari's feet on the stairs. A second later, she was by my side.

Hark looked to the prince and gave a haughty smile. "But I see the prince has beaten me to it. And I can see why—so many women under one roof . . ."

The prince didn't answer. It was as if he were frozen in place, staring at me.

I wish she'd run, the prince thought. *There's still time. Use your magic. Please.*

I wanted to grant his wish. It would be so very simple. The prince and me away from here in a single wish. But I couldn't leave my sisters or Cinderella to face whatever wrath came after we disappeared.

"I imagine the Queen's Right Hand already filled you in on our errand."

"He did. I find it all so very romantic," Galatea said.

"Isn't it? Love at first sight is supposed to be a thing of fairy tales. But here we are," Hark said.

"Yes, it really is quite something," the prince said, his voice harsh, but he did not look away from me.

"Pardon our haste, but we must have every woman in the house try on the shoe, and then we must move on. As you can see, the prince is very anxious to find her too. There are so many ladies, and so little time," Hark said cheekily.

"Well, I for one find it the most romantic thing I've ever heard," Amantha said, pushing her way to the front of the crowd. She removed her own shoe.

"I see we have our first victim," Hark said, making a show of putting the slipper—my slipper—in front of Amantha.

Prince Mather kept his eyes on me.

Did he really know it was me all that time? And could he really love me?

There was a yelp from the footman's direction. He was looking down at Amantha's foot.

The shoe fit, but through the glass you could see that all her toes had disappeared.

Amantha shrugged, feigning innocence. Galatea glared at her. She had taught her to be smarter with her magic. But Amantha had been too impulsive, too eager. And her magic may have just exposed us all.

Hark and Mather moved to get a better look. But as they did, Galatea slipped her hand into her pocket where her wand was. The crystal shoe filled with blood.

"Take it off, Hark!" the prince exclaimed.

When Hark removed the shoe, Amantha winced in pain, and we all saw what Galatea had done. Amantha's skin was jagged, as if her toes had been removed with a serrated knife.

Amantha looked at her own foot in horror and confusion.

"I'm afraid, Your Highness, she just wanted it too much," Galatea said, her tone somber. "I will call our family doctor."

Amantha bowed to the prince, but I could see that she was really looking at Galatea. "I am sorry I deceived you, fair prince. Being your bride meant so much to me, to our family."

"It is I who should apologize to you. I never wanted this for any woman in the Queendom," the prince said.

The footman helped Amantha toward the stairs, but not before she cast another apologetic look at Galatea.

I wish I could make them see that was magic, thought the footman.

Hark blinked hard and shook his head. "You do realize that magic is outlawed in Hinter . . ."

"I believe you are mistaken, Hark," the prince said firmly. "There is no use of magic here. Just bad judgment."

The prince was choosing to look the other way. He was choosing to protect us. To protect magic. Just like he had done in town at the Black Glass factory.

Galatea's hand went to her pocket again, ready to take action if need be.

"Very well, then . . . ," Hark said with doubt. "Now, who is next?"

I wish everything were different. I wish that poor girl hadn't hurt herself for me. I wish that I were on that dance floor again with you—anywhere with you.

The prince glanced at me as he wished it, his eyes full of knowing. It was almost as if he wanted me to hear his wish.

CHAPTER 66

Hark looked straight at Cinderella. "You, in the back. Come forward."

"That is my stepdaughter. But I know for a fact that she was not at the ball. She wasn't feeling well. She stayed home," Galatea said.

"Madame Gray, please tell me that you are not disobeying the directive. Every girl in the Queendom must try on the shoe."

"I merely wanted to spare you some time. Cinderella wasn't at the ball. But she will try on the shoe, as you wish," Galatea said, knowing she would not win the argument.

When I was small, I learned that the world could turn on a single moment.

We can all be saved or lost by a kiss or a kill. Either takes seconds and changes everything, Hecate had said.

For so long I thought the words applied to the royals, not to one of us. Not to me. But I realized now was one of those moments.

"The prince is looking for the girl he danced with at the ball. He intends to marry her and take her away from this place. He could make all her wishes come true," I said, trying to send a message to Cinderella.

I imagined that Galatea already knew the truth of Cinderella's recent Past and my role in it. She would consider all that I had done a series of hostile acts—ones that my sisters could not overlook, but ones they could not address either in the presence of the prince. Lucky for me, she could not know what I was about to do.

Cinderella looked down at the shoe, understanding, but not all at once. She inhaled sharply, remembering clearly that she had spent only a dance with Mather, while I had spent most of the night.

I know it's not me, but I wish it were. I wish the shoe fit; I wish I were free of them, Cinderella thought.

Being a princess was not what she'd wished for. But being a princess was possibly going to be the thing that saved her.

As Cinderella slid her foot into the shoe, I touched my wand and cast the spell:

As she sits,
Make the shoe fit.
Give the prince his future queen.
Let him know she is the best the Queendom has ever seen.
In time she will win his heart.
Let the shoe be the start.

"It fits!" Hark exclaimed. "Prince Mather, you have found your new princess."

It was done.

While being with Prince Mather was all my heart yearned for, I knew I would never have a place with him—especially if my sisters took over the Queendoms. I didn't need Hecate to tell me that we could not have a future. But he and Cinderella could.

She could help him rule. Together, they could save the Queendoms.

Suddenly a barrage of arrows hit the open door. Their Black Glass tips stuck deep into the wood.

"Bring me the witches!" Queen Magrit cried, stepping out from behind another army of soldiers. "They're mine."

"No, they are not!" South cried from the sky, landing between us. His wings folded upon his back. "You will never defeat the Entente."

CHAPTER 67

Amantha, Bari, go to our sisters," Galatea ordered.

Bari's eyes flashed. She turned into a column of crows and flew away.

Amantha sighed and disappeared into a blur.

Galatea waved her wand and South fell to the ground, unconscious. I rushed out the door and to his side. I was relieved to see his chest rise and fall.

"What did you do?" I shouted. "Bring him back!"

"Why don't you make a wish?" Galatea said bitterly before she raised her wand and disappeared.

"I wish Farrow, South, Prince Mather, and I were in the Enchanted Forest," Cinderella said aloud.

With a wave of my wand, we were.

Cinderella knelt over South. I tried to wake him, but Galatea's spell still held.

"I danced with you only briefly, didn't I?" the prince asked Cinderella. "I danced with Farrow, right?"

I revealed my face to him. I wanted, needed him to see me.

"Yes," I said, stepping in. "But Cinderella's the one you want.

She's the person the Queendom needs. She's good and true. Unlike me. She's who you need," I repeated.

"Don't I get to decide that?"

"What we want doesn't matter."

"*We?* You feel the same way?"

There was hope in his voice, like my confirmation was all he wanted. I told myself that it was enough that he wanted it. I would always have that.

"I thought it was you every time because of your tell, but I didn't know for sure until you kissed me."

My heart felt like it was beating on the outside of my chest.

"It has always been you. You think I don't know what magic is, what your kind can do, how you can change your appearance? I do. Your face may have changed, but your body is the same. The way you move. I always know you."

My heart leapt. Once, Mather had suggested that he wished we could meet without our Pasts and just have our Presents and our Future. But here he was wanting me, loving me, knowing exactly who I was. And me knowing exactly who he was. I had spent a lifetime with limits on love. And yet here it was on my doorstep.

"But why? Why do all this? The ball? The Couterie?" he pressed on.

"At first it was for revenge. Your mother killed my Hecate . . . my mother . . . She was the Entente your mother burned in the square."

The prince's eyes widened, then filled with sadness.

"It was you in the hallway . . . Your mother froze the soldiers . . . and you refused to play with me. Oh, Farrow . . ."

"It was me . . ."

We held like that for a few seconds. The next part was harder to say.

"I was planning to kill both of you on the night of the Becoming..."

"You what?"

"I thought it was the best way to hurt her. To take from her as she'd taken from me. But then I got to know you. I couldn't do it," I admitted finally. I owed him the truth. But I hated seeing it reflected on his face. He had to be hurt. He had to think less of me. There was no way he couldn't. I continued, the words tumbling out faster so that I could try and explain. Even though there was no excuse for what I'd wanted to do.

"Surely you must blame me for what I came to the palace to do. I almost killed you." I waited for him to admonish me for what I had planned. I was sure that my words had changed his heart.

"And instead you woke me up. And it sounds like maybe I helped wake you up. So I'd say we are even," he said with a smile.

"We're far from that... But because of everything that's happened, because of you, because of Cinderella, my mission has changed. And I guess, I've changed... I want to find peace between the Entente and the royals. That's what's best for Hinter and the Queendoms. And for the people, even if they don't see it now. And to protect you. I realize that now. Galatea was right when she said there is more than just Queen Magrit that's wrong with our Queendoms. For so long, all I wanted was to see Magrit dead. But revenge won't end this war. And peace can't happen if we don't find a way to stop Galatea. She wants to have power over every person in the Hinter and beyond. Over everyone without magic."

"Maybe we deserve it," the prince said. "We've stood by while your people were persecuted. We did not stand up to my mother."

"You were a child on the day of Hecate's Burning. And there are millions of people in the Queendoms. They are not responsible for the Queen's actions."

"But they are responsible for their own fear. Fear I admit I shared. Fear and standing by," he said resolutely.

"The Hinter can be better precisely because you acknowledge where the Queendoms have fallen short. You can rebuild the Queendoms and make them the world you described to me the night of our Becoming. One where Couterie and royalty and Entente and regular people all get along. All have a part . . ."

"You really believe that? How do we begin?"

"Galatea and the Entente are going to go after your mother. You have to be out of the line of fire and ready to take her place. I can't save your mother, but I can spare the other Queendoms as much loss as possible."

"You want me to run away?"

"I want you to regroup with Cinderella. An alliance with a commoner will bring the people of Hinter new hope."

"I could say the same about us. Imagine the message it would send to the Queendoms and Hinter if I married an Entente?" he reasoned.

"Marry . . ." I let the word sink in, and some part of me fluttered in response. I shook my head. "The Queendoms aren't ready for that. The Entente are feared. And given what my sisters have been up to, that fear is more than warranted."

"You are not your sisters," he said. "What if I'd rather have you than the Queendom?"

I shook my head again. There was part of me that wanted this. To be more important than the world. To be more important than the Queendom. To be first in the eyes of someone. I had never been first with Hecate. Or my sisters. But here was a prince, my prince, choosing me above everything else.

I was tempted by the prospect. I was tempted by him. My time in the Couterie and my time with Cinderella had taught me that humans were no different from us except for the magic. And I had been both with and without it. It did not define me, even though I had missed it fiercely when I had been without it.

But in the end, in my heart of hearts, I knew there was only one answer. It wasn't just about me. I had to pick my sisters. I had to pick the humans. I had to pick the Hinter. I could not pick me. I could not pick him.

"I'm sorry, Prince. You must go. Go with Cinderella. Find the Rookery."

His face fell. He had just laid his heart out to me. Offered his hand despite his mother. Despite history. And I had turned him down.

"Farrow . . . it's okay to choose us," he offered, still waiting, hoping he could sway me.

I rolled on even though every word hurt me. I knew it was the right thing to say. I knew it was the right thing to do. I needed to explain it to him and to my own heart.

"South is certain that the Rooks will help us. He knows every Present, and in every one, they want us to live. You are our best hope to convince the other Queendoms that there is a place for magic and humans to coexist. We need help. Get to the edge of the Thirteenth Queendom and you will find it. We each have a path to take. This Fate, this Present, is not ours. This is where we must part," I said, hoping my firm words did not betray how much I wanted to say the opposite.

Prince Mather held my gaze for a beat, defeat washing over him.

He broke away and turned toward Cinderella. In those seconds, I felt a part of me sink.

"Cinderella, is this what you want?" Prince Mather asked quietly.

Cinderella looked from one of us to the other, seemingly taking in the tension between Mather and me.

"I will do what's right for my friends and my land. We cannot go on like this, and if my fate is with you, then yes, that's what I want," Cinderella said finally. She threw her arms around me. "But what will you and South do? How will you end this war?"

"The best way for me to help is to stay close to Galatea," I assured her. "I can't have one dictator replacing another. I am in the unique position to stop her. I can't do that if I am not by her side."

"But if she is anything like Queen Magrit, there is no stopping her, Farrow," Cinderella said, worried.

"I have an ally here in South. And there are others of us—other Entente spread out among the Queendoms. There is a chance to change their minds, to save them, and to save all of us, humans and Entente alike."

"And if you can't?"

"Then I will stop them," I said resolutely. "And then I will come find you. Both of you."

"What is it like? To have all that power?" Cinderella asked.

I looked at her, surprised. I had spent so much of my life without my magic. And now that my magic was back, it paled in comparison to that of my sisters.

"Once upon a time, it felt like magic could make anything possible. Now it feels like something else. A last opportunity to make things right so Hecate didn't die in vain. I only hope that I am enough."

"Does having magic feel like you're filled up with stars and lightning and thunder? Like you're about to burst?"

"When I was young, I could feel the magic inside. But I didn't know what I could or would do next. Now it's different. It takes a key to unlock my magic. It takes a wish. And when I grant that wish, it's like all this pent-up magic is finally released for its exact purpose. And I feel a rush of something else. I think it might be peace."

Cinderella hesitated, and then kissed me on the cheek.

Prince Mather leaned in so that his lips were a mere inch away from mine.

"I will go with Cinderella, but my heart remains with you," he said.

And then, with the same wish from the prince and Cinderella, they were gone.

The spell had worked. I exhaled sharply. I had granted a wish, but none of us truly had what we wanted. My own heart ached.

They were safe for now. That was all that mattered, I told myself.

CHAPTER 68

One thing done. One to go.

I looked at South lying so peacefully under the apple tree in the orchard. I wondered if he would approve of what I had done. It felt like the right thing, and yet somehow everything was wrong. I thought of the prince and Cinderella making their journey to the Rookery. At least they were on their way. And they were safe for now.

There was only one way to find out what South thought. I had to break Galatea's spell. She had cast it once before, when Iolanta had died and passed her magic to him. He was stuck in a moment that he loved more than any other. What if I showed him something or someplace he wanted more than the perfect place she'd trapped him in his mind?

I took a deep breath, leaned down, and placed my lips gently over his. It was just a peck, but I knew it was also a violation. I knew how he felt about me, and I knew I felt that way about someone else. But this was the only way I knew to wake him up. I needed him, and all of Hinter needed him.

"I'm sorry, South," I whispered when my lips left his.

His eyes slowly fluttered open. "What happened?" he asked.

"Galatea put you under a spell, and I broke it. I replaced the dream kiss with a real one."

His face fell as he read mine.

"I could feel everything that was happening to you. I could feel your heart breaking over Prince Mather. And I could feel his—"

"I'm sorry, South . . ."

"I know," he said, forcing the corners of his lips upward. "So, what do we do now?"

"We need to find Galatea and the Entente. They need to believe we are on their side again so we can stop them from taking over the Queendoms."

"She just put me to sleep. She thinks we betrayed her," South protested, stretching his wings out behind him.

"They're our sisters, South. Whatever problems we have between us we will resolve. But we all have to live to solve them," I vowed.

~

There was only one place Galatea would go right now: the Reverie. As South and I slipped through the Veil, lightning crackled. I knew it was Galatea. She was welcoming us home.

When South and I joined her in the courtyard, she gave me a withering look.

"We might not agree, but we are Entente," I said firmly, half expecting her to spell us to sleep right on the spot. "We have come to stand with you."

"Why shouldn't I punish you with twin bolts of lightning?" she asked.

"Because Entente do not kill Entente. And because you loved our mothers."

"Very well. But that does not mean I trust you to stand with me."

"What if I told you I had a way to save us all . . . ?"

"And how do you propose we take over the Thirteen Queendoms?" Galatea asked.

I leaned in and whispered to her the one piece of information I could offer up to earn her trust.

Galatea's lips turned up into a wicked smile. "My, you've certainly changed your tune, Farrow. Perhaps you are Entente after all. We shall see if that's the solution."

She gave me a long look. and then said, "It's time to storm the palace."

CHAPTER 69

Queen Magrit's palace was heavily fortified by her army. We had come out in force to meet it: Galatea, me, South, Amantha, and Bari.

But surprisingly, the soldiers parted.

"The Queen demands an audience with you," Hark called from the palace steps. He waved us forward, through the troops.

I snarled at Hark, the boy I had seen by the Queen's side when Hecate had burned. The boy who was a traitor to his friend. Hark looked through me like we were strangers. If he felt guilt for his betrayal of the prince, I could not see it. Perhaps the Queen had raised him for this.

He led us right through the royal palace's front door. We made our way to the throne room.

Is this a trick? I wondered. *Why would she let us walk in?*

Is it a trap? I thought as I caught our reflections in the Black Glass that covered every wall. Even the ceiling and floors. We were wearing our own faces, so it made no difference. It offered no danger. I felt one of the walls and it was cool to the touch. Without heat, we were in the clear. But what if there were soldiers holding lighted Black Glass arrows behind the door?

"It's too easy," I whispered to South.

I wanted to know what he felt. If he could sense a plan. I tried to read the Queen before we reached her.

When the door swung open, we could see her sitting in her Black Glass–covered throne. Her posture was regal. But when she registered our presence, she leaned forward and sneered at us. There were two guards at her side. Each stepped forward protectively.

She nodded at them as if to say she could handle us. And then she finally addressed us.

"Witches!" Queen Magrit said with contempt. "Where is my son?"

"The girl and your son are innocent. And they are gone," Galatea said finally.

"If you give up, I won't kill you or your progeny," Queen Magrit offered.

"You'll just cage us and use us against one another?"

"Once magic is contained, there will be peace. Just put your wands down," Queen Magrit added.

"Never!" Galatea shrieked. "The Entente will live on!"

The air flickered around us. Amantha appeared behind a cluster of guards. Her wand was drawn.

Another flicker and Horatia was there on the other edge of the quadrant of soldiers. I wished she'd brought her spindle. We needed all the help we could get.

There was another flicker and another and another . . . until all the sisters had surrounded the soldiers and the Queen.

I caught the tableau in the Black Glass, and despite the terror of the moment, the glass reflected back our unity and readiness for whatever was to come. But it also captured the Queen and her men, and they were not backing down.

"Did you really think you could walk in here and expect to walk out again? We are not so dissimilar. We both have used our years to plan for this day."

The Queen nodded, and one of the guards lifted a torch and touched it to one of the walls. They began to warm. The Black Glass blanketed every inch of the palace, and all the glass was connected. The walls glowed as they warmed. Outside the windows, we could see the soldiers lighting their Black Glass arrows. Just like in the glass factory, I felt an immediate sense of nausea.

A wand rose. A ball of fire formed in the air. The battle had begun, and it spilled out of the throne room to the grounds of the palace.

Before the day of the Burning, the Entente had never raised their wands against humans. Now there was no hesitation.

Xtina threw a fireball, which missed the Queen and hit the glass wall behind her—which was of course the exact wrong thing to do. The stench of the glass grew more toxic.

Each Entente used her own special skill to thwart a group of guards.

"Galatea, remember . . . Break the glass," I screamed. This was what I'd whispered to her in the Reverie: I said simply, remembering how the prince had set the factory on fire, "Black Glass reveals our identities, and it can also kill us. It killed Iolanta. Destroy it, and Queen Magrit is powerless. We must use force to destroy it if necessary."

They ran at us with their Black Glass–tipped swords, but we were everywhere and nowhere at the same time. The Black Glass–covered walls reflected our true faces as we attacked and deflected their advances.

Galatea raised her voice and the others followed suit. "Break the glass, and bring our power back . . ."

I joined in the chant as the glass walls of the palace began to crack and melt.

The Queen's face contorted as she watched the walls she'd had built for her protection turn against her. Meanwhile, the battle raged on.

I watched in amazement as Bari transformed. Her bun became a beehive, and when she opened her mouth, bees poured out of it. Her dress began to disintegrate and re-form as a full skirt made of bees. She lifted her wand and the swarm dispatched.

There were screams as the bees split into two clouds, and each hovered over a guard.

But even with the glass broken, the guards had not lost their will to fight. If anything, they were now fighting doubly hard as they watched their palace be attacked.

Bari swiped again with her wand and the clouds attacked the guards' faces, hands, and all visible skin. They made their way into the crevices of the guards' armor. The soldiers collapsed into heaps on the ground.

Galatea stepped forward. "Give up your Queen and I will spare every one of you. If you don't, you will perish," she vowed.

To punctuate her point, she raised her wand again and a bolt of lightning met it.

"If you just give up, then I will let the rest live," Galatea offered, echoing Queen Magrit's words.

"Never!" the Queen screamed, and the soldiers began to fight again in earnest.

Galatea moved her wand and half a dozen men fell dead before they could reach her.

"I can beat you without spilling a single drop of blood, or I can spill every single one . . . till there is an ocean made of you."

With that, she put a dozen of the guards to sleep with a wave of her wand.

She raised her wand a final time, and Queen Magrit rose into midair. The Queen gagged. Her hands flew up to her throat as if someone were choking her.

Is Galatea going to kill her? I wondered. This was what I had dreamed of for years. A whole life of planning came down to this, this one moment, this one action. But instead of feeling joy, I felt sadness and regret. This was not what I wanted after all.

I raised my wand, even though I was powerless to stop her without a wish.

"Remember this, Magrit," Galatea said, releasing her. "You are not stronger than the Entente. You cannot defeat magic."

The Queen fell to the ground. The Queen wished to live and to breathe and to kill all of us. And then she looked for her son. She wished for him. She wished for him to avenge her.

Galatea then turned to address Hark and the soldiers. "You have seen what we can do. There is no end to our power. If you submit, then we will let you live, but your Queen will die."

The soldiers' voices rumbled through their ranks. Some retreated, but others bowed down to us.

"There is not one moment in Magrit's life that is worthy of this Queendom or that is worthy of your sacrifice," Galatea said. "I know this because I am Galatea, Fate of the Past. And he knows it because he is South, the Fate of the Present."

South looked around awkwardly.

In the crowd, a couple of soldiers balked at the idea.

"South can barely hold a sword, let alone all our Presents," one of the soldiers taunted.

Galatea laughed. "You thought South was one of the Fallen. One of you. But he is one of us."

I could hear all the guards' wishes. There were so many. My head felt as if it were underwater as I listened to everything they wanted.

I wish we could trust her, but she's a witch.

I wish we could trust the Queen.

I wish no more daughters would die in the name of the Queen's witch hunt.

I wish the witch were dead.

Then I heard a new voice with a different wish.

I want you to live your lives under the thumb of the Entente. I want my revenge.

The voice was Galatea's. This was the first time I could see clearly into her heart's desire.

She wanted them all dead. But she would settle for ruling over them instead.

She had told me her plan. But seeing it in her heart was different. The closer she got to her revenge, the darker her heart got. And it was up to me and South to stop her.

The closer the plan had gotten to mine, the more conflicted I felt. Queen Magrit needed to be stopped. But I didn't like what it was doing to me in the process.

"I am offering you one chance to save yourselves. Just walk away. And leave your Queen to me."

"My people will never betray me," Queen Magrit gasped, lifting herself half off the ground.

But I could hear the wishes and hearts of the guards. And they were wavering. One stuck out in particular.

I just want to live.

The Queen looked around, waiting for her minions to step forward and lay down their lives for her.

The next few seconds passed without any movement. Then there was a rustling as the soldiers put down their weapons.

Queen Magrit glared around her wildly. "You fools! She spared your lives just to show her power. Now that you have laid down your arms, she will kill all of you. Will none of you protect your Queen after all that I have done for you?"

Hark stepped in front of the Queen to protect her and pulled out his knife, facing Galatea.

"I don't want to hurt him. But I will," Galatea offered.

The Queen stepped in front of Hark, stilling his knife. It didn't make any sense. Who was Hark to her—why would she want to save him? Of all lives, how could she put his in front of her own?

She whispered something to him, and he smiled a small, sad smile.

"Very well, then. You have won this round," she said.

Queen Magrit had surrendered.

This was not how I thought Magrit would end. I would have thought that she would fight to the death. And for her to essentially lay down her crown for Hark. I couldn't parse it. Was there another play she had planned that I could not see? I could not sense anything from her in her defeat.

I looked around at my sisters. I was relieved that we had escaped this battle without losing any of us and without killing any more of the guard. But I worried about what was still to come. My sisters were elated, and I could hear their wishes for futures full of wealth and power. But with every crown the Entente might wear and every Queendom they might rule, I feared the trade-off was their souls.

Feeling overwhelmed, not wanting to hear another mercenary wish, I glanced away toward the square, and my eyes caught on a smiling Galatea. It was more than seeing the incredible contrast between who I remembered her to be before the day of the Burning and today. I could finally hear her.

In her happiest moment, she had forgotten to maintain her mind palace. I could finally search her head and her heart. I heard her wishes.

I felt a chill overcome me. I could not find any light in her heart. She was lost.

CHAPTER 70

The Queen was kept in the same tower she'd kept prisoners in for years. She was pacing back and forth in front of the single window. Light flooded in around her.

Galatea destroyed all the remaining Black Glass in the Queendom.

The guards offered to lay down their arms, but Galatea insisted they keep them. That they use them to serve the Queendom. And now the Queendom was Galatea's.

She ordered them to search out Cinderella and the prince.

"What are you going to do to the Queen?" I asked.

"What was done to us. Surely, you don't object? This is what we worked for."

"We should have a trial," I said.

"Why would we do that?" Galatea asked, seemingly genuine.

"To show that we can be better."

"We are better. And the Queen is right about one thing. They will never accept us. The only way to keep them down is to rule them. It's that, or we would have to kill every single one of them."

"You don't mean that," I protested.

"They will never think of us as equals. Because we aren't equal.

We are better. We have magic. We know things that they will never know. Or at least we know them first. And we can do things that they can never do. They will always fear us. They will always resent us. This is the only way. You know that she deserves it. You know that they all do."

"I believe in justice. Not vengeance. It took me so much time to realize that."

"You have feelings for that boy. Once they are removed, you will see that what I am saying is right."

"Removed?"

"I am going to take the Crown. He has to be dead for me to do so."

"No, Galatea!"

"Here, let me make this easier on you."

She tapped her wand against my head. She was letting me in.

I could see what she wanted, what she wished for. It was each of us sisters, rising up, wearing crowns in each Queendom.

"I can't watch this. This is not what the Entente is."

"It is what they made us," Galatea said.

"We have a choice," I said.

"And I have made mine. And so have your sisters and South. What's yours, Farrow?"

I gave Galatea a smile that was filled with sadness. I loved her and my sisters. But this was where we parted. She smiled back.

"You will return to us. I don't need to see the Future to know that," Galatea said.

"Can I have a few minutes with her?" I asked.

She nodded.

"Tell me, is there a way I could have done it differently? Was there a way I could have escaped this?" Magrit asked, surprising me.

I was expecting her to be thinking of her son. Of his future. Of the Queendom itself. But Magrit cared about herself and the Crown.

"I don't know—only one person could know, and you killed her. If it's any consolation, you could have lived if you'd given up the crown."

Now Magrit laughed.

"Your Hecate told me that too. I changed everything else. I fortified the palace. I never had another child. I sent you all scurrying away like rats. I did everything I could to thwart you, and yet here I am about to ascend to the pyre," she said as if she was still somehow surprised by this outcome. "I did everything else . . ."

"This was your own choosing. Every step of it, Magrit."

"You asked for too much. What kind of life would I have had as a commoner?"

"One where you were a mother. One where you were not a murderer. One where you didn't steal food out of the mouths of your own people. One where you were loved."

She was a mother. She had the prince. She didn't care. The Crown was all that mattered to her.

My heart clenched for Mather. She didn't love him as much as she loved the Crown, and she did not regret one life that she took. She regretted only that she did not win.

"Oh, you poor thing, you may be Entente, but my boy got to you, didn't he? Love is for the common people. It is not for us."

"Us?"

"Entente and the Crown. On that we must agree."

I looked at her a long beat. And then gave her a deep curtsy.

"Goodbye, Your Highness," I said and turned and walked away.

The day had come.

South and I stood at the edge of the crowd. We looked up at the dais where the Queen and my sisters stood a few feet from the pyre. The Queen looked smaller than I had ever seen her as she looked to the pyre with understanding.

It was too much. I couldn't stay. As I began to move away, South stopped me and grabbed my hand. I looked down at his hand around mine, I knew what a big deal it was for him to reach for me.

"You can't go. This is the moment you have been waiting for, for years," he said urgently.

"I thought it would be different. Feel different. It's not right."

"For her to pay for what she did?" South asked.

I felt more certain with every step I took away from the crowd.

"For me to be here to witness it. I thought I needed to see it, but I don't," I said.

"Where are you going?" he asked, following beside me.

"I have to find the prince and Cinderella and protect them. I have to find a way to stop Galatea and all of them."

"Then I am coming with you," he vowed.

"I need you to stay with our sisters. See what Galatea does next."

"You can't do everything alone, Farrow," South insisted.

"I know that—but I need you to stay here. And I know you can see me and find me wherever I am," I said firmly.

I gave him a quick kiss on the cheek and turned to walk away.

"No goodbye, child?" the Queen yelled after me, still sounding high and mighty even though she was on the pyre.

South, I need to talk to her, I thought, looking at him.

South shook his head.

She doesn't deserve to talk to you. It won't bring our mothers back, South responded in my head.

I nodded firmly. *I need it for me. For Hecate. Please, South.*

South nodded, but I could still see the concern on his face. He was worried that the Queen, even bound and on a pyre, still might find a few last drops of poison to hurt me. But he honored my desire, slipped his wand out of his sleeve, and whispered under his breath.

Give Farrow the time she needs . . .
Before the fire feeds . . .
On the one who started all our grief,
I pray Farrow finds some relief.

I mouthed a thank-you to South before I walked up the steps to the Queen's place on the dais. My sisters, the crowd, and the guard remained frozen around her. I felt almost frozen myself when I looked at her. The words would not come.

"Tell me how you did it. How did you pass as human when we first met? Grant a dying Queen's wish . . ."

"This is exactly what you deserve, but the people deserve better than what you've done to them. To us."

"Don't pretend to care about the people—you only care about one in particular. My son."

I didn't answer. She was wrong. I did care for them. And since I had begun to hear their wishes, I cared more . . . understood more. But she was right too. I did care for Mather even more.

"If you want the Queendom to succeed—if you want him to succeed—you can take his side over these witches. You can save him. The other Entente want to kill him and take the Crown. You don't. You're not like them. I can see it," she said, changing tactics.

"Why should I believe that you suddenly want what's best for your son or for the Queendom?"

"Because I'm already dead. You're the Queendom's best chance for survival. I put his and its life in your hands."

"What do you want?" I demanded.

"Spare me the pain of the fire," she said.

I was surprised again, even though I shouldn't have been. She put her own fear of the fire over everything else.

"Tell me how you know about magic," I insisted, but the Queen kept her lips sealed. "I won't spare you the pain. But I will do everything in my power to save your son and the Queendom—though we may have very different ideas of what that means."

"It takes magic to find magic," she countered.

"What does that mean? Are you saying you have magic yourself?" I demanded.

Out of the corner of my eye, I saw Amantha begin to flicker. They were waking up from South's spell.

"Magrit . . ."

While Magrit remained silent, my sisters shook off the spell and continued on, oblivious to the time they had lost.

"It's time," Bari said as she and Amantha dropped their disguised faces. They knew the Queen would never bear witness to their true faces because she was, as she had proclaimed, already dead.

"I just need one more minute," I begged.

"Time's up, Your Highness," Amantha quipped.

The Queen looked to the pyre beneath her with understanding. Galatea registered her resignation and seemed annoyed by it. She wanted a bigger reaction.

Despite her initial objection, Galatea took my advice. The trial would not be formal; rather, Galatea invited all the Queendom to decide the Queen's Fate.

"When our sister Hecate was taken from us, the charges were

read for her, but no one was allowed to give testimony. We will give the people and the Queen the chance that our sister was never afforded."

Galatea asked for people to step forward and testify for or against their Queen.

There were countless tales of her atrocities: mothers whose daughters had been burned on the pyre, families who were going hungry after their parents had been sent off to the guard. And it went on and on.

"Her obsession with magic destroyed us all. Why could she not have been content with the peace we struck long ago? Now we must forge a new peace. But the Entente no longer serve humans. Does no one have a kind word to save their Queen?" Galatea asked, surveying the crowd.

Hark stepped forward finally. "Everything she did, she did for the Crown. She loved us the way she loved herself—selfishly and fearfully . . . the only way she knew how."

The Queen smiled at Hark as if she could not see the insult in his words.

She looked around again, perhaps expecting her son. But no one stepped forward.

"The word of the Queen's Hand is not enough to save her. Queen Magrit, I charge you with crimes against the Entente and humanity."

Galatea produced an opaque screen in front of the Queen, and the Queen was stripped of her Black Glass gown by Amantha and Bari. Burning Magrit in it would hurt us almost as much as it would hurt her. Galatea herself removed the shiny black crown.

Magrit kept her head high. But before she said her final words, I could hear her thoughts, her wishes.

I don't want to die. I want to live. I don't want the pain . . .

"I still wish you were with my son," she said finally.

She was using the pyre as another pitch for me to save her son. I assumed it was a tactic to gain my sympathy, but for Mather's sake, I wondered if some part of him would be comforted by her at least thinking of him before her death.

But something else happened at that moment. The air around Hark began to flicker, and he stepped back and disappeared into it, in the same way the Entente did when they traveled.

Hark was magical.

I thought back on that moment on the grounds where I couldn't read his thoughts or heart.

Hark had been somehow tied to the Queen all along. But before I could make sense of him and his role in all that had transpired, I heard the Queen's voice in my head again. It was a wish, and it was not meant for me. It was meant for Hark: *I wish for vengeance; I wish for you to give it to me, and when it is done, I wish you free—*

Hark had flickered away because of the Queen's wish.

It wasn't a wish; it was a curse—and he wasn't a Right Hand; he was a Rook. Perhaps the Queen had one last move after all.

I took South's hand and made sure he understood what had transpired. He read my Present and nodded. He knew I would have to find Cinderella and Mather before they found the Rooks.

Galatea spoke again. "The Entente sentences you to death for crimes against them and against your own kind and Fate itself. May this fire bring back some peace for all that you have taken."

I felt my insides clench. The moment had come. Magrit deserved the fire for all she had done. But fire had a way of destroying more than the person on the pyre. Galatea, me, South, Amantha, everyone who had been in the square that day, and everyone in the Hinter had been changed by that first fire.

And it was happening all over again. I looked at the cold anticipation in Galatea's eyes as the fire began lapping up toward Magrit.

I had to go.

I could not stay to watch the light expire in Magrit, as much as I had wanted it so very long. I had something else to do—something I finally was ready to do, something perhaps I should have done before.

CHAPTER 71

With the smoke from the fire still in my nostrils, I ran to the Reverie. I ran through the clearing where the Veil used to be and found myself at the cliff beyond the trees, where we had once upon a time stood together.

I opened the pouch and let Hecate's ashes out.

"Hecate . . . Mother . . . I know this won't bring you back. But I hope it can give you peace. Thank you for keeping me company. I will make it the rest of the way on my own. Well, not just on my own."

I thought of South and the prince and even Cinderella. It would be our fight.

"It's not fair for me to keep you with me. It's time for me to set you free."

My mother's ashes re-formed, and her silhouette hovered over the cliff.

"Goodbye," I said.

The tears began to come. I could hear cheers in the square: "Long live the Queen; the Queen is dead."

More tears fell. I had never imagined having the Entente return from the grave. I had never imagined having to fight them either.

I had heard so many wishes. But it occurred to me that I had spent most of my life thinking of only myself, my mission, and what I had lost.

I had not thought about what it must have been like for Hecate, being bound to me all this time. This half life in a pouch around my neck . . . My letting her out only for my company and amusement could not have been any life at all.

"I wish you were alive; I wish you were wholly here with me. But since you are not, I wish you your freedom. I wish you peace."

I wish I were alive too.

I looked up. It was Hecate's voice.

My heart leapt. I had waited and hoped and dreamed of knowing what Hecate was truly thinking all these years, and she could not or would not tell me a thing until now.

But she wasn't just sharing her thoughts with me.

She was making a wish.

My heart caught in my chest. Hecate had made a wish. And my power—my half power—was what could make my mother whole again.

I lifted my wand, closed my eyes, and granted it.

The ashes remained hovering in the air.

I sighed. I turned back toward the trees and began to walk to the Veil. It had been too much to think that I could have her back. Happily Ever Afters weren't for the Entente. I had known that all along. And Hecate's wish was the same as my own. And my wishes never, ever came true.

I heard the crunch of footsteps in the leaves behind me.

"You always were impatient," Hecate said.

Her words filled my ears and my foolish heart. I turned around to see something I never thought I would see again.

Hecate, in the flesh.

"You're really here," I said as she put her arms around me.

"We were always together, even when we were far apart," she said.

"Oh, Hecate. Hinter is a mess. I tried to do what's right. Have I taken the correct path?" I asked, knowing she knew for sure.

"What we do has consequences. Being a Fate means caring about everyone, not just the Entente. It means caring about everything in the Hinter and the Queendoms and beyond. It means that what you do matters. And what you undo matters. You did what you could, and now the rest is to be seen," Hecate said.

"I wish—" I began.

"Be careful what you wish for," she interrupted with a loving look.

When she'd said those same words all those years ago, I'd thought they were a warning. Now, as she smiled at me, I saw what they really were—a promise, finally fulfilled.

EVER AFTER

We were Entente. We were the whispers. We were the details, tiny arrows that you couldn't ignore. We were strings of moments, coincidences, and happenstances that led you to yesterday and today and tomorrow. We were the Fates.

For a long time I thought I was all that was left. But now I knew I was so very wrong.

I would have to stop my own sisters to save the Queendoms. But they couldn't possibly know that I had a Fate, I had Hecate at my side in the flesh . . .

ACKNOWLEDGMENTS

To my Chris Albers. Happily Ever Afters were only in books until I met you.

This book has been in my brain and my heart long before I wrote *Dorothy Must Die.* I have always wondered where fairy godmothers came from, but more importantly, I have always been obsessed with what they stand for. I have been lucky to have so many fairy godmothers in my life. From my own beautiful family, my mother, Shirley, whom I miss every day; my grandmother, Virginia Holt; and my father, Arnold Paige. (Daddies can be fairy godmothers too. And Daddy, you are incredible. You and Mommy gave me a love of books and art and all the love in the world.) And to my sister, Andrea, you were my very first friend and the most beautiful and best sister I could ever dream up. To my brother-in-law, Josh, thank you for always reading and rooting me on. I am so grateful to my fairy godmothers and all the magic that they have given me.

The tale I wrote is twisty and sometimes dark, but at its heart, I hope, is the spirit of fairy godmothering. As simple as a compliment or a gift of a pair of shoes or as big as a job, a kind word or a lifeline: what we do matters; how we touch others in small ways and in large can make a day or change our fate.

From Lauren Goodman Dell in that suite in Wallach Hall and

every day after to Jill Lorie Hurst and Nancy Williams Watt at my very first job at *Guiding Light* to Tina Sloan and Steve McPherson taking me into their home to my friend Paloma on the steps of Columbia . . . To Bonnie Datt, who helps me through every heartbreak and celebrates every dress and success. To Carin Greenberg, who inspires and cheers, and to Daryn Strauss, who is a literal fairy godmother . . . and for so many other fairy godmothers both personal and professional. I love you all.

For Sienna and Fiona. I love watching you grow up. And everything I write, I write with you in mind.

To my beloved second families: Annie, Chris, Fiona, and Jackson Rolland; Lauren Dell and Sandy and Don Goodman; Stephen McPherson and Tina Sloan; and Jill Lorie and Tony Hurst.

To Josh Sabarra, Michele Wells, Kami Garcia, Frank Lesser, Sasha Alsberg, Stephanie Garber, Leslie Rider, Paloma Ramirez, Jeanne Marie Hudson, Megan Steintrager, Lexi Dwyer, Lisa Tolin, Sarah Kagan, Kristin Nelthorpe, Leslie Kendall Dye, Crystal Chappell, Melissa Salmons, Laura Wright, Jordan Vilasuso, Valeria Tejada, Sasha Mote, Chris Lowe, Meg Cabot, Melissa de la Cruz . . . and so many more . . .

And to my dear Emily Williams! Thank you for all your help and love! I could not do this without you.

Thanks to my beloved agents, Jodi Reamer and Mary Pender! You are powerhouses and goddesses and rockstars!

To my brilliant editors, Mary Kate Castellani and Camille Kellogg. This book has been through so many iterations. Thank you for your steady hands and clear minds and insightful notes filled with fairy dust that brought our Farrow into focus.

And to Cindy Loh who wanted this book after a single conversation.